the criminal lair

PRISON FOR SUPERNATURAL OFFENDERS BOOK TWO

MEGAN LINSKI & ALICIA RADES

We the authors acknowledge that the United States of America is a country formed on stolen land. We respect and honor the indigenous peoples who have lived here for centuries, and we recognize there is still much work to do to make reparations and heal the damage caused to the many indigenous nations who were first here, both in the past and today.

May we remember the atrocities once committed, create a better world in the present, and look forward together for our future.

This book features characters with the following medical conditions. The information included is meant to educate readers on disabilities featured within the *Prison for Supernatural Offenders* series.

BIPOLAR DISORDER

Bipolar disorder is a mental illness that causes unusual shifts in mood, energy, activity levels, concentration, and the ability to carry out everyday tasks. Moods range from extremely elevated to extremely depressive, and can be intense. Psychosis, anxiety, eating disorders, and other conditions may develop. With proper treatment, people with bipolar disorder can lead full and productive lives.

BLINDNESS AND VISUAL IMPAIRMENT

Blindness is defined by an individual having severely impaired or absolutely no sense of sight. Total blindness is described as being unable to see anything with either eye. Vision loss typically affects an individual's ability to perform functions of daily living.

ONE

I never knew what two weeks without a man's soul could do to him. It'd been tortuous to be away from Ava-Marie and Oberi for so long. I was literally trapped in a prison— the Darke Institute for Supernatural Offenders— and that didn't seem half as bad as the prison I'd built up in my mind. The distance was agonizing, every second waiting for the pieces of my soul to return to my side... waiting to be made whole again.

I knew the moment Ava left the mainland, because I felt a sense of excitement swell within me. My pidge was coming home.

I paced the main entrance to the Institute for what felt like hours, awaiting Ava and Oberi's arrival. They were getting closer. I could feel it.

The doors to the Institute opened, creaking on the antique hinges. Cool air swept through the hall, and the sound of dozens of footsteps met my ears. Everyone who'd been allowed off campus during Christmas break had returned. There weren't many, as it required one hell of a donation from your parents to get permission to leave. But they had to let a few kids out every now and then, to keep up the appearance that they were in fact a school, and not a prison.

None of the inmates were buying that crap.

A dog barked, and I knelt with my arms spread wide. "Oberi!" I called.

He tore through the entryway, panting. Oberi slammed into me, nearly knocking me backward as he gleefully licked my face. I laughed and scratched behind his ears. It was the best I'd felt since the night of the Villain's Ball.

Heels clicked against the floor, and I swore my heart stopped. The scent of lilac and raspberries surrounded me, and my soul once again felt whole.

I stood and faced her. "Pidge," I said breathlessly. "You're back—*oof!*"

"Charlie!" Ava cried, throwing her arms around me. Her duffel bag hit me in the side. I went still in surprise, before relaxing into the embrace. I wrapped my arms around her and inhaled her scent.

She drew away far too soon, sounding amused. "You sound surprised I'm back. You think I could escape this place forever? I get into so much trouble, they'd send me back in a heartbeat."

"In true pidge fashion," I teased.

Ava shifted, hoisting her bag up on her shoulder.

"Do you want help with your bags?" I asked.

"I only have the one," she told me. "But you can walk me to my dorm to drop it off."

"Sure." There was literally nowhere else I'd rather be right now.

Ava and I fell into step side-by-side, and Oberi trotted along ahead of us, panting happily. He seemed to miss me, too, and was happy to be back. As if magnetized, mine and Ava's fingers intertwined, but only slightly— as if we were trying to hide what we were to the rest of the world.

We weren't really *anything*— not officially. Though we shared a soul, Ava wasn't exactly my *girlfriend.*

But I'd be damned if it didn't feel good to hold her hand like she was.

"How was your break?" Ava asked while we walked to the Elementai cellblock.

I shrugged. "I bummed around with Marcus and Kallie. We snuck into the chapel on Christmas for a gift exchange. Marcus gave me a used roll of toilet paper."

Ava laughed out loud. "That sounds like him. I'm sure he stole it from the men's room."

"Honestly, my break was pretty boring," I admitted. The truth was, I'd spent most of it just waiting for her to come back. "I hope your break was better."

"It was nice seeing my parents and my siblings again," Ava remarked. "I had to check in with an officer every day, so that sucked a pair of dragon balls. But otherwise my break was... productive."

"Oh? Productive how?"

Ava slowed outside her room and lowered her voice. "I can't tell you here."

My stomach sank. If Ava found something she couldn't talk about out in the open, it might have to do with the prophecy. The last thing I wanted was to play a part in this prophecy coming true.

The words her aunt Maddie had spoken to me echoed in my mind, like a voice recording on repeat. I didn't think I'd ever be able to get them out of my head.

A choice will be made by the twin of her soul
To save her and damn the realm
Or curse her, and save us all
A fate worse than death
Is the chosen one's destiny.

Maddie had visited me the night of the Villain's Ball and spoken the prophecy to me. She was a *naderei*, a Hawkei prophet, and I had to trust that what she said was true. She'd been very clear with me on what the prophecy meant. There'd come a day when I would have to make a choice— a choice between Ava and the rest of the world. For Ava, this would be *a fate far worse than death*, Maddie had said.

It was cruel to ask of me. Ava was part of my soul. I'd do anything for her—

Including hiding this from her.

Maddie had been adamant that Ava couldn't know, and that telling her would compromise the outcome of the prophecy. If Ava knew my part, it would only push her toward her own demise. I shuddered to think about it.

Ava dropped her bag off in her room, then took my hand. "Come on. I think I know a place where we can talk."

Ava led me through the halls of the Darke Institute, and Oberi followed at her side. The halls were lively with chatter, as this was our last day off before classes started up again, and no one liked being cooped up in their dorms. I paid careful attention to the twists and turns we took, and soon realized where we were headed.

"We're going to the balcony," I realized. It's where Ava and I had spoken of the prophecy before. The balcony was secluded and was difficult to get to, as its entrance was hidden down a maze of hallways. I didn't think I'd be able to find it again without Ava's guidance.

"It's the only place in the Institute where we can talk in private without being overheard or interrupted," she said.

We turned down a few more halls, and Ava opened a door. The air was chill but not totally unpleasant, as the Institute was located on a Pacific island. I was used to bitterly cold winters this time of year, so I didn't mind. With Ava here, my heart was warm.

Oberi pushed his way between us and barked happily as he ran out onto the balcony. Ava and I followed behind him, and I heard the door click shut.

We stopped at the end of the balcony, and I leaned my elbows on the banister. My heart hammered in anticipation of what she had to tell me.

"So, you made progress on the prophecy," I stated flatly.

"Yes," Ava said, sounding a hell of a lot more enthusiastic about it than I was. "Do you remember that door we found in the woods during the Darke Games?"

I nodded. It'd been strange, and obviously magical, though we hadn't had a chance to really explore or understand it, as there was a monster chasing us at the time. "I remember."

"Well, I don't believe in coincidences," Ava said. "Those runes we found on the door keep popping up— first on those ships we found in the alcove in Kinpago, then on that bow in the cave, and then on the door in the woods."

I didn't know as much about the supernatural world as Ava, but the way she spoke of these runes made it sound undeniable. They were too ancient and rare for it to be coincidence.

"What do you think it means?" I asked.

"They're Elven runes," Ava replied. "And I think the door is crucial to the prophecy."

I tilted my head. "How so?"

Pages began to slide over one another, and I realized Ava was flipping through a book. It must've been that journal she kept that detailed the wording of her prophecy. She began reciting a line. "*A discovery of the ancient ones on the island of shadow will change the course of our universe.* I already know the *island of shadow* is Darke Island. It's why I came here in the first place. The *ancient ones* obviously refers to the Elves. They're the oldest known supernatural race, and they died out a century ago. So this *discovery...* it *has* to be the door, or something similar."

"What do you think is behind the door?"

"I don't know," she admitted, flipping through pages again. "Maybe a weapon that will win us the war. I went back to those ships while I was on break. I can't translate the runes yet, but I wrote them down, along with any of the symbols I remembered from the door."

My mouth went dry. If Ava managed to translate those runes and got answers about that door, it would push her further toward fulfilling the prophecy— push her toward me making that decision between her and the world.

The sound of pages flipping stopped instantly. "Are you okay?" she asked. "You look a little sick."

I cleared my throat and reached for her hand. "Are you *sure* you want to pursue this, pidge?"

She drew away from me. "I *have* to, Charlie. The fate of the world is at stake."

So is your life, I wanted to say, but I couldn't.

"I know this is going to be hard, but I'm prepared to face that," Ava said. "And I was hoping you were willing to face it with me, after everything we went through in the Darke Games. I *need* your help, Charlie. I can't do this without you."

Hell. How could I deny her when she begged me like that?

"What exactly do you need my help with?" I asked warily. I was already being asked to choose the world over her, and I wasn't sure it was a decision I could make.

"I need you to find out everything you can about the history of the Elves on Darke Island. If the door *does* have something to do with this, we need to learn what it is, and how to open it. I bet they left something behind before they went extinct— clues of some sort. We need to find out what else they left here besides that door, because it's going to give us answers."

A lump rose to my throat. "What about you? What's your plan?"

"I need to work on decoding these runes and learning what the rest of the prophecy means," Ava said. "There's still so much of this prophecy I don't understand. You'll help me, won't you?"

I hesitated, and I knew she sensed it. "I just... I don't want you to get hurt."

She'd never know how deeply I meant that.

Ava sighed. "I wish I could promise you I wouldn't, but I can't. I know the possibility is there, but either way, I have to do this. I really don't want to have to do it alone, though, Charlie."

Her voice was soft, almost broken, and it tore my heart to shreds. I opened my mouth, but couldn't answer.

Ava blew a breath. "Well, if you're not going to help me, I'll figure it out on my own."

Ava turned toward the door, but I grabbed her arm. I couldn't stand to let her hurt for even one second. I spun her around and caught her in my arms. I didn't say anything, because I didn't trust my words to do it justice.

I wrapped Ava in my arms and pressed my lips to hers. She stilled a moment, before relaxing into it. Passion surged between us, and I lifted my hand to cradle the back of her neck. Ava wrapped her arms under mine and clung to my shoulders, dragging me closer until our bodies were pressed against each other. Her fingers dug into my skin as her tongue moved in and out of my mouth. A euphoric high took over my entire body, and my dick hardened in my trousers. I couldn't help but press my hips into hers, to show her just how much I was head over heels for her.

The kiss ended far too soon, though we were both gasping as we drew away. I rested my forehead on hers to catch my breath.

"I will *never* let you go through anything alone," I promised.

But the promise didn't feel like the saving grace it should've been. It didn't warm my heart or inspire me. Instead, it felt like a rock had been dropped onto my stomach. I realized how horrible a promise it was the second I made it. If I helped her with this, I pushed her closer to the end of the prophecy, where I—the twin of her soul—would be the one to hurt her most.

"Thank you," Ava whispered as she drew away. "That means a lot to me. With your help, I think we really have a chance of solving this."

"Hey, pidge..." I dared to ask. "What are we to each other?"

Ava froze. "What do you mean?"

"Well... I've never really dated anyone before. Kinda just messed around." I shrugged. "I was thinking—"

"I get it," she responded, almost too quickly. "But... Charlie, I'm not ready for that right now. I don't know if I ever will be."

My voice sounded crushed. "So you don't want to be my girlfriend."

"It's not like that," she rushed to say. "I just need to focus on the prophecy first. You understand, don't you?"

I understood she was afraid. And I knew she was pushing me away because she was worried I'd get too close.

She didn't want to get her heart broken. I didn't, either.

"Pidge, I'm gonna be here no matter what. If you just want to be friends, fine," I said.

"I want to be *more* than friends," she insisted. "But I don't know if I can put labels on... *us*, you know? Whatever we are."

Hell if I knew. I had a policy of not fucking my friends, but Ava wasn't exactly just a friend. She was so much more.

"Can we just see where this leads?" she offered. "I don't want to force anything. Why can't we have fun with no strings attached?"

I knew that wasn't going to work. There were *always* strings attached. More so with Ava and I, because we were bonded. Whatever we did would just bring us closer.

But I wasn't going to push her. She had trauma in her past. I had to wait for her to be ready.

"If that's what you want, I'm fine with it," I said. "We can mess around without any promises."

That was a lie. I was imploding on the inside. But this is what Ava wanted, and my heart craved to satisfy hers.

"I'm sorry," she whispered. "I just haven't dated since John... well, you know. I couldn't trust him, but I trust *you*. I don't want to do anything to screw up what we have."

"I don't want to, either," I said. "I'll always be here for you. No matter what happens, we'll get through this together."

Ava placed her hand on the side of my face, then stood on her toes to kiss me. I melted into the kiss, nearly forgetting everything we'd come out here to talk about. Adrenaline coursed through my blood, and I felt the passion rise within Ava through our bond. I couldn't help it when my hands tangled in her hair, begging for more.

Ava inhaled a deep breath, then shoved me backward, until my back was pressed against the side of the building. I drank her in like nectar from the gods, clinging to her as if she were my very life force— and she was. My tongue slid into her mouth, rolling over her tongue ring. She pressed her breasts against me like she wanted me *so* fucking badly.

I bet I wanted her more. It was pretty obvious.

My hands moved over her, though I was careful to avoid any areas that might make her uncomfortable. Apparently, she didn't have the same reservations, because she grabbed my hands and placed them on her ass.

Dear ancestors.

I moaned as I squeezed her ass, and my head spun as if the balcony had dropped out from beneath our feet. When she kissed me like this, I didn't give a damn about the labels. Ava-Marie owned half of my soul, and though it wasn't a choice I had made, it was one I would choose a thousand times. Nothing would ever change that.

That was something I could always rely on.

I just wished she didn't rely on me. Deep down, I knew I was lying to her. I couldn't help her with this prophecy the way she wanted. If I did, it pushed her closer to the prophecy Maddie spoke of to me. Every answer got her closer to her fate.

I realized then that the only way to save her was to stall her. The world was in danger, but damn the world, because I had to keep my pidge safe. I'd prolong this as long as I possibly could— and sabotage her if need be.

Because there was no way in hell I was letting this prophecy come true.

ava-marie
TWO

The Darke Institute might be some people's definition of hell. But if it was hell, I had to admit I was quite comfortable there.

And, if I was pressed to admit why, it was all because of a very handsome and very charming Mister Charlie Wahkin.

Oberi bounced at my side in his husky form as we entered our Supernatural Religions classroom on the first day of school. Charlie was already there, waiting at a desk for two people near the back of the room.

My heart stuttered when I laid eyes on him. Hot damn, the Great Spirit didn't make them like this anymore. Those eyes. That hair. That *body*. Someone better call a doctor, because I was in love, and that I was infatuated enough to admit it was enough to give me a heart attack.

Charlie sensed my arrival through our bond, and his whole form instantly lit up. That I could have that kind of effect on somebody made me want to glow. Charlie wanted to spend time with *me*. The notion that I actually made someone's pulse race caused my head to spin.

I slipped into the seat beside him, and Oberi crawled under the desk to lay on our feet. I put my hand on the desk, but before I could take things out of my bag, Charlie grabbed it. Our matching tattoos touched as he pressed his wrist against mine. I caught the sight of my name written across his skin, and it gave me a thrill. I'd traced the scrawling of his name on my wrist over and over during break, feeling like a piece of my soul was missing and longing to be with him again. Now that we were no longer apart, everything felt *right*.

"Good morning," I teased. "You're being awfully sweet."

"Because we're not alone," he said lowly. "There are more things I'd like to do than hold your hand."

My insides whirled, thinking of the way he'd grabbed my ass the other day. "Well, seeing as how we're in public, you're going to have to settle for holding my hand."

"For now." Charlie kissed the back of my hand, and I totally swooned. A couple of people looked our way, but most ignored us. For some reason, Charlie and I had gained a reputation last semester for being attached at the hip. I couldn't fathom why.

Ava, you're wasting time.

Stop what you're doing, Ava.

You don't want to hurt Charlie, do you?

Ancestors, this again. The voices were so loud, they were giving me a headache. I was seriously over this.

Charlie caught my distance. "What are you thinking about?"

"The voices," I whispered. "They've gotten even louder lately. I don't know how to shut them up."

Charlie mused on this. "How are you feeling?"

He was referring to my mood. I didn't want to tell him the truth—that it was like gray paint drying on the walls. "Okay," I lied.

Charlie could tell I was fibbing. I couldn't really lie to him through our bond. It didn't work very well. "Is something bothering you?" he asked.

I wondered whether to tell him. "Monica's birthday is coming up," I said. "Every year, it brings back all kinds of emotions."

"Oh." Charlie held back a moment. "I get that way around Marty's birthday, too."

It was nice to know I wasn't the only one, although I hated his pain. I'd prefer to go through it alone, rather than see him hurting.

"I'm just reminded of everything that happened, every year," I told him. "Sometimes I feel like I have to endure it, instead of just talking about it."

"Well, what if you *did* talk about it?" Charlie offered. "Let it out instead of letting it stew."

"What do you mean?"

"I think you should tell other people about what happened," Charlie started. "Maybe not everyone, but someone you trust. It might help you to start healing, instead of feeling like you have to conceal this big secret."

I mulled over the idea. Charlie was the only one who knew about my assault. It'd been hard telling him, but I'd felt better once I'd shared what had happened. "Maybe I will. Thanks, Charlie. For caring."

"Of course I care," he said. "You're my pidge."

That made my insides knot together. I couldn't help but squeeze his hand. I was *his* pidge. Right now, Marcus could dance across the room naked and I wouldn't even notice. I only had eyes for Charlie Wahkin.

The door slammed, breaking our tender moment as a teacher walked in. Professor Mazur taught this class. I really didn't like her. She was stuck-up and quite rude, not to add she'd denied Charlie accommodations all last semester. She was providing them now, but only because she'd been bribed by my dad. She was the worst kind of teacher.

"Take out your notebooks," Mazur barked. "I expect your notes this semester to be impeccable; otherwise, you will not pass."

Mazur pointedly ignored the recorder sitting on Charlie's desk, so he could take audible notes. She'd taken Daddy's money, though it was clear she wasn't willing to admit defeat just yet. I was sure she'd do something else to get back at Charlie later.

Mazur sneered when I hesitated to take out my notebook from my bag. I did it as slowly as possible. She noticed mine and Charlie's joined hands.

"Excuse me, but public displays of affection aren't permitted at the Institute," she sneered. "I'd like you two to stop this disgusting behavior at once."

Ancestors, lady, we're holding hands, not screwing on your desk, I thought.

Charlie let go of my hand, but I snapped, "Listen, Professor, just because you aren't getting any doesn't mean the rest of us can't either."

There was a bit of scared laughter that rattled around the room, and

Mazur flushed bright red. "Miss Mitoh, if you speak that way to me again, I'll have your tongue. Are we clear?"

I went to bite back something, but Charlie kicked me under the table, and Oberi let out a whine. I sighed and muttered, "Crystal."

"Good," Mazur sneered. "For the life of me, I can't understand why you girls today go for such pathetic men. Apparently being a caregiver is more interesting to you than being a girlfriend."

Charlie shrank down several inches in his seat. Her words humiliated him. I wanted to jump right up on the table and body slam Professor Mazur to the ground, like in some crazy wrestling match meant for television. I could hear the announcer in my head now. *Ancestors, she's got a chair!*

I went to do just that, but Charlie grabbed my arm. "Don't," he whispered. Oberi put a paw on my shoe, telling me to stay put.

I said nothing. Mazur's look was triumphant, happy she'd gotten to me. She gave me a death stare before stomping to the board to write down a few key points.

My blood boiled. If I wrote *Professor Mazur is a bitch* on top of my paperwork, think she'd grade me down?

Mazur rustled her feathery wings as she finished writing on the board. She paraded around with a long wooden pointer, which she smacked against the board. I was certain if she was allowed, she'd hit us with it. "Supernatural Religions is a requirement here at the Institute. Since multiple supernatural races reside at the Institute, you'll be expected to learn god what each magical race worships, so therefore, you can learn to... respect their beliefs."

Respect beliefs. Psh. I was half-certain Mazur taught this class because angels wanted to convert everyone to their way of thinking. The angels insisted their god was the *only* true god, and therefore, the only valid religion. In their eyes, all other religions were false. I expected to be indoctrinated the entire semester.

Imagine my surprise when Mazur turned and said, "To begin the semester, we will be studying demigods."

This caught my attention, and I leaned forward. Charlie cocked his head as he noticed me shift beside him.

Coyote's words that he'd whispered to me at the Villain's Ball came rushing back. He'd told me I was a demigod... and so were Charlie, Kallie, and Marcus.

But what did that mean, exactly? What was the Koigni god trying to tell me? I was determined to find out.

"Demigods are powerful supernatural beings," Mazur stated. "They are the offspring of exceptionally talented supernaturals. To breed a demigod, two supernaturals with extraordinary, special power to come together to make a child, although this isn't the only way— sometimes, mortals who mate with gods can *also* breed demigods. Unlike chosen ones, demigods are not picked by the gods for greatness. They can only be born."

Opal raised a hand. Being the shy mermaid she was, this surprised me she was interested enough to speak out loud. "So demigods are descendants of the gods, and have god-blood in their family line?"

"That's a misconception," Mazur replied, like she was stupid for asking. "A demigod does not *have* to be descended from a god. Gods were formed at the beginning of creation, and can produce offspring with mortals, creating a demigod. But this is much rarer than it used to be in the olden times. The gods rarely appear to us anymore."

"Then what does it mean to be a demigod, if you don't need god-blood to be one?" Opal asked.

"Demigod is a *classification* of a type of rare supernatural, not something that's in a person's bloodline," Mazur replied snidely. Ancestors, she hated answering questions. It's like she expected us to know it all already. "We know there are two main types of supernaturals— average, which most supernaturals are, and talented, which are typically supernaturals of unique power. The third and most powerful type is demigod, which means these individuals have magical strength beyond what even the most talented supernaturals can achieve. A demigod *can* be created by talented supernatural parents. Say, if a chosen one and a person born on a powerful magical day such as a solstice were to mate and have a child, there would be a chance, albeit slim, that the child would be a demigod."

That was *my* parents. My mother was a chosen one— my dad had been born during the Summer Solstice in the Year of the Sea Serpent, which was a powerful year in the Hawkei zodiac. It'd made him incredibly strong.

Mazur pinched her nose. "Something also important to note— demigods are often firstborn. Just because two talented supernaturals mate and produce a child does not mean all of their children will be demigods. In fact, there is a slim chance that *any* of their children would be demigods at all. It would be like winning the lottery to produce one, and demigod children are often difficult to raise. Strange things happen to them throughout their childhood— such as gods appearing to them throughout their lives, though they often don't understand what's happening."

That probably meant that Ezekiel, Alana and Maverick weren't demigods. Unlike me, they'd never had anything odd happen to them growing up. Strange things happened to me every day. I remembered the strange monster in the woods when I was five, and the blue eyes I'd seen when Daddy had been healed from near death when I was sixteen. Neither situations had been explained.

Kallie crossed my mind. I remembered she'd told me last semester how she'd seen a strange woman appear to her as a child during trances. My suspicions about her origins were confirmed.

"Also important to note," Mazur added, "To get a demigod, the child must be born on an important day in the astrological cycle. An equinox, a solstice, a comet, an asteroid shower, an eclipse, an alignment of the planets... something in that nature is *always* required to create a demigod. Heavenly bodies influence our births and lives significantly, and without them, demigods cannot exist."

Charlie was born on the Winter Solstice. I was born on Christmas Day, in between the Winter Solstice and the Anichi New Year on January first. That made us both pretty powerful. I wasn't sure when Kallie and Marcus had been born, but I was betting that both of them had been born when something important was going down on the astrological plane.

Mazur strolled around the room. "Although demigods aren't always descendants of the gods themselves, their powers are comparable. Demigods have the power to do things beyond what even talented supernaturals are capable of. They can push and bend the laws of nature to their command, and have even been recorded to work magic that is outside the natural realm. Demigods could stop time, change reality, and even... as it is rumored... build new worlds from nothing. The difference between a talented supernatural and a demigod is that a talented supernatural can store and use more magical energy than any average magic caster, at rates that would kill most other casters. But a talented supernatural cannot pull from energy or power that isn't there. Fae pull from Edinmyre. Witches pull from their afterlife, Alora. Elementai get energy from the earth, and their Familiars. And so on and so forth. But once this magical energy source is exhausted, there's nothing left to pull, and therefore, the magic of a talented supernatural dies. As you all know, energy can neither be created nor destroyed. However, this law of nature did *not* apply to demigods. They could create something out of nothing, and were capable of harnessing copious amounts of magical energy from thin air. *They* created it *themselves*, out of their own power. They need neither source, god, nor place to pull from, for they are their own magical source of energy. Their makeup is the magic of creation itself, and therefore, just like the gods, can create and access boundless sources of magical power."

Mazur smacked the board with her pointer again, and a couple of people flinched. "It is incredibly rare to find a demigod, and their offspring never exhibited the traits of their parents. More often than not, demigods were infertile, or produced children that had no magic whatsoever. Nature will only allow a race to grow so powerful before it will begin canceling that genetic line out. Demigods are magical anomalies, and nature did the right thing by driving them to extinction."

I scowled. Mazur almost sounded disgusted with the idea of demigods— like they were abominations that needed to be destroyed, and that such power only belonged in the hands of the gods.

"Demigods were usually plagued by certain... features," Mazur continued. "The primary aspect of demigod-hood was mental instability. You must understand, these people didn't think like you and I do. They were often deranged, driven to madness by the power they harnessed and their inability to control it. More often than not, they were delinquents of magical society, and menaces to the common good. They just weren't normal."

A jolt ricocheted through my gut as the voices in my head quaked and ebbed. Who was Mazur calling *unstable?* Jackass.

Mazur tapped the pointer in her hand. "Although the demigods are considered extinct, there is always a chance of one popping up, when talented supernaturals mate and produce offspring. More likely than not, if there are young demigods running around, they've most likely ended up here at the Institute, as a result of their instability meshing with their problems with authority. You must be aware, if there is someone at the Institute that you suspect to be a demigod, you *must* inform the Warden immediately, to protect yourself and your fellow students."

Yeah, right. That sounded like a joke. More like the Warden wanted to get his hands on that kind of power.

But why?

Mazur had us do some boring worksheet for the rest of the class period. She yelled at me when I wrote down Charlie's answers for him, until I asked her if she wanted me to call my father. She backed off, though the way her hands tightened on her pointer made me believe she'd like nothing more than to gouge my eyes with it.

My thoughts were racing. I'd talked to Daddy and Mama over Christmas break about the possibility of me being a demigod. I hadn't told them about seeing Coyote, though, because I was sure they'd think it was some bipolar moment and freak out. My parents, and others, had seen footage of me talking to Coyote during the Darke Games, but as Coyote had told me, the cameras couldn't catch him on film and it looked like I was arguing with myself. I'd made up some excuse about how it was all stress-related from being in the Games, and my parents had bought it. It wasn't that I didn't trust them with the information... more or less that I didn't want to worry them any more than what they already were.

Daddy had scoffed at the notion that I was a demigod— he didn't like any idea that put me in more danger— but Mama was pretty convinced. I was the firstborn daughter of two supremely powerful supernaturals, after all, the only Elementai that had mastered both Fire and Water. There wasn't much denying it.

"What's going on, pidge? You seem quiet," Charlie commented once we left class.

I chewed my lip as memories of the Darke Games fluttered through my mind. I decided that this was something I couldn't conceal— from Charlie, or my friends.

"I need to tell you something," I began. "Kallie and Marcus should hear it, too."

Charlie's expression became muddled. "Okay. Where?"

"We'll meet up after class is over for the day. We can think of a place then."

"Just what kind of scheme are you working on now, pidge?"

I took his hand again, to distract him. "Nothing that can't wait."

I thought it might make him happy, but his fingers went a little stiff in mine. I frowned. "What's wrong?"

"It's not unusual for people to wonder what a woman is doing with the blind guy," Charlie said sourly. "Trust me, I've heard it all before."

"You're not *the blind guy*," I said, irritated. "You're Charlie."

"Sure." He didn't sound too confident. "But when people catch on, I'm expecting backlash. It always happens when someone like me gets with a girl, particularly a hot one."

"You think I'm hot?" I perked up.

Charlie smiled and pulled me closer. "Probably the hottest dame I've ever been with."

That got my panties ready for some action. "So what's the problem?" I asked.

"I'm worried about someone seeing us and getting us in trouble for it. A teacher, most likely. I don't think I could keep my hands off you even if I was ordered to."

I smirked. "Then let's go somewhere no one can watch."

I took Charlie's hands and dragged him away. Oberi barked as I pulled Charlie into an empty classroom. I didn't bother to lock the door, merely dragged Charlie toward an empty alcove behind the teacher's desk at the head of the room.

"Oberi, stand guard," I told him. Oberi barked again, then padded to the entryway to keep a lookout.

When Oberi was gone, I wasted no time putting my lips to Charlie's.

I kissed him, drawing out the kiss and making it long and sweet. Charlie kissed me back, and when he opened his mouth so I could roll my piercing over his tongue, he shuddered in pleasure.

His scent invaded my senses as I bit down on his bottom lip and slightly pulled. He put his arms around me and held me, playing with the strands of my hair as my fingers caressed his back. I eased into the kiss, changing focus and pressure from the top of his mouth to the bottom. As I increased the intensity, we fell into a rhythm where when I retracted my tongue, Charlie came in with his. I playfully nibbled at his mouth, turning my head from side to side to revel in the way he kissed me.

This was how every girl *should* be kissed. It was the stuff of movies and fairy tales. Charlie made me feel more in one single kiss than I'd felt in an entire lifetime. The way he cradled my body so gently made me feel more than passion. It made me feel *loved*.

Charlie's breaths were ragged and full of lust. He tore away. "We shouldn't—"

I kissed him again. Once I did, he moaned and pulled me closer. A magnetic pull brought our bodies together, and I felt the bond flare and ignite, giving me a burst of pleasure behind my closed eyelids. My fingers trailed upward, to explore underneath his sweater. My fingertips graced the bare skin there, and Charlie gasped lightly. His light pants of desire totally made me want to melt. Who knew a prison could be heaven?

Charlie pulled away from my mouth and started kissing my neck. Ancestors, it felt amazing. Little jolts of electricity sparked up my skin at the touch of his lips. I shivered, and as I fell against him, his strong body held me up, preventing me from sinking into the floor. You could kill me now and I'd be a happy girl, because the slightest touch of Charlie's lips was bliss.

Then Charlie's mouth touched the wrong part. His mouth sucked on the edge of my collarbone, and that was all it took for everything to break in an instant.

I wasn't aware of what I was doing until it happened. All I knew was that desire had mutated to fear in less than a few moments. Charlie's touch felt like spiders crawling over my skin instead of soft and comforting. Alarm bells went off in my head, and at that moment, I couldn't *stand* him touching me.

"Stop!" I put my hands on his chest and pushed him away. He stumbled backward so violently he nearly fell over. I flinched and curled away, instinctively turning my back to him, though I didn't mean to.

Charlie froze. Oberi's nails clicked on the floor as he darted back to see what had happened. He stood between the two of us, looking anxious as I tried to catch my breath.

I wasn't back in Kinpago, but I might as well have been, for the terror that was racing through me. *It's Charlie*, I thought. *Just Charlie.*

Charlie didn't approach, just stayed where he was. He waited for me to say something, as if worried if he spoke, he'd scare me off.

"I'm sorry," I said. "I didn't—"

"It's fine, pidge." Charlie sounded like he really meant it. "Sometimes it happens."

I hated recoiling from him, but he could sense it through our bond that I was freaking out. "I really do want to kiss you."

"I know. I feel guilty. I didn't mean to set you off."

"I didn't think you would," I said. "It's... is something wrong with me?"

"No," Charlie said immediately. "There's nothing wrong with you. Let's just start over. You can make the moves. I'll hold back."

I was nervous that something horrible would happen again. But, I reminded myself, I was in control of this situation. Charlie was willing to let me call the shots. This was nothing like that night in the woods, when John had attacked.

I moved toward him, though every inch of my body was telling me to hold back. I went slow, and started with a peck on the lips. Charlie kept his hands at his sides, and I began kissing him deeper. The kiss was different this time, slow and sensual. By the time the alarm bells in my head stopped ringing, I felt at ease. I grabbed Charlie's wrists and put his hands on my hips. He sat them there, and began kissing me back. A warmth spread over my body, conquering the fear and setting it aside as we proceeded into gentler territory. When I finally pulled back, both of us were breathing heavily, but I was no longer afraid.

I licked my lips. "Thanks for being there for me."

"We'll figure it out," he said. "One step at a time."

Hollowness grew inside of me with how patient he was being. It was so kind, and I felt I didn't deserve it. I almost wanted to tell him, *See? This is why we can't date. I'm too messed up.*

But instead, I said, "We should go. We're going to be late for class."

"To hell with class." Charlie's voice was amused and low. "I want to stay here with you."

I wanted that, too, but the Institute had rules. "If we skip class, we'll get an infraction. We can pick this up later."

That seemed to change his mind. Charlie's hands trailed from my hips. I was relieved, and sad, when his touch was no longer on my body. My emotions for him were like a wave, pushing me toward him and away in one circular motion. I might get seasick.

"You gonna be okay?" His voice was worried.

"I always will be, so long as you're there."

Charlie smiled wistfully, and he parted from me. Oberi went with him as they left the room and went the opposite direction down the hall.

Despite the bad moment I'd had a few moments ago, our last kiss had lifted my mood. My head was still swimming with hormones and horniness when I sat next to Kallie in our Substance Abuse course.

The fae sorceress smirked as she caught sight of my goofy grin. She scooted her chair closer. "You seem happy to be back from break."

I couldn't hide my smile. "Let's just say Charlie was *very* excited to see me."

"Ooh," Kallie teased. "So what's the status on you two?"

"There isn't one." My smile fell a little. "We're just... you know... us."

"You aren't going out?" Kallie's tone was accusatory.

"I mean... no... maybe?" I said. "We're not putting labels on anything. I told him I want to see where it leads."

Kallie groaned and hit me in the arm. "Girl, you are *killing* me! Why haven't you made him your boyfriend?"

I paused as I considered her question. There wasn't an answer I could give that she would understand. I'd had a ton of boyfriends before, but to be honest, I blew through guys like money. I never got close enough to any of them to want anything deep. Two weeks would pass, or a month, maybe, and I'd get bored and want to be single again.

Charlie was so, *so* different. My feelings about him were complicated and numerous. Every thought I had about him seemed to expand into a galaxy. I couldn't say I'd ever been in love before. I'd had crushes and felt butterflies, but I'd never fallen so far I felt like I couldn't live without somebody.

And that was the problem. Being that vulnerable terrified me. I knew I didn't want to live without Charlie Wahkin. I loved him, but love was dangerous. It was how people got hurt.

After losing Monica, and being assaulted by John, I felt like an empty vessel. There wasn't anything I could offer Charlie. He didn't know that yet, but soon, he would.

My heart was already broken, to the point I didn't even want it anymore. Charlie could cut himself on the shards. Worse, he might shatter what was left. After years of gluing the pieces of myself back together, I knew Charlie could obliterate my hard work in one touch. If we didn't work out... I'd never recover from it.

And then there was the prophecy. The closer Charlie got to me, the more he was in danger. I couldn't stand it if loving me cost Charlie his life. I'd lose what little sanity I had left.

No. I wouldn't do that to him. I had to keep him at a distance. For his own sake.

Besides. It wasn't like he wanted to stay with a bipolar girl like me long-term. He thought everything was dandy now. He hadn't been around long enough to deal with one of my uncontrollable mania episodes.

And I could feel it coming, crawling over my skin and approaching on the horizon. It'd been like this ever since the Darke Games ended. I sensed the impending spiral, and knew it'd only be weeks before it got here. It only needed something to tip it off, and I'd throw myself right over the edge.

I knew the moment it approached, he'd take off running. No one could watch someone implode and not be affected by the aftershock. I couldn't blame him once he bolted. So I was doing some preparation for that moment, and making things easier before the final blow came. No need to break up if we never got together. Simple.

"You know how it is at the Institute," I said, as an excuse. "People find out you care about someone, and they use them to get to you. I don't want to put Charlie in that kind of danger. You know I have a talent for making enemies."

Kallie let out a sarcastic noise. "Like anyone would dare to go after Charlie. Quite a few people are impressed with his performance in the Darke Games. His reputation makes people avoid him."

"Why can't we be friends with benefits?" I asked Kallie. "That way, nobody has to get hurt."

"Because you already have feelings for him," Kallie pointed out. "Don't deny it. I know you do."

I swallowed. "Feelings don't have to mean anything. Trust me, Kallie. I'm making the right choice."

"Well, if you don't snap him up, some other girl might," Kallie said. "People want to get with him just for protection. When you were gone, I overheard a couple of girls gossiping about what it'd be like to sleep with the *hot blind guy.* You know that can only mean Charlie."

The thought of another girl touching Charlie, let alone having sex with him, made my worst inclinations come out. Murder sounded tempting.

"Charlie can do what he wants," I said offhandedly. "I'm not going to stop him."

"Okay." Kallie's voice was disappointed. "Just... think about it, all right? He really likes you."

Yeah, I liked him too. And that was the problem. When emotions got entangled, everything went to shit.

I changed the subject, because I didn't think I could talk about this without breaking into tears. "So what about you and Marcus?" I asked. "You two went to the dance together. Did anything happen?"

Kallie huffed. "No. He refuses to be alone with me. He'll hang out with me if Charlie or someone else is around, but whenever we get a moment by ourselves, he'll run off. We're just friends, though I thought I made it clear I wanted to be more. I don't know what his deal is. I thought he liked me."

"I know he does," I said. "Maybe he's just scared about being in a relationship."

Kallie's lips twitched. "Like you?"

I frowned. "Hey, I was asking about your love life, not mine."

"Which is nonexistent," she said. "If anything did happen, you'd be the first to know."

I tapped my pencil on top of my books. Romance would have to wait for the both of us, because I had prophecy stuff I needed to tackle. And I wanted Kallie and Marcus to be a part of it. I'd done a lot of thinking over break, and I knew if I was going to fulfill my destiny, I needed my friends. "Can you find Marcus and meet me in the prison yard around five? It's important."

"Sure." Kallie's eyebrows narrowed. "Is everything all right?"

"It's just something you need to hear."

Professor Gael started his lecture then, so I didn't say anything more. When class was over, I did homework until it was time to meet up with the others.

Charlie, Marcus and Kallie were already waiting for me. They sat on the benches in the prison yard, chatting in low voices. Oberi was chasing Rishi in circles. The cat yowled as Oberi stepped on his tail, and my Familiar whimpered an apology.

"What's up?" Marcus asked as I approached. He was trying to wipe a large stain of paint out of his sweater, and failing. Kallie rolled her eyes.

Charlie didn't speak. I was nervous being around him, after what happened earlier. I hoped he didn't think I was too damaged to deal with. But with Kallie and Marcus around, we couldn't talk about that right now.

"You guys should come with me," I said. "Kallie, make sure we're not followed."

Kallie didn't question anything, just nodded.

Marcus made a face. "Goddess, what are we getting into *this* time?"

"Nothing we aren't mixed up in already," I responded. "Trust me, you're gonna want to hear this."

Marcus went to object further, but Charlie elbowed him. I began heading toward the forest on the other side of the prison yard. Kallie looked behind us, but the other students on the grounds were either too busy playing games or talking to be concerned about where we were heading.

Oberi guided Charlie through the trees. Charlie used his Earth magic to move some of the branches and plants out of the way, though Marcus— the wonder he was— still kept tripping over them anyway. "Ouch! Ava, do you know where you're going?"

"It's not far," I responded. "It's just a secret."

"I'm half-convinced you're leading us out here to murder us," Marcus protested.

"Nah, you'd be dead already."

Charlie let out a chuckle, and Kallie hissed with laughter. Marcus scowled and grumbled, "I'd like to see you try."

Finally, we came to the large rock formation Charlie and I had found last semester. It loomed overhead, in the middle of the woods. Marcus balked about going inside, but Kallie dragged him in after Charlie and me. I lit a fireball for light, and once we entered into the giant empty chamber in the middle of the formation, both Kallie and Marcus gasped.

It was the same stone room I'd summoned the ancestors in. It looked as empty and forlorn as it had when we'd last been here. Kallie and Marcus circled the room, while Oberi sniffed the floor and Rishi ran after a mouse he'd found hiding in one of the rock's pores. Charlie's hands roamed the stone, and he smiled as he observed the structure with the use of his Nivita magic.

It was so nice to see him happy. This was as natural a place as any for him to be. It was the perfect spot.

"This place is like an evil lair," Kallie said as she looked around in awe.

"Yeah," Marcus added. "A *criminal* lair."

That sounded pretty damn good. "Okay, I think this place needs a name. All who are in favor of calling this place the Criminal Lair?" I asked.

There was a show of hands, and everyone agreed. I gave a nod. "Awesome. So now we have a code on where to meet."

"But *why* do we need it?" Marcus asked. "What did you bring us here to talk about?"

My mouth went dry, and I cleared my throat. "Take a seat. We might be here a minute."

I set my fireball on the floor. I sustained the flame as I sat cross-legged in front of it, and my friends sat around me in a circle. Oberi and Rishi preoccupied themselves with the mouse, though every now and then, Oberi's eyes flickered back to me.

"I didn't tell you guys everything that happened during the Darke Games," I began.

Charlie opened his mouth, but Marcus cut in first. "Oh, no," he started. "Not this again."

"Stuff happened when you guys were possessed by the lichen," I said.

"Was it when you were talking to yourself in the middle of the woods?" Kallie asked. "Because I reviewed the tapes, and I've got to be honest with you, that was a little weird."

"Because I wasn't talking to myself," I said. "The person I was talking to was actually a god. Coyote, the Koigni god, to be exact. He helped me figure out how to save you guys during the Games."

Charlie, Marcus and Kallie didn't say anything, and I worried they really did think I was crazy. I rushed to explain. "Technology wouldn't capture him on tape, and even if everyone else was there with me, no one would be able to hear and see him but me. And you guys, I think."

"Why us?" Kallie asked.

"Because he told me that I'm a demigod, and so are all of you."

Marcus blanched. Charlie shook his head no, like he couldn't believe it, but Kallie's look was introspective— like she might actually consider it.

I gave a frustrated noise. "Come on, guys. You can't tell me it doesn't make sense. All of us were using crazy magic during the Games, and we're all First Year students. We're more than talented supernaturals. We have to be."

"Are you *sure* Coyote came to you?" Marcus asked. "I'm not saying you were imagining things, but we were all pretty stressed out during the Games. You could've had a trauma response."

"No. She has to be telling the truth," Charlie said as realization crossed his face. "Because I heard Coyote, too. He was at the Villain's Ball after the Games, wasn't he?"

Kallie's and Marcus' mouths dropped open, and I said, "Yes. He came to me then, too. He said more gods would be along, and I'd have to look out for them."

"But why you?" Marcus asked. "No offense, but what god would want to talk to a couple of inmates? Why would they care?"

I sighed and reached for the journal in my bag. "Marcus, Kallie, you don't know this yet, but there's a prophecy written about me. I'm a chosen one who's destined to save the supernatural world, or destroy it. My aunt wrote the prophecy, but she doesn't remember what it means. All she could tell me was there was going to be a war of gods, and I'd decide the fate of it."

I ruffled through the journal pages. Once I found the prophecy, I began reading it aloud.

The balance between the light and the dark
Will be brought together by the light of the new dawn

A discovery of the ancient ones on the island of shadow
Will change the course of our universe

A second war breaches the horizon
Mountains will fall and villains will stand

The heavens will crumble and hell will open wide
Unleashing the demons that fester within
The path she will walk determines our fate
She dances the line both dead and alive

A new world formed from gods of old,
One from ashes or one from light
The choice is hers alone.

When I was done reciting, Marcus said, "This can't be real."

"Why not?" I snapped. Marcus really had to get with the program, here.

"Because my *mom* is a chosen one," Marcus replied. "How can I believe my friend is one, too? They're supposed to be incredibly rare."

"No fucking way," Kallie said immediately. "That can't be true."

"It is!" Marcus rebutted. "Why would you think I'm lying?"

"Because *my mother* is a chosen one," Kallie insisted. "She had her own prophecy she had to fulfill twenty years ago."

This was getting just too freaky. *All three of us* had chosen ones for mothers? Chosen ones were supposed to be incredibly rare.

Charlie broke the silence by saying, "Well, if all of you are the offspring of chosen ones, it makes sense why you're demigods."

"But what about you? You could hear Coyote, too," I pointed out. "You have to be a demigod as well."

Charlie shrugged. "I don't know. As far as I know, my mother wasn't a chosen one. There was never a prophecy about her. She was put to death years ago."

"Charlie, I'm sorry," I whispered. I didn't want to bring that up.

"It's fine, pidge. It's not like I knew her."

I heard the lie in his tone, but Marcus said, "This is all so crazy. It's hard to believe we're all at this prison at the same time, and we're all demigods, too. It's like fate led us together or something."

Kallie snorted. "Look, Marcus, I know you're pretty inept at magic—"

"Hey, my parents are pretty talented supernaturals!" Marcus protested. "Besides being the chosen one, Mom's the most powerful witch in the coven, and my dad's the Reaper's Apprentice— a legendary warlock. No one back home can match their power."

"Then what happened to you?" Kallie snickered.

Marcus wrinkled his nose, and I cut in. "Regardless, if you guys *are* demigods, I think Coyote wants you to help me with the prophecy. I'm not saying you have to, but this would be a hell of a lot easier if my friends were with me on this."

Kallie's eyes sparkled in excitement. "This sounds like an adventure. I'm totally in."

"An adventure where we could get killed," Marcus argued.

"Even better," Kallie said.

Marcus sighed and put his chin in his hand. "I guess I don't have much of a choice, being a demigod and all. I'm the only warlock with all five tattoos from all five Casts. Mother Miriam wouldn't have given me every power from the coven if I wasn't a demigod myself. I'll be dragged into this whether I want to or not. The question is, where do we start?"

"When we got separated during the Games, Charlie and I found a strange door in the middle of the woods on Darke Island," I said. "I've been studying the runes we found on the door, and I think they're Elvish. We believe the Elves are the *secret ones* the prophecy refers to. I've put Charlie up to researching the Elves, in case it leads us somewhere."

"But what if it leads to nowhere?" Charlie argued. "All the Elves are gone. We can't get answers from dead people."

"Charlie, I think this is important. I saw Coyote right before we found the door. I think he might've led us there. It *has* to be crucial to the prophecy."

Charlie tilted his head and scowled.

I raised the journal and waved it in the air. "While he's working on that, I plan to figure out a way to decode those Elvish runes. They have to mean *something*."

I got up from the circle and began walking around the room, conjuring a new fireball in my hand for light. I didn't find what I was looking for, until Oberi nudged my leg. I saw that he was carrying a thin wooden bow in his mouth— the same one I'd found here last semester.

"Good boy." I took the bow from him and patted his head. When I sat back down, I showed Kallie and Marcus the bow. "This is an Elven artifact. Charlie and I found it here last semester. That was after we found a bunch of Elven boats washed up on the shore in Kinpago. Why are all these Elven relics popping up, and why are most of them on Darke Island? It has to mean something."

I handed Charlie the bow. He ran his fingers over the runes, deep in thought.

Kallie sat back. "So what do you want me and Marcus to do? We want to help."

"Speak for yourself," Marcus grumbled, but Kallie punched his arm.

"I think if we are demigods, we need to look into it," I said. "Professor Mazur said something about our powers being unbound by the laws of nature, but that does us no good if we don't know how to use them properly. Can you guys try to find out more about demigods?"

"Definitely," Kallie said. "If I've got demigod powers, I want to start using them."

"Good luck," Marcus replied. "Most of the lore on demigods was destroyed by other supernaturals. We have no clue on where to look."

"Then we'd better get started," Kallie said in a cheerful way. Marcus groaned.

"One last thing. If we're talking about the prophecy, or us being demigods, it has to be here," I said. "Professor Mazur made it pretty clear that demigods should be reported to the Warden, and I don't want him to know anything about what we are, or what we're looking for. We can't risk the guards or teachers overhearing us talk about this stuff."

"Agreed," Charlie said. "We don't speak about any of this unless we're inside the Lair. Understood?"

Marcus nodded, while Kallie said, "I can put a ward around the Lair. It'll prevent anyone who isn't us from getting in or finding the place."

"That's perfect." I took the bow back from Charlie. "I need to get this back to my dorm, to study it."

"How are we going to sneak it in? No weapons on Institute grounds," Charlie said.

I handed the bow to Marcus. "Here. Subconjure this for me."

"Excuse me? I'm not your personal storage unit just because I'm a warlock!" Marcus protested.

"If you don't want to subconjure it, you could always stick it up your butt. I bet the guards don't check there," Kallie teased.

Marcus scowled. "You're *so* funny." He took the bow from me, and subconjured it into his magical stash.

I helped Charlie stand. "We should be getting back to school. We have to report for dinner."

As we made our way out, Marcus said, "You know, the Lair could use a little sprucing up. If we're going to be spending a lot of time there, we should decorate."

"Good idea. You provide the art, I'll provide the weapons," Kallie said.

"Weapons!" he squeaked. "Why do we need weapons?"

"It's an *evil lair*, dummy! *Of course* you need weapons!"

Kallie and Marcus argued about interior decorating ideas for the Lair all the way back to school, until Charlie told them to shut up. In the cafeteria, Charlie loaded a plate for both of us with fried chicken, mashed potatoes, and gravy. I shared food with him while Oberi watched us eat.

"Something on your mind, pidge?" Charlie asked. I hadn't said a word through dinner, but I'd managed to force down a whole drumstick and a couple of bites of potatoes. That was my heaviest meal in a week. I was really proud of myself.

I glanced to the side. Kallie and Marcus were arguing about something else now, and wouldn't overhear us. "What you said earlier, about me telling someone..." I said. "I think I want to do that after dinner."

"Oh. Are you sure you're ready?"

I nodded. "Yeah. It's time."

I'd been thinking about it all afternoon. I wasn't sure who I could trust with my deepest secret, until a familiar face popped into my head.

Ezekiel was my most beloved friend. He was more than my brother. He was someone I knew who was loyal to me, and he would be supportive no matter what. If I could tell anyone about this, and know they'd stay by my side, it'd be him. And a part of me wanted him to know, so I had one more person to help me carry this burden.

Now that I'd made the decision, I got a very demanding prompt in my spirit telling me not to wait. I should tell my brother now.

Inmates only got one phone call a week on Saturdays. It was Monday, but I felt like I couldn't wait that long. Once we were released from dinner, I ran down to the phone room and tapped on the glass that separated the phones from the guard's office. Charlie wanted to go with me, but I told him it'd be easier if I did this alone. I wanted a private moment with my brother.

"Can I make a call?" I asked the guard behind the desk. "It can't wait."

"If you call someone during weekday hours, it's two dollars a minute, and you get five minutes tops," the guard grumbled.

"That's fine," I said. "It won't take but a second."

I didn't care about the money. I just wanted to talk to my brother.

The guard scowled, but waved me forward. Orenda Academy students weren't allowed to have cell phones, so I hoped to the ancestors there was an off-chance my brother was home.

The phone rang. My nervousness churned and tightened in my stomach when no one answered.

On the last ring, someone picked up. "Ava, hi!" Ezekiel's cheerful voice resonated through the phone. "I didn't know you could call during the week!"

I was relieved my instincts had been right, and I'd gotten lucky enough to get a hold of him. It was like he and I were connected at the mind sometimes. "Uh, you can buy extra minutes," I stuttered. "Is anyone home?"

"Nah, Mom and Dad just left. They're at Maverick's dirt bike race."

"Oh. I didn't know that was today."

"Yeah. And Alana's staying at a friend's house. It's just me. I popped by to grab a couple things for my dorm. Do you want me to tell Mom and Dad you called?"

"Actually, you're the person I wanted to talk to," I began.

"Me?" He sounded surprised. "Okay, what's up?"

I twirled the phone cord around my finger. I felt so nervous I wanted to throw up. Maybe if I vomited out the words, and just got it over with, I'd feel better. "You know me and John had a falling out a couple of years ago."

"Yeah. Why does that matter now?"

I spoke before I lost my nerve. "I never told you why. He... do you remember that party I went to, a couple weeks after Monica died?"

"Yeah. You were acting really weird after it," Ezekiel began. "I asked if something was wrong. Was there?"

My throat was so tight I almost wondered if there was a Yapluma nearby, sucking air out of my windpipe. "Well... John got me alone that night, and... he raped me. I couldn't stop it."

The line was so quiet, I feared for a moment it'd gone dead. My brother was completely shell shocked. I'm certain ten seconds passed without a response.

Ancestors, just say something, I pleaded in my head. The silence felt horrible.

"Are you okay?" Ezekiel sounded on the verge of tears. But at least he spoke, and a weight lifted off my shoulders.

I sighed, and my back hit the wall. "Not really. But I've had a long time to deal with it."

Ezekiel didn't ask why I never spoke out about it, and I was relieved. Instead, he said, "That really explains a lot about the past few years. I'm so sorry, Ava. You never should've gone through something like that."

"It happened," I replied. "Not like I can go back and change it."

Ezekiel was quiet for a moment longer, before he asked, "Does... anyone else know?"

"I told Charlie a while ago," I admitted. "He actually encouraged me to tell more people, open up about it."

"Wow. And you chose me?" Ezekiel sounded honored.

"Yeah. Don't tell Mama and Daddy, okay? I'm not ready for the whole world to know yet. Just you and Charlie."

"I would *never*," Ezekiel insisted. "I won't say anything, I promise."

Ezekiel was a tattletale, and always had been, but he kept secrets under lock and key when it counted. I breathed a sigh of relief. "Thanks. I guess Charlie was right. It doesn't seem like such a big secret now."

"I'm glad. I don't want you to go through this alone." Ezekiel's voice cracked. "I love you, Ava. Like I *really* love you."

"I love you too, Ez. And I'm glad we could talk about this. It feels better, getting it off my chest."

An Institute notification pinged, telling me my five minutes was almost up. "I gotta go, Ez. Talk to you soon?"

"Sure, Ava. Bye."

I hung up the phone. When I did, I was certain I felt ten pounds lighter.

There was nothing easy about my past, or the road I'd have to take.

But with my friends and family beside me, I knew I could make it through just about anything.

Though a part of me wondered if telling my brother had been the right move. He was very protective of me. Now that he knew, I wasn't worried about what he might say.

I was worried about what he might *do*.

charlie
THREE

Me, a demigod? At first, I didn't believe it. I'd never been *anything* special.

But then I remembered the Villain's Ball. I had noticed something was different about Coyote when Ava spoke to him, but I hadn't realized what it was at the time. He was powerful, and I'd felt it. When Ava mentioned only demigods could see him, I knew the truth.

We were demigods. All of us. I couldn't deny it.

I mulled over the revelation for days, not quite able to wrap my head around it. I hated that Kallie and Marcus had agreed to help Ava with the prophecy. I just hoped Marcus was right and all the information on demigods had been destroyed. If they couldn't find anything on it, then Ava couldn't learn more about the prophecy. She'd be safe.

The one thing that took my mind off it was the mines. Over the past few months, the Institute had really grown on me. I mean, most of the students were shit, and the professors weren't much better, but I had everything I needed here— including *her*.

But if there was one thing I absolutely despised about the Institute, it was the mines. I didn't mind the physical labor; in fact, I found it relaxing. It took my mind off things and gave me something to do. It was the narrow tunnels and blocked passageways that got me.

Confined quarters didn't usually bother me, as long as I could feel the bigger world outside— a door, a window, *anything*. Down here in the noxite mines, it was a labyrinth of tunnels, one that was so difficult to navigate that no inmate would dare sneak off and try to escape. Your skeleton would remain here forever if you died down here— that was for certain.

It was the Yapluma in me talking, Ava had told me. We didn't like places where we couldn't control the air. In the tunnels, there wasn't much Air to work with, and it set me on edge every time my Work-Study class came down here.

The mines were located off campus, not far from the Institute. We had to take a bus to get there. I'd spent my first semester at the Institute learning about the mines in my Work-Study course. I knew my equipment and the safety procedures in place. Still, it took a few days to get into a groove, and stop worrying about hitting someone with my ax every time I swung it. Our powers didn't work well down here— if at all. Not with all the noxite around. So we had to work the old fashioned way, instead of with magic.

"I don't know why we bother with this," a Nivita kid named Thaddeus complained while we were working the mines. "They're just going to put this noxite into new fences, cuffs, and darts to keep us in line."

"I think this *class* is what they hope keeps us in line," Chancey replied. He was an angel, and one of the few people I got along with at the Institute. He was a rebel— always collecting money and making bets when it was against the rules. Then again, everyone here was a bit of a rebel.

I scoffed, wiping the sweat from my brow. "This isn't a class. It's cheap labor."

I swung my ax and felt it connect with the wall. A large chunk of rock broke free and tumbled across the ground near my feet.

Noxite was a metal present within the rocks beneath Shade Hills, one that had the ability to take magic away from supernaturals. It was incredibly strong on its own, but there was more rock than there was noxite, so the walls of the mines crumbled pretty easily after a couple swings of my ax. Once I knocked a few pieces free, I'd load them into a wheelbarrow, where the rock would be taken to another part of the mines. There, the noxite was extracted and melted down.

Chancey blew a breath, like he was ready for a break. "Does that bother you, Charlie?"

I shrugged. "The labor is fine. I just think we should all get compensated fairly."

Someone listening in on the conversation laughed. "Fair? Nothing's *fair* at the Institute."

"Go suck a dragon cock, Edwin," Chancey snapped at him. "You're just bitter you didn't win the Games."

It wasn't until Chancey called him by name that I recognized who'd spoken. It was Edwin Halloway, a warlock with an ego bigger than the mines. I'd just met him this semester, but according to Chancey, he'd competed in the Games two years ago and lost half his team before their first kill. I didn't like Edwin.

"What do *you* know about the Games?" Edwin sneered. "You didn't even compete."

Chancey ignored Edwin and turned to me. "You looking to make some extra cash?"

I swung my ax and frowned. "Even if I was, I don't have enough to enter one of your bets."

"That's just it, my friend," Chancey said smoothly. "There are more ways than one to make money inside the Institute. What do you weigh, Charlie?"

I groaned. "Don't tell me you're betting on my weight now."

It wouldn't surprise me, considering some of the stuff Chancey came up with. After we came in second place in the Games, he must be all over my team's stats.

"This isn't a bet," Chancey assured me, though I wasn't sure I believed him. "I'm just saying, they don't make muscles like *that* anymore."

I tossed a pile of rocks into a nearby wheelbarrow. "Great. Now you're hitting on me."

Chancey laughed. "You wish."

"He was totally hitting on you," Thaddeus snickered.

From a few paces away, Edwin scoffed loudly.

I was just about to say something, but Chancey beat me to it. "What's that, Ed? You got a problem with bisexual guys?"

"I didn't say nothing," Edwin shot back. "If anyone's got eyes for someone in this mine, it's not going to be the *blind kid.*"

My hands tightened on my ax, but I knew better than to respond. I'd heard that kind of shit enough times. It wasn't worth my energy.

"That's a shit thing to say," Chancey growled, taking a step forward.

I shot my hand out and caught him on the shoulder to stop him. "Don't worry about it."

Chancey hesitated. "Don't you want to beat his ass?"

I sighed. Sure, I didn't like Edwin much, and he was getting on my nerves, but I'd learned long ago to brush these comments aside. "He's not worth a trip to solitary."

Chancey stepped back and whispered lowly, "Edwin's a jerk. You should punch him, or I will."

"I'm not going to punch him," I said.

Chancey sounded amused. "I bet you have one hell of a swing."

"Get back to work!" a guard yelled in our direction.

Chancey's ax *clanged* as he picked it up and swung it against the wall. He made it look like he was working, but he mostly ignored the guard. "Charlie's got enough eyes on him," he announced to Edwin. "I hear the girls talk about him all the time in the hall. Apparently, it's a big deal to them that he came so close to winning the Games. What place did you come in again? *Last?*"

Edwin scoffed. "Like your place in the Games matters if you don't win. The only girl Charlie can attract is one as mental and broken as he is."

I lowered my ax and turned to him, nostrils flaring. "What the hell did you just say?"

Edwin chuckled. "Everyone knows you and Ava are screwing around. I've seen her visiting the nurse. We all know she's on meds for whatever loony weirdness she's got going on in the head."

"Ava's not *loony,*" I growled.

"Then what's she doing with *you?*" Edwin laughed. He was obviously amused by how angry I was becoming. "How many run-ins has she had with authority now? First that... *creative* uniform stunt last semester. And let's not forget the time she was nearly strip-searched in the hall."

"That proves nothing," I snapped. "Say one more word about Ava, and I'll—"

"You'll what?" Edwin taunted, taking a step forward until he was mere inches from me. I could feel the heat coming off him in waves. He was a few inches shorter than me, but judging by the way he swung his ax, I'd bet he had just as much muscle on him. "You'll use your elemental powers on me? Good luck down here in the mines, surrounded by all this noxite. Or maybe you'll swing your ax at me. You'd like it down in Cellblock 9."

My hands shook at my sides the longer he talked. I didn't know what the hell Edwin's problem was, but I suspected he was jealous that a blind guy had done better than he had during the Games. I was never going to get this asshole off my back if I didn't teach him a lesson.

"Your girlfriend may be mental, but she's a hot piece of ass," Edwin continued. "With you down in Cellblock 9, I bet she'll be looking for some relief. She'll be screaming my name so loud, you'll hear it down in your cell—"

Clank! Thwack!

First came the sound of my ax dropping out of my hands, then the crack of my fist across Edwin's face. *No one* spoke about my pidge like that.

"You go, man!" Chancey cheered. I was sure Thaddeus said something, too, but I was fuming and didn't hear him.

Edwin stumbled back a couple of steps, but I didn't give him a chance to react. I grabbed him by the collar and shoved him up against the wall.

"You take it back!" I growled. "You take it back *right now.*"

Edwin only laughed, and the stench of his breath filled my nostrils.

I was so fucking pissed that I grabbed him around the throat, instantly killing his laughter. "If I ever catch you anywhere *near* Ava-Marie, so help me, I will suck the air out of your lungs so fast, you won't live long enough to regret it."

"Get off me!" Edwin yelled, shoving me backward.

The guards began shouting, but I was too riled up to make sense of it. Screw the consequences. Edwin deserved one hell of a beating.

I lunged at him and clocked him across the jaw again. He retaliated immediately by tackling me to the ground. He tried to wrestle me down, but I elbowed him in the nose. It gave me just enough time to gain the upper-hand, until I had him in a headlock. I bit down hard on his ear, until I tasted blood.

"Holy shit, Charlie!" Chancey cried, though he sounded more impressed than anything.

Then came the sound of footsteps as the guards came rushing closer.

"That's enough!" Chancey insisted. He swatted my arm before he started yanking on me, as if begging me to let up on Edwin. "Charlie, that's enough!"

Strong hands landed on me— several pairs. The guards pulled Edwin and me apart, but I was still out for blood. I yanked an arm out of one of their grasps and swung at Edwin again, but he was too far from me now.

"Filthy Elementai!" Edwin sneered, before he spit at my feet.

"You're headed back to the Institute," a guard with a deep voice snapped. "All three of you."

Chancey sucked in ragged breaths. He didn't even fight the accusation that he had anything to do with the brawl. Instead, he simply said, "Charlie's with me."

"You're coming, too," the guard barked back at him.

Shit. Did I just drag Chancey down with me?

Someone yanked my hands behind my back and slapped noxite cuffs on my wrists. I stopped struggling as the guards began dragging me away. Reality sank in, and I realized where the guards were taking me. I'd started a fight within the prison, which meant I'd have to answer to the Warden. I'd end up in Cellblock 9, just as Edwin had threatened.

Fuck, what had I done?

I chastised myself the whole way back, out of the mines and onto the bus that transported inmates to and from the school. I'd just ruined everything good I had going on at the Institute. And Ava and Oberi...? I didn't know when I'd see them again. No one who went into Cellblock 9 got out. They either died down there or were transferred to the adult penitentiary. All for... what? A fight that barely brought me satisfaction? I'd have done a lot more than draw blood if I were given the chance.

The guards led Chancey, Edwin, and me inside the school. Edwin yelled profanities, like that would somehow convince the guards the fight wasn't his fault. They dragged him down a hall away from Chancey and me, until his voice faded. Maybe they *did* believe him, seeing as he wasn't going wherever the hell we were.

"Keep walking," a guard snapped, shoving me forward.

I quickened my pace and heard the sound of a heavy door open.

"Stairs ahead," Chancey told me.

The air was damp as we stepped into a wide stairwell, which went downward. Fuck... we were headed straight to Cellblock 9.

"Don't I get to appeal to the Warden?" I asked.

One of the guards chuckled. "The Warden doesn't deal with cases like yours. Consider yourself lucky."

"Lucky?" I practically choked on the word.

No one responded. They kept leading me down hall after hall, until I couldn't make out where we were anymore. It was somewhere in the basement of the school, but a place hidden so deep in the maze of hallways, I was sure I'd never find my way out.

The Institute's basement consisted of several chambers— one of them being the pool for merpeople, the other being Cellblock 9. But wherever the guards were taking me didn't seem to be either of them. I didn't hear the splashes of the siren pool, or the screams that I was certain had to be the background for Cellblock 9.

A door opened, and I was sure it was my new cell. But I realized immediately this was no cell at all. The air expanded to a large room. I heard the sound of various footsteps shuffling around, along with ongoing *thuds* that sounded like fists hitting a punching bag. Voices overlapped one another.

"Give me all you've got, Damien," a gruff voice said. "Mama didn't raise no pussy."

"Your punch is weak, Deuce," one student said to another.

"You hit like a little bitch! Think you'll win your next fight with that technique?"

Holy hell. This wasn't Cellblock 9. This was a fucking *training center*.

"Don't quit on me now, Damien—" the man with the gruff voice said, before cutting off abruptly. "Chancey," he greeted— like the two were great friends. "What have you brought me today?"

"Elementai, sir," Chancey announced. "He's blind, but one hell of a fighter."

The guard who'd been dragging me along released the noxite cuffs on my wrists. I leaned over to Chancey and growled, "What the hell is this?"

Chancey clapped me on the shoulder. I wasn't sure he'd ever been wearing cuffs to begin with. "This is the greatest opportunity of your life, my friend."

The man with the gruff voice approached us, his footsteps heavy against the concrete floor. I could tell he was huge by the way the air moved around him— definitely the body-builder type, or perhaps ex-military. He was a vamp, best I could tell. He sounded thoughtful, like he was sizing me up. "I recognize you. Charlie Wahkin, is it? You nearly won the Darke Games."

I cleared my throat. "Yes, sir."

The man terrified me, though in a different way than the Warden. I'd met people like him on the street before. His tone held authority, but he also sounded friendly... like he was the kind of guy to have your back until you stepped out of line. And if you did, so help your soul.

"Mm..." he mused. "A very interesting choice, Chancey. Why Charlie?"

Chancey chuckled. "He likes money."

"Always a good motivator," the man replied, sounding amused.

"Excuse me," I said. "If you don't mind me asking, who are you? What is this?"

"Call me Captain," he replied.

Yep, definitely ex-military.

"I'm the head of security here at the Institute," he explained. "Chancey here is one of my best recruiters."

"Recruiters?" I questioned. "For the fight club?"

It was obvious by the training sounds going on around me that's what we'd just walked into. I knew there was an underground fight club here at the prison, and it was rumored Chancey was involved, but I'd never experienced it myself... until now.

"Exactly," Captain said proudly. "And I'd like to bring you on board."

I furrowed my brow. "Why? Because I started a fight in the mines? What's going to happen to Edwin?"

Captain laughed. "I think a few hours in solitary will do it for him. I'm offering you this opportunity because you intrigue me, Charlie. Will you fight for us?"

I crossed my arms. This sounded sketchy as hell. An underground fight ring all for... what? The guards' amusement?

Profit, I realized immediately. Chancey wasn't just recruiting for Captain. He was taking bets for him, and I bet Captain walked away with one hell of a payday.

"What's in it for me?" I asked.

"Money, status, girls, you name it," Captain said.

"It's great," Chancey raved. "Every time you win a fight, you get money deposited into your account that you can spend on campus or take with you when you graduate. The referral money is amazing, too, if you're asked to recruit."

"Does the Warden know about this?" I asked.

Captain scoffed. "He doesn't take an interest in the club itself, but he lets us have our fun, provided we keep things quiet and under control."

I turned to Chancey. "What makes you think I'd want to do this?"

Chancey laughed. "Why *wouldn't* you? I like you, Charlie. I thought you'd appreciate being a part of something bigger at the Institute. And don't forget about the privileges."

I tilted my head. I admit I was intrigued by the money, but my curiosity piqued even more at the mention of privileges. "What *kind* of privileges?"

"There's a lot you can get away with when the guards are betting on you," Chancey explained. "Get into a brawl? Forget about punishment. Failing your classes? Expect extra accommodations. We even get to go on extra field trips every now and then— get some fresh air outside of the

Institute. You can do whatever you want when you're a fighter, and the guards will just look the other way."

I barely heard what Chancey had said about the field trips, because I was so focused on the extra privileges and accommodations. I could really use accommodations for my disability. And earning a place at the Institute where the guards ceased to target you could prove useful—especially with the way Ava attracted trouble like a magnet. I could use my new position to protect her and Oberi.

It almost sounded too good to be true.

"What's the catch?" I asked.

"No catch," Captain replied. "Though there are rules. Rule number one, no attacking with magic. Everything else is free game."

They wanted better bets. It was too easy to bet one supernatural power against another. They just wanted to watch us beat the shit out of each other.

"Rule number two, you don't go snitching," Captain growled, like the thought made him bitter. "The only people who know about the fight ring are those putting in bets. You tell someone else, and your ass gets booted. And I don't have to tell you what my security team is like when they've got a grudge against you."

I shivered.

"Rule number three, you show up for your training hours every week," Captain continued. "I'm not interested in anyone who isn't taking this seriously."

"It's not that bad," Chancey told me. "You can come down whenever you want to get your hours in."

"Oh," Captain added. "And you've gotta win your fights and keep your stats up. I don't take pussies. You get three fights to prove yourself, and if I spy any signs of a losing streak, you're out."

"What if I don't take the offer?" I asked, just to cover my bases.

"If you walk right now, nothing will change," Captain said. "The guards will treat you the same as always, and your pathetic bank account balance will waver on the negative. You'll receive a memory-wiping potion, so you'll forget everything you've seen here today. So... what will it be? Will you take the offer and join the club, or will you walk away?"

It wasn't even a question. I needed to be able to get away with stuff inside the Institute, so I could investigate the prophecy and protect my precious pidge and my Familiar. Four years of winning fights could give me enough cash to actually get a fresh start when I graduated. This fight ring was my one chance at having a future beyond the Institute.

And I'd be damned if I didn't want to kick ass while I was here.

"There's no reason to waste any memory-wiping potion on me, Captain," I stated confidently. "I'm in."

ava-marie
FOUR

It was rare I didn't have much to say, but on days like today, the words just wouldn't come. My thoughts slipped away as quickly as I conceived them.

"Pidge, you okay? You're really quiet." Charlie's voice broke me out of my stupor.

I blinked and realized I was in the Villain's Den. I sat on one of the couches, my legs flung over Charlie's lap, while Kallie and Marcus sat on the floor across from us. Marcus was working on a drawing. Kallie, strangely enough, was playing with Rishi. Weird. I thought she hated that cat. Oberi lay across Charlie's feet as a husky, snoring loudly as he took a nap.

I knew it was just past lunchtime. We'd gotten done eating and must've come to the recreation room to chill out before class.

Problem was, I couldn't remember the walk from the cafeteria to the Villain's Den, or sitting down next to Charlie. The last thing I recalled was walking through the double doors of the mess hall.

Shit. If I was forgetting simple things like walking across the school, that wasn't a good sign.

I shook my head. "I'm okay, Charlie. Just a little distracted."

My brain slipped from one thing to another. I could watch in my mind's eye as ideas fluttered by like birds, winging from this way to that. My head followed them as they zoomed back and forth. A couple people passing by watched as my head tilted from left to right, then whispered to each other that I was crazy.

I knew I was crazy, but people needed to mind their own damn business. Unfortunately, I was the talk of the prison ever since Charlie had gotten into trouble. He'd beaten the crap out of some guy for threatening me— rumor was, he'd nearly bitten off the guy's ear.

Okay, it was kind of sexy, thinking about Charlie going psycho on some asshole. I knew I was messed up for being attracted to violence, but hot damn, Charlie was like an uncaged animal when he lost control. It made me wonder if he was as much of a beast in the bedroom as he was when he was fighting some douche for my honor.

Charlie told me he'd gotten off with a warning, which shocked me. I was certain he'd get in big trouble for starting a fight, but I guess the guards let him off easy. I couldn't imagine why, but he got lucky. Who knew why anything happened around this joint?

Chancey passed by and stopped in his tracks. "Well, hello there. Aren't you two a sight for sore eyes?"

It was almost one o'clock in the afternoon, but still too early for Chancey's endless flirting. I would've liked it to happen *never*. His eyes flickered from me to Charlie, like he was sizing both of us up. Kallie looked upward at us, but Marcus' eyes narrowed, like he was annoyed.

"Oh, stop bothering us," I said, half-playfully, and half-irritated. "We're not interested in being your next conquests."

"I'm the kind of guy who likes a two-for-one," Chancey swooned. "And you two look like a couple that could really ruffle my feathers."

Charlie choked, before he forced out, "Not really what we had in mind."

"Don't forget I already got you in on one sweet deal, Charlie-boy," Chancey said. "I'm just the grand prize."

Charlie frowned, and my interest grew. What was he talking about?

"Can't you do this someplace else?" Marcus complained from the floor. "We're right here."

"This isn't a special offer. Chancey will fuck anything." I laughed.

"Nuh-uh," Chancey rebutted. "I'm not blind, sweetheart— no

offense to you, Charlie. But I only sleep with the hottest pieces on the market, and both of you are high rollers in that department."

"You're not convincing us, Chancey. Go away." I waved my hand and smirked.

"Well, if you change your mind, you know where to find me," Chancey teased. He winked, then sauntered away.

Charlie leaned in. "Did Chancey just... offer to have a threesome with us?"

"Ignore him. He's a harmless ho who likes to play around," I joked.

"I still can't believe he hit on me," Charlie said.

"You *are* pretty cute," I teased. Charlie didn't smile, and that bothered me.

Then something crossed my mind. "Hey... what was he going on about? He said he got you in on a sweet deal."

Charlie flushed. "Uh, it wasn't anything. Just talked the guards down when I got in that fight."

"Oh, so that's why they let you off easy. I see."

"Yeah." Charlie loosened his tie. "Sure."

Charlie stood, and my legs fell off of him. Oberi grumbled when the movement woke him up. "I've uh, gotta get to class, pidge. See ya."

Charlie walked off with Oberi, and I narrowed my eyes. He didn't have class for another thirty minutes. I knew his schedule.

Kallie sauntered closer, like she was excited at the idea of teasing me. "He's keeping something from you."

"What? No he's not!"

"He's acting suspicious as all hell," she argued. "He just walked off after you confronted him about Chancey. What do you think that means?"

I shrugged. "I don't know."

"I'm saying *something else* is happening behind closed doors," Kallie whispered. "And since I know you care about him, you should figure it out."

I glanced at Marcus for confirmation, who just blushed and looked down at his sketchbook. "Don't look at me. I know nothing."

"You know *something*. Charlie tells you everything," Kallie argued.

"If he *did* say anything, I'm sworn to secrecy," Marcus pledged. "You won't get it out of me."

"Wanna bet?" Kallie lunged toward him. Marcus immediately jumped up, clutching his sketchbook like he would a set of pearls. Kallie chased Marcus out of the room, and he yelped as she ran after him into the hall. Rishi followed, giving yowls and mews.

As I gathered my things to head to Supernatural Explorations, her words caused my thoughts to race. What was this *something else* she was talking about, if anything at all?

It struck me as I was walking down the hallway. *Oh, ancestors. Charlie must be sleeping with Chancey. That's why Chancey talked the guards out of putting him in Cellblock 9 after that fight. Charlie's giving him the goods.*

I didn't think Charlie was bisexual, but I mean, it wasn't like I'd ever asked. After all, he and Chancey had been sneaking around a lot lately, and I knew Chancey swung both ways. I wasn't sure where they went. Charlie always dipped out late at night, and didn't come back until curfew was almost called.

Ancestors, they were *definitely* screwing around. I can't believe I'd been so oblivious. I couldn't be mad about it. After all... like Kallie said, I hadn't claimed him. We weren't technically dating, so Charlie could mess around with other people.

Though... it was kind of different, thinking about Charlie being with another guy rather than a girl. I don't think my poor little heart could take it if I knew Charlie was out there sexing up a woman that wasn't *me*, although I understood that was hypocritical... I'd given him full permission to do that.

Maybe Charlie had to get his needs met elsewhere after I'd pushed him off me the other day. I didn't know.

How could I *support* Charlie in this? I wished he'd told me about it, but maybe he was embarrassed. Hadn't I made it clear I wanted an open relationship? If he was messing around with both me *and* Chancey, he had to be polyamorous, right? I'd never been in a polyamorous relationship before, but I was open to trying anything... I think?

Oh my *ancestors*, THAT'S why Chancey had offered to have a threesome! He was trying to warm me up to this whole poly-thing!

Wow. I couldn't believe I'd been so stupid. And I'd turned him down. I bet that had just crushed Charlie's poor feelings. He wanted to break it to me easy. *Ancestors*, that Charlie couldn't tell me the truth about his sexuality twisted up all my feelings and made me sad. I had to be the problem.

I must be a bad girlfriend— or bad partner, since I'm not a girlfriend, or whatever the fuck we are. Is this my fault, because I told him I didn't want to date? Is Chancey a better kisser than me? I should ask. I wonder which of them are bigger.

Too bad I couldn't talk telepathically to Oberi yet. I bet she had the dirt.

My thoughts were so jumbled about Charlie and Chancey, I almost walked into the door when I got to the Alchemy classroom. I sat down at my desk and tried to clear my thoughts. I didn't have a potions class this semester, but I had a class with Hemlock, and this was her designated room. Supernatural Explorations sounded interesting, and Hemlock was my favorite teacher, so I was planning on this being my best class this semester.

As people continued to flood the room, my nerves got worse. *Ancestors, can't there be fewer people in this class?* The number of students closing in around me felt suffocating. I began scratching my arms through the fabric of my sweater, feeling like my skin was crawling.

Things were getting bad again. I barely remembered last week. I was bored all the time and couldn't pay attention to a lecture for more than five minutes. My perfect grade point average had plummeted at the start of the semester, because I couldn't be bothered to finish my homework or tests. Nothing interested me like it had before.

Maybe I needed my meds adjusted. But I was scared to do that. The last time I'd adjusted my lithium, I'd gone into a full-on black hole of depression and hadn't left my bed in six days. I'd nearly starved to death. I didn't want that to happen again.

Opal sat beside me, and I nearly shied away from her presence. "Hi, Ava," she said. "Did you get the homework done last night?"

"Didn't bother." I'd have nothing to turn in to Hemlock.

"Oh." She frowned. "I was kind of hoping I could copy off you, since there were a few answers I didn't understand—"

"Give it here." I snatched the paper out of her hands, then wrote down the answers she'd missed quickly before handing it back to her.

Her eyes widened. "I didn't ask you to do that. You didn't even do your own homework. You shouldn't be worrying about my grade."

"It's fine, Opal. Just take it."

Her look was reluctant. "Okay..."

She fidgeted as she took out her pencils and laid them out precisely. "I got a few laps in at the pool this morning. There's a tear in my mermaid tail, but I don't know where it came from. I think Melody has scale rot, though. She was telling me her scales were falling off in the locker room this morning..."

Opal talked on and on. I didn't have much to offer in the way of conversation, but she kept chatting like it was any other day.

That was the best thing about Opal. No matter how bad my symptoms got, Opal never treated me any different. She hung out and had conversations with me whether I was completely sane or three sheets to the wind. It was nice.

Hemlock walked in, and the conversation in the room died away. "I hope all of you finished the worksheet I handed out," she began. "Otherwise, there will be severe consequences for your grade."

Whoopee. Like I cared.

Hemlock tapped on the top of her chest, just beneath her chin. As she did so, a light began to glow underneath her skin. It was round and radiant, a tiny purple ball that resonated within her body. The class awed at the prettiness of her fae light.

"As many of you know, this class is about exploring unusual aspects of the supernatural world," Hemlock said. "It's a bit of an odds and ends catchall for things that aren't expansive enough to elaborate on in full classes, but are interesting enough nonetheless. There are many things supernaturals share across the board. Certain powers of magic are available to everyone, though they're typically so minor, they go ignored in the magical community. Intuition is one of those abilities."

Hemlock gestured to the ball of light that shone under her skin. "You don't need to *see* your intuition to know it's there, but I've created an illusion to show you an example of the magic that lies inside. Each of us has a small light within us, guiding us toward what we believe is right.

This is called our sense of intuition. Usually, it shines the same color as your aura— a different lesson for another time. Intuition can be used for many things. It can help us make a choice when we aren't sure which path to take, or warn us of danger before we even know it's there. Our intuition comes from our highest selves, the part of us that resonates within our deepest souls. It connects us with our true purpose and guides us onward toward it, whether it be right or wrong, but can be used for other means. For example, magical explorers would use their intuition in order to locate artifacts and search ruins."

That was interesting. My Grandpa Elliot often said he "had a hunch" whenever we were exploring caves together, and we'd follow his suspicions wherever they led. Daddy complained that my grandfather didn't know what he was doing, but maybe there was something more magical to his process that we didn't understand. Grandpa's weird hunches had led us to find some interesting discoveries when we'd gone exploring quite a few times— whenever they didn't lead us into booby traps or dead ends, as Grandpa was likely to do.

Ghost raised his hand— he was a warlock student who was in this class with me, who'd gotten his nickname because he was scared of everything. "How does it work, if it's an innate skill?"

"It's quite simple," Hemlock replied. "To follow your intuition, you must look inside. The more you practice using it, the more effective it will be. You must learn to trust yourself, and cast away doubt. The most talented supernaturals are always the ones who can follow their instincts with trust and faith. If you ignore your intuition, it will cease to appear, and may even fade over time. However, if you practice using it in even the simplest situations, it will show up for you when you need it the most."

Hemlock levitated the ball of light outside of her body and sent it outward. It began flying around the room, and she followed it in a circle. "You can practice amplifying the power of your intuition by being creative, such as through dance or art, or through meditation. Keeping a journal on your instincts will also prove helpful, and show you a record of where your intuition was right and where you might've gone wrong. The gods gave supernaturals the power of intuition so that we might use it, not let it sit idly by. Sometimes, they know what's best for us."

Hemlock continued on, but as much as I tried to listen, her words fell away. I tried to take notes, but they turned into doodles as her voice droned on in the background, and my eyes went glossy. Fuck, this was a subject I was *interested* in, and I couldn't pay attention. I hoped it didn't look to Hemlock like I was spacing out. I *wanted* to learn this. Why couldn't my brain just work right?

"Miss Mitoh? Miss Mitoh, you've been sitting there for ten minutes."

I blinked a few times. "Huh?"

I looked around. The classroom surrounding me was completely empty. All the seats were vacant. Hemlock sat at the front of the room behind her desk, appearing concerned.

Fuck. I must've phased out again. Who knew how long I'd been sitting here, completely gone while Hemlock lectured? Class had probably been dismissed a while ago. The last thing I recalled was Hemlock talking about the gods giving supernaturals intuition. The rest of the hour had passed in a blur.

Hemlock raised an eyebrow. "I thought you wanted to ask me a question, but you haven't spoken in some time. Is there something wrong?"

I dug my fingernails into my palms, to wake myself up. "Actually, I did want to ask you a question. Do you have time?"

"My next class is in another hour," Hemlock said. "What is it you wish to ask?"

I scampered up from my desk and dug in my bag. I'd been planning to talk to Hemlock all week about the Elven gate. I didn't want to tell her about the prophecy— didn't know if I could trust her that far— but I was sure if anyone knew something about that gate, it was Professor Hemlock. I'd looked up her teacher's biography, and she'd been on Darke Island for over twenty years, longer than any other teacher. Maybe she knew what it meant.

I took out the journal Aunt Maddie had given me on the prophecy, as well as Charlie's recorder. I had borrowed it because I wanted Hemlock's words on tape. I didn't trust my bipolar brain to remember anything she said to me right now, and if we found out something crucial, it would be best to have a recording of it we could review later.

"Do you mind being recorded?" I asked. "I don't want to miss anything."

Hemlock cleared her throat. "Miss Mitoh, I noticed you didn't turn anything in today. I know you are more than capable of doing your homework. Please don't ask me for a pass, because I know you don't need one. You could answer those questions in your sleep."

"It's not about that, actually," I said. "I'm doing research for a private project, and I thought you might be able to help."

Hemlock raised an eyebrow. "Was this... research so engrossing that you forgot to do your work?"

"Yes," I lied. "I'm sorry, I won't forget next time."

Hemlock sighed, then gestured to the chair across from her desk. "Take a seat."

I sat in front of her, then pressed *record* on the machine. I began shuffling through the pages of the journal, careful to hide the contents from Hemlock as I spoke. "When I was in the Darke Games, Charlie and I came across a strange doorway in the middle of the woods. I was wondering if you could tell me what it means."

I opened the journal to a page where I'd drawn the gate from memory. It wasn't fantastic like Marcus' drawings, but it was enough to know what I was referring to.

Hemlock adjusted her square spectacles as she observed the drawing. "I've been there many times. It is a relic, from when the Elves were still living on Darke Island."

"So it *is* an Elven artifact," I insisted.

"Yes. Most likely a portal from long ago, though I'm certain it no longer works," Hemlock said. "It is a curious thing. I'm not surprised you're obsessed with it."

"But why would the Elves make it?" I asked. "A door that has seven keyholes— why would the Elves want to keep something locked up so tightly?"

"You're not asking the right questions," Hemlock stated. "Don't ask why it's there. Ask where it might *go*."

My heart pounded several times. "But you said if it's a portal, it probably doesn't work."

"For us, yes. But if it's an Elven door, it could possibly work for an

Elf," Hemlock pointed out. "Provided they had the seven keys to open it."

My mouth went dry. "But all the Elves are dead."

"Unfortunately." Hemlock sighed. "And there lies the tragedy. We will never know what is behind it, because we destroyed our only chance of solving the mystery. But one does have to wonder... why would the Elves need to build something like that in the first place?"

Hemlock was silent for a moment, and I said, "This is something you've investigated."

"Many times, yes," Hemlock said. "I am a bit of an expert on Elven lore. It was a fascination for me when I attended Arcanea University."

Excitement climbed in my belly, but I forced it to stay put. "So, might you be able to tell me what these mean?"

I turned the page of the journal, one where I'd written down a couple of Elven runes from memory. A few were from the door, and others were from the Elven shipwreck in Kinpago. I'd gone back over break and copied down what I could.

Hemlock's fingers skimmed the page. "I know a few of these, but this one I understand the most. It's on the center of the gate."

Hemlock pointed to the biggest rune I'd written down.

"Can you tell me what it means?" I asked.

She nodded. "That particular rune is the Elven symbol for *demigod*. Put together, all the runes on the door say, *What is hidden remains secret from all but the demigods, forevermore.* Strange, considering I wasn't aware of any demigods at the time of the Elven genocide, but interesting nonetheless."

It was very difficult to keep myself in my seat. The gate on Darke Island wasn't a door for Elves at all.

It was a door for demigods. Which meant Charlie, Kallie, Marcus and I needed to figure out how to open it. But why had the Elves built a door for people like me in the first place?

"The rest of these runes look like the names of ships," Hemlock said as she read them.

Hemlock looked toward the door, as if she was worried someone might walk in. Then she waved a hand, and a lock on her desk clicked open. She opened the drawer, then placed a very old and very worn book in front of me.

She opened the book and began turning the pages. "This is a translation guide for Elven runes. With this book, you should be able to decipher any Elvish you come across."

"Where did you find this? It's extraordinary," I marveled. No one knew how to read or speak Elvish anymore— everything of Elven lore had been destroyed by the fae during the Great Supernatural War.

"I came across it when I was crawling around in a cave years ago," Hemlock said fondly. "It's my greatest discovery... and probably the last living relic that the supernatural world has of the Elves."

My awed voice became horrified. "You can't give me something so valuable. I won't accept it."

"I have read that book so many times the pages are bare," Hemlock replied. "The knowledge goes nowhere if it dies with me. I wish to pass it on to you."

I wanted to refuse again, but to do so would be foolish. My prophecy was connected to the Elves somehow, and Hemlock was doing me a great favor by supplying this to me. I needed this book. "Thank you," I said as I slipped the book into my bag, along with my journal and the recorder. "This means so much to me."

"It's more than just a gift. I'm giving you this as an opportunity that you'll hopefully learn it, so one more person in the world can remember what we supernaturals have forgotten," Hemlock said. "I don't have to tell you that book is contraband. If you're found with it, there will be extreme consequences by the Warden. The supernatural world can't afford to lose that book. Keep it secret."

I hugged my bag, which contained the book. "I promise."

"I know you'll do right by it." Hemlock sat back in her chair. "I haven't come across a student as passionate about history as you in a very long time. It's a refreshing change."

"Did you teach it at Arcanea University?" I asked. A knowledgeable fae teacher like her should be instructing at a high-profile college in Malovia, not this dump. For the millionth time, I wondered why Hemlock was here.

"For a few years, but most of my time teaching has been spent here.

Before I was a professor, I was a great anthropologist, but this is one enigma I've never been able to solve. I've been to that site dozens, perhaps hundreds of times, and I've never been able to determine just what that gate was used for."

"You were an anthropologist?" I brightened.

"Oh, yes. I traveled all around the world, having many adventures in many countries. I have studied many different cultures in my time," Hemlock said.

"I wanted to study anthropology, before I came to the Institute," I said sadly, thinking of my lost dream.

Hemlock raised her chin. "You're the granddaughter of Elliot Baine, aren't you? A wonderful, clever man, if not a little odd. He's had some... *interesting* discoveries over the years. I very much enjoyed his book on supernatural societies. I went on one or two explorations with him in my younger years, and I daresay they were far from... ah... boring."

That was a nice way of saying she was glad she'd kept her head on while exploring with my grandfather, a sentiment many shared.

"Yes." I sighed. "I wanted to follow in his footsteps. It was my goal to be an explorer."

"Whyever can't you?" Hemlock asked. "The Institute has a major in Anthropology, small though it may be. I am the director of the program — though we haven't had an enrollee in years."

"Really?" I sat up. "So you mean, I could graduate with a degree in Anthropology?"

"Yes, if you complete all the requirements. Of course, the program requires an internship with me over the summer semester at the Institute, and it's *very* intensive. There's no time for friends or relaxation. We only take breaks for meals and sleep. Most students don't make it through, I'm afraid."

"I can. I can do it," I insisted. "I want to be in the program."

Hemlock smiled. "If you're interested, I can give you the paperwork to fill out, so you can decree your major."

"Yes! I want to do it right away!"

Hemlock smiled, then dug in her desk for a few papers. She blew off the dust that was on them, then handed them to me. They looked like they hadn't been touched in years. "Once you've completed the application, turn it in, and I'll alert the Warden to your choice. I'm sure he'll be thrilled to finally have an applicant in the Anthropology program again."

That soured my mood. I didn't want the Warden to know anything about what I was doing, even if it was as innocent as declaring a major.

As we finished our conversation, a guard came in. He stooped down and whispered something to Hemlock. Her eyes widened.

"Miss Mitoh, you have an emergency call from your mother," Hemlock said. "You should head to the phone room immediately."

I immediately felt so sick that the room started spinning. Whatever happened had to be *bad*, if the Institute wanted me to take this call. Something must've happened with Daddy. Ancestors, what if he was in the hospital again? I couldn't leave the prison to visit him. What if there wasn't enough time to say goodbye?

Tears sprang to my eyes, and I jumped out of my seat. I barely remembered to grab my stuff before I dashed out the door.

When I got to the phone room, a guard handed a receiver to me with a cold look. I snatched it out of his hands and pressed it to my ear as he walked away. "Hello? Mama, is that you?"

"Oh, Ava, thank goodness," Mama breathed. "I was worried we wouldn't be able to get in contact with you."

The minute I picked up the phone, I heard shouting echoing in the background— men's voices.

"What's going on? Is Daddy okay?" I blurted.

"Your father's fine, though he's a little... well, *unhinged* at the moment, is what I would call it."

"What?"

Daddy's voice broke in. He had to be on the other side of the house, but he was shouting so loudly I could hear it through the phone. "I don't understand what's gotten into you. Attempted *murder*?! Do you understand what this means? I have no choice but to send you to the Institute!"

"*Good!*" Ezekiel's voice responded back. "I'd rather be with my *sister* anyway!"

My stomach plummeted. "Mama, what's going on?"

"Your brother's gotten into some trouble," Mama said. "We knew he was struggling in his classes, but we didn't think it'd go like this. He's behind in magic, and was *so* frustrated, but your father and I couldn't have guessed it'd end up this way."

Mama was talking like she needed excuses for my brother's behavior.

"What does that got to do with—?"

"Ez was walking to class at Orenda Academy this morning when he passed Johnny Smith in the hallway. You remember Johnny, don't you, dear?"

Did I ever. My intestines knotted together as I squeaked, "And?"

"Well, it looks like Rosary and Johnny are dating now," Mama admitted. "I overheard that they'd been kissing when he passed by, and your brother didn't take it very well."

What the fuck? My brother's abusive ex-girlfriend and my rapist were sleeping together? This was so gross. I swallowed a lump in my throat. "Okay, so what happened?"

"That's just the thing. It's hard to explain," Mama said slowly. "From what I understand, Ezekiel tried to use his magic on Johnny, and when his powers didn't work, he grabbed Johnny and started..."

Mama trailed off, like it was hard for her to say out loud. I didn't have to wonder. Ez had beaten John to a pulp.

"Your Uncle Jonah split them up, but by the time Ez was done with him, Johnny was in a very dire state. He's in the hospital on oxygen. A couple bones in his face are broken. It was a miracle Ez didn't kill him," Mama admitted. "Ez has your father's temper, but I never believed he'd take things this far."

I knew my brother better than that. He'd be hurt about Rosary, sure. But what he'd done wasn't about that. Ezekiel had been delivering justice on my behalf, in revenge for John attacking me.

Ancestors, I felt guilty as all hell. Maybe I shouldn't have told him.

Mama sighed. "Your father tried to talk it down to aggravated assault, but the injuries Johnny sustained were so severe, the Elders couldn't let it pass. Ez is coming to the Institute, Ava. He's leaving in the morning."

She sounded heartbroken. I couldn't imagine how she felt, losing two kids to the Institute.

I didn't say anything, but Mama rambled on. "This *can't* be all there is to the story. I knew Ezekiel was upset after Rosary miscarried their baby, but I refuse to believe he'd take things this far because she decided to date someone else."

"Maybe it's not about her." The statement slipped out of my mouth, and I berated myself to be quiet.

Mama noticed. There was a long pause.

"Ava, is something else going on?" Mama sounded very worried. "It's not like Ezekiel to go off like this, and I know the two of you spoke not too long ago."

I had to lie. If I told the truth, it'd make everything worse.

"Everything's fine," I said. "I don't know why Ez would act that way."

"Hm." Mama mused for a time, before she said, "Well, I called because I want you to keep an eye on Ezekiel, show him around and explain how things work at the Institute. You know he has a gentle heart. I'm worried he'll get eaten alive in there. He can't stand his ground like you. At least, I thought he couldn't, until today."

Ezekiel was basically a marshmallow. He'd attacked John to protect me, and not for any other reason. Up until this point in his life, he couldn't hurt a fly. I worried about how he'd handle prison, too.

"I'll watch over him," I promised. "He'll be okay."

"Good." The shouting between Daddy and Ez grew louder, and Mama said, "I have to break this up. Stay safe, Ava. Your brother will be there by tomorrow."

The phone clicked, and I hung up the receiver. Dread grew in my chest with every passing moment, and I couldn't do anything to suppress it.

My little brother had been sentenced to the Institute. And for what? Defending me?

It was like I'd told Charlie months ago. The people around me were collateral damage. I was a blazing star that torched everything in my path, and Ezekiel got burned.

Though a tiny bit of me felt justified. I hadn't been able to get back at John for what he did, but my brother had. He'd taken justice into his own hands and fought for me.

I just wished there wasn't a price he had to pay.

I WAS nervous all throughout class the next day, waiting for my brother to arrive. I figured he'd be there early in the morning, but when I checked for new arrivals, the prison bus still hadn't shown up.

I suffered through a long ass morning, then rushed back to the Elementai cell block before lunch. My legs nearly became water when I slid to a stop at the end of it. Ezekiel stood in the hallway of the cell block, looking like he didn't know what to do. He wore a new Institute uniform, and was completely lost. He must've just gotten back from the Warden's welcome speech.

"Ez!" I shouted, and he turned. Relief shone on his face when he saw me. I flung myself on him. Ezekiel squeezed me so tightly it felt like my lungs were going to burst.

"Ava," he gasped. "I'm *so* glad you're here."

He almost sounded near tears. I looked around. There was no one here, but it was better to have this conversation in private rather than out in the open.

"What cell are you in?" I asked. "We should talk."

Ezekiel led me to a cell only a few doors down from my own. After he closed the door behind us, we sat on the bed. His face broke into a smile.

"I know it's only been a few weeks since I saw you, but it felt like forever," he confessed. "I hate being away from you."

"But now you're away from the rest of our family," I pointed out, and Ezekiel's smile slunk away. "Ez, why did you do that? What I told you, I said in confidence. I didn't want you to go after John."

"I couldn't stop myself. The first time I saw him after you told me what he did, I just lost control," Ezekiel admitted.

"But what happened to me is *my* trauma," I said. "It wasn't right for you to take it into your own hands."

"I really didn't want to invalidate you, or anything like that," Ezekiel said. "After it was all over, I felt really bad about what I did— not because

I hurt John, because fuck him, but because I worried you'd think I was trying to blow your secret, or that I wasn't letting you handle what happened to you on your own terms. I really fucked up, Ava. I broke your trust because I couldn't control my emotions, and I'm sorry for that."

I sighed. It was really hard to be mad at Ez for beating the shit out of my rapist. When Mama had told me John was in the hospital, I felt like cheering.

But not at the expense of my brother's freedom.

"I understand," I said. "Your feelings got the best of you, and I know my past doesn't affect just me. I only wish it hadn't come to this. I feel like I put you in here."

"Don't say that. It's not your fault. None of this is. My actions were my own, and he fucking deserved it," Ezekiel raged. "Do you think I would just sit around and let him attack other girls? If he's done it to you, who's to say he won't try to hurt somebody else? The bastard got what he deserved. Maybe he'll think twice next time."

His words made me want to vomit. That was my worst fear— the thought of John attacking another woman. I'd been praying to the ancestors I was the only one, but I was all but certain there had to be more victims. Hopefully my brother's actions *would* cause John to pause before he cornered another girl again.

"Still," I argued. "The Institute isn't a great place to be."

"Maybe it's not such a bad thing," Ezekiel said with a shrug.

He was an optimist to the point of his own detriment. "Ez, you're in *prison*! This isn't a good situation."

"I was failing at Orenda Academy. My magic sucks," Ezekiel insisted. "I couldn't keep up in my Toaqua classes. I can't even levitate a ball of water."

"It can't be that bad," I scoffed. "Last semester, Mama said you were casting Water like a natural."

"She was exaggerating to try and boost my confidence. I'm shit."

"I don't believe you."

Ezekiel pointed to the condensation on the window and raised an eyebrow. Then he moved his hand toward it, in a way that should've commanded the droplets to move.

They didn't budge an inch. He made a gesture toward the window, and I blew out a breath. "Okay, so you're new at this. Big deal."

"At my age, I should be able to do more than what I'm capable of," Ezekiel said. "The Elementai program at the Institute is at a slower pace. I might do better in an elemental class that's easier than the ones at Orenda Academy."

That was putting it lightly. The elemental class at the Institute was a course for beginners and people who couldn't do magic. Charlie and I were bored out of our minds during that class. It was just too simple.

But maybe Ez was right and that's what he needed.

"I'm sorry about Rosary," I offered. "I knew you were hoping you two could work things out."

Good thing they hadn't, though. I hated that bitch.

"I don't care about *her*," Ezekiel said, in a way that sounded like he was repulsed. "You should've seen the way she looked at me after she got done kissing John, like she wanted to brag about it. She loved rubbing it in my face that she'd moved on. Really, Ava, it doesn't bother me that she and John are together. I went after him because he hurt you, but that was the only reason."

I chewed my lip nervously. "Ez, what if you had killed him, in the public where everyone could see? You'd be doing life right now."

"I didn't care at the moment. I just wanted him dead. I saw the look in his eyes as I was wailing on him. He knew exactly what he did and why I was doing it," Ezekiel said darkly. "I think he was terrified I was going to tell everyone what he'd done. But I wouldn't do that to you."

"It sounded like you and Daddy really got into it," I pressed. "What did you guys say to each other?"

Ezekiel wrinkled his nose and crossed his arms, hunching his shoulders. "I don't want to talk about Dad. He really pissed me off after I was arrested. He said some shit he shouldn't have."

"He probably didn't mean it," I said gently. "I imagine he was devastated at the thought of sending you here."

"Yeah, well, I get that it doesn't look good for him. He's a chief, and two of his kids are in prison," Ezekiel admitted, scratching the back of his head.

"It's not about that. He's going to miss you."

Ezekiel huffed. "Yeah, well, could've fooled me. There was some stuff said that he can't take back."

Their argument must've been bad. I redirected the conversation. "What about the rest of the family?"

"Well, you know Mom. She's just trying to hold everyone together," Ezekiel said. "Alana just seems... really confused. You know she's smart. She might piece it together."

I nodded. I didn't really mind if my sister knew, but I hoped she didn't figure it out before I told her on my own, and I wasn't ready yet. Not after this fiasco with Ezekiel. "And Mav?"

Ezekiel frowned. "I, uh, had to tell Maverick," Ezekiel said reluctantly. "He was *really* upset when you left, and when I got sentenced, he practically lost it. He's just a kid, Ava. It's not fair to him to lose two siblings to prison at such a young age and not know why."

"I wanted to tell him myself, Ez."

"I get that, but he was in a rage. I thought he might hurt himself. I had to calm him down somehow. He took it pretty well, actually," Ezekiel said fairly. "He thought that I did the right thing and it was good I was coming here, to protect you. He promised not to say anything."

"That's a big secret for an eleven-year-old to carry around."

"Yeah, but you know Mav. He's a stoic old man in a little kid's body. He'll take it in stride."

I knew Maverick was super serious, and really mature for his age. But still... what he knew now, no kid should have to deal with.

But what John had done caused ripples to resonate through my family and friends, whether they knew the truth or not. There were consequences for everyone when people got hurt, not just the victims. I could try to shield my loved ones from the damage, but no matter how much pain I took, there would always be pieces that fragmented off to cut them.

My shoulders relaxed. "I'm really glad you're here, Ez. It's nice to have family around. Even though I wished you'd kept your freedom, your presence makes me feel like I'm not alone."

"You're never going to be alone. You'll always have me," Ezekiel promised.

Ez stood. "Now, where's the cafeteria? I'm starving."

That was Ez— always worried about food. "I'll warn you, it's not Mama's cooking."

"I don't care. I'm so hungry I could eat a moose. *Two* moose, even."

I laughed, but the sound was wary. Ezekiel didn't know what he was getting into at the Institute. This place wasn't a game. There was only so much I could protect him from.

But at least he'd shown he could defend himself. It would be enough to keep him alive in here.

I hoped.

charlie

FIVE

Ava had me worried earlier. Sometimes, she wouldn't talk for hours, which was so unlike her. But the second her brother Ezekiel arrived at the Institute, it was like a switch had been flipped inside of her. I didn't know if it was her bipolar— and if it was, how long it would last— or if that was just the effect her brother had on her. I could feel through our bond that she was more at ease around him, and I noticed she was eating more at dinner.

Oberi had picked up on it, too, as he constantly begged her for a grooming. I didn't know if she'd noticed, but he didn't bother her much when she was down. It was one of the ways I assessed her mood, even when she wouldn't outright tell me how she felt.

Ez was great and easy to get along with. He quickly melded into our group and ate with us at every meal.

"How's your first week been?" Marcus asked Ez at breakfast one morning.

He hesitated. "It's, um... interesting."

"Interesting how?" Kallie asked.

"I didn't know what to expect, to be honest," Ez admitted as he poked at his food, the fork scratching the plate. "Some people are really nice, like you guys. Others are... a little scary."

I heard the hesitation in his tone and realized he must've been shooting glances around the cafeteria.

"Pft." Ava blew a breath. "Forget about Mad Dog. We kicked his ass during the Games, and that's not even the first time."

"And probably won't be the last," I teased.

Kallie clapped Ez on the back. "As long as you stick with us, you don't have to worry about him. He's not coming anywhere near us."

"Though you might want to steer clear of Deuce and his goonies," Marcus added.

"Why's that?" Ez sounded instantly intrigued.

I nearly winced. "We had a confrontation during the Games. His team stole our first-aid kit, and I choked out a merman on their team. I don't think he's the kind to drop it."

He was also in the fight club alongside me, though we trained at different times. I tried to avoid him as much as possible.

Ava swatted me lightly. "Don't go scaring my brother. Deuce has left us alone for weeks. We can handle him."

She reached over and grabbed a grape off our shared plate, then popped it in her mouth. "Besides, it's not the ones who *look* scary that you need to worry about. Be worried about trickster fae like Kallie."

Kallie gave a wicked laugh. "I think the most dangerous inmates are the hotties who might steal your guy."

Kallie, Ava, and Marcus snickered, like they had some inside joke going on. I didn't understand the reference.

"Did I miss something?" I questioned as Oberi nudged me for another piece of French toast.

Kallie giggled under her breath. "Not at all. In fact, I think you understand *far* better than any of us."

Her tone was teasing, but I didn't know what she meant. "Understand what?"

"I think they're implying *somebody's* getting some," Ez said.

"What?" I balked. Hell if I was getting *any*. I only wanted one chick in this place, and we hadn't made it that far yet. "I don't even talk to any girls besides Ava and Kallie."

"Nobody said anything about *girls*," Kallie practically sang, and she and Marcus started laughing again.

I titled my head, totally lost. "What are you talking about? Did someone slip some laughing potion in your breakfast, because you two are acting weird."

"Hey," Marcus said quickly. "We have nothing to hide. But if there's anything you want to get off your chest... now's a fine time."

My breath stalled momentarily. Did Marcus know about the fight ring? I hadn't told anyone yet, because I didn't want to get kicked out before my first fight. I wanted to be sure I was ready before I asked them to bet on me and let them in on the secret.

"What are you trying to get me to say, Marcus?" I demanded.

"Nothing," he said innocently.

"Oh, don't look," Kallie said quickly. "Chancey just walked in."

My fingers tightened around my fork. Shit! They *totally* knew about the fight ring! And they wanted me to admit it out loud to Ava.

"Will you guys stop it?" I snapped. "If there *was* something I wanted to share, I'd do it at my own pace, thank you very much."

Kallie whispered something to Marcus, though I didn't hear it. They both started laughing again. Ancestors, they sounded like high school girls.

Ava leaned closer to me. "If there *was* something you were keeping secret, you'd tell me, right?"

"Yeah, of course," I said as I shoveled food in my mouth.

I *was* going to tell Ava about the fighting... eventually. She'd been in such a low period lately, I wasn't sure how to approach the topic, and I didn't want a social-justice lecture either about how unfair it was that Captain was using me for his own personal gain. It was coming. I just knew it.

"You don't have to hide *anything* from me," she assured me softly, placing a hand on mine. "I won't judge you."

The way she said it sounded like she was talking about something else entirely. I figured she didn't know about my new hobby yet. I wondered if she'd be supportive when she found out. I thought about telling her now, but not in front of Ez. I liked him, but I didn't know how far I could trust him. I couldn't have him running off and blabbing about it to other people.

"Pidge, you know I tell you everything," I assured her. "Just... let me work through this one on my own."

Ava gaped, and I felt her breath rush across my skin. "I... um... take whatever time you need. Just know that I'm not mad... whatever it is. We never agreed to be exclusive."

Ava wasn't my girlfriend— she was right about that. But I hated that she thought it meant she didn't get an opinion. I wanted to tell her about the fight club, because girlfriend or not, we were a team.

But I also feared she wouldn't support me, regardless of what she said now.

"Hey, Charlie," Ez cut in. "We should probably head to Ancient Magical History. Class starts in ten minutes."

I almost laughed. Ten minutes early, and Ez was worried about getting to class. Almost everyone here waited until the last minute before class to tear their way across campus and slip in right before the professor. Prison was going to change Ez, that was for sure.

But I was glad for the distraction, because I suspected Ava would press me about my secret, and I couldn't go telling her in the middle of the dining hall. I stood, leaving the rest of the food on the plate for Ava and Oberi.

"Yeah, we should probably get going," I said. "I'll catch up with you guys at dinner."

I left Oberi with Ava, since I knew my way to class, and I had Ez to help. He'd been placed in my Ancient Magical History class, and although he missed the first few weeks, he seemed to be catching up quickly.

"What was all that about?" Ez asked as we started down the hall.

"Kallie and Marcus?" I questioned, shaking my head. "No idea. Those two can be... strange sometimes. You learn to brush it off."

"Hm," Ez said thoughtfully. "Marcus seems nice, but Kallie actually scares me a bit."

I chuckled. "She has that effect, but you don't have to worry about her... actually, on second thought, don't agree to anything she offers unless you know the terms."

Ez sounded wary. "I take it you have some experience with that?"

I'd told him the story about our Darke Games training session last semester, when Kallie had roped Marcus into volunteering to be a guinea pig for a possession by a demon. A horny sex demon, as a matter of fact. By the time we reached the classroom, Ez couldn't stop laughing.

"Now *that* part of the Games should've been televised," he teased, before getting really quiet.

We took our seats in the back of the class before he continued. "It wasn't easy watching my sister fight in the Games, you know. To be honest, I couldn't watch most of it. I thought I might lose her."

"They broadcast the Darke Games all the way back to Kinpago?" I asked. I'd thought it'd only been for Shade Hills residents only.

"Mom and Dad streamed it for me, since I asked," he explained. "The picture was really poor, considering the crappy reception here on Darke Island."

I nearly snorted. "Tell me about it."

The library computers helped *some* in getting me through my classes, but it was a minor accommodation at best.

"I'm just glad you were there," Ez added. "It looked like you guys really worked well together. I don't know if she would've made it out without you and Oberi."

The thought sent a shiver down my spine. Ava could handle her own, but our team had only pulled through by working together during the Games.

Voices filled the room as more and more students filtered in. Ez and I went quiet, and I heard him scratching away at his notebook while we waited for our professor to arrive.

It wasn't long before Professor Warbright entered the room. He was a warlock who taught most of Marcus' classes. I'd heard from Marcus he was an easy teacher, and so far I had to agree with him. Warbright had no issues with me recording his lectures or receiving any extra accommodations when I needed them. He'd quickly become my favorite professor. Marcus claimed Warbright's necromancy magic was terrible, but the guy sure knew his magical history.

"Today, we'll be moving on to Elven history," Warbright announced.

I immediately perked up and leaned forward. Ava had asked me to learn what I could about the Elves, in order to better interpret the prophecy. I was still wary about helping her out, because I didn't want her to get hurt. Even so, I couldn't miss a second of this lecture. Maybe I'd learn something that would help me to protect her. I pressed *record* on my device and set it on the desk in front of me.

Someone toward the front of the room piped up. "I thought the Elves died out."

"Yes," Warbright confirmed. "But why should that mean their history is unimportant? Elven magic has many influences on our own magic— no matter your magical race. If we hope to understand our own magic, we must understand where it all began... with the Elves."

Ez slumped in his chair, like he didn't care about the lecture. I, on the other hand, was on high alert, my spine straight as I drank in every word Warbright spoke. I don't know why, but the subject of Elves had always been... intriguing to me. Even before I'd found out about Ava's prophecy, from the moment I'd learned about the Elven Union, I wanted to know more about them. Something about their former existence called to me, and drew me in.

"The Elves are considered the original supernaturals— the first magical race to evolve outside of the gods' realm," Warbright began. "They are older than any other supernatural race alive, even the fae. Before they were killed off, they were considered to be the most powerful supernaturals of all time."

"If they were so powerful, why would anyone bother trying to go up against them?" a guy asked.

"Ah, a good question," Warbright said. "The Elves were targeted during the Great Supernatural War because they were the most feared. They were known as the crime lords of the supernatural world, but it was their power that ignited fear the most."

"What kind of power?" the same guy questioned.

"Among their powers, they could cast illusions and battle magic, much like the Arcanean fae," Warbright answered. "Each Elf was also said to have their own specialty, one power that set them apart from other Elves, such as mind reading— though such a powerful gift was reserved for the strongest of the Elves."

"That doesn't sound so scary," a girl said, her insect-like wings fluttering slightly. "They don't sound much different from the fae. The fae can shift into animals that could tear the Elves apart."

"Yes, of course," Warbright agreed. "But there was so much more to the Elves. One thing to note is that the Elves were born with their powers. Unlike other supernatural races, they had no coming-of-age ceremonies, and so their children were stronger than the other races. But there was a power much more terrifying and unique to the Elves."

I leaned forward in my chair, practically sitting on the edge of it.

"The mark of the Elves was the ability of energy manipulation," Warbright said, and a shiver ran down my spine. "The Elves had the power to siphon magic from any other supernatural race— save from another Elf— and use it for themselves."

The fae girl spoke up again. "How's that any different from the Curse Breakers of the Miriamic Coven? Can't they siphon magic, too?"

"Yes, but their powers are limited," Professor Warbright explained. "A Curse Breaker can only siphon witch magic, or move enchantments from one object to another. At times, they can draw out a monster's magic, but only if they are more powerful than the creature. They can't steal from another race, because they'd have to overpower them. Only someone as strong as an Elf could do that— such as a demigod, as the Elves themselves were originally demigods."

I thought about what Marcus had done in the Darke Games, how he'd pulled magic from Ava and me to defeat the malumuto demon. We should've realized then that Marcus was a demigod.

"If an Elf took your magic, you would be left powerless, and they could perform any magic you were capable of," Warbright continued. "The effects, of course, were temporary, but powerful enough to be feared in war. An Elf could steal an Elementai's weather magic, or steal a fae's ability to shift into an animal, or take the super strength and speed of a vampire— even steal the wings of an angel so they could use it to fly on their own. They could steal any magical power from any other race, and use it for themselves, and whoever they took that magic from would be weak and helpless. Eventually, the magic would return back to whomever the Elves stole it from, but by that point, the damage would be done and it would be far too late for anyone to stop them."

Ez piped up, clearly interested in the lesson now. "How were they killed off then, if they were so powerful?"

"A very good question," Warbright said, sounding delighted we were so interested. "The fae and their allies, the angels and the vampires, developed a plan during the Great Supernatural War to target the most powerful Elves first, leaving only the weakest alive. You see, energy manipulation was something every Elf could do, but only the strongest could harness it for lengthy periods of time— something crucial in war. Once the most powerful Elves were taken out, the remaining members of the Elven Union could not defend themselves when so vastly outnumbered."

"How outnumbered were they?" the fae girl asked.

"Well, there are a lot of factors to consider," Warbright said thoughtfully.

I wanted to learn more about the plan to overpower the Elves and how the fae did it, but Warbright went off into a tangent about the power split during the Great Supernatural War, who was allies with who, how many troops each side had, and so on. He didn't get back to mentioning the Elves until the end of the lecture, then abruptly cut off when he realized we'd reached the end of the class period.

"We'll continue with the fae next week," Warbright announced. "There is no homework for today."

I snatched up my recorder and hurried out of the room to find Ava and tell her what I'd learned, only to stop in my tracks halfway down the hall. If I told Ava, it would put her closer to figuring out the prophecy— and closer to her demise.

But I couldn't keep hiding things from her. She'd feel it through the bond, I was sure. If I wanted to hide information from her, I had to find a way to lie around our bond. Practically impossible to do.

I guess Warbright's lecture didn't *really* mention anything directly related to the prophecy. If I told her what I'd learned, at least it looked like I was helping and not trying to lead her astray.

Hell, keeping secrets from pidge was the worst. I didn't know how long I could keep it up.

I decided to tell her, but I didn't go out of my way to find her, either. I expected to see her at dinner, but she didn't show. It wasn't until I was leaving the cafeteria to head to the training center in the basement that I felt her and Oberi approaching through our bond. Oberi's hooves padded gently on the carpet, and the unicorn nickered politely.

"Hey, Charlie," Ava greeted, stopping just in front of me. "Are you on your way to dinner?"

I shook my head. "I already finished. Where have you been?"

"I got carried away studying," she said.

I knew Ava had been missing assignments, so I didn't believe her. "Studying for what?" I asked skeptically.

She didn't answer right away, like she worried someone might over-hear. She lowered her voice. "Studying the prophecy. I've been trying to decipher that book Hemlock gave me. Have you learned anything about the Elves?"

"Some stuff," I admitted. I listened to the sounds around the hall and noticed a few footsteps coming and going from the cafeteria. I took Ava's arm, and we went down a secluded hall. Oberi followed.

"Warbright lectured today on Elven magic," I told her, before diving into what I'd learned. As I explained the powers of the Elves' energy manipulation, Ava remained silent.

"Mm..." she mused when I'd finished. "This could be important, but I think we need to know more. Have you tried searching other sources?"

Hell, no! The more I learned, the more it put Ava in danger. Though I couldn't tell her that.

Against my better judgement, I got defensive. "Like what, pidge? You want me to pick up a book and read it? I'm doing everything I can."

Everything I could to protect her, at least.

"You could talk to Professor Warbright again," she suggested, sounding a bit annoyed. "We need more information. This isn't enough."

"I'm trying," I growled. I hated lying to my pidge, but more than that, I hated everything her aunt had told me about the prophecy. It pissed me off just thinking about it. "You should go eat."

Ava huffed, obviously taking note of my harsh tone. "You're making excuses. What's up with you?"

"I just don't know what you expect from me," I insisted.

"I *expect* you to help me with the prophecy, like you promised," she pressed.

"Don't you trust me?" I snapped. I wasn't truly mad at Ava. I was only taking my anger out on her, and it wasn't fair. I had to cool down, and shoving my fists into a punching bag sounded like the perfect way to do it. "You know what? I have plans. I'll catch up with you later."

The fabric of Ava's uniform rustled as she crossed her arms. She sounded skeptical. "What kind of plans?"

"I'm headed to the prison yard to work out."

At least I wasn't lying to her. I had to be in the best shape I could for my first fight, because if I impressed the guards now, it was more money in my pocket later.

"Since when did you start *working out?*" Ava asked.

I squared my shoulders. "Since now."

Ava must've noticed my harsh tone, because she blew a breath. "Ancestors, are the guards spiking your meals with testosterone? You're acting like a jerk."

I pressed my lips together. "No, I'm acting like a guy who should've trained better for the Darke Games. I need to be ready for anything in this prison."

And *that* was the truth. Prophecy or not, I had to do everything I could to protect Ava. I couldn't do that unless I was a better fighter.

I didn't give her a chance to argue. I whirled around and started toward the prison yard.

Whether she believed it or not, I really *was* doing everything I could to help her. Just not in the way she wanted.

ava-marie

SIX

Charlie Wahkin was hiding something from me... and it was bigger than whatever he had going on with Chancey.

It wasn't like him to go off on me without being provoked. I could always tell when the guy had something hidden up his sleeve. I just wasn't sure what it was yet.

I was damn well certain I was gonna find out, though.

The subject of Charlie's questionable secrecy had gears turning in my head. Opal, Kallie and I walked to Substance Abuse together after lunch one afternoon, but while they chatted, I couldn't get my head on straight. Oberi walked behind us as a unicorn, tossing her head every time I had a new theory about Charlie, and what it possibly meant.

My stream of thoughts were interrupted as I realized someone was sitting at my desk. A new person had arrived at the Institute. They had shaggy white hair that fell into red eyes, with a matching streak of red blazing through their bangs. They were wearing the sweater, tie, shoes and socks of the boys' uniform, but the girls' skirt draped over their long legs.

The person looked male, but I didn't want to assume, because that was rude. Opal started beside me when she saw the person— as if she couldn't believe it. Oberi nickered and tapped her hooves happily.

"Uh... okay," I muttered. Kallie usually sat next to me, but her seat was clearly occupied by the new guy. She took a spot behind mine, next to Opal. I slid beside the person sitting at my desk, and played with the pages of my books.

The person next to me eyed me curiously. "I know that look. If you're asking, I'm nonbinary; pronouns *he* and *they*, but I don't mind if you use male terms."

His voice smacked with a slight Italian accent. It was intriguing.

I relaxed. "You must be new here. I'd remember if I'd seen you around."

"Damn right you would, precious." His eyes sparkled, and I instantly liked him. "My name's Ivy. I'm a freak. Half-vampire, half-mermaid. Don't be asking for my real name, cause you ain't getting it."

"I'm Ava-Marie," I offered, before gesturing behind myself. "This is Kallie and Opal. We've been at the Institute a while."

"I know Ivy. He's a very distant cousin," Opal said fondly. "We grew up together, before he moved to Chicago."

Ivy grinned. "I *do* miss Hawaii, but it wasn't really my scene. Not enough action. Or money."

"What are you in for?" Kallie asked, propping her elbows on the table.

"Illegal prostitution. I'm a sex worker," Ivy said. "I was making bank as an escort. You should've seen the dollars I pulled in. They never woulda caught me if I hadn't overdosed."

"Overdosed?" I blinked.

"I have a *slight* problem with nightshade," Ivy admitted.

I'd heard of nightshade from my Uncle Jonah, but he'd told me the Miriamic Coven had stopped producing it years ago, when I was just a baby. It was a magical drug that was very dangerous. "I didn't know nightshade was still a thing."

"Oh, you mean from when our parents were young?" Ivy asked. "It's a different formula now, synthetic, but the effects are similar. Anyway, once I came out of the coma and did a fresh round of rehab, they sent me straight here."

Opal frowned, like this was a common problem with her cousin. I rushed to say something. "Are you still—?"

"Nah. I'm off it now," he said. "My last stint in rehab was enough, trust me. I'm clean."

Opal made a sound like she didn't believe him.

I hurriedly changed the subject. "I love your outfit, but I'm surprised the Institute let you wear it like that."

"School rules. The Institute can't dictate what a student wears, as long as all components of the uniform are there. It's discrimination against gender identity, and no matter what the Warden thinks, he can't do a thing about it." Ivy flashed a fanged smile. "Besides. I wear what I want."

Ivy and I would get along just fine. He drummed his nails on the table. I noticed they were painted a violent shade of red. "You had the most *confused* look on your face when you walked in. Let me guess. Your man fooling around with a bit on the side?"

I sighed. "You could say that."

Ivy leaned in. "If you're interested, I know a couple moves that'll have him eating out of the palm of your hand."

I raised an eyebrow. "Really?"

"Of course," Ivy purred. "Any friend of Opal's is a friend of mine. Just say the word."

I was considering accepting his offer when Professor Gael strode in. His monotone voice rang out over the classroom as he told us to open our textbooks to the current module.

Ivy rolled his eyes, like this was already pointless. Gael dove into his lecture, and it took all of five minutes for my attention to start wandering. Ancestors, Professor Gael was the most boring teacher at the Institute. He could make any subject dull. I was willing to sign a contract never to try drugs at any point in my life, if the exchange was I didn't have to hear him lecture about them ever again.

No one was really paying attention. A couple of people had fallen asleep. The rest were either doodling in their notebooks or throwing paper wads at each other across the room.

Professor Gael didn't notice. The guy was kind of self-absorbed, and therefore, oblivious. I was certain I'd witnessed a drug deal in this very class on our first day. He hadn't seen a thing.

"This class is boring," Kallie huffed quietly. Opal stirred sleepily next to her, like she'd nodded off.

"It's not like we have to stick around," Ivy sang under his breath. "What do you say, girls. Wanna ditch?"

I glanced forward. We were at the back of the room, near the door. Professor Gael was so engrossed in his lecture, he wouldn't even notice us sneak out. "Gladly."

Oberi shifted into a husky, so he could slink out of the room without being noticed. Ivy, Opal, Kallie and I got up and crept toward the door. Ivy used his vampire speed to open the door in a flash. We ducked out, and he shut it behind us just as quickly— and quietly.

"So, you wanna learn how to keep your man?" Ivy asked when we were out in the hallway, and he put his hands on his hips. "If so, follow me."

"I want to come, too," Kallie offered. "There's someone I'd like to impress."

"The Ivy School for Debauchery is open," he offered, and he flung his arms wide. "Let's see if you have what it takes to get a passing grade."

He headed down the hallway, and we followed. Oberi changed into a unicorn, and Ivy observed her flaming mane with awe.

"Your unicorn is beautiful, by the way. I was always jealous of Elementai. I'd love to have an animal companion follow me around," he said.

Nobody ever said they were jealous of us. It was nice.

"You can pet her," I said. "I don't mind."

"Really? Oh my gosh." Ivy reached out and felt Oberi's velvety coat. She nickered politely and nosed Ivy's fingers. He laughed.

An alarm bell went off in my head, but it wasn't from me. It took me a moment to figure out where it was coming from. I'd never been able to feel Charlie through our bond from this far away before. He had to be on the other side of the prison.

A twinge of annoyance crossed from him to me as he felt Ivy's hand skim Oberi's coat, but I brushed it off. He took my indifference as a sign everything was okay, but I still felt him seethe as his mental presence faded away from my mind. He didn't want to share Oberi with anyone but me, but ancestors, other people could pet her every once in a while if I gave permission. It wasn't a big deal. He didn't *own* her, after all.

"I saw her shift," Ivy said. "What kind of a Familiar is she?"

"She's a *mutabeecha,* a changeling Familiar," I explained. "She has as many as five different forms, but so far, we've only discovered two. She doesn't have a particular gender, either. She changes it depending on which form she's in."

"A Familiar after my own heart. I like her even more," Ivy said.

Ivy led us through a twisting realm of back hallways, which got tighter and tighter the further we wandered. We had to walk single-file, and Oberi had to squeeze through. "Where are we going?" I asked.

"There's a secret tunnel of rooms the prison uses for storage," Ivy said. "I found it when I was trying to figure out where security had taken my stuff."

Ivy opened a door, and I gasped. We stepped inside. The room was a large, open area, with a few metal poles stationed around the room that looked like supportive beams. It was empty, like the school had been planning to renovate it to use as a classroom, then abandoned the idea halfway through. Our shoes echoed as we walked around the large space.

"This place would be perfect for a nightclub," Kallie said as she roamed around the room. Her fingers skimmed the metal poles.

Ivy hissed with laughter. "That's the plan, eventually. Just have to get my bearings around here. I plan on calling it The Devil's Playground."

That was a badass name. There were a couple things inside, like a wooden chair and a large cardboard box. Ivy ruffled through the box. I gasped when I looked inside and saw that it was full of all kinds of fun things— corsets, whips, and even heels.

"How'd you sneak this in? All my heels were confiscated when I came to the Institute." They'd been expensive too, the fuckers.

"You can get anything into the Institute if you're willing to do *favors* for the guards," Ivy said with a wink. He ruffled inside the box before he found a pair of size sevens, then handed me the heels. "Here, put these on."

Ivy gave a pair to Kallie as well. He tried giving some to Opal, but she waved him off. "Ah, no. You know dancing's not my thing. Not in *that* way."

Ivy huffed. "Opal, your innocent schoolgirl routine is getting old. No guy at the Institute wants to be with the girl next door."

"*Some* guy will," Opal snapped. "You'll see."

Ivy rolled his eyes. "Suit yourself." He kicked off his own shoes and snapped on a pair of heels before he said, "All right. The most crucial thing is to have *confidence*. Observe."

Ivy grabbed one of the metal poles. He twirled around it, spinning in a circle before he dipped down and rose back up again. The movement was so fluid, it was clear he'd done it a million times.

I tried to copy his movements, but I felt clumsy. I spun around the pole too fast and had to grab on to it to keep from falling down. Kallie staggered forward and almost hit her head on the pole.

Ivy leaned against the pole. "I can see we have a lot to learn."

He demonstrated the move again. I studied his movements and noticed they were much slower than my own. I attempted it the second time and found I moved better when I took my time.

"Like this?" Kallie stuck her boobs out and spun around the pole. The way she dipped down almost made her cleavage spill out of her bra, and she had to flounder to catch it. I cracked up as she stuffed her breasts back inside her shirt.

Ivy shook his head, and Opal sighed impatiently. "No, like *this*."

Opal strutted forward, grabbed the pole and copied Ivy. She moved around the pole like she was swimming in the water, twirling her body upward like a sea serpent. Mermaids had a natural grace that was hard for the rest of us to copy. My jaw dropped open when I watched her dance like a pro. She wasn't even wearing heels, and she looked sexy as all hell.

"Damn, Opal, you've been hiding things from us," Kallie teased. "We didn't know you could rock that body."

"Just because I'm good at it doesn't mean it's something I like to do," she countered. Ivy looked vaguely amused.

Kallie and I kept watching Ivy. As we danced, he circled around us, observing the actions and barking out tips like a drill sergeant. He really took this kind of thing seriously.

"Use your ass," Ivy said. "Don't be afraid to stick it out when you dip down."

Kallie and I moved at once, and this time, the movement was fluid. I rounded my back after I dipped, and a surge of confidence raged through my core. I was getting it!

"*Yes*, queens!" Ivy shouted. "That's what I like to see!"

Oberi whinnied and twisted herself around one of the poles, walking in a circle. She twirled around it so many times she got dizzy and lay down on the floor. She rolled on her back, wiggling her hooves in the air.

I giggled. "You're so funny, Oberi."

"Remember, girls, the key isn't in the moves. The key is in how you *feel*," Ivy stated. "You're a goddess, and you can use your femininity to make men worship you at your feet. If you don't believe in yourself, you can't believe in anyone else."

His words brought me back to a place I didn't like to be. Sexuality was hard. It was a part of me I'd shoved down and ignored for years. In my teen years, all I'd ever done with boyfriends was some heavy petting, always with clothes on. It wasn't much of anything.

Then I'd been assaulted, and intimacy was off the table. I was no longer interested in anything having to do with sex. I enjoyed looking at hot guys, and envisioning having a relationship again, but that only went so far in my mind before I shut it down. I couldn't imagine wanting to have a sexual experience with anyone.

But then Charlie had come into my life, and from the first moment we'd met, he'd made me curious again. I wanted to explore. I just didn't know how I could experiment without accidentally triggering something and making all those bad feelings come rushing back.

Ivy made sex and sensuality sound like fun. More than that, it was like he promised I could have total control. I had to learn everything I could from him.

"You girls are doing much better," Ivy said. "But if you really want to drive him wild, you'll have to get him alone first."

"Show them *the move*," Opal insisted, clearly getting into this.

"Opal!" Kallie laughed, and Opal blushed.

"Ah." Ivy's eyes sparkled. "*That* one. There's a signature move I always perform when I'm trying to get them to do what I want."

He turned toward me. "How flexible are you?"

"I was head cheerleader," I said.

"Perfect. Kallie, are you okay with being part of the demonstration?"

Kallie walked forward. "I'm here to learn. Teach me your secrets, oh wise one."

Kallie sat in the chair, and Ivy moved around her. "Start by massaging his shoulders. Twirl around him in a circle. Don't go too fast. The slower you go, the more intrigued he'll be."

Ivy straddled Kallie, and she let out an *oof* as her legs supported his weight. Ivy continued to instruct. "Sit on their lap. Grind your ass into their legs, and move your hips in a circle. Make sure you press down on their package, but not too hard, because you don't want it to hurt. Just enough so they know what you got. Once you're in position, lean down and show him the goods. I promise it'll drive him wild."

"He can't see," I explained. "He's been blind most of his life."

"Then take his hand and put it where you want it," Ivy said simply. "He'll feel his way around your real estate, and trust me honey, he'll want to make a purchase."

Kallie's face made me snicker as Ivy leaned his flat chest against her. She scrunched up her nose, and Ivy said, "Listen, you want to impress your man, or not?"

"He's sort of shy," Kallie said. "He'd probably be running away at this point."

Opal and I shared a giggle. Marcus was petrified of Kallie when she did something as simple as walk into a room. The thought of her giving him a lap dance was probably enough to scare him to death.

"Oh, he's one of *those*," Ivy said. "No biggie. Just takes longer to soften them up."

Ivy sat up. "Now, turn around and grind your ass against them. Then spin back around, and do *this*."

Kallie gasped as Ivy put his ankle on her shoulder. He leaned down, until he was practically doing the splits. The uniform skirt barely covered what he had underneath.

"See?" Ivy purred. "Flawless. In this position, you have everything on display. And that means you're ready to trap your prey."

"This doesn't leave the room," Kallie growled under her breath. Opal cracked up.

Ivy scoffed. "Trust me, honey, you ain't got the parts I like."

He swung his ankle off of her, then gestured to me. "Now you try."

I balked. I mean, it looked fun and all, but I was worried about looking stupid. It was fine, practicing all these moves and pretending like it could happen in real life.

But who was I fooling? I couldn't handle a hot and heavy makeout session without freaking out. Imagining doing this to Charlie... it would never happen. I'd chicken out before I even started.

I waited too long to respond. Ivy tilted his head, like he sensed something was wrong.

Ivy got off Kallie's lap and strode right up to me. He grasped me by the shoulders and looked me in the eyes. "Ava, *you* are the only person who gets a say on what happens to your body. You never, ever have to do anything you don't want to. Don't let some asshole from your past or in your present dictate what you want to do with someone you love— or even just someone you're interested in. Give in to desire and take control. You have all the power, and *you* call the shots. Don't ever let anybody tell you different."

Ancestors, it was like Ivy knew. Oberi nudged me, as if encouraging me to give it a shot. Kallie observed as I swallowed nervously. "Okay. I want to try."

I approached Kallie, then began to circle her. I carefully put my ankle on her shoulder and leaned in, hoping I didn't break a leg, or show off my hoo-ha. I slid into the splits, though Kallie burst out laughing.

"What?" I asked.

"Your face," she giggled. "You're concentrating so hard, it looks like you're constipated."

My mouth dropped open. "Screw you!"

"Focus, ladies," Ivy reminded us. "Ava, lean forward. Slowly, so you drag out the tension."

"Don't suffocate me with your giant tits, bitch," Kallie mumbled, leaning away from me.

I huffed. Kallie was far from a good participant.

"Make sure your hair drapes across his shoulder," Ivy said. "Men *love* that."

I tilted my head so some of my hair fell across Kallie's shoulder, but most of it ended up in her face. Kallie got a chunk of my hair in her mouth and gagged. I drew my ankle off of her, because I didn't want to get spit on me, but I swung my leg to the side so quickly I accidentally ended up kicking Opal in the face. I gasped and put a hand over my mouth.

"Ow! What the hell!" Opal said, holding her nose.

"Sorry!" I said. Opal brought her hand away from her face. Her nose wasn't bleeding, but it was a little pink.

Ivy sighed. "Ava, turn around. Try shaking that cute butt of yours on Kallie's knees. Men like that."

I bent over, but Kallie put her foot on my ass and pushed me over. I went sprawling forward, and she and Opal laughed.

"Hey, that wasn't bad!" I said with a giggle. Oberi whinnied, like she thought my tumble was funny.

"Not bad at all," Ivy confirmed. "You're nearly a pro."

"I'm just worried about messing up," I confessed as Ivy pulled me to my feet.

"Don't worry about it. The first lap dance I gave, I stuck my heel into the guy's foot. Ruined the whole thing," Ivy said. "Now look at me. I'm a natural."

I blew a wayward strand of hair out of my eyes. "I just don't know *where* I'm going to do this. I don't want a guard to walk in and ruin it."

"Feel free to use the room. It'll be available around four o'clock," Ivy offered. "Just be a good little bad girl and make sure not to miss curfew."

"What are *you* using it for?" Opal asked, though it was more like an accusation.

"A boy's gotta make money," Ivy said with a shrug. "I'm already accepting new clients, if anyone's asking."

Opal scowled. She clearly didn't approve, but before she could say anything more, Ivy clapped his hands. "Now, let's get to work!"

Ivy HAD Kallie and I bending, twisting, and shaking our butts for the better part of an hour. By the time he finally let us loose, I was exhausted. Pole dancing was a *workout*. I didn't have to wonder how Ivy kept such a great figure. If we kept these secret lessons up, I was going to be built by the time I knew how to dance like a master.

The Villain's Den was packed this time of day. We didn't have much time to hang there, but Ivy had asked us to show him where it was, so it wasn't much to swing by. Ivy took in the recreation room with interest, surveying the crowd like he was sizing each person up.

There were a couple of loud shouts on the other side of the room. Chancey was playing a dice game with a few guys in the corner. The group around him let out a couple yells when Chancey tossed the dice and got snake eyes. As his angel wings fluttered, I saw Ivy eyeing him up and down.

"Who's the tall cannoli over there?" Ivy leaned in and asked me.

I made a *pshing* noise. "Him? Oh, that's just Chancey. He's nothing special."

Ivy's eyes glinted. "I think I need to introduce myself."

Ivy sauntered across the room, weaving his hips in a way even I was jealous of. He planted himself into the group of guys like he'd always been standing there, placing himself right next to Chancey.

Chancey gave a double take when he saw Ivy. He immediately abandoned the game he was playing and looped his arm around Ivy's hips.

"Where'd you come from, kitten?" Chancey asked, his tone full of excitement.

"I'm new around here," Ivy said, batting his eyelashes. "I was thinking a big, strong angel like you could show me around."

"Gladly." Ivy and Chancey left together. Looks like Ivy had gotten his first new client. Kallie gave me a dumbfounded expression.

Good. Maybe Ivy could keep Chancey distracted long enough that the angel would keep his hands off Charlie for a while. Or permanently, hopefully.

"Ivy can charm anyone he wants! What the hell?" Kallie shouted. "Why can't it be that easy for us?"

"That means he knows what he's doing. It's good he's giving us tips," I said.

Opal was quiet. I nudged her and asked, "What's wrong?"

She frowned. "I love Ivy. He's my favorite cousin, and he's family. But I've been worried about him for a while now. He's a good person. But he doesn't make good choices."

That bothered me to hear, but Kallie shrugged it off. "Hey, he's at the Institute now, which means he can't fuck up that badly, right? Everything's regulated."

"I don't know..." Opal's tone was wary. "There are still plenty of ways to get into trouble here."

We didn't discuss it further, because Ezekiel entered the room. He saw me and gave a wave. He was carrying a load of papers, which he almost dropped. He scrambled to pick them up and bumped into a vampire, who sneered at him. Ezekiel gave a hurried apology and stumbled toward us.

Opal stiffened as he approached. Her green eyes got wide as she looked my brother up and down. It was like a freight train had fallen out of the sky and slammed into her as she watched my brother get closer and closer.

"Hey, Ava," Ezekiel said breathlessly. "You know, there was a gang fight by the angel cellblock, and I didn't really know what to do about it—"

"Yeah, just ignore it," I told him. I hadn't missed the way Opal was trying to hide herself behind me, and I wasn't about to have that. I grabbed her by the arms and steered her in front of me. "Opal, this is my little brother, Ezekiel. We call him Ez. Ez, this is Opal. She's a mermaid here at the Institute."

"Oh, hi!" Ezekiel gave Opal a bright smile, like he'd just noticed her standing there. "I like your hair. Blue's my favorite color."

Opal touched the strands of her hair delicately, like Ez had just told her they were made of gold. "H-hi."

Ezekiel sighed. "Ava, could you take me to Professor Ellender's office? It's not on the map the office gave me, and I have no idea where it is."

"I wish, but I actually have a counseling session," I said. "It's on the other side of the prison. Oh, but you have a class that way, *don't you,* Opal? You could show him."

Opal squeaked, "I—"

"I'd appreciate it," Ezekiel said, turning to her. "I'm totally lost around here."

Opal's look was pleading, but I wasn't about to save her, and she knew it. She caved, her shoulders falling slightly. "Professor Ellender's one of my teachers. I can take you there."

"Really? Gee, thanks. You're the *best,*" Ezekiel said. Opal let out a soft squeak.

"Well, no use in standing around," I said, putting a hand on each of their backs and pushing them out the door. "Better get to it."

Opal shot a despairing glance over her shoulder, but by the time I'd shoved them out, Ezekiel was already chatting her ear off. She nodded as they walked away, appearing out of her element.

Opal was too shy to say much, but it wasn't like Ez needed much input when it came to talking. The guy had whole conversations with himself. He'd keep the conversation going until he got to Professor Ellender's classroom.

"Who are you, the prison's local matchmaker?" Kallie asked me.

"My brother needs to be with a good girl. I'm tired of seeing him hook up with giant bitches. Opal's perfect," I responded.

"She obviously likes *him,* but that doesn't mean he likes her. He was practically oblivious to her presence," Kallie pointed out.

"Give it some time. I know my brother."

Kallie sounded skeptical. "If you say so."

We left then, because our counseling session with Professor Takahashi was supposed to start soon. Marcus was already there, sitting in one of the chairs in the therapy circle. Charlie, though, had yet to arrive.

It was strange he wasn't early. I swear, the man drove me fucking nuts lecturing me day in and day out about how I needed to show up on time— because, you know, I was a better-late-than-never kind of person.

Where *was* he? He was never around anymore. I saw him during our shared classes and at meals, but other than that, it was like he always had somewhere to be.

When Kallie saw Marcus, she straightened up. She threw her boobs forward and pushed her butt out, prancing from side to side as she deliberately strolled in front of Marcus's vision. She was trying to be sexy, but it came off totally awkward.

"Uh... what are you doing?" Marcus asked, completely clueless.

Kallie's expression was aghast. "This... this is just how I walk, Marcus. Gods!"

"No, it isn't," he replied. "You're walking like you have a stick up your butt."

Kallie's face turned bright red. "Well, screw you, Marcus Taylor!" She plopped down in her seat and crossed her arms with a huff. Marcus gave a questioning look to me, but I acted like I didn't know anything. He took a drawing pencil out from behind his ear and fiddled with it nervously, avoiding Kallie's pouting.

Takahashi came in at three o'clock and sat at the head of the circle. His beautiful bird companion sat on his shoulder, lifting pages from his clipboard for him with her beak.

Takahashi glanced around. "Where's Charlie? He's usually the first one here."

I was worried he wouldn't show up, until the door opened behind me. "Sorry I'm late." Charlie hurried in at the last second. Oberi nickered when she saw him coming. "I got held up."

Doing what, I wonder.

Charlie took the seat next to me, while Oberi changed into a husky and nuzzled his head in his lap. Charlie petted the top of Oberi's head absentmindedly, like his thoughts were anywhere but here.

"The four of you have made good progress since your entry in the Darke Games," Takahashi said. "I have to say that I'm proud of this group for continuing to be so open."

Takahashi's praise was nice to hear. Since the new semester had started, we hadn't really discussed anything deep, but all of us had been contributing to conversations that Takahashi chose the subject on— things like learning how to overcome procrastination, deep breathing exercises, and how to get along with others without punching them in the face— a good Institute life skill. I think we all found it easier to muse on stuff like that rather than go too deep.

"I believe it's a good idea if we try something new," Takahashi started. "I've noticed with this group in particular, the four of you have difficulty connecting with your feelings."

Oh, great. Here we go. And things had been going so well.

"We have emotions for a reason," Takahashi continued. "And sometimes, those emotions can overpower us and cause us to make harmful decisions. But this happens when we shove down what's bothering us and do not confront how we are feeling inside. At some point, those emotions must come out. To avoid allowing them to erupt in a destructive way, it's best to face our emotions, and allow ourselves to feel what we are going through without trying to block it, for fear of being uncomfortable. I would like each of us to go around the circle and explain how we're feeling today. Marcus, why don't you start?"

He always picked Marcus to go first, because Marcus was the easiest to open up. Marcus cleared his throat. "Uh, I'm feeling confused. I finished this painting— took me all week— but I think it's kind of shit, so I don't know if I'm going to paint over it or not. I just can't decide."

Takahashi nodded. "Ah, I see. Being creative can be very difficult at times."

Marcus sighed. "Sometimes I want to just throw it all in the trash and give up. I'm never happy with anything I make."

"What are you talking about?" Kallie asked. "Your paintings are amazing. All your art is."

"No, it's not. I'm a terrible artist," Marcus replied glumly.

"That's not true. I've seen your paintings. They practically look like photographs," I said.

"But there are people out there who are *better,*" Marcus pointed out.

"Comparing yourself isn't going to help you be a better artist, though," Kallie objected.

"I think your paintings are incredible. *Really* detailed," Charlie said with a hint of amusement.

"Thanks Char— hey!" Marcus said.

That got a laugh from the rest of us, but Marcus frowned and kicked at the floor. "Jokes aside, it's really hard trying to find inspiration when you're in a place like... this. And I know it sounds dumb, but I put a lot of myself into my art. It's like I cut out a piece of myself every time I finish a project. Sometimes I wonder what's going to be left of me if I keep pouring everything I have into my work."

"Your art is incredible, Marcus. You have an amazing talent. I'd be really sad if you gave it up," Kallie said gently.

Marcus hugged his arms around his torso, like her words had comforted him somehow.

Takahashi said, "It's understandable if you struggle to find inspiration in your current environment, but what may help is a shift of perspective. There's always inspiration to be found in even the smallest and most unexpected places, if only you have the desire to seek it out. Don't be so hard on yourself. The only person's expectations you have to meet are your own, and you can adjust those expectations if it means achieving your own version of happiness."

Marcus stared at the floor, and Takahashi shifted in his chair. "Kallie, how about you?"

Kallie's answer was bitter. "I'm feeling frustrated."

"And why is that?" Takahashi probed.

"Because I just want people to *like* me," she shot out. "My own country kicked me out, and I lost the Darke Games, so I figured I could start over and make a new life here. But it seems no matter how hard I try, I can't get people to notice me."

Marcus flushed, like he knew she was talking about him. This exercise was going south fast.

"We all want to be accepted and loved," Takahashi said. "That's not an uncommon feeling."

"It's more than about just fitting in. I want to earn people's approval," Kallie said.

"Don't we matter?" Marcus asked harshly, gesturing to all of us. "It's like we aren't enough."

"I didn't say that," Kallie said quickly. "I appreciate you guys, I really do. I'm just trying to be good enough for everyone."

"You don't have to be loved by everyone, Kallie," I said. Personally, I cared very little what people thought of me. There were very few people in my life whose opinion mattered to me. Everyone else could suck it.

"That's not true," Kallie insisted. "I have a responsibility not to fuck up again. Everyone looks up to me, or at least, they used to, and I let them down when I got sentenced to the Institute. So I *have* to be perfect going forward, because I..."

Kallie bit her lip and said, "You know what, never mind. I don't want to talk about it."

She was retreating back into herself in a way that I'd found was common for her. Kallie had this obsession with perfection that I just didn't get. All of us were defensive over our hang-ups, but Kallie acted like being vulnerable was what she was most afraid of. As her friend, I wanted to understand her, but as of yet she was a closed book.

"Fair enough," Takahashi said. "Charlie, what are you feeling today?"

Huh, good luck. Getting Charlie to talk was like forcing blood out of a stone. I was very grateful for the few times he'd opened up to me.

Charlie sighed and leaned back in his chair. "Tired. I'm always tired."

I didn't think that was a very deep answer, but Takahashi pressed him for more. "Go on."

Charlie crossed his arms and slumped in his chair. "For most of my life, it was all about myself. I was the only person I needed to worry about. But things are different now. I feel responsible for others."

"Responsible how?" Takahashi asked.

"Like I need to protect them." Charlie sank lower. "I didn't know what it was like to care about someone else, because nobody cared about me. I had someone I was close to once, but Marty could manage on his own without me. Now it's completely different. There are people in my life I need to provide for, people who couldn't get by without me around."

I knew he was talking about Oberi and me, but his words weren't meant for just us. Charlie was speaking about Kallie and Marcus, too. I knew he felt responsible for us as a group, not merely because he was the oldest, but because we more or less followed his lead.

"Caring for others is good," Takahashi said. "Have you given it any thought that maybe you don't have to do it all by yourself?"

"Yes, but I want to. I've never had to provide for anyone. It feels good," he countered. "I *like* being depended on. It means someone gives a damn."

"You don't have to do anything for me," I spoke up. "I can take care of myself."

Charlie shook his head. "I don't want you to do that, pidge. I can handle things for all three of us. I just want you to sit back and keep those pretty little nails clean. You and Oberi don't have to worry about a thing. Not anymore."

There was almost a promise in his tone— like he'd found what he considered a way out. It was really setting me on edge.

"Be that as it may, be aware you don't have to carry the entire world on your shoulders," Takahashi said kindly. "It shows you have empathy for others, but make sure to reserve some compassion for yourself."

"I've been living for myself for years, and it's gotten me nowhere," Charlie rebutted. "I don't... have a family. I never did. My friends are the best I'm ever gonna get. Ava and Oberi are the closest thing I have to a family, because we share a bond. And I'll be damned if I'm ever gonna let that go."

Oberi whined, and I felt tears brimming at the corners of my eyes. Charlie felt like that about *me*? I hurriedly dotted at the corners of my eyes with my sweater sleeve, and was glad for the millionth time Charlie couldn't see it, but he felt it anyway. He reached out his hand across the gap that was between us, and I took it. A rush of warmth rushed across my hand to his, and Oberi barked as he bumped his head under our arms.

"I'm glad to hear you've found some semblance of family here at the Institute," Takahashi said. "Just be sure you're making the right choices."

Charlie didn't say anything, but I knew by his stony expression he was done talking.

Takahashi didn't push him further. Instead, he asked, "Ava, is there anything you'd like to add?"

I froze. I'd been thinking about what I was going to say at this counseling session all week. I wanted to open up to more people about my past experiences. Ezekiel hadn't taken the news about my past the best way, but maybe Kallie and Marcus would.

"I am..." I took a breath. "I'm worried about my brother."

"And why is that?" Takahashi asked.

"Because he was sentenced here for beating up my rapist, and I feel like it's my fault."

My heart beat so fast that I thought it would rip out of my chest. My voice cracked when I made the statement out loud, and tears threatened to well out of my eyes, but I refused to let them spill. Time froze as I waited on what everyone might say. As hard as it was to admit what had happened to me out loud, it was worse waiting for everyone's reaction.

Kallie let out a strangled gasp, and the blood drained from Marcus' face. Even Rishi looked up. Tears started forming in Kallie's eyes, while Marcus hovered somewhere between shock and disbelief, as if hoping he'd misheard me.

Takahashi was the only one besides Charlie who remained calm, though a slight shadow of sadness passed behind his black eyes. He was a therapist at a reform school for troubled kids, so I was sure he heard stories like mine all the time, but it was clear by his expression that the thought of one of his students getting hurt bothered him.

"I thought Ezekiel got sentenced because he beat the crap out of some guy that got with his ex-girlfriend," Marcus said apprehensively.

"That's what he's telling everybody," I replied. "But that's not the real story. I went to a party a couple of years ago when I was still in high school. I'd gone because... because my best friend had died after we'd run away from home. I thought trying to have some fun would get my mind off her, but I ended up getting cornered by someone in the woods that I knew. I didn't tell anyone about it for almost two years, until I got to the Institute. The only people I ever told were Charlie and my brother. And now you guys. My parents don't even know."

It was a very short summary of what had happened, but the details felt too raw to go over with anyone but Charlie. He squeezed my hand, and the comforting feeling made a wave of relief wash over me. Telling the story the third time was already much easier. It was like the more I talked about it, the less power it had over me.

"Oh gods, Ava." Kallie got up and gave me a hug. I had to let go of Charlie's hand to embrace her. Her hold nearly suffocated me. Ancestors, the girl had a grip. She could squeeze monsters to death no problem.

Marcus' face was drawn tight. "I'm so, so sorry that happened to you. I don't even know what to say."

"You don't have to say anything. It just feels better that you know," I replied. "The more people I have to help me carry this, the less alone I feel."

"I wish this pervert was here right now. I'd enjoy ripping his balls off and feeding them to Oberi, before I shoved a flaming sword up his ass," Kallie growled. Oberi barked, like he approved of the idea.

"Kallie," Takahashi said gently, telling her to settle. She stomped back to her seat and flopped into it, looking peeved.

"Ava, what you said was very brave," Takahashi said. "I'm honored you chose to share this story with us."

"Is there anything we can do?" Marcus asked. "I know we can't make up for it, but I feel we should do *something* to make it better."

"I don't need anyone to do anything for me," I said, shocked that he would offer. "I just need someone to listen."

"We're your friends. We're always going to be by your side, no matter what," Kallie insisted.

Kallie and Marcus were taking it so well. It made me feel so loved. Maybe ending up in prison was worth it, just to call these guys my friends. You couldn't find a better group anywhere.

"I'd just like to move on," I confessed. "It happened so long ago, but it seems like it still affects so much of my life."

"Ava, what happened to you was very traumatic, and I'm deeply sorry for that," Takahashi said. "I do want you to grasp that you are not a prisoner to the man who attacked you. Don't allow him to control you. Every day, you have a choice to take back your life. And although it might be hard, and sometimes painful, the best revenge you could ever have is to live a life that's full and happy. He has taken enough from you. Refuse to give him anything more."

Charlie nodded, and Takahashi's words resonated with me. It wasn't like I purposefully wanted to give John power. I was a strong Koigni woman, after all. I had my own opinion and way about things, and I was damn stubborn about living life on my own terms.

But as much as I hated to admit it, John had driven a wedge between Charlie and me. We were close, but there was so much more I wanted to explore with him. I didn't want to just share my soul with Charlie. I wanted to share my body, too. I didn't want anything, past or present, holding me back.

"Ava, I can't even imagine what you went through," Kallie said. "I've never been... you know... but I've been through some things that were similar, and that was horrible enough."

"Like?" Marcus' voice rose several pitches, like he was scared to find out.

Kallie shrugged. "That shifter I told you about— the one I chose to fight beside me in the King's Contest— he was pretty creepy. He wouldn't leave me alone. There were a couple of times he cornered me and touched me in places I didn't like. I had to use magic to make him back off. I don't know what would've happened if I wasn't able to defend myself. The last time he got me alone, I hexed him."

Marcus turned beet red, and his hands began to shake. I remembered what he'd told us during the Darke Games— that he'd lost his temper and his magic had exploded out of him, killing eleven people. It was what he was in the Institute for. I was suddenly wondering if our counseling session would end with the room in a crater, and us in several pieces.

Charlie spoke up, because it was obvious if no one said anything, Marcus was going to lose it. "Good for you for using your magic on him."

Kallie laughed darkly. "Should've made it more permanent."

"What a creep," Marcus finally spat. "I can't believe there are guys walking around like that. And you were willing to be with someone like him, for the rest of your life, to rule your country?"

"For Malovia? I'd do anything," Kallie replied. "My nation is my home. Back then, it meant everything to me."

"I don't want him anywhere near you ever again," Marcus growled. The drawing pencil he'd been holding in his hand snapped.

Ancestors, *somebody* had a jealous streak. You couldn't convince me or anyone else in the world Marcus didn't have a crush on Kallie now.

"Well, that's one good thing about the Institute. He can't bother me here," Kallie replied.

I adamantly agreed. Things at the prison weren't always coming up roses, but at least behind these walls, John was far, far away.

Takahashi wrote down a few things on his clipboard, then set it aside. "I think we should end our session early today. We made a lot of progress, and we should give it some time to let you all adjust to what we've shared. Please remember to take care of yourselves."

Marcus and Kallie gathered their things. They had a study session for some class later they had to get to. Kallie looked around, like she suddenly realized something was missing. "Shit. My bag! I *swear* I brought it in here... or maybe not? Where could it be?"

"You didn't have it with us in Substance Abuse this morning," I said.

Her face fell. "That's right, I didn't. I have no idea where it could be," Kallie worried. "My project for Fae Illusion was in there. It's due tomorrow."

"I'll help you," Marcus volunteered. "Guys, can we borrow Oberi? His nose might help us find it."

"Go right ahead," I said, before Charlie could say yes. I wanted some private time with my man, and though I loved our Familiar, it was best he wasn't around for what I had in mind.

Charlie didn't object. He was fine if Oberi was with Kallie and Marcus, but nobody else. Kallie and Marcus hurried off with Rishi and Oberi. Oberi's nose was already to the ground, on the hunt.

Takahashi gave me a kind nod as we left, and the gesture touched me. I smiled at him slightly as Charlie and I wound down the spiraling tower and to the main floor of the Institute.

"I'm proud of you, pidge," Charlie said. "I know that had to be tough."

"It wasn't as hard as when I told you," I said. "And now that Kallie and Marcus know, I can keep moving forward."

A loud chime rang throughout the school as the hour changed, and my heart beat wildly. It was four o'clock. Ivy's secret room was open and up for grabs.

Ivy's words came back to me— his advice on *owning* my sexuality, and not allowing John to have control of my life. I wanted to have domination over my body, my feelings and my power. What had happened to me was in the past, and I had a brand new world of sex and feelings to explore. I wasn't going to let my trauma ruin what I had ahead of me, or destroy my future. The therapy session had really helped me to feel like I was freer than before. Things were out in the open, my friends knew, and it was no longer a secret. Therefore, it didn't have a strong hold on me. I had been refraining from letting my sensuality flow because I was scared of it, but I didn't want to be afraid anymore. I wanted to feel in control.

And I wanted to show Charlie Wahkin just how much he meant to me.

I took Charlie's hand. "Anyway... there's something I want to show you."

"What is it?"

"It's a secret. You like secrets, don't you, Charlie?"

"Not particularly."

"You'll like this secret. Trust me."

He instantly got my meaning. "Where do you want to go?"

"Come with me." Chills ran up and down my arms as I began dragging him down the hallway. A couple of people glanced our way and smirked. One of the guards eyed us in annoyance as we passed, but didn't stop us, like he was too busy to bother stopping a couple of kids from fooling around.

"What is this place?" Charlie asked as we got to the twisted realm of hallways in the back of the school. I led him carefully around the pillars, into Ivy's secret room.

"It's a sort of storage space, though it's unused," I explained. "I found it today and thought we could use it to... explore."

"Explore what?" he said in amusement.

"Uncharted territory," I said, then I cracked up. Okay, that was a bit too corny.

My blood raced in my veins when I saw the chair we'd been practicing lap dances with earlier. I pulled Charlie toward it and pushed him into the chair. He fell into it, a surprised expression in his eyes.

I dug in Ivy's stash and found the heels I'd been wearing earlier. I slipped them on, while Charlie said, "I'm waiting, pidge. What exactly did you bring me here for?"

His tone was teasing. I took a steadying breath. "I thought we could try taking things a step further. Are you okay with me touching you in places I never have before?"

"I'm ready to go wherever you'll take me."

Charlie answered instantaneously, like he didn't have to think twice. It left me feeling satisfied. Professor Takahashi was right. John *had* been controlling me. He'd been living in my head and dictating my life ever since he violated me years ago.

Well, he could go to hell. I *wanted* to mess around with Charlie, and I wasn't about to let that bastard stop me.

Charlie stiffened as he heard me remove my clothes. I did so slowly, dragging the moment out. I stripped down to a black push-up bra and a matching pair of lacy panties that barely covered half my ass. Glee shuddered through me as I saw a bulge rise in Charlie's pants at the sound of my clothes being removed. He couldn't tell yet if I was wearing underwear or if I was fully nude. It made the game more fun. There were perks to being with a blind guy.

"You're breathing quickly, pidge," Charlie taunted. "Your breaths are pretty shallow."

His damn Air magic would give some clues away, but I couldn't help it if I was nervous. I tossed my uniform to the side and strutted forward like the sexy bitch I was.

I was a bit too bold and tripped. I wavered on my heels and barely caught myself. Luckily, it was before I got to Charlie. *Confidence*, Ivy repeated in my mind. I gathered myself and continued forward. I put my hands on Charlie's chest, skimming my long nails over his uniform. His shoulders felt tense as I began to massage them. Slowly, they loosened up. As I came around to his front, I turned around and sat on his knees, rubbing my ass on his legs. Charlie's hands twitched, like he wanted to feel my ass but was waiting for my permission.

"You can touch," I said. "I don't mind."

Charlie reached out and brushed his fingers against my ass, before grabbing it lightly. A desirable thrill ran through me at his touch. I pushed against him harder, and he cupped my ass in his hands, daring to make his grip a little firmer.

I'd never done a lap dance before. This was so thrilling. Charlie had slept with a lot of girls. I knew he didn't exactly enjoy it, but all the women that had come before me were most likely more experienced. Whatever he had been through with other girls, I wanted to make sure I was the one he remembered.

I wanted more. This wasn't enough. I turned and straddled Charlie's lap, pressing my core against his dick. He was already hard. His zipper looked ready to bust open. A bit of anxiety rolled through my gut as I felt his dick press against my vagina, but I reminded myself we still had clothes on, and I was in control. I began making circular movements against his dick, leaning forward and pressing my breasts to his torso. Now *his* breaths were quickening. He slid his hands up and down my sides, brushing his fingers at the undersides of my breasts. His dick strained against me, and when I dared to push down harder, Charlie let out a soft hiss.

Lust welled up in me, making me want more. This wasn't enough. I took Charlie's hand and put it against one of my breasts. He explored the area before he slipped a hand underneath my bra and began playing with my nipple. The sensitive area made sensations rush from his fingers to my core, and I let out a soft moan. Charlie's breaths increased, becoming low and shallow at the sounds I made. He put his other hand on my opposite breast and slid it inside my bra so he could play with that nipple, too. The movement made me delirious. I fumbled around behind myself and unhooked my bra, letting it fall to the floor so he had free rein.

This was different from what I expected. Other girls often complained that their boyfriends were clumsy and too rough. From what I'd head, I'd expected my boobs to be mashed the first time I was touched like this by a guy.

That wasn't the case with Charlie. His touch was so delicate. He played my body like he played the organ in the cathedral's loft, softly and with tender sweetness. It was like he could bring me to the edge with little effort.

I didn't know it'd be like this. I didn't know I could feel this way at *all*. I thought my body was broken, but clearly, that was far from the case.

While he was kneading my breasts, I leaned down and kissed him. I put my tongue into his mouth and began sliding myself up and down his hard dick. The noise of pleasure he made when I did that drove me wild. I was acutely aware that I was more nude and more vulnerable than I'd ever been with a man before, and even so, I wanted to go farther.

I broke the kiss and began to stand. Charlie made a gasp of disappointment, but I put a finger to his lips to signal we weren't done yet. I guess I'd used up all of my mistakes practicing with Kallie earlier, because dancing against Charlie felt natural. As I rose to my feet, I supported myself with my hands on his shoulders, and slowly ran one leg down his dick. His body quivered. With that same leg, I lifted it over my head and placed it on his shoulder. Charlie froze completely, and I leaned forward so that I balanced on my tiptoes, lunging into the splits. Charlie's expression was mystified as he ran a hand up and down my thigh, feeling the heels I wore before continuing upward. He paused just before he got to my panties.

"I'm *very* flexible," I told him. "You can have me in any position you want."

Charlie swallowed. He looked nervous, which baffled me. Hadn't he done things like this before? "I think you're the one that's got me."

I gave a throaty laugh. *Thank you, Ivy.* I moved forward, so my knee was hanging off his shoulder, and my breasts were pressed up against Charlie's face. His mouth began to move over my breasts, kissing them like he'd been enchanted by a goddess. I allowed myself the indulgence of letting out a few more delicious moans. I let my hair fall across his shoulder, and thankfully, none of it got in his face.

"Ancestors, you smell so good," he breathed. He sucked one of my nipples into his mouth, and it made my head spin. I had to remind myself that this was about giving him a good time, and not me, but damn if I didn't want him to continue. Charlie continued to lavish attention on my breasts. He brought me to the edge before retreating backward, teasing me before he dove right in again, alternating his attention between one breast and the other, using both his hands and his mouth. My mind fell into a buzz, and even the ever-common voices faded away to nothing but static as I fell into Charlie's lustful touch.

The moment snuck up on me. One second, I was enjoying the feel of his tongue against my nipples, and the next, I was spiraling into a climax. My head fell backward, and I let out a loud cry. Charlie continued to play with me as I let go, and one of his hands wrapped around my back to bring me even closer. He didn't pull back until I was panting, completely brittle in his arms.

Holy. Fucking. Shit. He'd made me come by touching my breasts *alone*. He was some sort of fucking sex god.

I expected our first time fooling around to be a lot of awkward fumbling, maybe some pleasurable moments thrown in. After all, I didn't know what I was doing.

But it wasn't like that. It was like we'd done this a million times, and were just coming back to the memories now. I could hardly believe we hadn't done this before. This was some kind of magic.

I managed to bring the dizziness of my orgasm to a close. I slid down his body, removing my leg from his shoulder so I was straddling him again. I tried to go slowly, though my hands shook nervously as I unbuttoned his pants and slowly drew his zipper down. Ancestors, his dick looked fucking huge right now. I didn't know what I was going to do with the thing.

Before I pulled down his boxers, Charlie grabbed my wrists. "You sure about this?"

"Yes," I said. "Absolutely. I want to touch you."

Charlie let his grip drop, so he was feeling my thighs again. I pulled down his boxers slightly, and his dick sprang free. I gasped once I saw it.

Oh. My. Ancestors. It was *perfect*. Like, people *said* dicks were ugly, but Charlie's was a work of art. I didn't even know how to approach it.

Charlie sensed my trepidation. "Just play around with it. It all feels good."

I reached out and took his dick into my hand. His skin felt so smooth underneath my palm. I played with it carefully, stroking his most sensitive parts with care and concern. Charlie let out a couple of noises of satisfaction, but they made me hesitate instead of continuing on. Was I doing this right?

"You can go a little faster," he said. "You aren't going to hurt me."

I didn't want to. I knew a guy's junk was sensitive. I'd worried somehow I was going to rip it clean off. But he didn't seem too bothered. I picked up the pace. When I began to go faster, Charlie put a hand on the back of my head and pulled me forward. He kissed me, and I worked his body up to a stupor, feeling his dick jerk in my hand.

"Ava," he gasped against my mouth.

I nearly stopped, thinking I had done something wrong, until I realized he'd said my name out of passion. I increased my speed and held him a little tighter, and that's when I felt it. Charlie's excitement surged through our bond, and before I knew what was happening, stars exploded behind my vision. Charlie said my name again, and I felt his climax coat my hand. At the same time, a rush of exhilaration and euphoria coursed through my blood. My body wasn't having an orgasm, but in my head, my mind experienced the same rush of pleasure. I continued to stroke him through the end, urging myself to continue forward even as I was riding the same waves of delirium he felt.

Both of us were gasping when it was over. I pressed my forehead against his.

"Hell, pidge," he muttered. "You ruin me."

I bit my lip. "So... was it good?"

Charlie scoffed. "Was it good? You made me feel like a fucking king."

My insides glowed. Charlie took a handkerchief out of his pocket and handed it to me, so I could clean off my hands.

"Who carries a handkerchief around anymore?" I teased. "What are you, an old man?"

"I always come prepared," he replied slyly. "Never know when you're gonna need one. They're good for cleaning up blood."

He paused, like he'd said something too revealing. He rushed to explain. "People are always getting into fights at the Institute. It's important to have something to get the blood out of your eyes."

"I know you got in that fight at the start of the semester, but you need to be careful. I don't want you getting hurt," I said.

"I won't get hurt, pidge. I always win."

I rolled my eyes. He could be *so* cocky.

Charlie jiggled his legs, bouncing me up and down. "You seem like you're getting comfortable."

"I don't want to get off," I replied. Being on Charlie's lap was by far one of my favorite places.

"I don't object." He leaned back, like he was content with having me close. "Ava, being with you is unlike anything I've ever felt before. What we have together means everything."

His words brought me some comfort, but still... I felt apprehensive. There were things about being with me that Charlie couldn't possibly understand until they happened. And once they did, and I went on the warpath, I was concerned he'd remember what it'd be like to be with somebody else.

But he couldn't dump me if we weren't really dating. I'd done my homework. I'd protected myself.

"I know you've been with other people before," I said. "That has to make a difference. I know I'm not your first, but I'm okay with that. I just want to meet your expectations."

"They were transactions," Charlie explained. "I was giving something away to get something else. The women I was with always wanted me to pleasure them. I never got anything in return, except a night off the streets."

"Wow, that's rude," I said. What a bunch of selfish lovers.

"I had to learn pretty quickly how to make a woman feel good if I wanted a warm bed and a roof over my head," Charlie said.

"So... how many women have you been with?" I asked. It wasn't really my business to know, but I was a little curious. I hoped he didn't find my question invasive.

His cheeks tinted red. "A dozen," Charlie spat. "Yeah, uh, let's just say it was a dozen."

Well, that sounded like a lie, but I wasn't going to press. After all, that was in the past.

"Have you ever made a woman come by just touching her breasts before?" I asked. It couldn't be just me, right?

"No," he said. "I mean, girls have told me I'm good, but that was on another level."

I'd say. Our chemistry was off the charts. I didn't know if it was our bond, or just the way we felt about each other, but the connection we had while sharing our bodies was intense.

Charlie studied the quietness between us. "I know what you're thinking. I felt it when you came, too. I didn't even think such a thing was possible."

Me neither. I'd never heard of something like that before, even in cases of fated mates like the fae had. Did the fact that we shared a soul made our sexual experiences that much more powerful?

Charlie reached up, like he wanted to brush back my hair. As he swept a few strands away, I noticed the red and purple armband I'd woven for him as his birthday present around his wrist. "You're wearing the armband I made you," I said.

"I don't take it off," Charlie said. "It's the best gift I ever received."

That got to me. My eyes watered for the second time that day, and I choked out, "Did you mean what you said in therapy? About Oberi and me being your family?"

"Of course I did, pidge. It's you and me for life. Nothing's ever gonna tear us apart. I won't let it."

I wanted to believe him so badly. After the powerful moment we'd just experienced, I needed to think we'd last forever.

But at some point, the fairytale would have to break. He wasn't aware of the oncoming tempest, but I knew it was coming. I could feel it brewing inside my emotions like a hurricane, just waiting to burst.

Until it did, I'd cling to him. Charlie was the only way I could bear to weather the worst before it struck.

After then, I'd be on my own.

Unless he chooses to stick around, a voice in my head offered.

I'd typically push such fantasies away, but I couldn't this time. I wanted to hold on to hope that once Charlie saw the monster inside of me, he wouldn't be afraid to face it.

Yet I knew better. No one could tame me once I'd been let out of my cage. I hurt people. Unintentionally, but when the worst came and I crashed, I did damage and wrecked whatever was in front of me. Charlie wouldn't be able to stand against the storm. No one would willingly choose this kind of life.

Even so... I dared to dream.

I wasn't sure Ava-Marie could surprise me anymore. With my pidge, I'd come to expect the unexpected.

But I never could've predicted what happened that afternoon in the abandoned storage room. Ava-Marie had *really* surprised me, and in all the best ways. Feeling her body against mine made my head spin, until I didn't know which way was up and which was down. My hands against her skin, my lips on her breasts, and her sensitive areas pressing against my hardness... it was overwhelming and exhilarating and... *perfect.*

Ava had performed with nothing but the utmost confidence. It'd been so hot. It was like connecting to a part of my soul that always seemed inches out of reach. Now I had it in the palm of my hands... and I would never let it go.

"What's up with Ava lately?" Ezekiel asked the following week.

Ez had joined me in the prison yard after class to work out. I curled my fingers around a narrow brick ledge on the edge of the building and did three quick chin-ups. I dropped back to my feet and felt my cheeks flush when he asked the question.

"What do you mean?" I asked innocently, though I knew exactly what he was referring to. Ava had been nothing but bubbly and happy since that day in the storage room. To anyone else, it might seem like she was high on drugs, but I knew it was her bipolar. I just hoped she stayed in this happy state for a long time.

"She's been acting... weird," Ez said. "I mean, weirder than normal. Her highs aren't usually like this."

I shrugged. I wasn't about to tell him I was screwing around with his sister. Ez and I got along, but not *that* well. "You know her mood swings better than I do," I replied vaguely.

"I guess so," Ez grunted while he tried to do a chin-up. I could feel with my magic that he barely got two inches off the ground. He continued talking while trying to get through his first chin-up. "I didn't expect her... to be so happy... in prison."

Ez dropped to the ground and blew a breath. "Whew. Three in a row."

I laughed under my breath and clapped him on the shoulder. "Just because I'm blind doesn't mean you can fool me."

His shoulder dropped beneath my hand.

"I won't tell anyone," I teased. "If you want to impress the ladies with your lies, I'll let them believe anything."

Ez shrugged me off. "I'm not trying to impress *anyone*."

My eyebrows shot up. "Not even a pretty little mermaid?"

"No way." Ez shoved me.

I laughed. "I didn't mean to embarrass you, kid."

"Who are you calling *kid*?" Ez jumped at me, swinging out his fist in a playful way. I felt him coming and blocked him. He gasped and flung out his other fist, but I caught his wrist and yanked him forward, until I had him in a headlock. He slapped at my arms and shouted, "Not fair!"

I snickered and messed up his hair with my knuckles. "What's not fair? That a blind guy can beat you?"

I let him go, and he took several steps back. "Let's try to avoid getting caught fighting, okay?" he suggested. I noticed he purposely avoided answering my question.

"It's no big deal," I told him. The guards would look the other way for me, now that I had Captain to back me up.

"I don't want to get into any trouble," Ez said. "There's a field trip into Shade Hills at the end of the semester for good behavior. I intend to be on that bus."

"Cabin fever already?" I asked. Oh, boy. This kid had a lot to learn about the Institute. I was half surprised he'd lasted this long. "I hear the trip isn't that great, anyway. It's supervised, and the schedule is really strict. You're allowed to go shopping, but can only buy *approved* items. It's hardly a field trip."

"I'm just not interested in getting an infraction on my record, okay?" Ez said.

I shrugged. "Fair enough, but I suggest you learn how to defend yourself regardless. Avoiding fights in this prison only gets you so far. One of these days, you might end up in the middle of a fight you never saw coming."

I thought of my first encounter with Mad Dog. There were ruthless guys inside this prison that would pick a fight for no reason. I hoped Ez didn't get caught in the crosshairs, but he had to be prepared if he did.

"I can teach you to fight," I offered.

"Thanks for the offer," Ez said genuinely. "But you're forgetting why I'm in here. I know how to handle myself."

"You held back on me because I'm blind," I realized.

I was met with silence, which was nothing short of a confession. "You can't do that, Ez. Not in here. If someone picks a fight, you give it all you've got, okay? You have to do whatever you can to protect yourself in here, you hear me?"

"Yeah, I hear you," Ez grumbled. "You make it sound like I'll be getting in a fight every other week."

I smirked. "If you want to."

"I don't," Ez practically snapped.

I sensed something in his tone— guilt, perhaps. I didn't think he felt sorry for what he did to John, just sorry that he got caught. If you asked me, the kid was a fucking hero. I'd beat that motherfucker's ass too if I ever ran into him.

Ez quickly changed the subject. "What do you say we run a lap?"

"You sure you want to challenge me? I might beat you," I teased.

Ez laughed, sounding in a better mood. "We'll see about that."

Ez took off running toward the track, and I immediately bolted after him. I heard the sound of his shoes hit the pavement, then felt the soft grass shift to hard asphalt as I joined him on the prison yard track. I took note of the sound of a basketball *thwacking* against the concrete nearby to gain my bearings, then turned my attention to Ez's heavy footsteps ahead of me. I sprinted after him, but he was quick. For fun, I shifted the air currents around us so that the wind came at my back and a gust blew in Ez's face.

"Now *that's* unfair!" he shouted, already panting hard.

I laughed as I passed him. "I didn't know there were rules."

"You're still a cheater!" Ez called after me.

I kept close to the edge of the track, so I could easily follow the curve of it through my magical senses. I sensed trees ahead with my Earth magic and knew the first turn was coming. Ez's footsteps were long behind me, but I pushed forward anyway. I loved the adrenaline rush of the race and the rush of endorphins that came from working out.

I heard the familiar *twang* of the basketball and voices of players up ahead, and knew I was coming to the end of the track. I slowed as I completed my first lap, then waited for Ez to return. The kid must've given up, because he'd started out fast but took forever to complete the lap. I must've been waiting a full minute before his footsteps approached.

"Okay, so I cheated," I admitted. "At least I didn't give up."

"I... didn't... give up," Ez said through heavy breaths. He coughed loudly, practically hacking up a lung, and I heard him drop to the grass. His body gave a heavy *thump* as it hit the ground.

My stomach lurched, and I immediately knelt at his side. "Ez, you okay?"

He lay on his back and sucked in deep breaths. "Fine. Totally fine."

"You don't sound fine," I pressed. "What's wrong? Did you pass out?"

I reached out for him, but he shrugged me off. "No," he insisted. "I just haven't worked out in a while."

He took another few breaths before adding playfully, "If you didn't *cheat*, I could've kept up."

I frowned, because I sensed there was more to it than that. I could feel the air moving in and out of his lungs, and it was more labored than it should've been. I worried about him, but it didn't help to press. I was all but certain he'd lost consciousness.

Whatever it was, Ez didn't want to talk about it.

"We'll run laps another day," I offered. "Let's move on to push-ups."

"Yeah, sure," Ez said, rolling over onto his stomach in the grass.

I positioned myself in a plank position and began doing push-ups. I made myself look busy, but really, I had all my attention on Ezekiel. He tried to hide the strain from his voice, but I could sense it in his breath. I used my Earth magic to feel the grass beneath him, and he barely made it to the ground before it seemed like he was about to collapse.

I got to my knees. "I think that's enough for today."

Ez breathed a sigh of relief, and I heard him rise to his feet. "Sounds good. I—"

Ez stopped dead in his tracks.

"You what?" I asked.

"I, um, gotta get to class," he said quickly. "I'll meet up with you later."

"Okay..." I said skeptically. I was pretty certain Ez didn't have class right now, but for some reason, he was eager to hurry away. Probably thought I was going to suggest more chin-ups or something.

Or so I thought... until I heard the sound of footsteps approaching. My heart surged with happiness as I felt Ava's presence through the bond. I hadn't noticed her and Oberi at first, because I'd been so focused on Ez. Now I sensed them draw near as if I were touching them.

That was weird. Why did Ez hurry off when his sister showed up? It was like he didn't want her catching on to something— or calling him out.

What was he hiding?

"Pidge," I greeted, getting to my feet. Oberi barked and twirled around me, nudging his wet nose into my hand. I stroked the top of his head. "What's up?"

"What's up with *me*?" she asked innocently. "Since when do you and my brother work out together?"

I shoved my hands into my pockets. "Since now, I guess."

I felt Ava's skepticism through our bond. The more time I spent with her, the easier it'd become to feel her emotions. They were starting to get stronger. Sometimes it felt as if they were my own. I was really going to have to figure out how to manage that.

"Is that a problem?" I asked, a little harsher than I meant.

"No, it's just... weird. You're always in the prison yard lately," she admitted.

I should've explained myself. I could've told her about the fight club and why I'd been working out so much. But I felt something else through our bond beyond skepticism. Ava was anxious— about what, I didn't know. I sensed that if I told her about this, it would set her off. Ava would want me to quit so I didn't get hurt, and I wasn't going to do that, especially not before my first fight.

Ava apparently didn't care for an explanation, because she changed the subject quickly. "Anyway, Oberi and I came to find you, because I need your help."

Before I could respond, she grabbed me by the wrist and began dragging me behind her.

"Help with what?" I asked. Those were the only words I could get in before Ava started talking a million miles a minute.

"I'm bursting with ideas, but I don't have the time to do it all! It's driving me insane. So I asked Oberi, *how are we going to get this all done,* and of course the answer was *Charlie.* I hope you're not busy. Too bad if you are. You'll have to help me, because there's *no way* I'm getting this all done on my own." Ava opened the door to the Villain's Den, and we stepped inside the building.

"Get *what* done?" I asked. "You're not falling behind on homework again, are you, pidge?"

Ava snorted. "Homework is the least of my problems. It's at least half-done. Okay, maybe a quarter... I don't know. I really don't care. This is more important."

Ava took my shoulders and guided me into a chair by a study table. My elbow brushed against something, and a pile of papers scattered across the floor. Curiously, I reached out to feel the tabletop and found all sorts of odd things piled atop it— papers, glue bottles, tiny little balls of fabric from the craft room, and tubes that rattled when I touched them. I could only guess those were glitter. Oberi sniffed one of the tubes and sneezed.

"Oh, don't mind this," Ava said in a rush as she bent to pick up the papers I'd knocked over. "I'll get all this mess cleaned up."

"What is all this, pidge?" I asked.

"It's nothing," she assured me. "I thought I'd do some crafts, but I forgot what I wanted to do with them."

"You *forgot*?" I questioned. Ava was starting to worry me, because I felt her anxiety rising.

She tossed the papers on the table and plopped down across from me. "Honestly, it's too bad they don't let us have scissors. If I could snag some from the craft room, I would cut all my hair off."

"Cut it off?" I balked. "Pidge, what are you talking about?"

"You know. I just want a *new look*. I'm sick of the boring same old, same old. I've always thought it would be brave of me to shave my head."

"No way," I stated firmly, shaking my head.

Ava huffed. "Who are *you* to tell me what I can do with my hair?"

"I want you to do whatever makes you happy," I assured her. "But I know you. You'll regret it the second you do it, and it'll take years to grow back."

I didn't mention that I really liked her long hair. I loved pressing my nose into it and inhaling her scent. I'd really miss that if she chopped it all off.

Ava drew in a sharp breath, the idea of shaving her head totally forgotten. "You know what? I have a better idea! Let's visit Hawaii!"

I frowned. "Great idea, pidge."

"I'm serious, Charlie. We'll break out of the Institute— tonight!" she cried. "We'll go to Hawaii and hide away, where the Institute can't find us. We'll drink mimosas on the beach and spend every Saturday morning at the spa—"

Ava started talking so fast I couldn't understand a word she said. Ancestors, I didn't know how to deal with her like this.

"Pidge," I pressed, but she didn't stop talking. "*Pidge*," I tried again.

She didn't acknowledge me. She quickly switched from the topic of moving to Hawaii to what she was going to wear for next year's Villain Ball. Nervousness flashed through her quickly, so fast it was hard to make sense of it through the bond. My heart rate increased the longer I listened to her.

"Ava-Marie!" I snapped. I jumped out of my chair and grabbed her by the shoulders, shaking her a little.

She went silent for a beat, and I didn't waste any time getting a word in.

"Calm. Down," I insisted.

She shrugged me off. "You think it's dumb, don't you?"

I didn't know what part of it she was referring to— shaving her head, moving to Hawaii, the dress she'd been describing, or one of the other things I hadn't caught.

I sat in the chair beside her but remained close enough to take her hand. "Take a breath, pidge," I said gently. "You're looking for a solution that isn't there. I can feel your anxiety through the bond, and none of these ideas are going to fix anything."

"I'm not looking to *fix* anything," Ava objected. "And I'm not anxious!"

I frowned. "You can't lie to me about how you feel, because I feel it, too."

Oberi let out a high-pitched noise, as if agreeing with me.

"Not true. I feel great!" Ava countered.

"That's good," I assured her. "And I'm glad you do, but you have to see that these ideas are a bit irrational."

"No, *you're* irrational," she teased, poking my nose. "You don't *want* to go to Hawaii with me?"

I gaped at her. She *had* to see that we couldn't, even if we wanted to. No one escaped the Institute.

"Maybe one day," I finally answered. *When we got out of this place...* "But we still have the prophecy to deal with, and we both know the answers are here."

"The prophecy doesn't matter," she responded in a flippant way.

I'd never heard that come out of her mouth before, so now I *knew* something was wrong. "It doesn't *matter*? What's gotten into you? The prophecy is the whole reason we're here!"

"Oh my ancestors, can you like, just chill out for a second? I'm totally fine. I'm seeing things clearer than *ever*!" she cried. "Look, this is how it'll go. I'll shave my head as a disguise, we'll dig our way out of the Institute using a spoon— it works, okay, I've seen it in movies— then we'll go to Hawaii, and just like, hang out with the mermaids, and I'll wear a cute shell bra, and we'll run from the law, and it'll be *so* fun, and—"

Ava dissolved into a mess of babble that I couldn't make out. Oberi started to whine. It was like she was in her own little world, and I didn't know how to break her out of it.

"I've already snuck a spoon out of the cafeteria in my sleeve," she gushed. "I've started chipping away at a hole in my dorm. It'll be big enough for us to crawl through in no time, okay?"

I had to do something to stop her from attempting this ridiculous idea. She was acting like she was actually planning to go through with it, and with Ava being Ava, I knew she'd fucking try. Once she was caught, she'd be even more closely monitored by the Warden than she already was, and that couldn't happen.

"What about Kallie and Marcus? We can't just leave them," I flung out randomly.

Ava completely pivoted at my suggestion, and let out a great gasp. "You're *right*, we *can't*. We need to take my brother, too. And Opal, and Ivy, and I suppose you'll want Chancey to come along too—"

"What does that mean?" I asked. Shit, she was on to me. Had she found out about the fight club?

"Oh come *on*, Charlie, we all *know*," Ava said in a scathing voice. "Get with the program."

She was implying something, and I didn't think it had anything to do with the fight club. I was totally confused, but she left me no time to think about what she said, because she surged into a completely different vein of conversation.

"You know what we're missing here at the Institute? A theater program," she said confidently. "Marcus was a theater kid, you know, he told me, so I think we really need to get some acting classes around here. I don't *know* if I'd be good at it, but like, why can't I be an actress? That's a thing I can do after I graduate, right? I've read three books on acting in the last two days, so I think I can handle it."

"What about anthropology? Did you finish your application for your major?" I asked.

Ava froze beside me. "Anthropology? Hm... yeah, I forgot that was a thing. I guess I'll just quit. It's not like I'm doing well enough in class for Hemlock to accept me into the program, anyway."

She'd forgotten about that, too? Professor Hemlock's anthropology program was all she'd talked about for days after she'd found out about it. Now she was getting obsessive about acting, something she'd never indicated an interest in before, and giving up on her lifelong dream of being an explorer.

Whenever she got impulsive, that wasn't a good sign. "Ava, you can't just tank your grades," I started. I didn't know how to go about this, but someone had to bring her back down to earth.

She giggled, then gave another huge gasp, as if she'd forgotten yet another critical piece of information. "Oh, shit! I told Ivy I was going to do the— oh, but I also promised Kallie that I'd— you know what, never mind, I'm already late to see them both, I'll just have to make up some excuse. I have to go, I'll see you later, Charlie!"

My heart sank as I heard her skip off. Oberi remained by my side and whimpered. The heavy truth formulated around me as I was faced with reality.

Ava was sicker than I wanted to admit. I knew her bipolar was bad, but it was starting to get out of control.

She couldn't take care of herself when she was like this. Hell, she could barely function. I had to be the one to look out for her.

Protecting Ava became more important than ever. She was a loose cannon right now— who knew what she'd say or do, and if I didn't have immunity from the guards, I couldn't shield her from the consequences of whatever her mood swings provoked her to do.

Staying in this fight club was my only means of keeping both of us safe in this hell. Which meant that if I wanted Ava to be safe at the Institute, I needed to win my first fight.

I had no other choice.

I bounced on my toes and shook the nerves from my shoulders. The locker room was quiet, but I could hear the voices of a thick crowd outside the doors. My first fight had arrived, and I was itching to get into that boxing ring and beat someone's ass.

"You nervous?" Chancey asked.

I threw a few punches into the air and felt the air particles move around my fists, then across my bare chest. I didn't wear gloves, because I couldn't feel the air as well through them, so I'd just taped up my hands. There were no rules that said I couldn't use my magic to enhance my senses. I just couldn't use it against my opponent— like suffocating him to gain the upper hand. The guards wanted a show, not a slaughter.

I scoffed at Chancey. "Me? Nervous? Hell no."

I'd been ready for this since the day Captain offered me a spot in the ring. Hell, I'd been itching for a fight long before that. I'd gotten a taste of it during the Darke Games, and I wanted more.

Problem was, you couldn't get in a fight around here without repercussions, and I wouldn't let Ava and Oberi get caught in the crosshairs. Which was why Oberi wasn't here. I'd insisted Ava take him for the night. I didn't want him seeing this. I'd made up some lie to her about where I was, and I hoped that she believed it, but to be honest, I wasn't even sure if she'd remember by tonight. She was in a really complicated headspace right now.

Down here in the basement of the Institute, there were no such repercussions. I could let out all my pent up rage and beat the hell out of my opponent, and no one would do shit but cheer for me. Call me crazy, but I was ready to taste blood. I was ready to be *bad*.

"Good," Chancey told me. "You have nothing to worry about. Just make sure you give them a good show. You have one shot to impress the guards. I know Captain said you get three fights to prove yourself, but truth is, this first fight is where you have to impress them. Lose this fight, and you'll be hard-pressed to get on the roster again. Win, and your bets will skyrocket. You'll be making more cash than you've ever laid eyes on."

"Haha," I said dryly, though Chancey sounded amused at the joke.

"But hey, no pressure," he added.

I chuckled under my breath. "Yeah, man. *No pressure*."

The pressure didn't scare me. I'd made it through the Darke Games fighting monsters from hell. I knew I could handle another supernatural inside a boxing ring.

The door to the locker room creaked open, and Captain's deep voice boomed through the empty space. "Wahkin, you're up!"

Chancey placed a hand on my shoulder. "I'm right beside you, buddy. Let's give them one hell of a show."

I nodded firmly, then followed the sound of Captain's voice out of the room. The air expanded to the large training area, but my magic met resistance against a crowd. There must've been over a hundred people encompassing the boxing ring, all waiting to see how their bets panned out. Some of the voices came from above me, and I heard the sound of something clink against metal. I realized the crowd was seated in bleachers that weren't usually there during training. I could make out the voices of students as well as guards, though I couldn't pick anyone specific out of the crowd.

Cheers erupted as Captain entered the room. He must've been encouraging the crowd, because the cheers only grew louder. I followed Captain down an aisle toward the ring.

"Give us *bloood!*" someone shouted as I passed them.

"A blind fighter?!" someone else balked. "I've *got* to see this!"

"He's savage!" another student added. "Didn't you see him during the Darke Games?"

The voices grew so loud they began to blend together. Then I heard it— the sound of my name being chanted across the room.

"Charlie! Charlie! Charlie!"

People were cheering... for *me*. I didn't know who the voices belonged to, but I didn't have to. A wide smile spread across my face. I shouldn't have been thrilled by this, but I was. The adrenaline rush was exhilarating, and I hadn't even stepped into the ring yet. I was addicted to the sound of them cheering my name, and I wanted more.

On the other side of the room, the chanting became louder, though they cheered another name. *"Damien! Damien! Damien!"*

I'd heard of Damien before, but never met him formally. I quickly leaned over to Chancey. "He's Atlantean, right?"

"Yeah," Chancey confirmed under his breath. "The rules say he can't use his sonic scream against you, but remember that mermen have enhanced strength and senses. Find a way to use it against him."

"How many fights has he won?" I asked.

"Two," Chancey said. "This is his third. Make sure he loses."

I nodded firmly. "Got it."

"Oh, and don't hold back with this asshole," Chancey added. "He's one hell of a jerk."

I smirked. "Perfect."

Captain's heavy footsteps sounded as he climbed a set of stairs onto a platform. "Let's hear some noise!" he shouted with the voice of a showman. His deep voice filled the entire room like he was speaking into a microphone, but there was no buzz of speakers to accompany it. He must've been using fae magic to project his voice.

The crowd roared even louder.

"Are you ready for a fight?" Captain shouted. The crowd screamed in exhilaration, and I bounced on my toes, ready for whatever came my way.

"Are you ready for *blood*?" Captain continued. My ears rang from the loud cheers, but I welcomed it with the adrenaline.

"Ladies and gentlemen, the moment you've all been waiting for—the main event of the night," Captain announced. "You've seen him fight. You've seen him dominate. Give it up for the Barracuda, Damien Lee!"

I could barely hear Damien step into the boxing ring over the sound of the crowd cheering his name. But Damien himself was into the attention, obviously absorbing every last drop he could get.

"I can't hear you!" Damien screamed from the center of the ring. People cheered even louder as he encouraged them.

After the crowd settled a bit, Captain continued in his confident announcer voice. "You saw him fight monsters during the Darke Games—a balur, a malumuto, and a deceptem. But is he a match for the Barracuda? Well, folks, you're about to find out. Welcome to the ring for the first time—"

Captain cut off abruptly and leaned down, his tone soft enough that it didn't ring over the crowd. "Shit. What's your stage name, kid?"

I gaped a moment. Hell, I hadn't come up with a stage name.

Before I could answer, Chancey spat out something for me. "The Blind Bandit."

"*What?*" I balked. "Are you fucking kidding me? That's offensive as hell."

"You gotta give me something," Captain pressed.

"It's good marketing," Chancey insisted. "He's the Blind Bandit. Just go with it, Charlie."

"The Blind Bandit it is," Captain agreed.

Captain straightened and projected his voice across the room again. "Please welcome the Blind Bandit, Charlie Wahkin!"

I turned to Chancey, totally pissed. "That's a lame-ass stage name."

"One that you're stuck with now," he said, like it wasn't a big deal. But I knew it was. People would remember this name forever. "Besides, it's a good thing you're pissed off at me. Channel that into your fight."

I didn't get another chance to respond, because Chancey shoved a mouth guard past my lips and pushed me toward the ring. I caught myself on the ropes. The crowd was already chanting my stage name, and I knew there was no turning back now. I had to fight. I had to prove myself. I had to earn my place in this prison— not as Charlie Wahkin, but as the Blind Bandit.

Stupid ass name that it was.

I climbed under the ropes of the boxing ring and jumped to my feet to face my opponent. The air moved around Damien as he shifted his weight from one foot to the other, amping up for the fight. Someone else moved through the ring— a referee.

"A blind Elementai?" Damien laughed. "Taking you down will be easy."

I chuckled. "You'd be surprised."

"Ready?" the ref called. "Fight!"

I didn't hesitate, because I knew if I did, the fight would be over far too soon. Damien and I lunged at each other and met at the center of the ring. He threw the first punch, and though he was quick, I felt it coming through my Air magic. I ducked, and his fist went over the top of my head. I jumped back as he swung again.

Each of my moves were calculated. I didn't go in for the shot right away, but rather stuck to dodging his attacks. My strategy was simple. I was learning his fighting style with the help of my Yapluma senses so I could use it against him.

"Coward," Damien spat at me. He didn't seem to notice what I was doing, and it would be his downfall.

Damien was a simple fighter, I quickly realized. He'd go for any shot he could, whether it would work to his advantage or not. All he wanted was for his fist to connect to something— *anything*.

And so I let it.

Damien's knuckles cracked into the side of my jaw, and the crowd screamed a mixture of cheers and boos. I smirked in satisfaction as the pain radiated through my face. I already felt the bruise forming. Chancey hadn't been lying about Atlantean strength. They were no vampires, but mermen were *strong*.

As my hands came up to block my face, Damien aimed lower. He landed a punch to my ribs, just as I predicted he would. I knew the punch was coming and quickly calculated my counter-attack. Before Damien could draw his fist away from my ribs, I grabbed his wrist and yanked him forward, while simultaneously swinging my knee up into his gut. I knew by the way the air left his lungs that he felt the blow. We'd see how much *enhanced strength* he had after that shot.

My opponent recovered quickly and jumped back to where I couldn't reach him. He began circling me, and I followed his movements, tracking them with my magic and the sound of his feet on the floor. Nothing outside of the ring seemed to matter— not the crowd, the announcers, or anything. I barely heard them as I focused all my attention on my opponent.

"The clock is ticking, my friend," Damien sneered through his mouthguard. "I'm undefeated. It's time to end this."

I scoffed. "What are you doing standing around talking about it? Bring it on, fish boy."

"Fucking savage," Damien sneered as he jumped at me.

I blocked his first punch, but it hurt my forearm like a son of a bitch. I retaliated quickly, landing a punch to his gut, then to his jaw.

I quickly learned that Damien didn't back down. He was all about the offense and barely bothered to block my attacks. His fists started flying at me so fast, I had a hard time making out where they were coming from. His knuckles connected with my body in five consecutive blows, first to my guts, then to my face. My ears rang as his fist slammed into my eye. I instantly felt my eye begin to swell and blood drip down my face.

It should've left me stunned, but all it did was ignite a fire inside of me. The pain wasn't even mildly inconvenient. It was *exhilarating,* and I welcomed it with open arms. It reminded me that I was alive— and I wasn't just here in the Institute *surviving* anymore. I was having the fucking time of my life. And it motivated me to *win.*

Defending myself was suddenly off the table. My only choice was to do more damage to him than he did to me. I kicked Damien in the face so hard that he stumbled back a few steps, far enough that his arms couldn't reach me. I kicked him again before he could recover, but that was all I managed to do before he jumped at me again.

Damien's fist met my jaw once again, and the coppery taste of blood filled my mouth. I smiled in satisfaction and spat the blood in his direction. The crowd went fucking nuts.

The feeling of blood spraying all over his face must've distracted Damien momentarily, because I managed to gain the upper hand. I landed blow after blow to his jaw, enjoying the sweet satisfaction of beating him up. Hell, I was actually *good* at something for once. And the crowd was loving it.

Damien shoved me backward, and I stumbled to the outer edge of the ring, catching myself on the ropes. He grabbed for me, wrapping his arms around me so tightly I could hardly breathe. He tried to knock me over, but I refused to be taken down so easily. I jumped and wrapped my legs around him, throwing off his balance. Damien growled as he fell forward. The bastard nearly crushed me, but I used his momentum to roll the two of us over until he lay flat on his back.

I knew from my many fights on the streets that gaining a dominant position like this could easily be short-lived, so I did everything in my power to deliver as much damage as I could while Damien lay on his back. I landed punch after punch to his face. Blood spurted from his nose and onto my knuckles. *Satisfying as hell.*

As predicted, the position was short-lived. Damien's legs curled tight around me so that I couldn't move. He wrapped an arm around the back of my neck and yanked my face toward his. He was strong, and I couldn't get away. I heard Damien spit something from his mouth, then the thud of his mouth guard landing several feet away. Damien's teeth latched on to my ear, and he bit down hard. I screamed as pain radiated through my ear and warm blood trickled down the side of my face.

So he wanted to play dirty. I could play dirty.

I punched the side of his face a couple of times, but he didn't let up on my ear. The fucking bastard was going to bite it off!

Hell no. If I was going to lose an ear, this asshole was going to lose an eye.

I hated to play *that* dirty, but I had to defend myself, and there were no rules here in the underground fight club. I felt around his face until I felt his eyes, and I shoved my fingers into the sockets.

Damien reared backward and cried out. His hands left my body, and I thrust an elbow into his upper thigh so hard his legs loosened around me, too. I jumped to my feet and hurried to the other side of the ring, where I could calculate my next move. It was hard to make out what Damien was doing, because the crowd was so freaking loud I could hardly hear myself think.

I have to win this fight. I have to win this fight.

The words echoed in my mind. Every moment I let this go on was another chance for Damien to win. We'd already given the audience a good show. It was time to end this and earn my place.

Chancey's words came back to me. *Remember that mermen have enhanced strength and senses. Find a way to use it against him.*

Perfect. How'd I do that?

"What are you standing around for?!" Chancey's voice came from outside the ring. "You've blinded him! Finish him off!"

A moment of shock hit. I'd *blinded* him? Not for good, obviously, but I must've done enough to swell his eyes shut. Victory surged through me, and I hadn't even won the fight yet. No one navigated this Institute without sight better than I did.

I'd found my chance to win. I wasn't about to waste it.

I stepped toward the center of the ring and focused my attention on my Air power to get a feel for Damien's location. I quickly realized he was still on the ground, but he must've heard me coming, because he jumped to his feet. He shook out his hands, and sweat and blood splattered all over my chest.

"Come at me!" Damien yelled.

I chuckled. "Gladly."

I lunged at Damien, intent on delivering one last blow. But he was ready for me. I'd underestimated just how well his other senses would make up for his temporary blindness. Damien caught my arm as it was headed toward him, and he used my momentum against me. He yanked downward and spun around, twisting my arm behind my back so hard something popped. A sharp, ungodly pain twisted through my shoulder as the joint dislocated. I cried out in pain but barely heard my own scream as the crowd went fucking nuts. They loved it.

Hell, I'm done for, I thought. There was no way I was fighting back with a dislocated shoulder.

But then I felt *her*. Ava's fear flashed through our bond as she recognized my pain. She could feel that something was wrong with me, and she was worried.

I hated when Ava worried. All I wanted was to keep her safe and happy. If I gave up now, I gave up everything I could possibly give Ava inside the Institute.

My Air magic sensed Damien's arm drawing backward. He was going in for the final blow— the one that could end this all for me.

It simply wasn't an option.

Damien's fist flew forward, and I reacted as fast as I possibly could. I ducked and grabbed his arm with my good hand. I pulled him forward, accelerating his momentum toward me. At the last second, I rolled onto my back and shoved my feet up into his abdomen. His momentum kept him tumbling forward over top of me. I thrust my feet upward, flinging him into a flip. The sound of the ropes twanged as Damien flipped over them, then came the loud *thud* of his body as he landed outside the ring.

The crowd went freaking insane.

"You did it!" Chancey shrieked. "You knocked him out!"

A whistle sounded, and the ref hurried over to me to grab my good hand. He shot it into the air and announced, "Winner!"

"Ladies and gentlemen!" Captain's voice boomed over the room. "The Blind Bandit!"

That was all I heard as the shock of victory swept through me. Despite the pain, the blood, and the bruises— not to mention the dislocated shoulder— I'd won. It didn't quite seem real.

"Way to go, man!" Chancey screamed as he rushed into the ring to congratulate me. He clapped me on the shoulder, and I winced.

"Whoops. Sorry," he said sheepishly, before quickly adding, "It's so going to be worth it. That fight was incredible."

I couldn't help but beam as I soaked in the cheers from the crowd. "Totally worth it," I agreed as I tried to catch my breath.

"You looked so badass out there," Chancey continued. "You were so strong and fast. I honestly wasn't sure you'd make it against an Atlantean, but you proved me wrong. You proved us *all* wrong."

"Hell yeah, I did," I said proudly.

I'd prove them wrong time and time again. Because I was the fucking Blind Bandit. I was lawless— an outlaw and an outcast.

And there were only so many rules I could follow. I was planning on breaking each and every one.

ava-marie

EIGHT

As I woke up Saturday morning, my first thought was of Charlie. Oberi lay at the end of my bed and watched me as I sat up, his tail giving a slow, cautious wag as he observed my wild hair.

I rubbed my arm. Last night, I'd felt Charlie's pain. It came through our bond— a sharp ache radiating through my shoulder, like someone had almost wrenched it out. I knew immediately the pain had come from Charlie. I'd nearly cried, it'd been so painful. I was so concerned, but it was like Charlie was ignoring me. He didn't even brush against my consciousness afterward, to let me know he was all right. I wanted to go to him, but by that time, the door on my cell was already locked for the night, and I couldn't leave.

I immediately went to check in with him, but didn't get any sort of acknowledgement back. I could feel his presence just on the other side of the wall that separated our cells, still and silent. He was sleeping.

I didn't want to wake him if he was recovering from some kind of injury. Maybe he'd fallen last night and hurt his shoulder trying to catch himself. I didn't know. I'd leave him be... for now.

My second thought was I had to clean my room. I had to clean *everything.*

I was, by nature, a slob. My clothes, books, papers and anything else I had lay scattered around my cell, lying in piles and thrown this way and that. I sat up and realized how absolutely bothersome it was. Strange, considering I'd never noticed before.

I sprang out of bed. I organized my books, I took my clothes to the laundry, and I even made my bed. Oberi got up to help, pushing things into piles so I could put them away faster.

But it wasn't enough. I polished my desk with an old washcloth I had, I dusted the curtains.

Meanwhile, in the back of my head, the voices taunted. Oberi whimpered as he watched me scrub and scrub at a black spot on my windowsill that had probably been there for forty years and just wouldn't come off.

It's so dirty.

You're a filthy, nasty person.

What if Ez came in here? He'd get sick, and it'd be your fault.

It wasn't good enough. *Everything* had to be clean. Sweat beaded across my brow, and my arms began to ache as I scrubbed at whatever was in sight. The germs had to be gone. It was the only way to be safe, to be sure.

I'd been working for hours, and yet, I didn't feel tired. After my room was spotless, I got a taste for something sweet. I went to the med area, then headed down to the Arts & Crafts room. I signed in and wound around the room to the kitchen area.

There were all kinds of stations in the Arts & Crafts room. There were areas for sewing, a tiny kitchen for cooking, a paper crafting station, a yoga and meditation area, and others. The entire room was monitored at all times, to be sure students who got their hands on kiddie scissors didn't hide them to stab someone later. Marcus was usually in here more often than not, painting in the corner where the art supplies were.

I took a few supplies from the dingy old fridge. The kitchen in the Arts & Crafts area was stocked, but not well. I'd have to improvise on some ingredients. As I baked, Professor Celosia, who ran the room, watched me with a stern eye. She was a grouchy old woman who covered her hair and never put down her knitting, unless she had to stop a student from doing something stupid.

Her attention was taken away from me when a couple of guys in the corner started poking each other with sewing needles. She and a couple of guards had to escort them down to the Warden's office, leaving me unattended.

I put in one batch of cookies, but I figured that wasn't enough, so I made another— and another, and another. I fed Oberi cookies after they'd cooled from the oven. He lapped them up, until his belly was full and he spread out on his back, groaning from all he'd been fed.

Professor Celosia still wasn't back, giving me free reign— which was probably a bad thing. Just before lunch time, my brother walked in. His eyes widened at all the cookies spread out all over the countertop as I finished washing the last of the dishes I'd used to bake.

"Ez, look, I baked all these cookies!" I cheered. "Two-hundred of them! You want one?"

He frowned. "Why did you bake so many?"

"Um, well, I got to thinking I wanted some, but then I didn't know *what kind*, so I figured I should just make a bunch, but I didn't want to stop, so I ended up with two-hundred." I grimaced. "Professor Celosia is probably going to be mad at me. We're only supposed to bake a dozen at a time. I used all the sugar."

"What are you going to do with two-hundred cookies?" he asked flatly.

I blinked. "I'm not sure. But we're going to find out!"

I took a basket from the weaving area and began placing the cookies inside. Ez followed me as I walked out of the Arts & Crafts room. I waltzed around the prison and started handing out cookies to anyone who passed by— even the assholes. Cries of *Thanks, Ava!* rang out over the halls.

"Look at me, spreading so much joy," I sang. "What an amazing morning!"

"You didn't take your pills today, did you?" Ezekiel asked flatly.

"Haven't for a week." I'd been hiding them in my cheek when the nurse checked, and I spat them out later.

"Ava!"

"It's fine! I don't need them!" I said excitedly. "I feel *so good* right now, Ez. I'm in a great mood! I have been for days!"

"That's because you're becoming manic," he grumbled.

"If I was manic, would I be helping this many people? I *love* helping my friends," I swooned.

"Yes, but—"

"I don't know why you're so worried, Ez. I'm just having fun. Aren't you happy I'm not moping around?" I asked.

Ezekiel's mouth twisted. "Ava, just tell me the truth. Is it getting bad again?"

"It's fine, Ez. I can handle it," I told him.

"You can't just... think your way out of being sick," Ezekiel said.

His words caused something in me to snap. "You're one to talk."

I didn't mean to let that slip out, but it did anyway. Ezekiel paled. "There's nothing wrong with me."

"Well, there's nothing wrong with me, either." We were both liars.

He huffed. "Whatever. I have better things to do than babysit you." He stomped off, around the corner and out of sight.

I'd definitely touched a nerve. Oberi let out a low whine. I sighed and continued handing out cookies, like the magical cookie-fairy I was.

Deep down, I knew Ez was right. I was becoming manic, if I wasn't there already. A fun, hypomania bipolar episode *always* resulted in a huge dip in mood later.

I just hoped this high lasted long enough for me to get everything done this week. I was so behind on homework. Maybe if I stayed awake for three days straight, I'd be able to get it all finished in one go.

"Hey!"

I barely registered the guard's voice, but I definitely panicked when I felt his harsh grip on my arm. A bulky vampire guard towered over me, his nose twisting as he caught sight of my basket. Oberi immediately sank down into a crouch and started growling.

The guard ripped the basket of cookies out of my grasp. "What are these? Distributing *nightshade* cookies on prison property? Just who do you think you are?"

"They don't have nightshade in them!" I insisted. "I just wanted to be nice!"

"Inmates aren't allowed to share food," the guard snarled. "You're heading to the Warden!"

"I didn't know!" I shouted. The guard began dragging me away.

Oberi whined, not knowing whether to attack or stay put. I froze, wondering if I should fight back, or if that would make it worse. I didn't want to go anywhere near the Warden— not now or ever. "Let me go!"

The guard snarled, and he reached for the handcuffs on his belt. I felt my stomach twist, until I heard someone say, "Don't take her in. I can handle this."

My eyes narrowed immediately when I saw him, while Oberi's tail wagged. *Charlie.* I had a bone to pick with him. His arm hung in a sling, and clearly, he hadn't hurt it from falling— he'd been attacked. Charlie had yellow and purple bruises all over his face. The area around his eyes was swollen, and he moved gingerly.

Somebody had beat Charlie up. And when I found out who, I was going to make them eat dirt. Nobody put their hands on *my Charlie* and got away with it. I'd tear them apart— my heels were going straight into their eyeballs.

The moment I got some answers from my bonded partner, that is.

The guard stopped yanking on me when he noticed Charlie. "You vouching for her?"

"Yes. It's all right. She just made a mistake," Charlie said coolly. "It won't happen again."

The guard sneered. "You're lucky this one's your girl, Wahkin." The guard let me go, but took the basket and the cookies with him. Oberi began licking Charlie's fingers, and he stroked the dog's ears lightly.

I fumed. "Since when do the guards listen to you? And who hurt you?" I asked. "Give me a name, so I can drive a foot straight up their ass!"

"Not here, Ava." Charlie's tone was short. Oberi barked, like he wanted us to follow. Charlie moved slowly as Oberi led us to a deserted corner of the prison.

Once we were alone, I said, "Charlie, you look awful. What happened last night? I was so worried."

"Don't be." His tone was sullen. "It's nothing to be concerned over."

"Nothing to be— Charlie, your face!"

"I got in a fight. You should see the other guy." He smirked.

"Who the hell is the *other guy?*" I threw my arms up.

"I fought Damien."

"The crazy-ass Atlantean?" I spat. I'd seen him put a kid into a pretzel just last week. He was still in the infirmary.

"Yeah, and I put him in his place," Charlie said firmly.

"Why?" I put a hand on my hip. "You aren't one to go around starting shit just because you can." That was, effectively, my job in the relationship.

"Let's just say he had it coming." Charlie's smirk grew wider.

I began poking him in the chest. "Listen here, buddy. You're hiding something from me, and I think it's time we get it out in the open. Did Damien hit on Chancey or something? Is that why you're mad?"

Charlie's look was blank. "Chancey? Why would I care?"

"*Come on.* You don't have to hide it. I already know," I said tiredly. "You and Chancey have been banging on the side. I get it. Where else would you be going so late? You're always with him. You can stop creeping around on me. I don't mind, really."

Charlie sputtered. "You think I've been sneaking off at night so I can *fuck Chancey*?!"

"Obviously," I said, rolling my eyes. "I know we're not exclusive, so I have to be okay with it."

"I'm not fucking Chancey! I'm not even bisexual!" Charlie shouted.

"You don't have to sit here and convince me you're only into women. Who *doesn't* want a good dick now and then? By the way, how big is—?"

Charlie pinched the bridge of his nose. "Ava, I *promise you* I'm not into Chancey. I've never seen his dick, nor do I want to."

"Then what have you been doing with him, running around at all hours?" I asked. "I demand to know!"

"I'm just trying to keep you safe. But I guess if the alternative is you thinking I'm sleeping around, then…"

Charlie hesitated. "You… know about the underground fight club, right?"

Oberi gave a groan, like he knew what was coming. I put several things together very quickly. Then, I fucking exploded.

"The *fight club*?!" I shrieked. "Are you *insane*? Charlie, do you know how many guys get really hurt down there? Do you know how many people don't make it out alive?"

"I can take care of myself," Charlie said, and Oberi began to whine.

"Did Chancey get you into this? Ooh, I'm gonna have a *word* with that angel," I growled.

"Chancey runs the bets. He's been training me, says I can make good money."

"You don't need to do that. My family is rich. They'll help us with whatever they need."

"I don't want to rely on your parents. How many times do I have to tell you this? I want to be my own man, make my own way in the world!" Charlie's voice grew angry— like he thought asking my parents for help was some kind of charity.

"You said we're family. And family helps family," I insisted. "My parents wouldn't care if we asked for help."

Charlie scoffed. "Yeah, sure. Because I've definitely made a good impression on your dad already. Let's just go asking for handouts."

"Why are you being so stubborn?" I stomped my foot. I knew Charlie had relied on himself his whole life, but didn't he realize he didn't have to do that anymore? He had me, and I had resources. I just wanted him to use them!

"I'm fucking poor. I have nothing to offer you, and I know you're used to a certain kind of lifestyle," Charlie said. "This is gonna set us up once we graduate. I'll have money tucked away for us."

I felt gravely insulted. So I liked nice things, but they were nothing compared to Charlie. We hadn't really talked about this, but it was an unspoken understanding that wherever we went once we got out of here, we'd go there together.

"I wouldn't care if I lived in a cardboard box, so long as I was with you," I said.

"You say that, until you've lived in a cardboard box." Charlie crossed his arms bitterly. "It's different when you actually have to. Trust me, I've been there."

"Why would you even want to fight?" I shook my head. "You can't tell me it's just for the money. I know you. Getting your face turned into a pulp for a few bucks isn't worth it."

"It's my hobby. I like to fight," Charlie insisted.

"Getting the shit kicked out of you is *not* a hobby!"

"Tons of people fight for a hobby! There's boxing, mixed martial arts—"

"Those are all regulated sports," I said. "The fight club is an illegal ring, where guards manipulate inmates for entertainment! Charlie, they're exploiting you!"

"I don't need one of your social justice lectures, thanks. I know how it works."

"Ancestors, I'm not fucking protesting at a rally or some shit. I think the fight club is a bad idea because I *care* about you."

"So they're using me. What's the harm, as long as there's a benefit?" Charlie asked. "I get paid. The guards let me do whatever I want — they look the other way when I ask. That's beneficial for both of us."

A sick feeling settled in my gut. I knew part of this was my fault. I was always getting into some kind of mess with the guards.

Oberi whined again, like our arguing was bothering him.

"If you're trying to protect me, you don't need to," I insisted. "We can be safe another way, without you putting your body on the line." This was too similar to how Charlie had sold himself to those women for a place to stay, and it made me sick.

"It's not like that. Fighting makes me feel powerful. It gives me a rush," Charlie insisted. "During the Darke Games, I was finally in my element. I don't feel alive unless I'm in danger. And once my arm gets better, I'm going back out there."

I hated to analyze him, but he was just repeating the same patterns he'd been stuck in all his life, because he didn't know any better.

I wouldn't say that to him, though, because I didn't want to make him upset. "It's not safe. If I had known this is what you'd been doing, I would've tried to stop it. I only gave you space because—"

"Because you thought I was sleeping with Chancey?" His voice was harsh. "It makes me pissed you think I'd mess around with someone else. I'm only interested in *you*, Ava."

I felt a blush creep over my cheeks and breasts. "I said we weren't exclusive."

"Big fucking deal. Like it means anything." His words implied something that was too much for me to handle.

My voice got small. "Isn't there some other way you can feel... alive?"

"You don't get it. My whole life, I've been invisible. Nobody cared if I lived or died. But in the ring, when the crowd is calling my name, I *mean* something. I'm no longer worthless. I'm making my mark on the world."

"You don't have to fight to earn love," I said quietly. "You're not worthless to me. You never have been."

Why wasn't I enough?

"I just... I want you to come and see me fight. Cheer me on." He sounded so defeated. "Just watch one fight, and then let me know what you think. Okay?"

It hurt me to hear him sound that way. He really wanted my approval to keep doing this.

And if he liked it... what was the harm? I just wanted him to be happy. "Okay. One fight. I'll give it a chance."

Maybe it *was* like boxing, and the bad things I heard about the club were just rumors. Maybe the fight club wasn't as bad as I thought—though the proof I was right was smashed all over Charlie's face.

Oberi gave a couple barks of relief, and Charlie relaxed. He didn't say another word about it. Instead, he reached out to stroke my arm. "I've been looking for you since I got up. Ez said you were having... issues."

My snitch brother was asking for it. "I'm completely fine," I said. "I just have a lot to do. I have three papers I'm behind on that I should get done by midnight."

"All in one day?" His tone was doubtful.

I whooshed out a breath. "Look, you don't get it. If I don't get everything done right away, when I crash later, *nothing* will get done. I have to do it all now."

"What you need is a consistent schedule on the weekends," Charlie said firmly. "Your symptoms get worse if you don't have one, I noticed. We should make one together."

"Prison is already so structured!" I complained. "I can't wipe my ass without someone knowing about it! I want to be *free*."

"Don't whine, pidge. Just do as you're told."

"Make me."

Charlie's mouth twisted humorously. "You're a brat."

"But I'm *your* brat," I said innocently, batting my eyelashes.

Charlie wrapped a hand around my hip and squeezed me to his side. "Yep. You're mine."

A funny feeling went through me then, when Charlie called me *his*. Oberi spun around our legs, like he wanted to press us closer together.

Charlie bent down to kiss me, and my body instantly melted when he did. I slipped my hands under his shirt and roamed his chest, feeling his abs— and maybe looking for any other injuries he might be hiding from me. He thought he could distract me with a sexy makeout session.

Well, maybe he could. I wasn't complaining. Charlie's mouth was warm and soft— his lips were a little swollen, probably from being clocked last night. I was gentle with him, so I didn't hurt him further, but the way he pressed harder into me told me he didn't care. He wanted me close, discomfort be damned.

Charlie pulled away all too soon. "We should probably eat something. I need to maintain weight for my next fight."

Oberi was still full up from cookies. I couldn't tell if he was walking or rolling. But at the mention of food, he began to drool.

Was everything about fighting, now that I knew? I forced my voice to sound light as I said, "Sure. Let's get some lunch."

Charlie couldn't see me smile, so I didn't have to plaster one on for him. It felt good.

They were serving chicken parmesan today— loaded with carbohydrates, starch, a ton of cheese, and a bunch of other things that just weren't healthy. I was feeling massively guilty about the cookies I'd baked earlier and wished I hadn't eaten any. I had the thought I was a shitty person for even making them— for even having the craving for sweets in the first place.

"I shouldn't eat that," I said quietly as we got in line. "It's bad."

"What?" Charlie paused.

"It's not healthy," I insisted. "And if I *do* eat it, it means I'm a bad person, because I'm eating bad food."

"Food is just food," Charlie said. "It doesn't have any power. It's not good or bad. There's no morality attached to it."

"But it *is*. You don't understand." It was so hard to articulate into words what was going on in my head.

His tone grew softer. "Okay. If it upsets you, we'll go with something else."

Relieved, I put plain baked chicken and salad on our plate instead. Even so, Charlie's frown remained in place. He thought my symptoms were getting worse, but what did he know? I'd lived with bipolar for years. I could ride the waves.

As we ate, I looked around for any stupid guards that might harass us about the dumb *no sharing food* rule, but none of them paid attention to us. They didn't even look Charlie's way. I guess the fight club really did provide perks.

Ivy's laugh trickled over the cafeteria. He was here, hanging on Chancey's arm. Those two went everywhere together. Chancey said something loud, and Ivy laughed harder.

"Who's that guy Chancey has with him? He's always around whenever we train," Charlie asked.

My eyebrow twitched at mention of the fight club again, but I brushed it off. "He didn't give me his real name," I said. Hardly anyone did, around here. "He has a stage name, though. Ivy."

"Ivy? As in, *Black Ivy*? Like nightshade, the magical drug?"

I hadn't thought of it that way. "Maybe. But he's clean now. He said he's off it."

Charlie didn't seem convinced. "Chancey hangs out with some shady people."

Irritation edged at my tone. "Ivy is *not* shady."

He nodded thoughtfully. "Just be careful, pidge. I don't want you to get hurt."

Yeah, well, that went both ways, but he was clearly ignoring my wishes to keep his face intact.

When we were done eating, Opal popped by our table. "Marcus and Kallie are in the Villain's Den. They want to talk to you," she said. "It seemed pretty important."

Charlie brushed my hand, which I took as a sign that it must be about the prophecy. "Thanks, Opal. We'll check in with them," I said.

The Villain's Den was crowded when we got there. Kallie and

Marcus lounged on the couch, surrounded by a bunch of people. I wanted to ask what they'd called us up for, but it was probably best to wait until all these people weren't around.

I didn't understand what the crowd was for, until I saw that Kallie was sitting on top of Marcus, bent over him so their faces were close together. I thought they were kissing, until I realized Kallie was carefully applying a strip of wax to Marcus' forehead. Rishi perched on the edge of the couch and mewed.

I giggled. "She's waxing Marcus' eyebrows."

"What? How?" Charlie laughed.

"Kallie knows how to steal honey, sugar and lemon juice from the cafeteria. It's all you need for a sugar wax. She gets me my supplies when I need them," I said with a shrug.

"Marcus sounds nervous," Charlie said. We could hear his protests from here.

"I'll say." I sighed. "This is about as nerve-wracking as the first time I gave myself a Brazilian wax."

Charlie went rigid. "You... wax your..."

"Vag-area, yeah. Just breathe in, breathe out, and pull. And now it's silky smooth. Wanna feel?"

He was temporarily speechless. I grinned and left him with the thought of my perfect pussy as I romped to the edge of the couch.

"Why'd I let you talk me into this?" Marcus whined, looking up at Kallie.

"You *said* they were too bushy! I'm just cleaning them up!" Kallie insisted. "I promise it won't hurt."

"Let Ava do it! She's a certified cosmetologist!" Marcus whimpered, giving a desperate glance at me.

"I can do it just fine," Kallie insisted, and she grabbed the strip. "Hold still, okay?"

I was about to tell Kallie to stop, because I'd seen her apply the wax wrong. But as I opened my mouth, I knew it was already too late. Marcus yelped as a giant chunk of hair was pulled off his face. Kallie held up the strip in victory, but her face fell when she realized her mistake. Marcus slapped a hand to his forehead, horrified as he felt bare skin.

"Dude, she took off your *entire eyebrow!*" a guy roared. The crowd died with laughter.

"I can fix it!" Kallie insisted, flapping her hands. She cast a spell, and a new eyebrow formed on Marcus' face. She put her hands on her hips and said, "There. The illusion will hold until your eyebrow grows back."

"Gee, thanks," Marcus said sourly.

I giggled. "Let me clean up the other one, Marcus. I promise I won't take it off."

Kallie handed me the wax bowl sheepishly, and Marcus' nose scrunched up grumpily.

As I worked, a shifter nearby said, "What a fucking loser. Waxing his face like some kind of girl. You really are a fucking peacock."

Marcus flushed red, and Kallie jumped right up off of his lap. She lunged for the shifter and punched him right across the mouth. The shifter went flying to the floor. His jaw dropped open as Kallie towered over him, raising another fist.

"Hey! No one's allowed to pick on the warlock but *me*, got it?" Kallie snapped.

"Got it," the shifter whimpered. He scampered off. Kallie's outburst had made the crowd scared of her, so they wandered away.

Marcus sat up. "Thanks for sticking up for me."

"These assholes need to know not to mess with what's mine," Kallie growled under her breath.

"Huh?" Marcus blinked. This time, Kallie was the one who blushed.

Charlie sensed the awkwardness, and spoke up to put a stop to it before it got worse. "What did you guys want to talk to us about? It sounded important."

Marcus and Kallie searched Charlie's face. They appeared shocked by his ragged appearance, but thank the ancestors, didn't mention it. They glanced at each other.

"Not here," Kallie whispered. "We should go to the Lair."

My eyes widened, and Charlie nodded. "Good idea," he said.

We headed out that way. We got into the prison yard and turned toward the trees, but before we reached the forest, a booming voice cried out, "Kalina!"

Kallie's face went pale. "Fuck," she mumbled under her breath. She turned around.

A big man was walking in our direction, a visitor's tag clipped to the front of his suit. He looked like a very important person, an official of some sort. His black hair was mussed, and there was a spark smoldering in his dark eyes. If I had to guess, he was a dragon shifter, and he knew Kallie.

Kallie turned toward the dragon shifter with clenched teeth. "Hello, Uncle Stefan."

This guy was Kallie's *uncle?* Weird. I thought she said her family didn't care about her. But by the cheery look on the shifter's face, he seemed happy to see her.

"What? No hug for me?" Stefan said playfully. "That's fine. I only *slaved away* to get here."

"You took a portal," Kalina said flatly.

Stefan grinned. "So what if I did?"

He glanced at us. "Are these all your new friends? Huh. Didn't know you'd taken to hanging with a warlock."

"What are you doing here? Checking up on me?" Kallie asked accusatively.

"Your parents sent me," Stefan said, crossing his arms. "They just found out about the Darke Games, which you failed to inform them about. Neither of them are very happy."

"Funny. I thought they didn't care what I did anymore," Kallie replied sharply.

"Oh, please." Stefan rolled his eyes. "*Someone's* being dramatic. You're the one who didn't want to come home for Christmas."

That was a surprise. Kallie had all but implied her parents didn't want her around. Was that a lie? Marcus' eyes narrowed.

"If they wanted to lecture me, they could've come here to do it themselves," Kallie complained.

"They thought I'd be a good... go-between." He shrugged. "Your father doesn't think you want to see him."

"See *him?* He doesn't want to see *me!*" Kallie burst.

He groaned. "You two are cut from the same damn cloth, I swear."

"You have no right to talk! You voted against me! You didn't want me to be queen!" Kallie bellowed.

"As if you gave me a choice." Stefan's look was stern. "Kalina, what you and Valen had planned for Malovia was ridiculous. What the two of you said during your Trials of Competency ruled both of you out by default. Malovia can't afford another rule by a mad queen. We hardly survived the last encounter."

"Is that what you think I am? *Mad?*" Kalina sneered.

"I don't think you have a mind to run a country, no," Stefan replied shortly. "I'm sorry if that offends you, but duty before heart and all that bullshit."

Kalina was fuming. "I just wanted to make Malovia better. My father improved it, but we could be an incredible nation!"

"I know your heart is in the right place. You want Malovia to be a great country, where everything is fair and just, and the people are cared for, just like your father," Stefan said. "But you can't force people to do things at the threat of great penalty. You have to let people have choices."

"I was going to," Kallie said bluntly. "Either make the choice to be a good, kind person, or face the rack."

Stefan rubbed his face. "This is where I blame your father. Too many vigilante stories."

"It's *justice!*" Kallie rebutted.

"You can't do whatever you like whenever you feel like it," Stefan insisted. "You're the daughter of a king!"

Marcus audibly gasped. I felt surprise radiate from Charlie to me. Similarly, I was shocked. Kallie, a *princess?* She didn't seem the type.

But then... she'd admitted during her therapy sessions last semester that she'd tried to kill the son of the current king... then said that the person she'd tried to kill was actually her brother. Which made the king her father as well. It was odd that none of us had put it together. I guess we were so wrapped up in winning the Darke Games, we hadn't *really* thought about what Kallie had told us.

Kallie's eye twitched. "Being a princess has nothing to do with it."

Marcus looked at Kallie in awe, like she was his own personal goddess. Kallie caught his stare and held it for a few seconds too long.

Stefan caught the glance. He gasped, like he'd just heard some riveting gossip. "*Kalina.* This is quite an interesting development. I wonder what your parents would say."

"It's not what you think!" Kallie yelped, waving her hands.

Stefan's look was sly. "I'm sure. Well, even a warlock is certainly better taste than that Valen prick."

"You know why I chose him," Kallie grumbled.

"I can't say I do. No crown is worth looking at that ugly mug for the rest of your life." Stefan pretended to gag, and Kallie's hands clenched into fists.

"Can you give us some space?" she asked. "We were in the middle of doing something."

Stefan sighed. "I see you're busy with your friends. But can you *please* make a moment to talk to me? I didn't come here just to visit, you know."

Kallie's face burned. "I just need a minute."

"Well, don't keep me waiting around," Stefan said sternly, before he nodded to us and strolled off.

Marcus burst the moment he was gone. "What was all that about being a princess? Is he telling the truth?"

Kallie sighed. "He is. My title before I was banished was Grand Duchess Kalina Alexandria Nowak. Princess Kalina, for short."

"Your highness!" Marcus dramatically dropped to the ground. He began bowing to Kallie, and Rishi copied him, prostrating against the ground. Marcus reached out to kiss her hand, like he would a monarch's ring. She wrenched it away.

"Stop! I'm not a princess. At least, not anymore." Kallie dropped her head. "If I was, I wouldn't be here."

"You told us you tried to kill your brother because he stole the crown from you," Charlie said. "And that the governing body in Malovia wouldn't let you be queen because they didn't want a girl in power."

Kallie looked guilty. "I might've... *exaggerated* a little when I said that."

"Kallie!" I shouted.

"I wasn't all lying! There are *some* sexist pigs on the council, some that don't think women should rule," Kallie said. "But there are others who aren't, and they didn't approve of me because I didn't pass my Trials of Competency in order to take the throne. The Circle didn't vote me in because they thought I would be— too aggressive and unstable a monarch."

"Imagine that," Charlie said fairly.

"So when I didn't pass, the crown passed to my brother, the runner-up," Kallie admitted. "And at the time, I was very mad about that. I shouldn't have gone after Kaz like that, but I did it for the good of Malovia. At least, that's what I convinced myself of at the time."

"You certainly didn't prove to anyone you were *stable enough* to be a queen with that decision," Charlie pointed out.

Kallie let out a harsh laugh. "No. I guess not."

Kallie turned away from us. "My ideas to rule Malovia weren't *that* extreme," she ranted. "I mean, the world is terrible, and I just needed to rule it to make it better. With an iron fist. Right?"

I nodded, because I understood, but neither of the boys looked like they agreed.

Marcus took a step closer. "The truth this time. Why are you really here?"

"Eh, I was sent here for more than just trying to kill my brother," Kallie admitted reluctantly. "After that happened, they connected me to a lot of... um... past crimes."

"Past crimes?" Marcus raised an eyebrow.

"I wanted to start an assassin's guild," Kallie confessed. "It was just me for a while, though. I hunted down a lot of serial killers, sex traffickers, and the like. You know, people who the police never catch, or who get off with a slap on the wrist. I considered it cleaning up society. It was because of me the crime rate in Malovia went down by ten percent. I put a lot of evil people in the ground. And I would've kept at it, too, if I didn't get caught."

"Wow." My eyes widened. "I'm surprised you didn't hang for that in Malovia."

"If my parents weren't the king and queen, I probably would've. I got a break." Kallie shrugged. "But I mean, my dad did it, so why can't I?"

"Oh, yeah. The Phantom. He was a really famous vigilante twenty years ago, wasn't he?" Marcus asked.

"Yes. He acted like he was disappointed in me, for the public eye, you know, but I could tell he was proud I was following in his footsteps."

She sighed. "Until I went after Kaz, of course. Now it's like he doesn't want to know me."

"It can't be easy, being caught in the middle of both of your kids," I said.

"It isn't. And I know I screwed up, because I was the one who tried to take Kaz out. I mean, which side is my dad *supposed* to take?" Kallie's eyes watered. "But this really sucks. I was really close to my dad, and ever since all this happened, we don't talk anymore."

I knew how Kallie felt. I was a daddy's girl through and through. I couldn't imagine not speaking to Daddy. He was my rock.

"It was like I wasn't in control of my actions when it happened— I just lost it," Kallie went on. "I love my brother. I can't imagine trying to kill him. I can't even *remember* doing it. And yet, I did. I know I did, because I got caught."

Professor Mazur's lecture came back to me— how demigods were prone to lapses of judgement and power. Had that happened to Kallie?

Marcus put a hand on Kallie's shoulder and squeezed. "I know what it's like to lose control," he said gently. "I understand."

Kallie's face softened. She put a hand on Marcus'. "I do have one regret, besides trying to kill Kaz. There was a serial killer in the city. He targeted young girls, sometimes even children. It was my mission to take him down. I spent months hunting him, and never caught him. Then, when I lost the crown, I stopped thinking. I acted rashly instead of deciding to kill this fucker first. He's probably still running free around Malovia."

"That's not your fault," I said. "You can't be responsible for stopping every bad guy in Malovia."

"But I *did* try," Kallie said. "And in the end, my uncle is right. It drove me mad and made me unfit to rule. All hunting down criminals did was turn *me* into the villain, in the end."

Marcus reached for her again and squeezed her hand. It was clear he was dying to comfort her. "I'm sorry, Kallie."

"It's too late now. What's done is done." Kallie pushed away from Marcus. "Ugh! We won't be able to sneak off to the Lair now, not without my uncle watching me like a hawk. He'll want to talk to me some more. We'll have to wait until he leaves."

"We should go tonight, then, before they lock the doors to our cells," Marcus suggested. "This can't wait."

Charlie nodded. "Then tonight it is."

CHARLIE HAD CONVINCED the guards to skip our cells for bed check, and since he'd won his last fight, they'd agreed. As much as I hated to admit it, him being a fighter for the club had perks.

When Charlie and I arrived at the Lair that evening, Marcus was floating through the air. Kallie was levitating him with her wolven telepathy magic, and he was getting flecks of paint on his face as he spray-painted the only bare spot left in the Lair, which was the ceiling.

Marcus had spray-painted the entire interior with cool designs. There were pictures of a city skyline, of all kinds of magical creatures, of skulls and wings and faces, and all kinds of graffiti art. Everywhere you looked, on every wall, there was a unique design to look at, colors blending seamlessly into each other. I wasn't sure how Marcus had managed to smuggle so much paint from the Arts & Crafts room, but apparently he could do anything, if it was for his art. I ran my fingers over the impression of a door he'd painted on the rock. The flower arch spanning the doorway almost looked real.

The rest of the stuff we'd stolen from Contraband was scattered around the room, along with spray paint cans, snacks, and other stuff we weren't allowed to have at the prison. Kallie had conjured illusions of plushy purple couches to sit on, along with a stone fireplace that she'd created to be real. The fireplace cast the entire room in an eerie glow.

It looked pretty wicked in here now, and was a badass place to hang out. It was a shame we couldn't come here every day.

"So, what's up?" Charlie asked. I led him to the couch, and we took a seat. Oberi, who was in her unicorn form, lay beside the fireplace and made little fire butterflies rise out of the hearth with her horn, while Rishi immersed himself in a bag of catnip.

Kallie levitated Marcus down from the ceiling. They took separate armchairs, and Kallie said, "You guys wanted us to look for information on demigods. There wasn't much to go on."

"Until we figured something out," Marcus said. "The material in the library on demigods is rare, but we found every time a demigod was mentioned, it always led back to the Elves."

"The Elves?" I blinked. "Why is that?"

"We aren't sure," Kallie said. "The two are connected, but we don't know in what way."

"There is something we figured out, though," Marcus said. "Ava, you were able to translate the words on that bow, right?"

"Kind of." I got up and walked across the room, to where we'd stowed the Elven bow. I placed it on the table in front of the couches. "The runes on the bow roughly translate to, *Beneath the bones lies our forevermore.*"

I'd thought it rather gruesome when I'd interpreted it. It was a similar inscription to the Elven gate we'd found in the woods during the Darke Games; *What is hidden remains secret from all but the demigods, forevermore.*

The runes on the ships in Kinpago were all names, but underneath each ship name was inscribed the same word; forevermore, over and over.

I blinked. "Do you think *forevermore* was a code word amongst the Elves?"

"See, we think *Forevermore* is a location," Kallie said. "Not a warning."

"A place?" I asked.

"Yes. Otherwise, why would it be mentioned over and over, on the gate, the ships, and on the bow? It's a clue," Marcus said.

"Look at this book we stole from the library on the Great Supernatural War." Kallie placed a book on the table and rifled through a few pages before pointing to a paragraph. "This passage says, '*The Elves are gone to forevermore.*' I thought it was a mistake made by the writer, and that the sentence was supposed to read, '*The Elves are gone forevermore,*" but what if it isn't? What if Forevermore is a *place,* and the author didn't capitalize the name, in order to keep it safe from people who didn't know about it? *The Elves are gone* to *Forevermore.* It makes sense!"

"Who's the writer of this book?" I asked.

"Aeson Decimus. He's long dead and gone," Marcus said. "But when he was alive, he was an expert on Elven lore, and the Great Supernatural War. During our research, we found out he might've had Elven blood. If there's a hidden place of the Elves, he would've known about it."

"And that's what we're looking for. A secret, lost city of the Elves," Kallie said confidently.

My mouth twisted. "Are you guys sure about this? It isn't a lot to go on."

"I have a gut feeling. We know the Elves used to live on Darke Island, but if that's true, where are the ruins, the artifacts?" Kallie asked. "There aren't any."

"That's because the other supernatural races destroyed them all. They wanted to erase the Elves from history," I said.

"They couldn't have gotten rid of everything," Marcus insisted. "Even after genocides are committed, there are always traces left behind of former civilizations. Why aren't there any on Darke Island?"

"There are," I said, excitement surging through me. "The gate Charlie and I found during the Games had Elvish runes on it. *What is hidden remains secret from all but the demigods, forevermore.* The city must be behind the doorway!"

"Then we have to figure out how to get through it," Kallie stated with conviction.

"Agreed," Marcus said.

Charlie had been awfully quiet throughout all this. "Charlie? What do you think?" I asked.

He shifted uncomfortably. "We're making assumptions. How can we be sure of all this?"

My heart dropped. I really needed him to be with us. "We can't know for sure until we unlock the doorway. I get we don't have all the answers, but it's progress. We're one step closer to solving the mystery of my prophecy."

"You don't even know what's inside the city," Charlie said. "Whatever is behind that door could be dangerous."

"I know it has *something* to do with my prophecy," I insisted. "The prophecy says there's a war coming. Whatever we find in Forevermore must be something that will help us win the war."

"Or start it," Charlie grumbled. "What are you hoping to find? An Elven weapon? Think about it, pidge. Whatever the Elves hid behind that doorway is so powerful that only demigods can handle it."

"Maybe it isn't a weapon," I theorized. "Based on what Marcus and Kallie found, we know the Elves had knowledge about the demigods. Maybe Forevermore holds clues on how to use our powers, and *that's* why the doorway was made for demigods."

Charlie gave a skeptical expression.

I swallowed. "I'll never know what I'm looking for if I don't go out and find it, Charlie."

He fell silent. I ran my fingers over the bow. If this lost city was truly real, I had no choice but to find out how to get there. I was a demigod, but I had to know what that was, and why I was one— what my purpose in the prophecy meant.

No matter how dangerous this city could be, getting through that gate was the only way.

NINE

My knees shook the whole way back to my dorm from the Lair. We were making more sense of the prophecy. We had another clue. In normal circumstances, I should've felt relieved. Instead, I felt a storm stirring in my guts. I wanted to vomit just thinking about getting closer to answers— because that meant we were one step closer to Ava's demise. I wouldn't let the prophecy come true. I *couldn't*.

I lay awake all night, brainstorming ways to sabotage our search for answers. If Ava found how to unlock the lost city of the Elves, it was over. I'd become destined to be her undoing— to *end* her, as Maddie had said. I had to lead her astray, or at least as far away from answers as I could.

The answer became clear as I woke the next morning. It wasn't a sure thing, but it was one step in the right direction. I sensed that Oberi could tell I was on edge, because he padded slowly beside me as he guided me to the library. It was early morning, before breakfast, so there weren't many people in the halls yet. I listened carefully when I entered the library, but I only heard the librarian behind the main counter shuffling books around. I approached her and cleared my throat.

She gave a sound of surprise. It was unusual for students to visit the library so early. The Institute didn't exactly attract the book-smart crowd. Most students steered clear of the library as long as they could, usually only visiting it the night before a paper was due. Madame Rayne — the librarian— knew me by name, since I often had to come in to use the computers.

"Oh, Charlie," she said kindly when she recognized me. "If you're here about the computers, I've already informed the Warden that the one on the end is down. You'll have to use the other today."

"Actually," I said smoothly, "I'm looking for books on Elvish lore."

Before she could ask what the hell I intended to do with a book, considering I couldn't read, I quickly added, "It's for a group assignment. Since I can't read, my job was to check out the books."

"Oh," she said brightly. "Yes, I heard about this assignment. A girl came in a few weeks ago looking for books on Elvish lore as well."

Kallie, I thought immediately.

"I hope she left some for the rest of us," I said with a laugh.

"Unfortunately, most Elvish records have been destroyed," Madame Rayne replied. "But I stumbled across a few more after the other girl requested them. If you'll just wait here a moment, I can get them for you."

"That would be great. Thanks," I told her.

Madame Rayne's footsteps faded down a long aisle. I leaned against the main counter as I waited for her. Oberi nudged his wet nose against my hand and whined.

"It's for the best," I said, though knots twisted in my gut. I immediately threw up mental walls, so Ava wouldn't sense I was up to something.

Madame Rayne returned a few minutes later, and a *thud* sounded as she dropped a stack of books on the counter beside me. "It's not much, but this is all we have left on the Elves."

I gave her a kind smile. "I'm sure it will be enough for my paper. Thanks."

"Best of luck, Charlie," she replied kindly.

I grabbed the stack of books and rushed out of the library before she could check them out for me. I was out of the doors too fast for her to protest.

Oberi followed dutifully beside me and helped me navigate the halls. Madame Rayne had only found me three books, but it was enough. They might contain answers about Forevermore that I didn't want Ava to uncover. Kallie could keep her other books, since they hadn't provided any more answers than what we had, but no way in hell was she getting her hands on these.

I made my way to the prison yard out one of the side doors, where I wouldn't be seen. The grounds were eerily quiet this early in the morning. The air was chilly, and I felt the first few rays of the rising sun touch my skin. I listened carefully for the sound of guards, but I heard no one.

"Keep watch for me, Oberi," I commanded.

Oberi whined and nudged me again with his nose.

I sighed. "What do you expect me to do? The prophecy says I'll deliver a fate to Ava that's *worse than death*. I can't let her unlock that doorway. I won't lose her."

I ran my fingers through Oberi's fur, and he dropped his head. I could feel the conflict within our bond, but it was hard to decipher where it was coming from— whether it came straight from Oberi, or it was some sort of discord between Ava and me.

Ava didn't know what I was doing, though. She had no reason to be mad at me... yet.

Hell, I hoped she never found out.

When I was confident I was alone, I knelt down and set the books beside me in the grass. The earth felt so familiar beneath me. It was easy to command it to move to my will. I let out a breath, and the ground opened up beneath me. I felt the dirt with my hands. The hole was no wider than my forearm, but it ran deep underground.

"Sorry, pidge," I whispered under my breath, but I barely heard my own words over my pounding heart. This was the right thing to do. It *was*.

I dropped the books into the hole. The sound of a door creaked open. I quickly shoved the dirt back together with my magic, burying the books so deep no one but a Nivita could retrieve them. I held my breath and got to my feet.

"Charlie?" Chancey's voice met my ears. His hand landed on my arm, and he helped me up. "What are you doing on the ground?"

"Tripped," I lied. "What are you doing out here so early?"

I paid close attention to his tone to see if he'd witnessed anything, but he spoke so evenly that I didn't think he suspected anything. "Same thing you're doing," Chancey said. "Getting in as much training as I can. The second the sun hits the horizon, I'm on my feet. Can't waste time when I've got a fight coming up. What do you say we see who can do the most sit-ups before tapping out?"

"You're on," I agreed. I had a lot of nervous energy to get rid of, anyway.

Chancey and I spent the better part of the morning doing sit-ups in the yard. Oberi rolled around in the grass, protesting any sort of workout of his own. Chancey and I must've been out there for over an hour, and neither of us tapped out.

"We should probably head to class," Chancey said through heavy breaths.

"You giving up?" I teased.

"Nah, just don't want to get written up," he said. "Fighters or not, the Warden isn't going to excuse us from class."

"True. But it's *Criminal Justice*," I complained with a groan. "The class is nothing but a guilt-trip to make us *feel* like criminals."

Chancey laughed as he did another sit-up. "But you *are* a criminal," he teased.

"Touché. But you're right— we probably shouldn't skip."

I finally sat up and stretched my legs out in the grass. Chancey clapped me on the shoulder and offered his hand, helping me to my feet. My abs ached in protest.

"Thanks," I said. "You've got some real stamina, by the way."

"You, too." Chancey's voice held admiration.

"Dude, I wasn't hitting on you," I said flatly.

"Too bad," he stated, though it didn't seem to wound his ego at all. "I like it when guys hit on me."

Oberi barked and pranced to my side, sounding happy I was finally done. We started toward the door to the Institute.

I elbowed Chancey in the side. "Like it all you want, but that's not what it was."

"Ow," he complained, but he sounded slightly amused. "You can't tell me you're not flirting with me, Charlie."

I gaped. "I am not— ancestors, no wonder Ava thought we were banging."

"Ava thought—" Chancey burst into laughter. "Your *girlfriend* thought you were banging me on the side? Can you imagine?"

"Ancestors, Chancey!" I cried. "You're imagining it. Stop!"

Chancey placed a hand on my chest to stop me. His voice turned serious. "Look, bro. You're one of my best mates. You're the kind of guy I can hug and shit like that, but I know you have no interest in me. I will *never* make a move on you, okay?"

My shoulders relaxed. From an outside perspective, I could kind of see where Ava got the idea that Chancey and I had a thing. He could get pretty handsy, but in a totally platonic way— often touching my shoulder to help guide me down the hall and stuff like that. But that was all it was. I wasn't used to it yet, but I could appreciate it. Chancey just wanted to help a blind friend out.

"Thanks for that," I told him.

He cleared his throat. "No problem, bro."

Chancey and I arrived at class a few minutes later. We were the last ones there, and were left with two seats at the front of the class. I begrudgingly took mine, and Oberi rested his head on my knees.

Professor Allen, a warlock with psychic powers, cleared his throat at the front of the room. He was middle-aged and tough to read. Some days, I got the sense that he thought his students were nothing but low-lives, but every now and then, it seemed like he really cared and honestly felt sorry for us— like he really believed each of us had the power to reform, and were just dealt some really shitty hands in life.

"We've been discussing the hierarchy of power within the supernatural criminal justice system," he began. "Today, we will discuss how supernatural bounty hunters fit into that."

Usually, I barely paid attention in this class, but Professor Allen's lecture intrigued me today. It was like sitting at the front of the room made his lesson come to life or something. I sat straighter in my seat. I'd learned about supernatural bounty hunters last semester, but only sparingly. Ever since, I wanted to hear more about them.

"Supernatural bounty hunters are highly skilled individuals hired by the United Supernatural Union," Professor Allen said. "Their purpose is to capture and deliver the supernatural world's most wanted. It's a dangerous job that unfortunately, many do not survive."

I leaned forward in my chair the longer he spoke. For so long, I'd been hiding from danger, running from any threat that came my way. But when Professor Allen said that supernatural bounty hunting was dangerous, I felt a surge of excitement wash through me. It was like when I stepped into the ring, charged and ready for every fist that flew in my direction. *That* kind of danger, I wanted to be a part of.

"As you can imagine, the pay is phenomenal," he continued. "The higher profile the criminal, the bigger the paycheck. Supernatural bounty hunters are the most talented fighters and magic casters of their race—"

My hand shot into the air, and Professor Allen cut off. "Yes, Charlie?"

"How do you become a supernatural bounty hunter?" I asked. "I mean, who would you have to talk to, in order to get hired?"

He paused for a moment, then gave a light laugh. "Mr. Wahkin, you don't mean you intend to seek *employment* after graduation, do you?"

I didn't understand why he sounded so confused. I was a hell of a fighter and had been told I was a talented Elementai, casting magic way beyond my training. If anyone was fit to be a supernatural bounty hunter, it was me.

"What, you think a blind guy can't do it?" I demanded.

"It's not that, Mr. Wahkin," Professor Allen quickly assured me, though it sounded like a lie. "This lesson is not given as a career objective. It's in the syllabus to..." He trailed off.

"To warn us," Chancey finished confidently, like he knew that was exactly what Professor Allen had meant.

"Warn us?" I questioned.

"Warn us that they're coming after us after we get out of here," Chancey said bitterly. "That is, if we don't shape up and change our ways."

"That's not what... this lesson is..." Professor Allen stammered.

He quickly changed the subject. "Please turn to page three-hundred and fifteen in your textbooks."

I heard the shuffle of pages as students flipped through their books all throughout the room. I just sat there dumbstruck by the conversation. For just a moment, I'd forgotten I was in this place— that I was a *criminal*.

But I wasn't like the other criminals— the ones on the Union's most-wanted list. Yeah, I'd done some bad shit, but theft was nothing like Professor Allen was talking about. If all criminals stuck to petty theft, Ava never would've been raped. Monica and Marty would still be alive, because they wouldn't have been murdered.

I spent my life being a criminal. Taking down murderers and rapists was my chance to do some good in the world. If I could stop just one person from dying at the hands of a murderer, or save one girl from her would-be rapist, or protect one child from a kidnapper, then it was worth it.

I mulled this over all period and barely heard Professor Allen speak another word. By the end of class, I was shaking at the thought of all those criminals— the *real* criminals— still out there doing harm.

"You don't *really* want to be a supernatural bounty hunter, do you?" Chancey asked on our way out of class.

"Yeah, I do," I stated bluntly. I felt kind of pissed that he didn't think I could.

"But you have a record," he pointed out. "They're never going to take you. The Union only wants the best of the best. They're not going to hire a criminal to hunt convicts, even if you graduate and get your record wiped clean."

I pressed my lips into a thin line, feeling as if my magic might explode out of me at any moment. "I don't care. I'm going to make it happen. You just wait and see."

Who are you, to be anything more than what you are?

You're nothing.

You're worthless.

The voices came at me from all angles, ringing in my ears like an echo.

"I'm not worthless!" I snapped.

"Whoa, man." Chancey chuckled nervously. "I never said you were."

Chancey hadn't heard what I had. My heart slammed against the edges of my chest when it hit me. Voices? It couldn't be. Ava was the one who—

My train of thought came to a screeching halt when I realized that the voices weren't meant for me at all. Ava's anxiety came through our bond stronger than ever, and I realized that the voices had been hers— the ones that lived inside her head.

You don't deserve this.

You're dead weight.

Everyone thinks you're useless.

Anger and frustration flared in my gut, and it seemed to grow as the voices became louder. I wanted to shove my hands into my hair and yank the strands out, just to get the voices to stop. Chancey said something to me, but I didn't hear what it was. Beside me, Oberi whined, but the voices drowned him out. Ava was spiraling downward, and the crash was going to be the most devastating low I'd ever seen out of her. I could already feel it.

"I have to go," I insisted. I wasn't even sure if I'd said the words out loud. All I knew was I had to get to Ava— and fast!

I grabbed Oberi's fur, to guide me. He took off running, leading me through the halls and closer to Ava.

Please be okay, I thought as the voices grew louder, but they drowned me out.

You're here for a reason.

Because they can't handle you in Kinpago.

They threw you away.

Like garbage.

Bile rose in my throat, and every nerve ending throughout my body seemed to work in overdrive. It felt as if the only way to stop it was to crawl into a deep, dark hole where nothing could touch me.

Hell, this wasn't coming from me. Is this what Ava felt like *all the fucking time?* My heart pounded so hard and fast, I might've mistaken it for a heart attack. Heat flared across my skin, but my bones felt cold as ice. My knees trembled beneath me. I kept pushing forward next to Oberi with a single thought in my mind. *I have to get to Ava.*

I rounded a corner and stopped dead in my tracks. The sound of sobs met my ears, and I heard someone sucking in shallow breaths.

"Pidge!" I cried as I hurried to her side.

She sat on the ground. I knelt beside her and placed a hand on her shoulder. Her body trembled, and sweat soaked through her shirt and covered my palm. She didn't even acknowledge me. She rocked back and forth, muttering something under her breath. It was obvious I'd only gotten a taste of what she felt.

"Pidge," I repeated. I shook her lightly, but she didn't respond.

She spoke a little louder, until I could make out her words. "I'm going crazy. I'm *not* crazy."

Oberi padded up and down the hall in concern, then barked loudly. Ava gave a start, and her words halted on her tongue.

"Pidge, you're having a panic attack," I stated. "What do you need me to do?"

Ava continued to tremble, but she reached out for me and grabbed my arm, as if using it to keep herself steady. "Nothing," she rasped. "I've got it handled."

She couldn't fool me. The way she shook told me she definitely didn't have this handled. I had to distract her somehow, and pull her back to reality.

"Ava, I don't know where we are," I said, coming up with a wild idea. "I don't know this part of the Institute. Where are we?"

"It's a hallway," she replied through ragged breaths. "Just a back hallway that's a shortcut to one of my classes."

"Which part of the school?" I asked.

"The West side," she answered, falling for my ruse.

"I can't see anything. Can you describe it?"

"It's nothing. There's nothing," she spoke quickly. Her fingers curled tighter around my arms, and I held back a gasp as her nails dug in.

"Tell me what you see," I pressed.

"Carpet. Red carpet."

"Like in the entry of the school," I replied. "What else?"

"Um... windows. Stained-glass windows."

"With bars on them?" I asked.

"Yes."

"What pictures are in the stained glass?" I continued.

Her breaths began to return to normal, and her grip on my arms loosened. "There's a woman... and a tree. The whole hall tells a story of a woman turning into a tree."

I could tell she was starting to come back to me, but I didn't think she was all the way there yet. "Do you know the story?"

"I've heard of many similar stories. Almost all races have a legend of a woman turning into a tree." Her arms stopped shaking, and her voice slowly returned to normal. "In our culture, a Nivita woman saved a man who'd been robbed and beaten. The ancestors gifted her magic, but the thief wanted her abilities for his own. He killed her, and out of her power sprouted a tree."

Ava finally calmed, and she sniffled. She drew away from me, and the sleeve of her shirt rustled as she wiped her nose. "Ancestors, Charlie. I'm so sorry."

"Don't be." I reached for her and wiped the tears from her cheeks. I hadn't even decided to do it until it was already done.

Ava grabbed my hands. At first, I thought it was to stop me. But she held on, like she needed to ground herself in the moment. Oberi pushed himself between us, and Ava dropped one of my hands to stroke Oberi's head. She pressed her face into his fur, and her voice came out sounding muffled.

"I'm so embarrassed," she admitted, before drawing away from our Familiar. Her voice became clear again. "I can't believe this happened."

"What brought this on?" I asked.

She sniffled again. "Nothing. I can't explain it. It doesn't make any sense."

"Try me," I challenged. I wanted to know everything.

Ava drew in a deep breath. "It's just something that happens some-times— without warning. I can't control it or predict it. I don't do it for attention."

"I didn't assume that," I assured her, but the way she said it told me she'd been accused of attention-seeking many times before.

"I *should* have a reason, though," Ava argued. The shame was evident in her tone.

"You're scared. That's all," I said gently.

"Maybe a little," she admitted, but I didn't have to be bonded to her to know it was a lie.

"What are you scared of?" I asked. "If I know, maybe I can help."

Ava didn't answer for several seconds. I didn't want to prod, but I was starting to think she hadn't heard the question. I opened my mouth to ask again, but she answered before I got anything out.

"I'm scared of... the Institute," she said in a small voice.

It didn't make sense. "We've been here for months, and you've never expressed your fear before."

"You weren't fighting before," she stated bluntly.

My whole body stilled. "You're afraid of me fighting?"

Ava gulped. "I'm afraid of losing you."

"Nothing is going to happen to me in those fights," I promised. I intended to soothe her fear, but I was afraid I was doing the opposite.

"You already got hurt," she objected. "I know magic is going to help you heal faster, but it still scares me. I don't know what's going to happen to you in that fight ring. I can't lose you."

There was an unspoken message in her tone.

"You're not talking about fighting, are you?" I realized.

Ava took a few breaths. "Sometimes it feels like I'm waiting for the day you get sick of me, or realize I'm crazy, and leave. What keeps me up at night is wondering if you're still going to be there in the morning."

My heart melted, and my shoulders fell. I hated that Ava thought I'd ever leave her.

"Pidge," I sighed. I pulled her close and placed a kiss on the top of her head. "I will always be here for you."

She curled into me. "Can we talk about something else?"

It was clear she didn't want to talk about her bipolar, and I could respect that. Instead, I brought up the first thing that came to mind.

"Have you ever heard of supernatural bounty hunters?" I asked.

"Yeah, sure. Why?"

"Professor Allen talked about them in class," I said. "I'm going to be one someday. After we get out of here, I mean."

I expected Ava to shoot back how that wasn't possible— the way Professor Allen and Chancey had responded.

Instead, she said, "It's really noble of you to want to take down bad guys. I think you'd be good at it."

It shocked me how Ava seemed to do a complete one-eighty in under a minute. She was just talking about how dangerous fighting was, and bounty hunting was *way* worse.

But it was never about that in the first place, I knew.

"After we get out, you can do whatever you want to do. I know you can be anything you want to be," Ava said. "I'll always support your choices."

My shoulders relaxed, and I felt totally at ease.

Until she added, "We just have to unlock the lost city and fulfill the prophecy first."

Every muscle in my body froze. My mouth went dry, and my voice came out raspy as I answered, "Yeah. Of course."

Ava showed no indication that she detected my lie. The truth was, we were going nowhere near that city. Regardless of what Maddie had told me, Ava's condition was worsening. I didn't think she could handle fulfilling the prophecy in the first place. She could barely get through the day without crumbling inside. No way she'd be able to save the world. It'd destroy her, and I'd be forced to watch.

And so I had to believe that I was doing the right thing— that this was the only way to save her...

By making sure she never set foot in Forevermore.

ava-marie

TEN

Opening up to Charlie was so hard. At the same time, it was the easiest thing in the world.

I knew that my voices were starting to bleed over to him. I didn't know how long it would be before he realized how fucked up my head was.

And in that moment of vulnerability, I'd shattered and told him my worst fear was that I would lose him, like I'd lost so many other people in my life.

Stupid. I'd learned to keep my guard up, but Charlie could take down my walls brick by brick. The more I tried to keep him out, the harder it was to avoid getting close to him. Some people in life could just chase away your shadows, no matter how desperately you tried to prevent them from seeing the darkness.

Charlie was that person for me. He made my soul quiet when it wanted to explode.

I was wavering somewhere between complete depression and total ecstasy when I sat down at lunch on Monday. I'd waited forever for Charlie, but he hadn't shown up, so I'd given up and gotten a chickpea wrap for myself. I didn't want to eat it, but Charlie was really working with me on eating well, and I wanted to try this time.

I took a seat on the other side of Ivy and Opal. Ivy was going on about how flaky angels could be when Ezekiel sat next to me. As he dug into his meal, he gingerly handled his fork, like it hurt to use.

I reached out and snagged his hand, turning it over. Ezekiel's palm was full of blisters and bleeding sores. My mouth dropped open at the sight.

"They haven't been letting us have breaks in the noxite mines," he explained. "My hands aren't as callused as everyone else's yet."

Ez wasn't the kind of guy who could work for hours on end. Charlie had said mining was tough, but I didn't know it was that bad. I was on laundry duty this semester, so I'd gotten off easy compared to this.

"We need to get you out of there. A medical exemption—"

"For what?" His tone was flat.

"Ancestors, Ez." I rolled my eyes. We really needed to stop playing this game.

"If I get out of working in the mines, the other guys are going to get pissed, then I'll become a target. It's not that bad," he insisted.

"Chancey said you almost fainted yesterday," Ivy said, popping a fry into his mouth.

"I did not," Ezekiel spat.

"Is that why Charlie had to catch you before you hit the dirt?" Ivy asked coyly.

"Ivy, shut up," Ezekiel growled.

"Obviously you've been keeping shit from me," I growled.

"I have not! Ancestors, I just have to get used to it," Ezekiel mumbled.

Opal blinked and watched Ezekiel with concern. She didn't speak up, but by the way her lips were pursed, she was thinking hard.

"You have no room to talk, by the way, because *you're* keeping things from *me*," Ez pointed out, to redirect the conversation. "You're clearly in love with Charlie."

"Hey, hey, hey. Nobody said I was *in love* with him," I protested. "It's... think of it as more of a *friends-with-benefits* situation."

"Hmm, let's see. You go everywhere together, you do everything together, you *do* each other..." Ezekiel counted off on his fingers. "Yep, you're definitely in love with him."

"We've never had sex," I seethed.

"But you've done other things, I'm sure," Ez shot back at me. "I'm not that dumb."

I scowled, and Ivy broke in for me. "Well, at least Charlie can be *honest*," Ivy seethed under his breath. "Unlike *some angels* around here. Ones who like to gamble, and play with your feelings, and—"

I was enjoying listening to Ivy rant, before a shadow fell over our table. My gut churned in distaste as Mad Dog stooped beside Opal.

"Hey, pretty lady," he rasped. "I've been looking to make a new friend, and word on the street is you're pretty damn friendly. You need a new man to call *Daddy*?"

Opal looked down and cringed away. She wouldn't stand up for herself.

But Ivy definitely would. He reached out and pushed Mad Dog's face away from Opal— a risky move, but Ivy didn't give a damn. "Can you *please* get your disgusting face out of our presence? You aren't wanted here," Ivy snapped.

Mad Dog's eyes flared. "Oh, yeah, I forgot. You two sluts sure love keeping it in the family."

What the hell was that supposed to mean? Tears beaded in Opal's eyes, and her lip trembled. She was seconds away from crying.

Ivy, though— when Mad Dog made that statement, he got *pissed*. I was certain I saw Ivy's fangs elongate just a touch when he spat, "If you want to take this outside, I'd be more than happy to kick your little bitch ass all over the prison yard. Then everyone will know you got the shit beat out of you by a whore."

Mad Dog sneered and drew away. "You know what? I'm not interested. Her blood probably tastes like fish. She sure smells like one. Fucking animals, mermaids are."

"Leave her alone!" Ezekiel stood up from the bench, ready to pick a fight. Opal had gone a deep shade of red.

"No one was asking you, tubby," Mad Dog shot at him.

Ezekiel's knuckles cracked, and my gut tumbled. He couldn't get in a brawl with a vampire. Ez would lose, and Mad Dog would put him in the hospital for sure.

So I, the queen of distractions, had to think of something fast. I picked up the food that was on my plate and tossed it at Mad Dog. He ducked, and it hit a shifter on the back of the head.

The shifter stood up abruptly. "Hey! Who threw that?"

He rounded on Mad Dog, who let go of Opal. The shifter took one look at Mad Dog and said, "Oh, so it was *you*, huh? Take this!"

He tossed his plate at Mad Dog. Half of it splattered all over his face. Opal had to duck away to avoid being hit herself. The rest of his meal was flung onto the sweater of a witch a few feet away, who screamed.

"Food fight!" Ivy screamed. Joyfully, he grabbed his tray and tossed it across the room. It splattered all over Ghost, who'd been eating a few rows down. The warlock grinned as he pulled Ivy's sandwich off his cheek, then threw it back.

In seconds, the cafeteria turned into a complete madhouse. Food flew everywhere. There wasn't anyone who wasn't hit. I flung up a water shield from a few of the cups lying around. I was able to protect the front of my uniform, but I got sauce in my hair and cream cheese all over my sweater.

Usually, I would've freaked— cause like, gross— but I didn't have time for that. I just wanted to get my brother as far away from Mad Dog as possible. He and Opal ducked underneath one of the lunch tables, watching food fly and trying not to get hit. The guards rushed into the room, trying to control the scene, but there was a lot of food flying around, and it was hard to tell who was tossing what.

I headed toward my brother. Someone grabbed my arm. I knew from the tight grip it was Mad Dog.

"You always got something planned, don't you?" he snarled. His breath smelled like sour blood. It made me cringe.

"You'd better get your hands off me." My Fire was damn ready to singe this fucker into oblivion.

"If I can't have the mermaid's blood, I want yours," he growled. "We can do this the easy way or the hard way."

I attempted to wrench away and failed. "You're damn lucky Charlie isn't here."

"But he's not," Mad Dog snapped. "And by the time he finds you, I'll have bled you—"

I smashed a fistful of Fire into Mad Dog's face. He let out an enraged sound and let me go, clawing embers out of his eyes. I took off into a sprint. I knew I couldn't outrun a vampire, but if Mad Dog got his claws in me again, I'd be in serious trouble. I glanced behind myself, but saw that Mad Dog was merely a blur. In milliseconds, he'd pounce.

Before Mad Dog could get to me, a huge gust of wind picked up in the lunchroom. It sent tables and benches flying. People screamed and got to the floor, to avoid being swept up in the windstorm. The gust sucked up Mad Dog in a powerful wind and slammed him against the wall twenty feet away.

The sound of concrete breaking echoed through the cafeteria. Before Mad Dog could move, the gust picked him up again, crushing him into the ceiling and making concrete chunks fall. The Air magic yanked him back down again, smashing him into the floor. The impact of his body made a small crater.

Charlie stood a few feet away, and it took one look to know he was fuming. Oberi was by his side in her unicorn form, tossing her head and scraping her hoof against the floor, like she wanted to charge.

Mad Dog trembled and tried to get up, but failed. Charlie had really hurt him this time.

I hurried to Charlie. "Pidge, you all right?" he asked, interlacing his arm with mine.

"I'm a mess. My hair is ruined," I said miserably as I pulled jelly out of my locks.

Charlie hauled me out of the cafeteria. I had to yank him out of the way of a couple of plates that were still flying. He took me to the nearest men's room, and Oberi's hooves clipped behind us. A couple of guys washing their hands looked up.

"Get the hell out," Charlie growled. Everyone immediately vacated the area, throwing nervous glances at Charlie as they left. Charlie leaned against the wall with his arms crossed while I worked on getting the mess out of my hair.

"Why is it every time I leave you alone, you get into trouble?" he asked.

"Because I get my kicks by putting assholes in their place," I replied. "And I honestly don't know when to keep my big mouth shut."

Oberi reached out and licked some of the food out of my hair. I'm sure she thought she was helping, but unicorn slobber wasn't exactly the shampoo I was looking for.

"Mad Dog has it out for you. He wants to get to me, but he's too afraid to go after me himself, so he's going to target you," Charlie pointed out.

"He was threatening Opal, and Ez stepped in. He can't do magic well, and he's not going to knock out a vamp. I'd like my brother not to end up in pieces, thank you."

"Ez is another one who needs to learn to control his temper."

"Our family has a talent of not being able to mind our own business," I said. "The saying goes *to see something, say something,* but the Mitoh family is more like, *see something, kick ass.*"

Charlie made a noncommittal, annoyed sound.

I turned toward him, and my heart dropped. "Charlie, you look awful."

He'd had a fight last night. A fresh set of bruises amassed his face. It was really hard for me to believe this was good for him, as he so insisted.

"Yeah, but I won again," he said. "I was up against another Elementai, so it was pretty fair."

I'd seen a guy from our dorms shuffling around this morning, looking like death warmed over. Charlie had really done a number on him. I really was convinced the guards were exploiting these people.

"I finally got permission from Captain to bring you to one of the fights. It's in a couple weeks." Charlie's voice was mixed with excitement. "Are you gonna be there?"

I'd promised him I'd show up. "Of course I'll be there. I want to support you."

"Awesome, pidge." Charlie puffed his chest out. "It's really gonna get your blood pumping, I just know it."

Yeah, once I have a heart attack when I see some vampire pummel you, I thought, but I said nothing. Oberi nickered, like she could read my thoughts.

I gave up trying to get the stuff out of my hair. "I'm gonna have to change and get a shower. This is hopeless."

"We should probably get back to the Elementai dorms anyway, just in case Mad Dog starts looking for us," Charlie said.

His tone held no fear, but I knew he was thinking about repercussions. The guards would look the other way when it came to him, but not if he started two fights in one day.

As we walked, I asked, "How's working down in the mines?"

"I'm fine. But I assume you're asking about Ez, not me."

"How is he, really? Ivy made it sound like it was bad."

"He almost passed out from the mine fumes yesterday," Charlie said quietly. "He's not doing good down there, pidge."

My stomach churned. "He's gotta get out of there."

"I can use some of my sway with the guards to get him working outside the mines instead of in them. They always need guys to load noxite onto carts once it comes out of the mines. He does that, he'll still be doing a lot of lifting, but at least he won't be inhaling all the fumes."

"You're a lifesaver, Charlie."

Literally. I knew Ez's health wouldn't hold up long, working in those mines.

We turned into the Elementai hallway, but were blocked by Kallie and Marcus. Marcus appeared nervous, while Kallie was about ready to blow her top.

"Are you okay?" I asked. They'd obviously been looking for us, if they were here in the Elementai cellblock.

"I'm pissed!" Kallie snapped. "All the Elven books from the library are missing!"

"What?" My eyes widened.

"Yeah! Some dickhead checked all of them out and didn't bring them back!" Kallie fumed. "I asked Madame Rayne who might've taken them, but she'd forgotten who wanted them, and they didn't use the library system to check them out, so there's no record."

"How are so many people asking about Elves? They're a really fringe subject," I said.

"A little bit is taught about them during the modules on the Great Supernatural War, and since not much is known about them anymore, the prison only has so many books in stock on Elvish lore," Marcus said.

"Some idiot probably took them for a paper and didn't bother to bring them back."

"Maybe, but this is too much of a coincidence," I pointed out. "All the Elvish books go missing right when we need them? Someone took them on purpose."

"That sounds like a stretch, pidge," Charlie said. "You're forgetting how careless everyone is at this school."

"Plus we're the only people who know about the prophecy, and what we're looking for," Kallie pointed out. "And it's not gonna be one of us."

"You're right." I trusted the people in this group. All of them had promised me they'd help me find Forevermore, and I had no reason to doubt them, nor did any of them have a reason to try and prevent me from fulfilling my destiny. After all, the sooner I did, the sooner we'd all understand what it meant to be a demigod, and that was information we were all craving to discover. Some moron had grabbed the books we needed for his dumb school project, then decided to keep them. Those books were probably languishing in somebody's cell right now.

"Can we buy the books?" I asked.

Kallie whooshed out a breath. "No. I already checked. They're out of print. And there's nothing valid online about Elves, not to mention every book that *is* available about Elves now is prohibited by the prison. It's on the restricted list. You can't order them."

"I swear the Warden is hiding something." I bet he was withholding information about Elves because *he* wanted to uncover Forevermore first, and didn't want to take the chance a prisoner would stumble upon it by piecing clues together.

"If we can't get our hands on those books, where else are we going to look?" Marcus asked.

"I can talk to Professor Hemlock again," I suggested. "She might know something about Forevermore."

"It's the best chance we got," Kallie moaned. "We're basically starting all over."

I took a shower and changed my clothes. I had to hurry to talk to Hemlock, because I had a class soon and there wasn't much time in between. Thankfully, Hemlock was alone in her classroom when I entered.

She shook her head when she saw me. "Ava-Marie, if you're going to ask me again about the functionality of some magical plants as objects of self-pleasure, I have to remind you that there are subjects that teachers shouldn't be discussing with students. Particularly when you ask the entire classroom at large what they use. During a test."

"This is actually about something else. But that would be *really* interesting if you knew. Phallic objects are very important aspects of supernatural culture," I said.

Hemlock couldn't fault me for asking why some of our potion ingredients looked like dildos. Opal and I had both agreed the magical underwater tuber we'd been given to examine in our Supernatural Anthropology course looked curiously like a dick.

Hemlock sighed. "Ask away."

I pondered how much I wanted to risk. "Have you ever heard any rumors about... maybe... a hidden city on Darke Island?"

"Forevermore," Hemlock stated, and my heart skipped a beat. "Yes, I've heard of it, but only in theory. The runes on the door you found speak of it, but I'm unsure if the runes are literal, or a metaphor. So many have turned this island upside down looking for ways to open the doorway, and nothing has ever been found. I think it's a wild goose chase."

"But how can you be certain of that?" I asked.

"We've had people surveying this island for the past one-hundred years, searching for the way through to Forevermore. Not a single clue has arisen that would lead us to passage. It's like the Elves didn't want us to open it," Hemlock insisted.

"Why not? The runes speak of the demigods, like the Elves wanted them to pass through." I was careful with my words, as to not reveal myself as a demigod.

Hemlock's expression grew concerned. "I understand, as an anthropologist, you'd be interested in discovering and studying such ruins of a forgotten city. However, if it is real as the legends say, it is best it remains undisturbed. There are some people in this world who do not have intentions as pure as you— people who would use Forevermore for their own twisted will."

"Does that mean there's someone dangerous looking for passage? Like the Warden?" I asked.

Hemlock paused. Her fingers thrummed upon the textbooks on her desk before she said, "Yes, the Warden is looking for a way into this city. Which is why you must abandon your quest to find it *at once*. This is dangerous, Ava."

"What's in Forevermore? What does the Warden want with it?"

"What wouldn't he want with it? Forevermore, if it exists, would contain all the knowledge the Elves had. There would most likely be information on demigods within, as well as all kinds of supernatural discoveries that other races have never gotten their hands on," Hemlock noted. "You understand the repercussions there would be if certain people managed to attain powers and information they didn't have before."

"But—"

"As anthropologists, we want to preserve and protect the ruins for future generations, but others would destroy the city in search of gaining power. If these ruins exist, they are all we have left of the Elves. People like us must be intent on keeping the city safe from others, even at the cost of our own research."

Hemlock straightened her papers. "You have a class, Miss Mitoh. If you do not move along, I will be forced to issue you an infraction. Now, hurry to it. And do not go looking for passage to Forevermore again. Not unless you're willing to face the consequences of what such a discovery might entail."

She was clearly throwing me out. I left her classroom disenchanted, wondering if she was right. That Hemlock was trying to warn me off uncovering the city made me nauseous. She was certain that if the doorway to Forevermore was opened, the discovery would be used for bad, and not good. If I was an anthropologist worth my weight, I'd do the right thing, and leave Forevermore to secrecy in order to keep it safe.

But I was a chosen one, too. I had a destiny to follow, whether I wanted to work out this prophecy or not. I was caught between the two.

If I had to choose between saving the world and saving a lost city, it'd break my little explorer heart, but I'd save the world.

Then there was the Warden. I was frightened to think that somehow, the Warden had worked out we were looking for Forevermore, and had taken those books himself. I knew he was watching me closely.

Yes, there was a risk that if I discovered how to get to Forevermore, others may follow and turn it to dust. But I didn't want the Warden to get to it first, and no matter how many years he'd spent looking for this city, he wasn't the type to give up.

I was going to keep searching for passage to Forevermore, even if there were consequences.

Because the consequences of not getting there were even worse.

Marcus and I were hanging out in the stands in the prison yard the next day. Kallie was in her shifter form, chasing around a dead mouse that Marcus had found and resurrected for her. The dead mouse scampered this way and that at Marcus' command. Kallie's eyes were fixated on the mouse, mouth watering as she dove this way and that, trying to catch it. Oberi was in his husky form, chasing the mouse alongside her with his tongue hanging out. Rishi sat in the stands beside Marcus, his tail flicking back and forth as he watched the mouse move.

"It's strange how much shifters act like actual animals, isn't it?" I asked. Kallie leapt into the air to catch the mouse, but missed and fell on her face. She shook off her fur and tried again.

"A bit," Marcus said, and he laughed. "She'd better hurry up and catch it soon, though. I can't keep this up for more than... five more minutes?"

"Why? You made that dead deer run during the Darke Games no sweat," I pointed out.

"Because we were going to die, and I had to," Marcus said. "Since we got back, I've only been able to reanimate dead mice. For fifteen minutes. On a Tuesday only."

"Wow."

"I know I have the most worthless powers in the world. No need to rub it in," Marcus grumbled.

Oberi jumped in front of the mouse, cutting off its path. The little creature turned and ran straight into Kallie's open jaws. She caught the mouse, then ate it in one bite.

Kallie changed back and put her hands on her hips. "You're gonna have to be quicker than that, Oberi," she teased. Oberi whimpered and stomped his paws.

"That was too easy," Kallie told Marcus. "You need to make it harder next time."

Marcus jumped off the stands and faced Kallie. "Do you ever do anything that's not... you know, physically exhausting?"

"I'm always ready for a fight," Kallie said. "You should be, too."

I scoffed. That was putting it lightly. Kallie would beat a bitch's ass on sight, versus Marcus, who avoided a brawl whenever he could. They were total opposites, which made them *so* cute together.

"I prefer to use my brains," Marcus replied. "You should try it sometime."

"No thanks," Kallie said. "When it comes to brains, I'd rather be spilling them."

"You're disgusting." Marcus wrinkled up his nose.

"And you're in prison. Most people would share my sentiment. Get used to it," Kallie shot back. Marcus huffed, but he wasn't half as offended as he pretended to be.

"Aren't you two adorable." Ivy approached and leaned against the stands. "I'm starting to think this prison is a hook-up pad."

"Uh, what?" Marcus said, and he let out a nervous laugh.

"You're the one that's open for business, so you tell us," Kallie said in a tease. "Any juicy details on new clients?"

Ivy hesitated. He chewed his lip before he said, "I, uh, haven't started looking for clients. I'm just trying to get settled in, feel out this joint, you know?"

Bullshit. He was trying to feel out Chancey's cock, and that was about it. Those two had a thing for each other, I was certain. They weren't just fucking to fuck.

There were a couple of laughs to the left. I turned my head, and was surprised to see Ezekiel playing basketball on the court with a couple of guys I didn't know.

What was he doing here? Didn't he have Work-Study?

"I think you need to prove to me you can handle your own around here," Kallie said to Marcus, and she took a wide stance. "Do they practice combat in the Miriamic Coven?"

Marcus went white. "Kallie, I—"

Kallie full-on tackled Marcus to the grass, and he let out an *oof*. Rishi yowled, hopping circles around them as Kallie wrestled Marcus into submission.

Which, you know, wasn't hard. He didn't know what to do. Marcus just laid on his back and took it. Kallie pinned his wrists to the ground. "Pathetic. I'm not always gonna be around to save your skinny ass."

Marcus smirked. "You know, this is the second time you've been on top of me this month. I'm starting to think you're looking for excuses to straddle me."

Kallie's cheeks reddened. "I'm trying to make you man-up! Fight me, you limp noodle!"

Marcus weakly tossed Kallie off of him, but she had him in a choke hold seconds after— which suspiciously looked like she was smashing her boobs into his face. I left those two to do... whatever they were doing, flirting or otherwise, and headed to the basketball court.

I waved Ezekiel over. "Hey. Aren't you supposed to be at the mines right now?"

"The mine we'd been working on collapsed yesterday after we got done working," Ezekiel said. "We won't be able to work for a few days."

"Really?" My eyebrows raised. "Was it an accident?"

"We dunno." Ezekiel shrugged. "We'd just left the mine to get back on the bus, then it crumbled to pieces right in front of us. It was totally random."

"Siren screams are powerful enough to collapse mines," Ivy chided. "And the sound of the mine collapsing would be loud enough to cover the scream."

"Yeah, but who would *do* that?" Ezekiel wondered. "My shift doesn't have any mermen on it. It's not like people are trying to get out of work."

Ivy and I gave each other flat looks, and I said, "No one, Ez. Absolutely nobody at all."

I knew Opal had been working inventory for the mines, recording how much noxite came out in the mining office. She was one of the few girls who was bussed out to the mines for her prison duties— on the same shift as Ez.

Opal had definitely collapsed that mine for Ezekiel. And my brother was completely clueless that she had.

"Anyway, I've gotta get to class," Ezekiel said with a shrug. "See you guys later."

Ivy turned to me as Ezekiel walked away. "I *know* your brother's not stupid."

"He's just oblivious," I said, waving my hand. "He never notices what's right in front of him."

Ivy let out a huff. "He isn't the only one."

That sure seemed like a dig at Chancey, but I didn't comment.

"What was Mad Dog saying yesterday about Opal?" I asked. "Those insults seemed... personal."

Ivy sighed. "Listen, precious. Opal's family— *our* family I should say — is messed up. Like, my mermaid side is so fucked, I had to move to Chicago to be with my vampire side just to get away from them. I didn't fall into prostitution because I thought it was a great career choice. It was what I had to work with. And for as sweet as Opal is, she's in here because our family... well, it's bad, no other way to go about it."

"What happened to her?" I whispered.

"You ain't getting the details from me," Ivy said, and he threw his hands up. "Just know, it's fucked up. Opal shouldn't be here. And if the person who put her here hadn't already faced justice, my first act after getting out of prison would be to make them pay. But they already got their penance, so, that's that. Just don't go poking your nose in. Otherwise, you're gonna find out some stuff you'd wish you hadn't."

Ivy sauntered off. What he'd said about Opal left a bad feeling in my gut. Whatever she'd been through, it was bad.

But I didn't want to make her more upset by prying, so I let it go. It wasn't my job to know what happened to her, only my job to be there for her.

I tapped my chin with one finger. Ez wasn't working in the mines, so I bet Charlie wasn't, either. I never got to spend time with him anymore since he'd started fighting.

I whistled for Oberi. "Come on, boy. We're gonna go find Charlie."

Oberi barked, then romped after me. We began searching the prison, but as we passed the main foyer, Professor Warbright stopped me. "Miss Mitoh, may I have a word with you, please?"

Professor Warbright was a warlock teacher whom we'd saved last semester from getting beat up by a couple of thugs. I hadn't spoken to him since, but he seemed a little more confident since that day.

"What is it, Professor?" I asked, certain I'd gotten in trouble for one thing or another.

"I heard you and Mister Wahkin are musically inclined," Warbright said. "Mister Taylor let me know the two of you favor music during his Miriamic Magic class."

Of course Marcus did. He babbled when he got nervous.

"We've messed around on the organ in the chapel a few times," I confessed.

"Yes, well, I felt like I needed to repay you all after what you did for me last semester," Professor Warbright said. "I was a music instructor at Miriam College many years ago, before I unfortunately lost my position. But I have convinced the Warden to let me operate a trial music program here at the Institute. I managed to cobble together a few old instruments in an abandoned classroom off the chapel. It's not much, but it's a start. I hope to start giving music classes next semester. I already told Mister Wahkin about it. He's there now, actually, if you'd like to see it."

A smile brightened on my face. "That's wonderful, Professor Warbright. Of course I would."

I hurried off. As I reached the chapel, beautiful piano music began drifting over the area. I pushed open the door to the classroom it was coming from, and the notes swelled around me. The classroom was small, but it was filled with all kinds of instruments— a little aged, but still able to make gorgeous sound. Charlie sat at a dusty old grand piano with aged wood, chipped black paint and a bent lid.

The sound lifted me up as the familiar sound of "Me & Mrs. Jones" echoed around the room. Charlie sang the first few lines, and I swear, my knees buckled. *Oh my ancestors.* Charlie's singing voice was going to make me come. I wanted to melt at the sound of it right then and there. His hair fell into his eyes as he played, and the way his hands moved over the keys made my heart swell. There was not a damn thing more sexy on this planet than Charlie playing the piano.

Oberi barked. I slid on the seat next to Charlie, and he smiled. "I was hoping you'd show up."

"This is such a beautiful piano." I dared to stroke the keys. That Charlie could make incredible music come out of such an old and beat-up instrument seemed magical. What it looked like didn't matter. What the piano could create made it beautiful.

Oberi stood up on his hind legs, then began mashing the piano keys with his paws. It made several loud, unpleasant noises.

"Oberi, stop. You're going to break it," Charlie scolded.

Oberi huffed, then changed into the Fire unicorn. She tapped her horn on the keys one by one delicately, as if to say, *Is this better, prissy ass?*

Charlie shook his head, and Oberi stomped off. She became distracted by sampling all the different instruments. She banged on a drum and threw a harmonica across the room when she couldn't blow on it correctly. Charlie continued playing, even with the noise in the background.

"I don't think anyone's touched this thing in years," I said. It needed to be tuned, but it still gave a resonant sound. "Probably because it didn't look the best."

"Yeah, well, looked like nobody took the time to see if it could play," Charlie said. "Turns out, it sings just fine."

"I always thought people judged with their eyes."

"Looks don't matter much to me." Charlie shrugged. "It doesn't matter what something looks like. What matters is what she's capable of."

"You think you can play me just like this old piano, huh?" My voice was teasing, but underneath that was something deeper and aching.

"You're not just a pretty face— hell, I wouldn't know one way or the other if you're beautiful or not. But I know you're the sexiest girl in this prison."

"How so?"

"By the way you speak. The most beautiful girls always have the prettiest voices, and yours is the sweetest I've heard yet."

"You're quite the charmer, Charlie Wahkin."

"That's what they tell me." Charlie took his hands off the keys. "You want to play?"

I hadn't touched a piano in years. But involuntarily, my hands began to move. I began playing a song Monica and I had written years ago as if it were yesterday. I had all the chords memorized. I figured I'd be rusty, but the song came flowing out of my fingers like it had been dying to get out.

I didn't sing anymore. Not even in the shower, or when I was getting ready in the morning. When Monica had died, my voice had dried up. I don't think I'd sung a note since that day, not even when my favorite song came on the radio. To sing without her felt like a sin.

It was different with Charlie around. When I played with him beside me, it wasn't like I was betraying Monica, but *honoring* her. I think she'd be proud if she knew I'd found someone to make music with again— someone who loved it as much as I did.

I didn't realize I was singing until I'd gotten through the first stanza of the song. Oberi stopped messing with the instruments and looked up to watch me. Charlie stiffened beside me, and my voice grew soft to match the notes I played.

"I'm slowly wasting away
Watching myself getting worse by the day
I'm always doing the wrong thing
No one ever hears all the songs that I sing.

I'm just my worst enemy
The girl in the mirror is still out to get me
I just can't stop lying
For them, I'll keep trying
Because I can't say goodbye

Where is my someone?
I feel like I'm no one.
Alone in an empty world, vacant world,
I just want to feel like I'm someone.

I don't just need anyone
I need someone, because I'm done
Feeling so empty."

I stopped playing and turned toward Charlie. I wasn't expecting him to grab me, but he did. He wrapped one hand around my hip and nestled the other in my hair as he brought me forward to kiss him, like he could not bear being apart from my lips for a moment longer. I kissed him back and found my hands wandering at the edge of his sweater and up his torso. His muscles welled up against my hands, and I was keenly aware that we were very much alone in here— and that anyone could walk in at any time.

As if that thought didn't make the ocean come spilling out of me.

Charlie clearly shared my sentiment, because I let my hand drop down, and he was hard. I went to unbuckle his pants, but he bit my lip, distracting me. I let out a moan as his tongue entered my mouth, making me effectively brainless. His hand slipped up beneath my uniform and under my bra to pinch and massage my nipple. His fingertips made rushing sensations pulse from my breasts all over my body. I swear Charlie stole my breath by the way he kissed me, taking it for his own. I almost thought he was using his Air magic to make us levitate off the bench. I felt so ungrounded and light. I always carried the weight of the world on my shoulders, but Charlie made me feel completely weightless. He could take my burdens from me and flick them away like a feather, and I was that feather, and I was floating away against him.

In lesser words, I wanted him. Now.

Charlie put the lid down on the piano, and it landed with a *bang*. He stood up, grabbed my ass and tossed me up on the piano lid, so I was sitting on top of it.

"Lay back," Charlie ordered.

"Or what?" My tongue popped out mischievously, though he couldn't see it.

"Be my good girl and do as you're told."

His words were a shot straight to the heart. I flopped back on the lid of the piano, because I'd been struck dead by his command. Charlie's hands massaged up and down my thighs, and he asked, "Do you want me to touch you?"

"Where?" My voice was breathy.

"Let me be clearer. Do you want my fingers inside of you?"

My first inclination was *fuck yes!* But then I had second thoughts. No one had been inside me since... well. I didn't know if it would hurt. I worried it'd be scarred down there, or it wouldn't feel good and I'd spiral into another freak-out.

But I'd touched Charlie, and experienced the wonders of his body. I wanted him to touch me, too.

I took so long to answer, Charlie said, "I can stop."

"I don't want you to," I replied. "We can try."

"Are you sure?"

"Yes. I want to see what it's like for you to be inside me."

Charlie's face flushed hungrily, and I wondered if that was the right thing to say, but he went on. "Tell me if you want me to back off."

"I will."

Charlie stood at the side of the piano. His left hand trailed up under my skirt as his right hand nestled in my hair and stroked it back. I felt him start to feather the outside of me, and the movement was so light and airy that it made my eyes close. He took his time circling the outside, dipping the tip of his finger in once or twice. I took an inhale when he did that, already feeling like I was going to blow. The anticipation was excruciating. I knew he was going slow for my sake, but at the same time, it felt like teasing. The feeling was immense, and powerful, building to something greater.

"You ready?"

"Yes." My hand stroked up and down his arm, though my eyes remained closed. I didn't need to see— I only wanted to feel.

Charlie inserted a finger, and I felt my back roll up off the piano. He slowly began moving in and out of me, creating a rhythm.

It didn't feel like I thought it would. It didn't hurt either, which was a major plus. It felt *good.* I gasped, and my breaths grew sharper as Charlie picked up speed, feeling me out as he coaxed me toward delirium.

Was I jealous of all those other women that had come before? No fucking way. It'd given Charlie a *lot* of practice. He made me feel like a goddess, the way he touched me. No offering or prayer could ever match up to the heat he was stirring inside of me.

"More?" Charlie's tone had grown deeper, and more throaty. The connection I felt between us was so strong, it pulled at my chest until I was sure my heart nearly burst.

"Yes!" I could certainly lay here all day long, enjoying the feeling of Charlie's hand rubbing the core of me.

Or at least, that's what my mind told me. This was such bliss that I felt myself falling for him fast and hard. When Charlie put another finger inside of me, I was nearly clawing at his arm. He picked up speed, and my body jolted as I realized—

Oh, *fuck.* He'd found my g-spot! Charlie pressed against it, and I couldn't hold on anymore. I rolled onto my side as I orgasmed, and Charlie worked me until my body stopped shaking, and the earth stopped quivering with the heaviness of my pleasure. I opened my eyes and looked up at him, studying his face as my chest heaved for air.

It was so intense. We were still locked in the moment. Without hesitation, I reached out and unbuttoned his pants. I yanked them down and grabbed his dick. I jerked him off, and Charlie hovered over me, his eyes shutting half-closed as he reveled in the waves of satisfaction I gave him. He was close. His body went rigid, and he bit the corner of his lip, like he was seconds from tumbling over the edge.

I looked down at his dick in my hand, and wondered what it'd feel like in my mouth. But that was a task for another time, because just as I thought it, Charlie came. He grabbed on to the edge of the piano to keep his balance, knuckles turning white as he gave a gasp of release. As before, stars burst behind my eyes, and I reveled in the amazing feelings that crossed through our bond.

A contented smirk made its way across my face. I played with him some more, but Charlie pushed my hands away. "Too intense. You're gonna make me lose control."

"Is that such a bad thing?" I asked as I turned on my back and stared at the ceiling, feeling very much proud of myself.

"Not when we're still learning each other. Maybe someday."

Charlie buttoned his pants and lifted me off the piano. Oberi gave us a judgmental look on the other side of the room, where she'd made a pile of instruments that was almost as tall as she was. I was sure she was saying, *Can you two stop fooling around long enough to come appreciate my cool mountain?*

"I was fiddling with a new tune when you got here," Charlie said as I sat back beside him on the bench. "I wanted to know what you thought of it."

"You were fiddling with me, too, and that had a happy ending."

"You're *very* funny, Ava."

"I'm a very funny person. I make myself laugh all the time. In fact, I laugh the most when no one else is around."

"That's not concerning."

I blew a lock of hair out of my face. "Yeah, yeah. Anyway, what's the song?"

Charlie played the melody, and I listened closely. "It's good, but it needs a bridge," I said. "And lyrics."

Charlie scoffed. "Okay, everyone's a critic. What do you suggest?"

I fumbled with my notebook and wrote down a few quick lyrics. I sang them out when Charlie played the opening. He said I didn't give it enough syllables, I told him he needed to clean his ears, we argued, then I rewrote the lyrics and we tried again. Oberi changed into a husky and lay at the foot of the piano bench, enjoying our banter.

Hours passed. I think Charlie and I stayed in the music room the rest of the day, and most of that night, writing songs until we had to go back for curfew. I was too happy to check the time. Playing music with Charlie was more than just songs resonating into an empty room.

It was coming back home. And for the first time, I dared to hope that maybe things would get better. That *I* would get better. It no longer felt like a wish, but something that could come true.

Charlie did that to me. He made me believe again. Mostly, he made me believe in myself.

Even when I didn't think there was anything left to believe in.

ELEVEN

The day in the music room stuck with me for weeks. I barely paid attention in classes, because I was fantasizing about meeting up with Ava during our free time. When I wasn't training with Chancey and Captain, I was usually in the music room. Ava and I fooled around about as much as we wrote music. It was during those times that I could forget I was locked in a prison. It was like inside our music, we found freedom.

I didn't realize how much I'd been enjoying it until Ava pointed out I'd been humming the same tune under my breath most of the day. We'd just left the music room and were on our way to Commissary to grab a snack before our last class of the day.

"What's that tune?" she asked curiously. "I don't recognize it."

I stopped humming and felt my cheeks flush. "It's something that's been stuck in my head for a while. I can't figure out how to end the last measure."

"Maybe lyrics will help," she offered. "Can you hum the tune again?"

I started humming while we walked, and Oberi tried to sing along, but it sounded more like howling than anything. "Oberi, that's not helping," I teased.

Ava laughed. "We'll figure it out later. What do you want to eat?"

Conversation buzzed around us as we stepped through the doors of Commissary. Ava took my hand to lead me around the tables.

"I'm not that hungry," I admitted. "What's on the menu for drinks today?"

Ava slowed as we stepped into line. She took a moment to read over the menu. "They've got fruit shakes, hot chocolate, coffee... the special today is Magical Mocha."

"That sounds good," I remarked. "Should we do two of them?"

"Can't," Ava replied. She took a step forward as the line moved. "Magical drinks mess with my meds."

"Right." I'd almost forgotten.

"What do you want?" a voice sneered from behind the counter. I couldn't pinpoint most voices, but it was easy to read Naya's by the rude inflection in her tone. We hadn't run into the succubus much since the Darke Games, and I wanted to keep things that way.

"A different barista, for one—" Ava started, but I squeezed her hand to cut her off. There was no reason to start a fight with Naya in front of everyone. I could only get us out of so many infractions before the guards got sick of me.

"I'll have a Magical Mocha, and Ava will have..." I waited for her to answer.

She sighed. "A strawberry-kiwi smoothie."

I heard Naya press a few buttons on the register before asking in a bored tone, "Will that be all?"

"Yes—" I started to say, but Oberi whined.

"Make that *two* Magical Mochas," Ava said.

Naya read us our total, then went off to mix our drinks. I turned toward Ava. "You're spoiling him. He's going to be up all night."

"No way," Ava chuckled, like the suggestion was ludicrous. She let go of my hand to kneel to Oberi's level. "You're not spoiled, are you, boy?"

Oberi barked, like he agreed with her.

She stood and spoke proudly. "Two against one."

"It's not a matter of opinion," I teased. "It's a fact. He's so spoiled, he's got mold growing behind his ears."

"I shampooed his ears yesterday!" she protested.

Oberi's tongue lolled out of his mouth, and he slobbered saliva down my pant leg. Apparently, he'd really enjoyed the bath.

I groaned. "No wonder he likes you so much."

"He likes me because I'm a *joy* to be around."

Naya snorted from behind the counter.

"You've got a problem?" Ava snapped.

Naya practically slammed our drinks onto the counter. "Yeah. I can't believe I'm locked up in this place with losers like you."

"Bitch, you're asking for it—"

I fumbled for Ava's wrist, then squeezed it tightly. "Pidge," I warned. We didn't need a repeat of the food fight in the cafeteria.

Ava huffed, then snapped at Naya. "I'm watching you."

Ava snatched up our drinks. She shoved a warm cup into my hands, then grabbed the other two. She nudged me slightly with her elbow to let me know her hands were full. I took her arm so she could help me navigate to an empty table.

"I don't know why you didn't let me light her hair on fire," Ava huffed as we sat. She popped off the top of Oberi's cup for him and set it under the table. He made loud slurping noises as he lapped at it.

"Because she's not worth it," I answered. I took a sip of my mocha and relaxed. It was really good— way better than what they served in the cafeteria.

"I'd just really like to kick her pretty little—"

"Hey," a voice sang as footsteps approached.

"Hey, Chancey," Ava greeted.

Chancey stopped at our table. "Didn't expect to see you two here. How's the Blind Bandit and his girlfriend?"

"I'm not his girlfriend," Ava said quickly.

To be honest, my heart sank a little when she said it, even though I knew we'd never officially agreed on labels.

"Yeah," I quickly agreed. "We're not dating."

Though we were doing all the things boyfriends and girlfriends did together...

"Sure you aren't," Chancey said skeptically. "That's why you have matching tattoos."

I always forgot about the tattoos until someone pointed them out, but when I remembered, a rush never failed to go through me. Ava-Marie's name was on my wrist, and my name was on hers. It was one more thing that connected us, and even better— it was permanent.

"That was a drunken mistake," Ava insisted, but I heard something else in her tone— and maybe even felt it through the bond, though perhaps that was just wishful thinking. Did Ava not regret the tattoos after all?

"You guys are together all the time," Chancey pressed.

"We have to be," I stated. "We share a Familiar. Would you drop it?"

He sighed. "Fine. I actually came over to tell you Captain's moved our meeting to tomorrow night."

By *meeting*, he clearly meant *training session*, but we couldn't talk about fight club like that out in the open.

"Thanks for letting me know," I said. As much as I loved training, it was nice to have the night off. "I'll see you tomorrow then."

"See ya." Chancey walked off.

I expected Ava to say something to fill the silence, but she didn't. I got the sense that she was still uncomfortable about the topic of me fighting. But we were going to fix that soon, once she saw me fight next week. After she watched me in the ring, she'd understand why I loved it so much.

Ava sipped her drink loudly. "So, um... you told Chancey I'm your girlfriend?"

"No," I said quickly, but only because that's what I knew she wanted me to say. It wasn't a lie, either. I *hadn't* told him Ava and I were dating, but I also hadn't corrected him when he'd called her my girlfriend before. "Chancey's just... well, you know how he is."

"I've heard stories from Ivy." She snickered.

I almost inhaled my drink. "I'm not talking about how he is in bed! Ancestors, it's like you're obsessed with Chancey's love life."

She laughed. "Don't you ever wonder?"

"Wonder *what*?"

"About people," she said nonchalantly. "Don't tell me you've never questioned how big Marcus' dick is."

"No!" I practically screamed, before lowering my voice. "Why would I ever wonder that?"

"You'd think it was small, but it's massive— maybe even bigger than yours."

"Did Kalina tell you that?"

Ava snickered as she slurped another sip of her drink. "No. She hasn't seen it yet. But I bet it's huge."

"I'm *not* taking that bet."

"So you think it's huge, too?" she asked. "Or do you *know*? What have you seen in the showers? Tell me."

"First of all, I haven't *seen* anything," I emphasized. "I'm blind, for the ancestors' sake. Do you really think I'm going around groping people in the showers?"

Her tone brightened. "Why? Are you?"

"Pidge!" I couldn't believe we were having this conversation.

"The Institute can get so fucking boring sometimes," she complained. "I need *something* to think about."

"And you automatically go to dicks," I stated flatly. "Of course you do."

"A girl can have hobbies," she teased.

"Yeah, but it shouldn't be every dick in the Institute. Just—"

I started to say more, but I cut off. The truth was, the only dick I wanted her thinking about was *mine*.

"Just what?" she asked curiously.

My heart started to pound, and I hoped she couldn't feel it through the bond. "Can we just stop talking about this?" I asked.

"Fine," she agreed. "I didn't know you were so anti-dick. Are you done with your drink?"

"Yeah," I said quickly. "Let's go."

Ava and I stood, and she reached out to take my hand. A red-hot sensation like burning coals seared my skin. I jumped backward, slamming into the corner of the table behind me.

"What is it?" Ava asked, sounding worried. It was clear she hadn't meant to burn me.

"Pidge, you're burning up," I said.

"I am?" She seemed so oblivious to it.

Ava gasped the same time I caught the scent of burning paper. Her cup clattered to the ground. "Oh, shit! I have to get out of here."

Ava ran out of Commissary. I rushed to follow, but it was so crowded that I couldn't get a good feel of my surroundings. I ran straight into an empty chair and tripped over it. I toppled to the ground, and people around me started laughing.

I didn't give a shit. I only cared about Ava.

Oberi barked, to let me know he was still at my side. I scrambled to my feet and grabbed his fur, so he could help guide me out of the room. We hurried into the hall and found Ava pacing back and forth. Her feet landed with loud noises on the carpet, and she sucked in deep breaths.

"Pidge, what's wrong?" I asked.

"I-I don't know, Charlie." Her voice wavered. "I didn't *try* to burn you. My Fire magic is coming to the surface. I can't control it. I ran out, because I was worried I was going to burn the place down."

I feared she was going to have another panic attack. I placed my hands on her shoulders to steady her. Her shoulders were hot, but her shirt helped insulate some of the heat. "It's going to be okay. Focus on me."

"I'm sorry I left you," she said in a rush. "I just had to get out of there. I didn't want my Fire exploding and hurting anyone— or hurting you."

"Listen to me," I said firmly. "You're not going to hurt anyone. I'm right here, and I won't let that happen."

Ava shook, as if trying to get rid of the extra energy inside her body. I could feel her anxiety through the bond and noticed she was trying to hold it back.

"Don't resist it," I encouraged. "That's what's going to make your magic explode out of you. Feel through it."

I demonstrated by drawing in deep, calming breaths. All I wanted to do was take her fears as my own. If I could do anything to make her feel better, I would.

My hands heated the longer I held on to her, and my arms began to tingle. Her shoulders turned to ice. The heat should've hurt like hell, but I barely felt a thing. It was as if her Fire magic was moving through me. I could feel her magic rippling along my form like my own did.

"Charlie!" Ava cried in alarm. "What are you doing?"

"I don't know," I admitted. "Is it helping?"

Ava hesitated a moment, like she was apprehensive about the whole thing. "Yeah, it's helping. I feel calmer now. Are you okay?"

I contemplated the question, paying close attention to the magical sensation tingling through me. I drew away from her, and the Fire seemed to settle into my gut. For a few moments, my abdomen felt warm, until the magic faded away.

"I'm totally fine," I said. "What just happened?"

"No idea," Ava replied thoughtfully. "It was like you just... *took* my magic from me. Must've been the bond."

Oberi barked, but I wasn't sure what he was trying to tell us.

"Strange," I thought aloud. We still had so much to learn about our bond. "Maybe we should take it easy the rest of the day."

"Yeah, that's probably best," she agreed. I was surprised to hear her say it, because Ava wasn't the kind of girl to *take it easy*. But whatever had just happened between our bond must've shaken her, because she remained quiet all the way to class.

We returned to our dorms that night without discussing the matter the rest of the day.

"I hope whatever happened earlier didn't scare you," Ava said softly while we walked down the hall in the Elementai cellblock.

"I'm not scared of you, pidge," I replied, thinking she was talking about how she'd almost lost control of her Fire.

"I was talking about whatever happened with our magic— how you just... took my powers from me. You're not Koigni. You shouldn't have been able to take my Fire. Will you check in with me in the morning? So I know you're okay."

"I feel fine," I assured her. "But I'll check in."

"Thanks." She turned toward her room, and Oberi tried to follow. "No, Oberi. Stay with Charlie tonight."

It was weird of her to give Oberi up so easily. I got the sense she was really worried about me. Whatever happened earlier wasn't normal— that much was for certain.

But then again, *we* weren't normal. Ever since Professor Baine showed up in my apartment and dragged me into this supernatural world, I'd come to expect the unexpected.

Oberi whined when I ushered him into my room. He tossed and turned all night. I barely slept. I must've managed to drift off, because I woke to the sound of Oberi barking loudly across the room.

I groaned as I sat up. "What is it, boy?"

He barked again, and his tail thumped loudly against the floor. It took me a few seconds to wake, but when I finally did, I suddenly became aware of a sinking feeling in my gut.

I scrambled out of bed and fumbled around for my pants that I left lying on the back of my chair. I yanked them on, then realized they were backward and tried again.

As soon as I had my clothes on, I hurried out into the hall and pounded on Ava's door. "Pidge?" I called. "You all right?"

Her emotions were all over the place. I could've been overreacting, but with Ava's high bleeding through, I was so overwhelmed. I didn't know which feelings were mine and which were hers.

"Ava!" I yelled, but no answer came. Beside me, Oberi whimpered.

"Hell," I muttered under my breath.

Footsteps approached, and I whirled toward whoever was coming my way. "Have you seen Ava-Marie?"

"I just passed her in the hall," an unfamiliar male voice responded. "She was headed toward the cafeteria."

Oberi guided me around corners, but he slowed when I heard the sounds of chatter coming through the cafeteria doorway. I started toward the doors, but Oberi sniffed the ground and started dragging me in the other direction. I followed quickly. We turned another hall, where all I could hear was the sound of footsteps as a few people passed through.

"Excuse me, madame," someone said in a high-pitched British accent. "Have you seen my brother?"

I stopped dead in my tracks. British accent or not, I'd know that voice anywhere.

"Sorry, haven't seen him," someone replied, then quickened their pace as they hurried away, as if they were frightened.

"Ava?" I called to get her attention.

"Oh!" she said brightly, without dropping the accent. "Hello, good sir! Have you seen my brother?"

"Is Ez okay?" My heart thumped in my chest.

Ava dodged my question as she approached me. "I'm looking for my brother. I must ask his permission to attend the ball."

"The ball?"

"Yes, the *ball*," she emphasized.

"Pidge, what are you talking about?" I demanded. Hell, was she delusional?

She gasped dramatically. "*Pidge*?! What kind of a foul insult is that? I expect better from a man of your status."

What the hell is wrong with you? You're not British, and there is no damn ball.

That's the first thing that crossed my mind, but I caught myself before I could say it. I already knew the answer. Something had gone wrong with her meds. It was the only explanation.

Ava had told me that in the past, her psychosis had convinced her she was a part of the circus, and that she'd swung from the chandelier in her house thinking it was some kind of trapeze. She'd almost gotten hurt. If she was going through something similar now, and experiencing some kind of delusion, it'd be best to play along— to keep her safe until I found help.

"You're right," I agreed. "A man of my status would call a lady by her proper name."

She huffed proudly. "Then you shall call me Lady Elizabeth."

"Very well, Lady Elizabeth. Shall we take a walk?" I held my elbow out to her, and she took it.

I couldn't understand what was happening to her. All I knew was I had to get her alone, before she could make a scene. The last thing I wanted was for her to come out of psychosis and realize everyone had seen. She'd be mortified.

Ava didn't lead me forward like she usually did. It was like she'd forgotten I was blind. I nudged Oberi, and he guided us down the hall.

"Tell me about this ball, Lady Elizabeth," I suggested as we started up a flight of stairs.

"You should *know*, Lord Henry." She snickered. "It's an annual event. Surely you've been!"

"I'm afraid I haven't." My mouth went dry. On a normal day, role playing might be fun, but this terrified me.

"Blimey! You must come. It is the most extravagant ball in all the land," Ava rambled. "I am to find myself a husband during this year's spring season. But I must ask my brother's permission first. He must approve of the man who is to take my hand. That's why I must find him."

She started to pull away from me, but I grabbed her hand, and she relaxed.

"Why don't *I* escort you to the ball?" I suggested. I couldn't have her running off on me now.

Ava snickered. "You know I can't, Lord Henry! That would be a *scandal*. I must have supervision from my brother."

Ancestors, where the fuck was Ez? I needed his help. He'd been with Ava when she was like this before. He'd know what to do, right?

Oberi stopped, and I sensed a wall in front of us. I reached out and felt a door. When I opened it, I realized where we were. Air swept past us, and I heard shouts coming from the prison yard below. Oberi had led us to our balcony, the one spot in the school where we'd never seen another soul. This was the perfect spot to help Ava find herself in private. Maybe I could talk her down.

I stepped onto the balcony and held my hand out for her to follow. "Perhaps we can discuss this further—"

Ava drew a sharp breath. "Oh, it's brilliant!"

I furrowed my brow. "What is?"

"The ballroom!" she squealed. "It's more beautiful than I could ever imagine!"

She was definitely seeing things. Ava rushed forward before I could react. She sprinted to the edge of the balcony, and Oberi barked loudly. My heart lurched, and I raced after her. I moved so quickly I must've reached the banister in three strides. I grabbed for her, only to realize in horror that she already had one leg over the banister— like she was ready to jump off.

"Ava!" I tried to yank her back onto solid ground, but she threw an elbow that sank straight into my gut.

Hell, we never should've brought her out here. I was done playing along. "Ava, get down!"

I grabbed her arm, but the last thing I wanted to do was hurt her. Ava shoved me off. "I must make my debut down the grand staircase!"

"You're going to hurt yourself!" I couldn't let that happen. I grabbed her so firmly this time that she couldn't pull away.

"Stop it!" she cried. "Lord Henry, you're hurting me!"

My heart broke when she said I was hurting her, but I knew it was better than letting her jump off the balcony. I tossed her over my shoulder, and she protested by slamming her fists against my back. For a girl her size, Ava had one hell of a swing, but I'd nurse my kidneys back to health another day. I had to get her out of here and to someone who could actually help.

"Put me down!" Ava screamed as I dragged her back inside the building. Oberi whimpered.

I pressed my lips together tightly as a knot formed in my chest. "Oberi, to the infirmary."

Oberi barked and led me down the stairs dutifully. Ava continued to punch me in the back. Her legs flailed so fast I could hardly keep a hold of her.

"You can't do this to me!" she screamed. Her voice echoed down the hall.

I heard other footsteps slow, and a couple of people gasped. The determined look on my face must've scared them off, because no one intervened.

"I am a duchess!" she shouted. "The king will have your head for this!"

Chatter met my ears, and I realized Oberi was leading me back through the hall that connected to the cafeteria. Hell, I didn't wish to humiliate Ava like this, but leaving her to her own devices was out of the question. She'd end up with a broken neck after jumping off the roof, or drowning in the pool beneath the school. Humiliation was the least of our problems.

We passed by the cafeteria, and I heard the chatter die momentarily as people turned to watch us.

"You're a traitor, Lord Henry!" Ava shrieked. "Put. Me. Down!"

The cafeteria chatter turned into laughter. Everyone knew Ava and I had a thing, and no one saw me as a threat to her. I moved as fast as I could, and Oberi led me down another hall. Voices filled the hall, and I bumped against a couple of people. Everyone must've been staring, because the area went silent as we plowed our way to the infirmary.

"This is injustice!" Ava shrieked.

A door slammed open, and several pairs of footsteps came rushing toward us.

"What in the name of the gods is going on?" a woman with a Slavic accent demanded. The accent gave her away as one of the fae sorceresses who worked in the infirmary. I guessed it was Lady Helga, the medical director at the Institute.

Ava kicked her legs, and I heard her heel connect with the woman's face. The woman gasped.

"I-I... think something happened with her meds," I stammered. "Bad reaction."

"Minerva, get a sedative," Lady Helga barked to one of the nurses.

My teeth ground together, and emotions whipped through me so quickly that I couldn't make sense of them. I felt as if I'd betrayed myself by dragging Ava here against her will. At the same time, there was conflicting reassurance, which I thought was coming from Oberi. Shame, guilt, pride... everything all came through at once.

"Help me, you imbeciles!" Ava screamed at the crowd. She threw her elbow back into my head so hard that it threw off my sense of balance. I had to grab Oberi to stay upright. "Don't you recognize a woman of noble blood when you see one? Consider this a crime against the crown. You will all answer to—"

Suddenly, Ava stopped flailing, and she fell limp over my shoulder.

"Get her into a wheelchair immediately," Lady Helga said in a rush.

The wheels squeaked as someone rolled a wheelchair over to us. I felt out for the armrests, then set Ava in the chair. One of the nurses rolled her away, and Oberi followed quickly behind. Everything had happened so fast that I could hardly process it. I slumped against the wall.

"She'll be okay," Lady Helga assured me kindly. She was one of the more gentle staff members here at the Institute. "We'll do everything we can to help. In the meantime, you mentioned she had a bad reaction to her medication. What can you tell us about that?"

I drew in a deep breath to bring me back into the moment. "Ava has bipolar disorder. She takes medicine every day to help regulate it. Yesterday she told me certain things could interact with them."

"Yes, that's true," Lady Helga confirmed. "Has she eaten anything unusual lately, such as potions or magical plants?"

"Not that I know of," I said thoughtfully. "I don't think she had breakfast yet this morning, and we ate dinner last night in the dining hall. Before that, we stopped by Commissary. *I* had a Magical Mocha, but Ava ordered—"

I stopped dead in my tracks. Fucking *Naya*. She'd been working behind the counter yesterday, and must've overheard Ava mention to me that magical drinks interacted with her meds. Naya must've mixed her drink wrong on *purpose*. My hands curled into fists.

"There might've been a mix up with her drink," I told Lady Helga.

"If that's the case, we'll be able to get her back to normal soon," she said kindly.

"Thanks." I meant it, but the word came out sounding more like a growl than anything.

Lady Helga excused herself and turned to go back inside the infirmary. I didn't have Oberi by my side to lead me back through the halls of the Institute, but I didn't give one flying fuck. I stomped away, bumping into people as I went. I didn't care— they'd get out of the way.

I made it to Commissary and marched straight up to the counter, knocking down a couple of chairs in my wake.

"What do you want?" Naya sneered once I got there.

I slammed my palms down on the counter so loud that the room quieted. Air magic swirled around me and rustled Naya's long hair so much that it tickled the end of my nose. My voice dropped to a deadly tone. "If you ever *think* of messing with Ava-Marie again, so help me, I'll make the Darke Games feel like a fucking daydream. This is your only warning before I beat your ass so hard your fangs will rattle around inside your skull. Don't hurt her again, or I'm coming for you."

A sense of calm washed over me, and for the first time I woke up, I could finally make sense of my emotions. I'd be damned if it didn't feel amazing to threaten this bitch.

Naya trembled so much a whimper passed her lips. I plastered a proud smirk on my face. Naya was scared of me, as she should be. Judging by the silence in the room, so was everyone else. Naya knew not to mess with my pidge. And now the rest of the school knew it, too.

So help any sorry bastard who tried.

TWELVE

It took me three days to come down from my psychosis. It took a few days after *that* until the infirmary staff was convinced I was well enough to be discharged.

I was so embarrassed. I couldn't remember what had happened from the time I'd transitioned into delirium until I came out of it a few days ago. I'd been informed on what I'd said and how I'd acted by the nurses, and I'd felt worse and worse with each word they told me.

I walked to class with my head down, keenly aware that everyone was talking about me. I could hear them whispering as I walked by.

The voices were strangely quiet, thank the ancestors. It was nice to get a little bit of peace every once in a while. It was as if they were satisfied they'd finally been heard.

Meanwhile, the rest of my body felt exhausted and worn. My thoughts progressed as if crawling through mud. As fast and high-paced everything had been before, now it was like the world was in slow motion.

I passed by a group of vampires in the corner, Deuce among them. I had to walk by in order to get to class. Deuce's eyes sparkled as he saw me coming.

"Would you like me to escort you to tea, *Lady Elizabeth?*" Deuce scorned in a corny British accent. His cronies howled, and my cheeks burned.

I went to bite back a response, but from out of nowhere, Ivy swooped in and looped his arm in mine. He threw his head back in pride as his scathing eyes landed on Deuce.

"Hey, Deuce, you should practice safe sex and go fuck yourself," Ivy told him. "Or is your name *Douche?* I can't really tell. It's not like you're important enough for me to remember."

Deuce blanched, temporarily speechless. Ivy escorted me away before anyone shot out a comeback. My hand on Ivy's arm tightened as we walked through the hallway together.

"Thanks," I whispered. At least someone would back me up around here.

"No one messes with my precious and gets away with it," Ivy said. He stroked my hair back, like I was his pet.

"Have you seen Oberi?" She had remained at my side until I'd woken up, and a few days afterward, but on my last day in the infirmary she'd left to be with Charlie. I wanted her so badly my heart ached.

"I'm sure your pretty little unicorn is around, along with your beautiful boyfriend," Ivy said, giving me a wink.

At the mention of Charlie, dread ran through my guts. I didn't even correct Ivy that Charlie wasn't really my boyfriend... whatever we were, we were definitely finished, after what had happened the other day.

I'd been purposefully avoiding Charlie ever since I got out of the infirmary. I already knew how this went. Once we met, he'd state the obvious and say we couldn't talk anymore, and I'd accept it, because how could I argue? I wanted to pretend that he could still be in my life— that he wasn't affected by the madness that infected me. So I'd draw it out as long as I could, even if it was only for a few hours more.

Even in my psychosis, I was drawn to him. I still felt safe around him. Despite being unable to recognize him, I recognized his soul, and he'd gotten me what I needed when I was at my lowest point.

I really missed Oberi, but if she was with Charlie, I wouldn't seek her out. I didn't know how I was going to face him again, so I was putting it off as long as I could.

Ivy didn't drop me off until I was in front of Professor Hemlock's classroom. I slid beside Opal at our shared desk and started taking out books silently.

"How are you feeling, Ava?" Opal asked kindly.

"I'm better now, thanks. They changed up my medication. Hopefully it doesn't happen again," I said.

Or, at least, hopefully it didn't happen again for a very long time. I wasn't sure if the new meds were working yet, but some of my symptoms appeared to be subsiding, so maybe this round would actually work this time.

"Did you talk things over with Charlie?" Opal asked.

"I actually haven't seen Charlie yet," I confessed. "I hope he's not mad at me."

"Of course he's not mad. He was very worried," Opal said.

I didn't respond to that. I started on busywork. Hemlock watched me carefully, until she turned to the blackboard to write notes.

Did she assume I wasn't stable enough to participate in the anthropology program this summer? I'd probably messed that up, too.

I kept my head down and got lost in academics until the hour was over. I ran out of class before Opal could stop me, but relief flooded into my veins when I saw Oberi in her unicorn form, standing outside the classroom and nickering to me.

I cast a few nervous glances, but Charlie wasn't around. She must've felt like I needed her. I ran my fingers through her flaming mane, and sparks tickled my skin. "Pretty girl," I cooed, and she let out a huff as I stroked her soft nose.

I laid a hand on her back as we walked to the prison yard. Once we were outside, I threw a leg over her back, and we took off. She surged into a gallop, and I held on tightly to her mane as her hooves pounded over the earth, my hair blowing back as the wind stung my eyes.

A couple of people looked our way, but I didn't care. We ran along the fence line, until we met a corner of the property underneath a guard tower. Oberi turned, and she bolted down the way again, until we came to an opposite corner and had to turn around.

Ancestors, this fence. I was so tired of being locked up. I just wanted Oberi to run across the length of the island, and then run over the ocean too, just keep running and running until we were alone and I didn't have to deal with life anymore.

Oberi's sides heaved, and she had froth forming on her coat. I patted her neck and walked her back to the prison, clinging to her neck the whole way.

"I'm sorry," I said as I swung off her back. "I know you need more room than this."

She only gave a gentle nicker in response. I wished she could talk to me, but she couldn't yet. She'd tell me what to do, how to handle everything. It's not like I had any idea.

As I passed the basketball court, a guy complained, "Women are such fucking prudes. They wouldn't dress like that if they didn't want it."

I wrinkled my nose as I recognized the loudmouth. His name was Digger. He'd put a worm down Opal's sweater last semester in Hemlock's class. He was a bully of the worst kind. For the most part, warlocks around the school were sweet, just like Marcus. He'd actually sent me a drawing of Oberi when I was in the infirmary, and it'd cheered me up. Even at the Institute, so many warlocks were kind.

But Digger wasn't kind. He loved picking on anyone who was within earshot. And there weren't any guards around, so it looked like he was taking his opportunity to try and incite some sort of fight.

His buddy didn't respond to his first dickhead comment, but Digger kept rambling on. "There's no such thing as rape— like, just be thankful someone found you attractive enough to want you. It's so ridiculous all these stories these girls make up to get men in trouble. Good thing Professor Mazur took *my* side."

My insides curled, and my skin felt itchy. I wanted to claw out of it. My stomach twisted with each word he spoke. I knew Digger was looking for trouble, so I forced myself to keep going. I wasn't going to say anything, but Digger had caught me glaring at him as I walked by.

He grinned wickedly. "Got something to add, Lady Elizabeth?"

Fucking *ancestors*. Could just *one* of these bastards leave me alone? It seriously wasn't that hilarious.

I rounded on him, and Oberi lowered her horn. She pawed her hoof into the earth as I said, "No one in their right mind would want to sleep with you willingly. You've got the personality of a rotting corpse."

"No one in their *right mind?* I guess that leaves you first in line," Digger said, and the friend at his side laughed. "I just have to wait for the right moment for you to lose it again, and you'll be all over me. I won't even have to put in the effort."

"I wouldn't go off with you even if I was brain dead," I seethed. "But if you tried, I'd stick your head right up your ass."

"Not the right call." Digger shook his head. "You should know better than to try me."

"And why's that?"

Digger's look was so demeaning, it made my whole body rot from the inside out. "You know *why* they call me Grave Digger?"

"Because you're dirty and disgusting?" I flatlined.

Digger grinned, and I noticed several missing teeth. "I killed both my parents and my sister, and had fun doing it, too. Threw 'em all in holes in the backyard. They would've never caught me if they hadn't found the graves— and I'd do the same thing to you too, in a heartbeat."

A shiver ran up my spine. This guy was fucking serious. He'd killed his whole family. He wouldn't bat an eye to hurt me.

I couldn't let him think I was an easy target. I ignited a fireball in my hand. "You think *you're* good at digging graves? I'll put you in one."

"Feisty," Digger replied. "You know, Wahkin must have a thing for crazy girls, because you're fucking psychotic."

I tossed a fireball at him so quickly, he barely had time to duck. It fizzled out behind him, but Digger rose to his full height with a huge smile. He tossed a battle orb at me, one black in color that had sparks like purple electricity whizzing around it. It looked deadly.

I avoided his spell, and the battle orb exploded into the building behind me, ripping out a chunk of the concrete. I flung out my arms. Water materialized out of the air and formed a long rope, and beside it, an identical one of fire grew. The two ropes twisted together until they were swirling as one. I shot the ropes at Digger, and he fell on his ass while trying to avoid them, scrambling backward as his mouth dropped open in fear.

"Ava, stop!"

Before I could burn this fucker to ashes, Kallie stepped in out of nowhere. She grabbed my arms and wrenched them backward, ending my spell before she hauled me away.

"What are you doing? Let me fry that bastard," I growled.

"You can't get in trouble again," Kallie insisted. "Trust me, I've got a temper, and it doesn't serve well around here. Walk away."

I let Kallie drag me off, because I'd already drawn enough attention to myself. Starting a fight would get me another one-on-one meeting with the Warden, and nothing was worth being alone in a room with that man.

Digger kept his eyes on me until Kallie hauled me out of sight. He got off the ground with a sullen look, and I knew I'd just made another enemy.

Let them come. I'd fight them all.

Oberi followed. She was so angry that fire came out of her nostrils. Kallie marched me back into the prison and down the hall. Her voice was cool as she said, "People know you're vulnerable right now. They'll do anything to rile you up, just to get some entertainment in here. You can't take the bait."

I was in half a mind to storm back there and burn the flesh off Digger's bones, on the verge of losing control. "I want him dead," I seethed.

"He's not someone to challenge," Kallie rebutted. "Digger deals drugs at the prison. What's worse, he gives the drugs to women— but he taints them with other things. Then he takes advantage when they're passed out."

I felt physically ill. "That's horrible."

"He's done it to dozens of girls here at the prison, but he never gets caught," Kallie said quietly. "You need to avoid getting his attention. I don't want Digger to slip something into your drink."

My stomach churned. "I need a distraction. Talk about something else," I rushed out. "Anything."

"Um..." Kallie bit her lip. "I went through Marcus' sketchbook this morning, because I thought I left my paper in there for my fae class, and he usually holds on to my stuff for me."

"Because you lose everything and are about as disorganized as I am?" I asked.

"Right. Anyway, in the sketchbook, there were a lot of... drawings of me."

That lifted my mood. "Naughty ones?" I giggled.

"Of course not!" Kallie's cheeks tinged pink. "Just like, of my face and stuff. I don't know if that's weird or not."

"It means he likes you, doesn't it?" I said.

"It doesn't matter," Kallie said mournfully. Under her breath, she added, "Not like it's going to make a difference."

The conversation she'd had between her and her uncle came back to me, and I began to smile. "Kallie, did you *bond* with Marcus?"

"No!" Kallie shouted, in a way that clearly meant *yes*.

I grinned in triumph. "Ooh, you're *mated*. That's a big deal in fae culture, Kallie."

"I can't have a *warlock* as my true mate. What would people say?"

"Does it matter? You care about him," I insisted. She'd made that clear during the Darke Games, though now I knew just how much.

"Well, he doesn't want me anyway, so there's that." She huffed. "It's fine. I'll just be forever alone."

"Don't be dramatic. Marcus is so shy. He's not going to make the first move. Just tell him how you feel," I said.

"It's not like that in fae culture. Telling someone you're mated is a big deal. You're supposed to make a public declaration, and vow to be together forever. It's like a marriage proposal. Marcus and I aren't that close."

"But you could be," I said. "The fae and the witches might hate each other, but that doesn't mean you and Marcus can't be together. Why not try?"

Kallie shrugged miserably. "I'm sure if he wanted to ask me out, he would've by now. It's just not meant to be."

"If that were true, you wouldn't have bonded with him. He's your soulmate. Don't give up, Kallie," I insisted.

She sighed. "At any rate, it's not like he notices. I've been giving him such obvious hints, and they fly right over his head."

"Then do something he can't ignore," I stated. "Then, once you have his attention, you can be honest with your feelings. I'm sure it'll all work out."

Kallie nodded thoughtfully. She passed by the chapel, in the obvious direction of the music room. I panicked, thinking she was taking me straight to Charlie, but I relaxed when I saw the only person inside the music room was my brother. Ezekiel sat in a chair and strummed an old acoustic guitar like the one he had back home. He looked up as he saw me enter, but didn't stop fiddling with the chords.

"I'm late," Kallie said. "But you *did* give me an idea, Ava. Thanks for the advice."

Kallie left, and I crossed my arms. "You all are passing me around like a hot potato," I grumbled. I didn't need a babysitter.

Or maybe I did, because without one, I kept getting into brawls.

"I just wanted to talk to you. The nurses wouldn't let me visit," Ezekiel protested.

I didn't clarify that was because I'd asked them not to allow visitors. "I didn't want you to see me like that."

"Not like I haven't before."

"It's still humiliating." I sat on the piano bench. It felt so empty without Charlie next to me.

"I'm your brother. I want to help."

"You can start by tuning that guitar. It's too pitchy."

Ez made a face and turned the pegs. "Kallie didn't escort you here without a reason."

"I nearly shoved Fire and Water down Digger's throat in the prison yard. She stopped me before I got into trouble. He was being a real bastard."

"I hate guys who pick on girls," Ezekiel grumbled.

"Yeah, we know. It's what got you landed in here. You're like the savior of women."

"Is that a bad thing?"

"No. It's one of the more charming things about you."

I began to fiddle with the piano. I played a song Charlie and I had written the other day, and it came out sounding like silk. Oberi bobbed her head, like she loved the tune.

Ezekiel strummed the guitar a few times. "You should talk to Charlie."

I groaned. "Ez."

"Come on, Ava. Don't let this wedge grow between you. He makes you happy— happier than I've seen you in a really long time."

"How do you know he makes me happy?"

"Because you started singing again," Ezekiel said softly.

I stayed silent, and Ezekiel said, "When I told Mom, she was so happy. She told me not to say anything to you, but she got all choked up and started crying, and—"

"Oh ancestors, Mama."

"All of us have been waiting for the day you'd start making songs again, and now you are, with Charlie."

A hard knot formed in my throat. "Pretty sure that's over now."

Ezekiel put his guitar down. "You think everyone is going to abandon you because of how your brain works, but all of your friends are here for you. We've all been here since you got out of the infirmary, trying to support you as best we can. That doesn't seem like we're running away."

A knot twisted inside of me. "Yet."

"No. Never. The people in here have been through a lot of shit, Ava. They've seen stuff, they know hard things, and they're not going to run away from it. Kallie, Marcus, Ivy, Opal... hell, even me, we've all got tough skin. People at the Institute like you, and they want to be your friend. And I damn well know Charlie wants to be more. All you have to do is let us in."

I let my fingers wander over the keys. I heard the door creak open, and Oberi changed into his husky form, giving a bark.

Ezekiel said, "Hey, Charlie. Ava's here."

My heart skipped nervously. Charlie was leaning against the doorway. Oberi ran to him. He jumped up and down, and Charlie patted his head, clearly waiting for me.

I got up slowly and walked to him. Charlie cocked his head, and we crossed into the empty chapel next door. Charlie sat down in the nearest pew, and I sat across from him as Oberi lay on our feet.

Oh, ancestors, here it was. The, *it's not you, it's me* talk. I wasn't ready for this in the slightest. My hands were sweaty, and I felt like I was going to hurl. No matter how many times I'd had this conversation with people, it didn't get any easier.

Charlie took my hands. "Pidge, you all right?"

I've been better. I cleared my throat. "I don't think I'm a debutante looking for a rich husband anymore, so I guess I'm good."

Charlie let out a low laugh. "Well, you played the part well."

"Spoiled rich girl really wasn't a hard reach. Sad my brain didn't pick something more interesting."

"It was interesting enough." Charlie squeezed my hands. "Were they able to help you?"

"I'm on a new medication. It's going to be a few weeks before we know if it works." I drew away. "Not like you're going to stick around for that long."

"Pidge, what are you talking about?" Charlie asked. Oberi gave a whine, and Charlie grabbed my hands again. "I want to be here."

My throat got tight. "Even after you saw me like... that?"

"I figured it was going to happen someday. I just wish I was better prepared for it."

"It's hard to prepare for that," I said quietly. I didn't know how to do it myself.

"Can you recall anything when you're in psychosis?"

"If I really force myself to think, I can somewhat remember minor details from when I'm delusional," I said. "I'll think in the third person, or I'll see colors really brightly, or all my senses will be enhanced by a thousand."

"And does this kind of thing happen... often?"

"It's pretty rare. I've only had a few extreme hallucinations like that in my life. And most of the time, when I have a psychotic episode, they're not really dangerous. It's only been twice I've almost hurt myself — this time and the time with the chandelier, and I've never been violent or hurt anyone else. They're always kind of scary for the people around me, because I'm not myself, but sometimes, they're a bit funny."

I gave a tiny giggle. "One time I thought I was a princess, and that my dad was my fairy godmother. I bugged him for hours to conjure me a pumpkin carriage with a pink pony. I wish I could remember it, because everyone said he was so annoyed. I bet it was hilarious to see."

I made a *pshing* sound. "My Uncle Jonah made a better fairy godmother, anyway. At least he had the dress to match."

Charlie smiled. "Well, if you're still interested in roleplay, I can be your Lord Henry."

I laughed a little. He wasn't being mean— more playful. "Only if you'll wear the coat tails and nothing else."

Charlie smirked. "Well, one thing that didn't change in the slightest was you still loved to back talk."

"I have a degree in sass," I said smartly. "My snark comes out in all forms."

"Is that why you tossed a fireball at Digger's head?"

Kallie must've filled Charlie in on what that creep was bragging about earlier. I fell quiet.

Charlie rolled his thumbs over the back of my hands. "You still thinking about what he said?"

"Not really. But he bothers me," I said, and I felt my body tense. "I don't want him anywhere near me."

"He won't come near you. He's not so stupid as to piss me off," Charlie said.

"He already threatened me, and implied something would happen. Kallie said he might slip something into my drink," I mumbled, and Charlie stiffened. "I was stupid for getting his attention. I bet he'll come after me now. He said he'd kill me."

"Never mind him." Charlie reached out to put his arm around me. "He'll get his soon enough. You still coming to my fight tonight?"

My heart dropped at the mention of it. That was tonight? I really didn't want to go.

But the look on Charlie's face was so hopeful, so I said, "Of course. I'll be there for sure."

He lit right up, and whatever I'd promised was worth it. I owed Charlie one. He'd been there for me, so now it was my turn to be there for him.

Even if I didn't agree with what he was doing.

We walked back to the music room together. I felt a thousand pounds lighter. Charlie hadn't given up on me. He still cared.

The feelings I had for him grew so strong inside my chest, I couldn't keep them inside. They were starting to well up and come out of my eyes, but I forced the tears back down, because I didn't want to let them show.

"I'm off to train before tonight's big fight," Charlie said. "Keep your hopes up, pidge."

Oberi bounced after him, giving a few barks. My heart felt a little lighter as I returned to the piano.

"Did you guys work it out?" Ez asked.

I gave a little sniff, and Ezekiel smiled. He struck up a song I hadn't heard in a while, and I opened my mouth to sing along.

Ezekiel and I played around with the instruments in the music room for hours. Eventually, he had a class, and I actually *wanted* to go to lunch. These new meds kind of made me hungry, which I guess was a good thing. I'd had my eye on the barbeque ribs— so not like me, but I was craving them— before Kallie zoomed up to me.

"I've heard you and Charlie are back on speaking terms," Kallie practically sang.

"I suppose." I smiled. "Though I found out roleplay might be something we're into."

Kallie scoffed. "You two are the definition of a brat and her dom."

"Oooh, really?" I gushed. I gave a giddy squirm. That was kinda hot.

"Yeah. But guess what! I told Charlie what that jerk Digger said to you," Kallie said. "He took care of it."

"How?" I blinked.

"Asshole got caught with a pound of nightshade in his cell," Kallie said, giving me a playful wink. "He's a plaything for the prisoners in Cellblock 9 now."

My jaw dropped open. "What?"

"Come on." Kallie grabbed my hand.

We ran down to the witch and warlock cellblock. A collection of students crowded the hallway, and a ton of guards swarmed around a cell. There was a brawl in the middle of the hallway, where the guards were trying to control one of the students. Kallie watched the scene with barely restrained glee.

"I didn't do it!" Digger screamed at the top of his lungs. He fought against the guards, but he was bound in noxite handcuffs and couldn't escape. "It's not mine!"

"Tell that to the Warden. You've wasted your last chance. It's Cellblock 9 for you!" one of the guards cried.

Digger screamed horribly as the guards hauled him down to Cellblock 9. I felt Charlie creep up behind me. His hair was messy, and he wore his workout clothes. His silence was all the confirmation I needed to know he'd done this.

"Where'd you even get a pound of nightshade?" I whispered. Now that the show was over, people in the hallway were starting to disperse.

Charlie shrugged. "Chancey needed to get rid of some evidence. I had the perfect way to dispose of it."

My eyes widened. "Chancey's no longer dealing drugs?"

"He said he's done with it. He's trying to get rid of all his stock."

That was surprising. Chancey would sell his own mother for a buck. What had convinced him to stop dealing here at the prison, where money from addicts free-flowed?

Charlie noticed my pondering and said simply, "Ivy."

"Oh," I said quietly. "Aren't Ivy and Chancey just... fuck buddies?"

"What Chancey says and how Chancey feels are two completely different things," Charlie told me.

My stomach flip-flopped inside of me nervously. "Was it your idea to get Digger thrown into Cellblock 9?"

"Someone had to take care of him," Charlie said with a careless shrug. "I was done hearing about all the tainted drugs he gave to girls, and no way in hell was I letting you be next. He made a major mistake threatening my pidge."

"But hiding the nightshade in his room was so risky. What if you had gotten caught?"

Charlie laughed. "I *rarely* get caught. There are easier ways to handle things than getting into a fight. Not to mention more effective. He won't bother you anymore."

"I can't believe you did that... for me." I turned toward Charlie, and he grasped my arms. I rested my hands on his forearms, and Oberi shoved his way between us, wagging his tail.

"I'd do anything for you, pidge. You don't even have to ask," Charlie said.

A strange sort of unease settled within me. I was honored that Charlie would go to such lengths to keep me safe. There was no one better I could trust with my safety.

At the same time, I was scared about what Charlie would do to protect me. Because clearly, to him, nothing was off limits.

I was a chosen one, which meant I was *supposed* to be a hero— I had a duty to put my relationships, my needs and my wants second, and the world first, because according to my prophecy, I had an obligation to save it.

But day by day, I doubted how far I'd go to save the world. Because if saving the supernatural community meant sacrificing someone I loved, I'd let Earth itself burn.

Like me, Charlie was no hero. He was a villain, and a villain would allow the world to crumble just to get one last kiss.

It made me wonder what else Charlie was capable of if it came down to saving me— if he'd get in the way of what I'd been chosen to do.

To be honest, I was frightened. I wanted to fulfill the prophecy, and save the world, but to Charlie... I *was* his world.

And today, he'd proven just how good he was at defending what was his.

⌢⌣

THAT NIGHT, I steadied myself to go to the fight club. I had on my favorite jacket, as well as the jeans my mother had given me for luck, because I really didn't want to see Charlie get hurt tonight. I hoped some of their magic worked.

Charlie got Marcus and Kallie passes too, because he didn't want me to go alone. I'd left Oberi in my cell. I felt really bad leaving him behind, but I knew that a fight club was no place for a Familiar... though I was sorely lonesome knowing he wasn't with Charlie or me.

It didn't feel right to have the three of us in separate places. That was asking for something bad to go wrong.

Marcus leaned against a gargoyle statue by what I assumed was a hidden door in the wall. Rishi wasn't with him— a fight club was no place for cats, either.

Charlie had given us details on how to get to the fight club, and I hoped we'd found the right place. Kallie hadn't shown up yet, so I sat on the statue beside Marcus.

"Thanks for the picture you drew of Oberi," I told him, and I squeezed him into a hug. "It was so nice."

"No problem," Marcus choked out. I was a tight hugger. "I can't believe Charlie's really doing this. It's such a big risk."

"I know." I sighed. "But it makes him happy, so I can't stop him."

Marcus eyed me. "Are you two being honest with each other yet?"

"What do you mean?" I parted my hair to the side.

"You don't want to call him your boyfriend, but it's obvious you two are together. Don't you think you're fucking with his feelings?"

"I'm not." I felt my stomach drop.

"He was really messed up when you were in the infirmary," Marcus said quietly. "It was rough seeing him like that. And with this back and forth between you two, it kind of seems like you're leading him on."

"I would never." To consider that hurt my soul.

"But you are, whether you want to admit it or not," Marcus said. "Don't you think if you really wanted to be with Charlie, you two would've agreed on something by now?"

My heart ached. "I'm a chosen one. My life's more complicated than that. The closer Charlie gets to me, the more danger he's in."

"But we're all in this now," Marcus pointed out. "We're all helping you figure out what being a demigod means. Doesn't that put us all at risk?"

"You don't get it. If Charlie is too close, he'll take unnecessary risks. You saw what he did to Digger today. What would he do if I made him something more? He'd put his life on the line day after day just to protect me."

"He's not gonna stop, Ava. That's what you need to understand. He's already too far in."

I let out a harsh breath. "Don't you think you're being a little hypocritical?"

Marcus lost a bit of color. "What do you mean?"

I smacked my head. "Kallie!"

"What about Kallie?"

I was tired of him playing dumb. "Marcus, she likes you! What is the fucking problem?"

"The *problem*?" he snapped. "The *problem* is that I *killed my last girlfriend*, Ava."

"Not on purpose!"

"Yeah, and it could happen again," Marcus insisted. "Kallie could get too close, I could lose control, and she could end up just like Anya. I'm better off alone."

I scoffed. Marcus was being a giant hypocrite. "So you're saying that you won't date Kallie because you're scared of your powers, but that it's okay for me to date Charlie, even if what I'm involved in could get him hurt?"

"You have no proof the prophecy will get Charlie killed. My magic already murdered someone," Marcus said.

"By accident," I whispered.

"So?" Marcus' tone was harsh. "Doesn't matter if it was an accident or not. Anya's still dead. And I'm not going to let the same thing happen to Kallie. Just drop it, Ava."

Marcus crossed his arms, a sullen expression written across his face. As fate would have it, Kallie came walking down the hallway.

"Hey. What's wrong with you two?" Kallie asked, looking between us.

"Nothing. Let's just go," Marcus grumbled. He jumped off the statue and pushed the hidden door in the wall open. The piece of the wall swiveled in place, and the three of us walked down the stairs and into bleak darkness.

The more stairs we descended, the louder the noise became. It was pounding, screams and shouts that shook the very walls of the basement. It was a crowd, hungry for blood.

A doorman waited at the end of the stairs. He was big, had a scar across his face, and was mean-looking. His lip rose to bare his teeth as he grunted, "Passes?"

We showed him the tickets Charlie had given us earlier, and he let us in. We stepped into the wide space, the roar of the audience swelling over us. The basement was packed with hundreds of people— mostly guards, but some students. There was a giant boxing ring in the middle of the room, surrounded by metal stands. The ropes on the ring looked worn, and blood stained the floor.

A balcony ran around the edge of the room, which guards leaned against to watch the fight from above. Little Fortune Fairies, which resembled small balls of glowing light, hovered above the area, blinking all kinds of different colors. I smelled popcorn coming from somewhere, and heard the sound of bets being called as money was passed around. It was dark in here, dank, and smelled of sweat.

My heart went straight to my gut as the three of us took empty seats as close to the ring as possible. I wanted to be near Charlie, in case something went wrong and I had to help, even if it was against the rules.

But fuck the rules. If it looked bad, I'd jump in and defend him. The fight club could suck a dick.

A fight had just ended. A merman was getting dragged off by a couple of officials while a shifter stood tall in the middle of the arena, his arms raised to the crowd. The merman's face was little more than a bloody pulp.

"First time?" a girl asked me. She wore a sports bra and boxing shorts, and she leaned against the ropes of the ring. It looked like she was up next. She had dark skin and a long black braid that went all the way down her back, along with deep red eyes. She was gorgeous, but seemed dangerous.

I knew by her sultry tone she had to be a succubus, but she seemed nicer than Naya. "Yeah," I said. "I'm here to watch my boyfriend fight."

The word slipped out before I could stop it, and both Kallie and Marcus looked at me. But the succubus smiled and said, "Ah, you're Charlie's girl, aren't you? He doesn't shut up about you. When he's not getting his face beat in, anyway. But we all take a few punches around here."

She reached out to shake my hand. "Name's Scarlet. Hope you placed a bet on me, because I'm going to win."

Scarlet grabbed the ropes and swung herself into the boxing ring. Kallie's eyes glittered as she bit her lip and looked Scarlet up and down. "She's kind of hot," Kallie whispered to me.

"*Her?*" Marcus spat. "Succubi aren't hot. If you don't want to get your face eaten off, I mean."

"She's clearly the hottest person in this room," Kallie shot back.

Marcus sat back and grumbled something incoherent. He was totally jealous, but Kallie didn't seem to notice. She was too busy checking out the succubus.

Well, good. Maybe if Marcus felt envious, he'd do something about his feelings for Kallie.

Scarlet stood across from a witch, who was bouncing up and down with her hands up. The official came between them and announced, "Introducing the Scarlet Letter, challenging our top female champion, the Tarot Mistress. You all know the rules. No magic— anything else goes. May the best fighter win!"

The bell rang, and both girls sprang at each other. The witch cracked Scarlet's head to the side with a few punches, but the succubus quickly responded by nailing her foot into the witch's face. The witch ducked and put her fists up to block Scarlet's hits, but Scarlet delivered a few fast kicks to her sides, which left the witch unguarded.

The fight was over in a matter of seconds. Scarlet knocked the witch out with a harsh swing to the jaw, and victory was declared. The witch was carried off stage by her coach, and the referee raised Scarlet's hand in victory.

"This looks like fun." Kallie's eyes glittered. "Maybe *I* should join the fight club."

"No fucking way!" Marcus shouted. I cringed between them.

"You don't think I can take it?" Kallie's expression burned.

"It's not about that," Marcus flustered. "I don't want you to get hurt."

Kallie rolled her eyes. As Scarlet walked off, two other fighters joined the arena, and a new brawl began. As I watched the latest fight,

Kallie and Marcus walked off to get popcorn. The taste in my mouth soured as a certain angel came slinking up to my side.

"Glad you could make it," Chancey said, shuffling dollars in his hands. "Want to place a bet? Charlie's the favorite, slated to win at six-to-one."

I still hadn't forgiven him for getting Charlie mixed up in all this. "Be glad I'm here at all," I stated. "This isn't okay with me."

"Relax. The man can handle himself." Chancey pocketed the money he had. "He's so good they put him in the main line-up, for crying out loud. He's not in any danger of getting hurt."

"Then bring Ivy down here if it's so safe."

Chancey went rigid. "No," he said sharply. "He don't need to know about all this."

I huffed, before I added quietly, "I'm glad you stopped dealing drugs. There are better ways to make money."

Chancey's mouth became a thin line. "Nightshade isn't something to play with. Overdose one too many times, and it'll get ya."

I didn't say anything. Chancey pinched his nose, prompted to speak up.

"Ives can't be around drugs," Chancey whispered. "He's pushed his limit one too many times. He gets back on nightshade, it'll kill him."

"And why do you care?" I asked, prodding for more.

Chancey strode off, clearly ending the conversation. "If you see Ives, tell him I said hi, okay?"

Sure, and I'll tell him how badly you've been pining away, I thought. Apparently, nobody at this prison acknowledged their feelings. I wasn't the only one.

Kallie and Marcus came back at that point, and the current fight ended, leading up to the brawl before the night's main event. Two angels swung themselves into the ring. They danced around each other before they faced off, taking swings and kicks.

I watched the fight with a fresh bout of nervousness. I just wished they'd hurry up. Charlie was up next. The two angels were really well matched. Neither of them could land a good hit, and I wasn't sure which would fall the other.

Then, one of the angels swung out his fist, and it sent the other guy reeling. He swung back his fists, pummeling his challenger over and over.

The crowd moaned as the angel delivered a particularly brutal hit. I swear I heard the guy's skull crack as the angel's fist collided with his face. Instantly, he dropped to the floor. My throat seized up as I realized that he wasn't moving.

Or breathing.

An official ran forward. He knelt down and placed his fingers against the guy's neck, feeling for a pulse. He looked up at the referee and shook his head.

"Take him out back," the referee said. A couple of guards dragged the limp corpse out of the arena, while the other angel's fist raised to a roaring crowd.

I felt ice run through my veins as my blood went cold and all color drained from my face. That guy had *died* right in front of us. The fight club had *killed* him.

This was barbaric. It wasn't a sport. There weren't any rules—anything was on the table, including murder, and these guards didn't care, so long as they got their entertainment. And we, the students, were disposable.

My whole body began to shake. All I could think of was finding Charlie and dragging him out of here. In moments, Chancey was back, his hands out in front of him like he wanted to calm me down.

"What the hell was that?" I demanded, throwing my hand at the ring. "The guards let people *die* here?"

Chancey grimaced. "It doesn't happen often—"

"*Often?!*" I shrieked.

"Just hold tight, Ava. Charlie's quick. He'll end the fight before you know it."

Chancey trying to talk me off the ledge wasn't doing any good. But before I could act, I saw Charlie walking toward the arena, flanked by someone who I thought had to be his trainer. His shirt was off, and he wore nothing but a thin pair of boxer shorts that clung to his form.

I would've been drooling if I wasn't so worried about him getting his head knocked off.

Charlie sensed my presence through our bond. He immediately beamed, and I felt him brush up against the edge of my consciousness, telling me he was happy I was here to watch.

His joy was obvious. I couldn't mistake it for anything else. This sick, twisted shit made him happy, as fucked up as it was. And who was I to get in the way of that? I had to trust that he wouldn't get hurt.

As Charlie jumped into the ring, he had a wild look on his face. I couldn't call it determined... it was more like... crazy.

And trust me, I knew crazy.

Charlie's opponent entered the ring, and my mouth went dry. He was at least a foot taller than Charlie, and fifty pounds heavier. He was corded with muscle, with arms that looked bigger than tree trunks. Kallie tilted her head when she saw him.

"I know that guy. His name's Tony. He's in my Fae class," Kallie told me.

Charlie was up against a freaking *shifter*? They were strong as hell! This was hardly a fair fight.

The official's voice came over the microphone as he shouted, "Newcomer, the Dangerous Dragon, is going up against our current reigning champion, the Blind Bandit!"

"Wow, that's not ableist," I mumbled with a growl, but Marcus nudged me.

"This is a fight for the ages. The Blind Bandit has never been beaten, folks!" the announcer cried. "Has he met his match tonight? The only thing left to do, is *fight*!"

As the bell rang out, signaling the fight was starting, I grabbed Marcus' hand. He squeezed it back, and I tried to loosen the tightness in my chest as I watched Charlie approach his opponent. The two danced around each other, until the shifter lunged out a massive punch. I gasped, but Charlie avoided it and smashed his fists into the face of the shifter in retaliation. The shifter went stumbling backward, until he ran forward, arms extended to put Charlie into a hold. Charlie avoided that, too, and landed a kick to the shifter's back. He went staggering forward. He barely had time to bring his hands up to block his face before Charlie brought his fist down again. The shifter socked Charlie in the gut a few times, but Charlie didn't even appear to feel it as he landed a couple of harsh kicks to the shifter's torso.

Charlie was *really* good. I was impressed with how well he could fight. He was fast, and nimbler than the other fighter. He dodged anything the shifter threw at him and retaliated just as quickly. The crowd cheered every time Charlie landed a punch, or groaned whenever he missed. Clearly, he was the top favorite.

I felt Charlie's ecstasy surge through our bond as he fought. He was right. He really didn't feel alive unless his life was on the line. This was exciting to him. It gave him a rush I already worried he was addicted to. Every time he landed a punch, he got a thrill. Every time the shifter punched him back, it just made him want to fight harder. I became more and more anxious as the fight dragged on, wondering when it was going to end.

The shifter knocked out Charlie's legs from under him, and he went down. The shifter lunged out, locking him into a tight hold Charlie couldn't escape. I watched Charlie's skin tinge blue as he struggled to breathe through the shifter's grasp.

He couldn't overpower a shifter. They were way too strong. I almost jumped out of my seat, but Marcus held me down. "He's gotta do it on his own," he whispered.

The referee stood nearby, almost ready to call the fight. But then... something weird happened. Charlie broke out of the shifter's hold. He threw the shifter's arms apart and scrambled out of his hold with so much power that it sent the shifter sprawling backward. The shifter was forced to set him free, as if he couldn't contain Charlie's strength. Charlie hopped back onto his feet, and the shifter was left on the ground, wondering what happened.

Charlie wasn't stronger than that shifter. It wasn't physically possible. Shifters were as strong as vampires. They could lift things like cars without breaking a sweat. Elementai didn't have that kind of strength. Charlie *couldn't* have overpowered that shifter.

But he *did*. And it was that moment I knew something wasn't right.

The shifter looked pissed that Charlie had gotten out of his hold. With rage, he surged forward, giving a giant yell. He sank his fist into

Charlie's face several times, and I gave a whimper as I watched the skin break above his left eye and under his cheek, sending blood splattering. Charlie got the shifter away from him by kneeing him in the gut, but blood poured down his face and over his eyes.

Charlie's face was starting to swell. He wiped his lip of the blood that was seeping from his mouth and put his hands up again, clearly not done.

Amazement still shone in the shifter's eyes, but he snarled as he attacked again. This time, Charlie was waiting for him. The shifter took a careless swing, and Charlie kicked him right in the head.

The shifter went down. His body collapsed to the floor in a clear knockout, and the crowd went nuts. Guards jumped up from their seat as they cheered, and the very floor shook with their cries of victory. The referee raised Charlie's fist into the air as the shifter struggled to come around. The smile on Charlie's face was so broad, I was sure it hurt. A light emitted from him through our bond that was warm and full of pride.

How could I take this away from him? Even if he was risking his life? I'd never felt this kind of emotion from him before. He was always so quiet, constantly suppressing his feelings. Fighting made him feel like he *mattered.*

We all had our chosen addictions here at the Institute. For Ivy, it was nightshade. For Charlie, it was the fight club. It might be bad for him, but he didn't care.

This was his chosen high.

Charlie hopped out of the ring. I ran to him immediately and sacked against his side. Charlie let out an *oof* as I wrapped my arms around his middle.

"Did you like it?" Charlie asked. His voice still shook with the thrill.

I swallowed down my anxiety and lied. "It was amazing! You were so great. I didn't know you could fight like that."

I yanked a handkerchief out of my pocket, because I knew I'd need it tonight. I started wiping the blood off Charlie's face, but it was hard, because there was so much of it. It stained my fingertips red.

"Let's get you fixed up," I said. "It looks pretty bad."

"This is nothing. I can't *wait* to get back in the ring next week."

My lips wobbled. "I really hate you."

Charlie laughed and squeezed me against his side. "I hate you too, pidge."

Marcus and Kallie joined us. Kallie punched Charlie's shoulder lightly. "That was some incredible fighting. You've really got your own style."

"Learned it on the streets," Charlie said proudly, and again, my heart fell.

"You're crazy, man," Marcus said, clapping him on the back. "Guess that's why we keep you around."

There was a medical area set up a few feet from the ring. Charlie sat on a stool while a guard worked on bandaging his wounds. The shifter he'd fought, Tony, sat on the other side of the tent, getting his own wounds mended. His gaze was resentful as he eyed Charlie up and down.

I turned my back and focused on helping Charlie. The guard was doing a shitty job of bandaging his head, so I took the gauze from him and did it myself. As I wrapped the area above Charlie's eye, I heard a small voice not too far away whimper, "I don't want to do it."

It was Ghost. I didn't know he was in the fight club— he was kind of small to be a fighter. He trembled as he held his arm, which was in a sling. It looked broken. He must've been in one of the earlier fights, before I got here.

A guard sneered as he towered over Ghost. "We had a deal. I didn't turn you into the Warden when you tried to break out last semester. You still have two more fights left before you've settled your debt."

"But I don't want to do this anymore!" Ghost protested. He was on the edge of tears. "I've lost every fight you've put me in!"

"Too bad," the guard sneered. "So long as the crowd likes watching you get kicked around, I'll keep putting you in."

Ghost broke into sobs. I couldn't handle this. I wouldn't let Ghost get bullied by some asshole guard.

"Pidge," Charlie said, but I didn't listen to him. I crossed the tent and stood in front of Ghost, shoving my way in front of the guard.

"Where does it hurt?" I asked him.

He showed me his arm with a sniff. I felt it gingerly, and he let out a yelp. It was definitely broken.

As I handled Ghost's broken arm, I felt a tingling sensation spread through me. My entire body began to grow warm, and pinpricks edged along my palm. It was a strange sensation... like magic was about to come out.

What was going on with me?

Ghost's eyes widened. He opened his mouth to say something, before a guard put their hand on my shoulder and wrenched me around. "Hey, girlie, you don't make the rules around here," he growled. "Don't forget, we're still in charge."

"If he doesn't want to fight, he shouldn't be forced to!" I insisted.

"Pidge, that's not how things work," Charlie said calmly. His tone told me to back down.

Tony stood. He was looking to get a rise out of Charlie, and I knew it as he said, "Wahkin needs to keep his bitch in line."

Charlie immediately jumped to his feet. My eyes narrowed as I faced Tony, and I said, "Don't you have another fight to lose somewhere el—?"

Tony's fist cracked against my cheek, and I went flying backward. Kallie caught me before I fell, but that was the only thing I noticed. My vision was thick with stars, and my head pounded, on the verge of losing consciousness.

There was shouting, and the sound of a scuffle. Kallie gently laid me on the ground, and I propped my body against Marcus, who knelt beside me. There was a lot of shouting, and it hurt my already aching head.

"Charlie, Charlie, stop, you're gonna kill him!" I heard Chancey plead. He and a couple of other guys were wrenching at Charlie, trying to drag him off Tony. Tony wheezed for breath. Charlie had put him in a headlock with one arm and was smashing his face in with the other. No matter how many guards tried to rip Charlie off of Tony, he couldn't be pried away.

I managed to stumble to my feet. Drunkenly, I put my hands on Charlie's arm. "Charlie, stop it," I slurred, pushing at him.

I had the strength of a mouse at the moment, but at my touch,

Charlie let go. He flattened on the ground, and the guards backed off. A couple of medics rushed forward to treat Tony.

"Pidge, are you all right?" Charlie asked, taking me into his arms.

I couldn't answer— my head was still spinning. Charlie tenderly felt my cheek, and I gasped. A bruise was already starting to form.

"Charlie, you need to get her out of here," Chancey said roughly, casting nervous glances at the guards. I didn't know if Charlie would suffer consequences for what had just happened. Charlie grabbed my shoulders and guided me away. Kallie and Marcus hurriedly followed.

"Over here," Marcus said. We trailed him to the empty staircase where we'd come in. Blood dripped on the floor from Charlie's hand. He'd busted open his knuckles pounding Tony's face in.

"Pidge, you can't speak up here," Charlie said in a strained voice. His thumb brushed my bruised cheek, and I almost cringed away.

"I was just trying to help Ghost," I pleaded. I only wanted to help people and do the right thing, but as I'd known all my life, me doing the right thing typically resulted in the *wrong* thing happening.

"I know, but there are rules," Charlie said. "He's only got two more fights. He'll make it."

"He shouldn't have to fight against his will—"

"It was a mistake bringing you down here." Charlie's voice was thick with disappointment. "I knew it was a bad idea. You got hurt by some jackass who was trying to get back at me for losing his fight. This is a rough crowd. Too rough for you."

"I can handle it!"

"No, you can't." Charlie let out a heavy sigh. "Just... go, pidge. You can't come here again."

My spirit physically dropped, and I felt like melting into the floor. Charlie turned his back and mumbled, "Take care of her, guys," before he slipped back into the fight club.

Marcus grabbed my arm and led me upward. I felt tears forming at the corner of my eyes.

"Let's get you to the infirmary. That was a bad hit," Kallie said. "You might have a concussion."

"I don't care." I wiped at my eyes. I can't believe Charlie had kicked me out.

"He just cares about you. He doesn't want to see you get punched again," Marcus said gently, but it didn't help.

I knew my friends probably thought I'd been poking my nose in where it didn't belong, again. But if I didn't say something, who would? I'd only been trying to stand up for someone who was in trouble.

So why did it feel like I'd let Charlie down?

Nobody touched my pidge. *Nobody.*

I'd have killed Tony if given the chance. He'd hurt my pidge, and as far as I was concerned, that warranted the death sentence. I was dead set on taking his life the moment I'd realized he'd hit her. At the same time, I was glad Ava pulled me off of him. I'd have ended up in Cellblock 9 if I'd taken things any further.

I should have known Ava's issues with fight club went far beyond my own involvement. She wasn't just scared of me getting hurt. She didn't want *anyone* getting hurt. That's how Ava was. She never wanted someone to suffer the way she had. She wanted to wipe suffering from the face of the planet.

But she couldn't. Even as the chosen one, such an effort was futile. She could live a thousand lifetimes with the same goal in mind, and it'd do nothing to save our souls.

There was no saving me, either. I was already in too deep, and Ava knew it.

She didn't mention fight club over the next few weeks, and neither did I. It wasn't a secret anymore, but we both avoided the topic as if it didn't exist. I would run off to train without telling her where I was going. Though she obviously knew, she didn't object.

It made me feel as if we were both living a lie. But Ava wouldn't talk about it unless she wanted to, so I didn't bring it up.

"Ivy's hired me to design him a dress," Ava announced on our way to class one day. I had my arm draped over her shoulder, and Oberi walked alongside us, her hooves clicking lightly against the floor. Ava bounced on her toes with every step, obviously in one of her better moods. "I should be done with the design by the end of the week and can start sewing it in the Arts and Crafts room this weekend."

"That's nice, pidge," I said. "I'm glad you're doing something you love."

Ava had been spending an awful lot of time designing clothes— so much that we'd barely spent time in the music room lately. I got the sense that she was avoiding me, but I wasn't interested in having that conversation right now.

"It's going to be gorgeous," she raved. "I'm thinking a red satin evening dress with a long slit up the side to show off Ivy's legs."

"I'm sure he'll love it," I said.

She scoffed. "Of course he will. My designs have never let anyone down."

Ava slowed outside our Supernatural Religions classroom and led me inside. We claimed seats at the back of the room, and Oberi shifted into husky form to curl up on the floor between us. Chatter buzzed around us as more students came into the classroom. As usual, people threw things like pencils across the room. A paper plane soared through the air and almost hit me in the face, but I sensed it with my magic and sent it flying off in the other direction.

"Settle down, please," Professor Jobe called to the class in a bored tone. He was an older warlock and a decent guy, but I had to imagine he was only here because he couldn't get a teaching job anywhere else. His lectures put most students to sleep. "Today, we'll be talking about the various ways the gods came into being."

Almost nobody heard him. Paper wads clattered to the ground as students tossed them at each other across the room, and a group of people laughed in the corner.

"Pay attention," Professor Jobe called. "This will be on the test."

The room finally settled, and Professor Jobe sounded slightly proud of himself.

"As I said, we'll be discussing the gods today," he began once he had everyone's attention. "We've previously discussed the gods that belong to each major supernatural religion, but with so many gods alive today, the question arises; what makes a god *a god?*"

He paused, like he was waiting for an answer, but no one responded.

Professor Jobe continued in a monotone voice. "Ultimately, a god is measured by their power and omnipotence. Their power is immeasurable, far greater than any supernatural alive, or any classification of demigod. But there are several ways they can get this power."

Ava faked a light snore from beside me, and I nudged her playfully. She snickered under her breath.

"The very first gods have existed since the beginning of time," he continued. "The Great Spirit in Hawkei culture, or the Seven Gods from Arcanean culture, are great examples of this. The second way to become a god is to be *made* into one. To ascend to godhood, an existing god must give a piece of him or herself away, gifting a piece of their godhood power to the individual."

"Guess your dreams of becoming a god are crushed," a girl loudly joked to one of her friends.

"You're no goddess yourself," he cracked back.

"Students," Professor Jobe tried scolding them, but it was a comical attempt at best.

Ava leaned over to me and whispered, "Could this class get any more boring?"

"Probably not," I whispered back.

"Ascension does not happen often, as the gods don't readily share their power," Professor Jobe continued. "However, there are several documented cases of mortals becoming gods, such as with the goddess of the Miriamic Coven, and one of the two Elven goddesses."

Ava grabbed my arm in shock, and I felt her whole body still. "The Elves!" she hissed at me under her breath. She shot her hand into the air.

Fuck.

"Yes, Miss Mitoh," Professor Jobe called on her.

"There are two Elven goddesses?" she asked in a bright tone.

I held my breath, hoping Professor Jobe knew nothing more about the Elves, but he launched into an explanation.

"Yes. The story is quite fascinating." He sounded more interested than I'd heard him all semester. "One thing you should know about the gods is that their power prevents them from having children of their own. That is to say that a god and a goddess cannot mate and birth new gods. However, the Elven goddess, Idril, fell in love with a female human from Edinmyre— Caralyn."

"A human from Edinmyre?" someone balked. "I thought only fae and Elves came from Edinmyre."

"This was millennia ago, at a time when there were humans in Edinmyre," Professor Jobe replied. "Caralyn eventually ascended, becoming an Elven goddess herself. Before she ascended, however, the two goddesses mated and birthed a child— creating an entirely new race known as the Elves."

Ava's hand tightened on my arm, and she leaned over to hiss under her breath, "The Elves were half-god, half-human!"

Professor Jobe didn't hear her. "As you can imagine, with the blood of the gods running through their veins, the first generation of Elves were considered demigods. That is to say they possessed great power, more than even the most talented supernaturals. The Elves were similar to fae, because like the fae, they drew their power from Edinmyre. But the Elves were different in that they drew magic from both Edinmyre *and* their goddesses. For many years, the Elves and the fae lived alongside each other."

His voice changed, almost sounding sad. "Unfortunately, there came a time when the fae became fearful of the Elves, for they were far more powerful. The fae struck first to protect themselves. With the help of the fae god Droga, they trapped Idril and Caralyn in hell, in order to weaken the Elves' power. Soon, the Elves were no stronger than the fae, and the fae killed off the most powerful Elves still left alive. Outnumbered, the Elves stood no chance. Those that remained were forced to mate with other races, like humans, for survival. Their power was diluted— up until the Elven genocide that occurred during the Great Supernatural War, when the last of the Elves died."

Ava's hand shot into the air so fast that her fingers brushed my cheek. She didn't wait to be called on. "Do you know anything else about the Elven goddesses? Or the Elves at all?"

"Most of their stories have been lost to history," Professor Jobe said. "I'm afraid there are very few stories left. This one remains because it is a part of the fae's story as well."

He continued his lecture on other gods and goddesses, but I could feel Ava's energy sizzling through our bond. As soon as class let out, she dragged me aside in the hallway.

"I have an idea," she whispered under her breath.

My guts twisted, and I threw up a mental wall to hide my response. I already knew it must have something to do with Professor Jobe's lecture and the Elves. "What is it?"

"Well, everyone says the stories of the Elves died with them, but they're wrong," she insisted. "It's like Professor Jobe said. Their story is part of ours— of all supernatural races. The Elves didn't live in a bubble. They traded and interacted with everyone else. The genocide wasn't just *their* story. It was everyone's— including the people who killed them off. We have to look through the history of *other* races and their interaction with the Elves to learn more about them."

My mouth went dry. "I know you want to find Forevermore—"

"*Someone* must have been at the gate at some point, right?" Ava insisted. "What if the other races knew how to get through the door? What if someone besides the Elves knew where to find the keys?"

I sighed. The last thing I wanted was for her to go to Forevermore and get one step closer to fulfilling the prophecy. "I don't know, pidge. I thought Forevermore was an Elven secret."

"Someone knows something." Ava was hardly listening to me anymore. "I just have to find out who."

She clicked her tongue, and I relaxed a bit. Ava thought she was on to something, but it was the same dead end we'd hit before. No one knew a damn thing about the Elves, and that was my only solace.

"I hope you find answers," I lied. "But in the meantime, we have a counseling session with Takahashi. We don't want to be late."

"Ugh," Ava groaned. "Do we have to do this *now*?"

"Takahashi will write you up if you skip," I pointed out. Truth was, I didn't care for the counseling sessions either, but I knew how obsessive Ava could get when she put her mind to something. I needed to distract her now, before she could dig too deep into the Elves and the story Professor Jobe had told us in Supernatural Religions.

"Fuck," Ava growled under her breath. "Fine, let's go."

Ava took my hand and guided me through the halls of the Institute with Oberi at our side. When we arrived at Takahashi's office, Kallie and Marcus were already there.

"You're delusional if you think you can beat me in an arm wrestle," Kallie laughed.

Marcus scoffed. "My biceps are the size of your calves."

I'd felt Marcus' biceps, and he was a liar with a capital L.

"And I'm a shifter," Kallie pointed out. "I bet I've got more strength in my pinky finger than you have in your whole body. Let's go right here, right now. We'll prove who's right."

Marcus squeaked. "Oh, here's Ava and Charlie."

Smooth.

Kallie huffed. "Another time then."

"Welcome, students," Takahashi greeted kindly as we took our usual seats. Oberi sat between Ava and me. "How are you, Charlie?"

The tone of his voice indicated he'd noticed the bruises on my face. I barely felt them anymore since my last fight, but Ava had told me this morning they were still visible. "Fine," I answered vaguely.

Takahashi cleared his throat, sounding displeased by the answer, but he didn't push it. "And Ava? How have you been since... our last meeting."

Ava sighed. "You can say it, Professor. Everyone else has already made a point about it. It's called a *psychotic episode.*"

Something came through the bond when she emphasized the phrase. It was hard to make out, but it was clear she was bothered.

"Very well," Takahashi said. "Let's talk about your psychotic episode. This is a safe space, remember."

"There's nothing to talk about," she insisted. Her foot tapped against the floor impatiently. "It's something that happens with bipolar— not to everyone with the diagnosis, but to me. I'm on meds that are helping."

Takahashi spoke softly. "I don't bring this up to upset you, Ava."

"I'm not upset," she practically snapped. It was pretty obvious she was lying. "It's just that my condition isn't something you can *talk out*. I'm not going to be magically cured through therapy."

Takahashi remained calm. "It's not my intention to *cure* you. I only suggest that discussing your experiences may help you understand them better, and allow you to manage your condition with ease."

"Any other suggestions?" Ava scoffed. She was obviously challenging him and didn't think he could help.

"I understand your resistance," Takahashi reassured her. "I myself have not experienced bipolar and simply cannot fully grasp what it's like for you. However, I have seen many students with conditions like yours come through the Institute. The ones who make it out of here better than when they came in are those who *embrace* their diagnosis."

"I am *not* my diagnosis," Ava snapped. "I'm so much more."

"Exactly!" Takahashi said proudly. "You are already on the right track. You are *not* your bipolar, but that does not make your bipolar *wrong*. Once you realize that and truly embody it, you can turn it into one of your strengths."

Ava laughed nervously. "I've been fighting my whole life to be normal. Hell, I take *medication* to stay sane. No way is that a strength."

"Perhaps that's the problem," Takahashi suggested. "You've been fighting your illness— resisting it. Instead of trying to fight your voices, thoughts, and moods, perhaps you can find a way to work with them rather than against them. Instead of trying to change who you are, you can accept it. You can learn what works during your cycles instead of trying to force yourself into the mold of what other people think you should be and how your mind should work. Your brain isn't wrong, Ava. It's just different, and you must find what works for you."

I expected Ava to respond, but she fell silent. The emotions I'd felt rising through our bond seemed to soften, like she was truly considering Takahashi's words.

After a few moments of silence, Takahashi changed the subject. "Let's talk about high school. Marcus, would you like to go first?"

He always started with Marcus after we touched on something heavy, because he was the most willing to talk.

Marcus scoffed. "What's there to talk about? I was a pothead with a bunch of fake-ass friends. Art was the only thing that made it better."

"I believe the term your mother used in your entry letter was *misunderstood*," Takahashi said kindly.

"I was such a poser. I had to fake who I was just to get by. It was all BS," Marcus said. "I was in theater, and that made me happy, but even when I was onstage I never found people who could just accept me for me."

"Why do you think you felt the need to fake who you were?" Takahashi asked.

"No reason, really," Marcus said. "I mean, my parents were great, my teachers were nice, and I was provided for, but I could never figure out who I was or where I fit in. Acting was easy, because I could just slip into someone else's life and not have to be myself, for once."

"Is that why you made a fake identity for yourself once you came here?" Kallie asked softly. She must've resonated with something Marcus said, because for once, she wasn't yelling at him.

"Kind of," he admitted. "I mean, I tried to be tougher than I was for safety reasons, because we're in prison and all that. But because of theatre, it was so much easier to pretend to be someone else rather than be my awkward-ass self. I realized back then that I'd never be able to find people I could just be weird with— because I'm a weird fucking person. I've tried not to be, and I can't, so I might as well go at it alone."

"You can be weird with us," Kallie suggested.

Marcus made a skeptical noise. "Yeah, sure. You're perfect."

Kallie blew out a soft sigh. "I'm far from perfect."

Marcus' voice had turned quiet. "My mom was the one who arrested me, you know? She was the first detective who showed up on the scene after Anya died. It was so messed up. She came in blazing, thinking she's gonna arrest some mass murderer, and it ends up being her kid."

Marcus sighed. "I guess I am a mass murderer. And she had to face that. I'm sure she always thought I was going to kill someone someday, but I bet she figured it'd be myself."

"Marcus!" Kallie gasped, and I cringed.

"Why not?" Marcus said. "My uncle killed himself when he was around my age. And my dad's got depression, too, so I know I'm predis-posed. My parents always want me to talk about my feelings."

"I'm sure that can be exhausting," Takahashi said.

"It is, because sometimes, I just don't have any— feelings, I mean. I wish my dad would stop freaking out about it. He constantly thinks I'm going to throw myself over the edge."

"He cares," Kallie said. "Better than having a parent who doesn't give a shit."

Marcus shrugged. "I guess. Then there's my little sister, Erica."

"I didn't know you had a sister," Kallie said.

"I try not to mention her," Marcus admitted. "She's great— really. I just can't help but... be jealous of her, you know? Even though I love her. She was so perfect at everything— school, dance, music, cooking, garden-ing, sports, you name it. And then there was me. I could barely pass a math class, I have two left feet, I burn *water* and kill every plant I've ever owned, and I trip walking across a basketball court. Maybe that's why I turned to art— because it was the only thing she wasn't good at. It was *mine* and not hers."

My shoulders grew heavy as Marcus talked. Marcus was the biggest talker in the group during these sessions, but he usually brought up stuff that didn't really matter, mostly to just fill our time until Takahashi dismissed us. But this was deep.

"I'm sorry you felt overshadowed by your sister," Kallie said, sounding genuine. "I know what it's like to compete with a sibling. My twin brother was the same way— perfect at every fucking thing while I was off getting into trouble."

"I wasn't getting into trouble," Marcus snapped. His soft tone instantly soured.

"I didn't say you were," she huffed back at him. "You don't have to get so defensive."

"I'm not getting defensive," he argued.

"I'm just trying to comfort you, and you're pushing me away," Kallie growled. "You always do this!"

Marcus huffed. "I do not! Name one time I've pushed you away."

"Literally every second of every day!" Kallie burst, stomping her foot as she shot out of her chair. "I've done nothing but try to be your friend, and you insist on keeping me at a distance."

"Didn't you hear anything I just said?" Marcus demanded, and I heard him jump to his feet beside her. "I don't *do* friends."

"Because you don't want them!" Kallie yelled. "You're so afraid you're going to hurt someone like you hurt Anya that you make *sure* they never get close enough for you *to* hurt."

"So maybe I do," Marcus seethed. "It's better than seeing them get hurt."

"You don't get it! Pushing me away is pretty damn hurtful. You could shove a sword through my stomach, and I would even *feel* it compared to the pain I feel waiting around for you to wake the fuck up and realize the kind of bond we share."

"Bond?" Marcus repeated nastily. "The only *bond* we have is as teammates in the Darke Games, and that's over!"

Kallie gasped, and sobs broke out of her chest. "But you— you said—"

Marcus took a step toward her, his shoes squeaking against the floor. His tone softened as he realized the mistake he made. "Come on, Kallie. I didn't mean it that way. I only meant—"

"Fuck you, Marcus!" she snapped, and I heard her push him away. "The only curse you can break is a promise!"

Kallie took off running, and her sobs echoed down the staircase as she left. My jaw dropped.

"Fuck," Marcus muttered under his breath. "Kallie, wait!"

He quickly followed after her, along with Takahashi.

"Excuse me, students," Takahashi said quickly as he passed Ava and me. "Session dismissed."

Within moments, Ava and I were left alone in Takahashi's office with Oberi.

"Whoa," Ava breathed. "That was intense."

"No kidding," I agreed. "I had no idea Kallie felt so deeply about Marcus."

"It's totally obvious," Ava said as she stood. A keychain on her bag jingled as she swung it over her shoulder. "And it's not like she can help it."

"What do you mean?" I asked as we left the room.

"Are *all* men this oblivious?" Ava groaned.

She paused a beat before adding, "We should probably talk about this somewhere private."

Ava led me to the balcony. It was quickly becoming our hideaway whenever we needed a moment alone, just the two of us.

I was a bit on edge after what happened the last time we came up here, but Ava was doing well today. Oberi hurried over to the banister and thwacked his tail against the ground as he looked out over the prison yard. He *loved* being outside.

"What's so secret we had to come up here?" I asked.

"Didn't you hear Kallie?" Ava practically whispered, though we were alone. "She admitted they're bonded."

"*Bonded?!*" I gaped. "Like magically? I thought she was talking metaphorically. They're mates?"

"That's what Kallie told me, but Marcus has no idea," Ava admitted.

"How's that possible? I thought fae only mated with their own kind."

"They're supposed to, but Kallie's different," Ava pointed out. "She's the only female shifter known to her people. Perhaps her bonding magic works differently, too."

"I guess that makes sense," I said thoughtfully. Between us, Oberi whined, and I felt his disappointment.

"What's up with him?" Ava asked. At the same time, we both reached out to scratch his head, and our fingers connected.

"He wants us to talk," I said without thinking about it.

Ava's fingers stilled. "Talk about what?"

My shoulders dropped. "He wants us to talk about fight club."

Ava began scratching Oberi's ears again. He started panting. "What's there to talk about?"

"I don't know…" I started gingerly. "You've been avoiding me. I thought you were still mad."

"I'm not mad!" Ava cried. "Ancestors, do *all* men need everything stated explicitly to them?"

"Yes," I stated flatly.

Ava laughed. "I thought you understood how I felt. I haven't been *avoiding* you."

"Then what's up with all the fashion designing lately? I thought you didn't want to do music anymore."

"Of course I do!" she insisted. "I thought *you* would rather train than do music. I've been designing so you had time to train. I... I didn't think you wanted to make songs with me anymore. That it wasn't important."

A weight fell from my shoulders. "I want both— fighting *and* music."

"Oh..." Her voice became soft. "It's just... you seemed so happy in the ring. I know we've fought about it before, but it doesn't matter how worried I am about what might happen to you. I want you to fight because you love it. I didn't want to keep bringing up how worried I get, because you'd think I'm telling you to quit, but I'm not. It's just... this is risky, and I care about you."

I entwined my fingers with hers. "I know. But you have nothing to worry about."

"I do!" she pressed. "Ghost broke his arm, and they're still making him fight."

"They're not *making* us fight," I argued. "Ghost signed up for this, same as everyone else."

"Yeah, but he wanted out. What if you want out at some point?"

"I don't. Besides, Ghost is fine. We were sparring the other day, and he was using his arm."

"Really?" Ava sounded confused, like she'd been *certain* his arm was broken.

"I think he was just trying to get out of his next fight," I said.

Ava took a deep breath. "Look, I don't want to argue about this. You're not going to convince me there's nothing to worry about, and I'm not going to convince you to stop fighting. So we're going to have to come to some sort of agreement."

I took a few beats to consider her words. "What kind of agreement?"

"A compromise," she suggested. "You let me be worried about you and tend to your bruises after your fights, and I'll support you, because this is your thing. I won't be the girlfriend who tells you what to do."

Every muscle in my body tensed, and heat pooled in my belly. "My... girlfriend?"

Just the thought of calling Ava my girlfriend— for real— made my head spin. A whirlwind might as well have come by and swept me off my feet, because I felt like I was soaring high above the prison yard.

Ava's skin heated beneath my touch. "I didn't mean that. Forget I said anything."

I quickly came spiraling back down. My elation immediately turned to irritation.

"Forget, pidge?" I blew a breath. "How can I forget something that makes me feel so damn good?"

She dropped her fingers from mine. "You sound offended."

"Of course I'm offended! You say men are oblivious, but if women are so insightful, you'd know how I feel about you by now."

Ava caught her breath. "How you... feel about me?"

I reached for her hands again, and they were almost too hot to touch. I didn't care. I loved the way her skin warmed with her Fire. "I'm crazy about you, pidge. But I'm sick of playing the friends-with-benefits game."

I could never open up to anyone else, but with Ava it came naturally. The words spilled out of me. "I care so deeply about you, but I don't feel like I can take care of you properly if you just keep stringing me along. There's too much uncertainty, and I've lived with that all my life. It's like being in a foster home all over again. I never knew when that was going to end, and now I'm not sure if you're going to stay or take off on me. At least if I were your boyfriend, I would know there was some stability. I could do better to protect you if everyone knew you were mine."

Ava spoke softly. "But Charlie... they already know."

"It's different if they think we're just a fling," I pointed out. "You mean way more than that to me. I want *more*, pidge. I want something permanent. Something I can count on to last."

Ava sniffled, and I reached up to feel tears streaming down her cheeks. My breath caught in my throat. "Pidge, what's wrong?"

"I didn't know you felt that way— about me feeling like another foster home." Her voice cracked. "You deserve better than that from me. You deserve to know how I truly feel."

I wanted desperately to know how she truly felt, but I was scared to know the truth. She might decide she didn't like me *that* much— not enough to be her boyfriend.

But at least if we settled this now, I'd know. I could stop waiting for the other shoe to drop. We might as well get it over with.

I swallowed the lump in my throat. "How *do* you really feel?"

The seconds seemed to stretch into minutes as I held my breath and awaited her answer. My body turned to stone, but my heart hammered.

Ava reached up to caress the side of my face. Her warm fingers sent tingles across my skin. Ava's voice sounded like an angel's as she said, "I love you, Charlie."

It was the last thing I expected to hear. I didn't know what to do. At best, I dreamed she might say she liked me... but *loved* me? Hell, no one had ever told me they loved me. Not a foster parent, or even a friend.

"L-love?" I slurred, barely present in the moment. I felt like the words had sent me to another dimension, one where I was disconnected from my body and couldn't decipher how to respond.

"Yes, Charlie," she chuckled through her tears. "I fucking love you more than I've ever loved anything— more than my own freaking element. I. Love. You. Charlie. Wahkin."

As she repeated the words, they finally started to sink in. I snapped back into my body, fully aware of the way my heart lifted in my chest— and how my dick hardened in my pants. Tears rose to my eyes, and one escaped down my cheek.

"What's wrong?" she asked in alarm.

She'd left me so starstruck that I couldn't speak. Instead, I swept her into my arms and crushed her body tightly to my chest. Oberi nearly got squashed between us, but he yelped and jumped out of the way. I buried my face into her hair and inhaled her sweet scent.

"Nothing's wrong," I mumbled. "Everything is perfect. I love you, too, pidge."

I planted a kiss on her lips, and if I thought I left my body a moment ago, it was nothing compared to making out with her. My spirit might as well have transcended to the Ancestral Lands, I felt so free and incredible. I didn't know what it was *like* to be loved— hell, nobody ever wanted me.

But Ava did. Ava threw her arms around my neck and dragged me even closer. She parted her lips, and my tongue slid inside her mouth. I cradled the back of her head and placed my other hand on her hip, pulling her into my hardness.

"I love you, Charlie," she gasped through the endless kisses I left on her lips.

"I love you, too, Ava-Marie," I breathed.

Her whole body began to shake in elated sobs, like she *loved* the sound of her full name coming off my lips. I began trailing kisses down her jaw and to her neck. She tilted her head back to welcome me in.

"I love you," she repeated.

"I love you," I muttered into her skin. Her perfect, angelic skin.

She must've really loved that, because she squeezed me so tight I couldn't drag her off me even if I tried. She wrapped her legs around my waist, and I grabbed her ass to keep her on me. I swayed on my feet as all my blood left my head, and I backed her against the wall to steady us. Ava drew in shallow breaths, like she liked it.

I sucked on her neck for a brief moment, just enough to tease her but not to give her a hickey. I drew away beaming. "So, is that it, pidge? Are you my girlfriend now?"

She giggled with happiness and ran her hands through my hair. "Yes, Charlie. I'm your girlfriend now. You're my boyfriend."

I never knew I could be so happy. Nothing beyond this balcony mattered, because right now it was just Ava and me— one couple, one being...

One soul.

ava-marie

FOURTEEN

"Ava, this is *perfect!*" Ivy gushed.

Ivy strutted around The Devil's Playground, wearing the red dress I'd made him. He'd already done a lot of work down here— there was a bar built at the head of the secret room, and a couple tables and chairs were scattered around the area. There was a stage built around a couple of the poles that went to the ceiling, and a half-finished dance floor in the middle of the space.

Ivy placed his hands on his hips and turned in place. The glittering red fabric fanned out around him, and he cooed, "This dress is going to be *amazing* at the nightclub's opening."

"You're welcome," I said. "I was sure the slit would show off your legs."

It went all the way up to Ivy's hip, like I knew he'd want it to. Oberi was with me, in her unicorn form and strutting about. She had insisted I make something special for her too, so I'd fashioned her a glittering red cape from the same fabric as Ivy's dress. She pranced around with her head thrown upward, like she was a queen in her castle. She stepped on the edge of her cape and stumbled forward, before righting herself with an embarrassed snort. I laughed.

Chancey sat at one of the nightclub tables, watching Ivy strut around as if he was drawn to him like a magnet. The look on his face was definitely desirous.

"What do you think, Chance?" Ivy struck a pose in front of the angel. "Do you think it'll draw attention?"

Chancey's lips upturned. "You look pretty amazing, doll face."

Ivy gave a sassy grin, and Chancey's face flushed, like he wanted to pounce on Ivy right then and there.

Chancey had turned from doing highly illegal things at the prison, to *slightly less* illegal things by helping Ivy get ready for the nightclub's big launch. I was very proud of him. I think Chancey was using the fight club to convince the guards to look the other way, when it came to Ivy. He was clearing pulling strings with the establishment to make Ivy happy.

"The Devil's Playground should be finished by the end of the semester," Ivy said smartly. "I can't *wait* to start taking in new clients. I'm gonna be raking it in."

"Why can't you run the club and not sleep with anybody?" Chancey growled. His previously bright eyes had turned dark, and there was definitely a jealous undertone to his words.

"I mean, that would be *fine*, but I'd be taking a huge profit cut," Ivy said. "Selling booze and tickets to the club would be a lot less profitable than being an escort for guards and prisoners."

Chancey let out an angry breath. "So what we're doing doesn't matter."

"Don't take it that way. It's just business," Ivy said with a casual shrug.

"Yeah, right, business," Chancey snapped. "I get it. Money is what's important."

Ivy's mouth dropped open. "Chance."

"I don't want to hear it, Ives." Chancey got up and shoved away from the table. His shoulders were hunched as he walked away and out of the room.

"What the hell's the matter with him?" Ivy asked, jerking a thumb at the door.

"Isn't it obvious?" I asked. "He's pissed off at the thought of you sleeping with other people."

"But it's my *job!*" Ivy whined.

"It doesn't have to be," I argued. "Everyone starts over at the Institute. You can reinvent yourself."

Ivy's eye twitched. "Well, if he wanted anything *more*, he should speak up. Before I change my mind. I've got a lot of options, all of them willing to pad my wallet."

"It's not just about that, is it?" I asked.

Ivy was quiet for a moment before he said, "When I showed up at the Institute, Chancey and I had an understanding. It worked well for both of us. He got off, and I got paid."

"But it turned into something more," I said.

Ivy sighed. "I *want* there to be," he confessed. "But I don't think he feels the same."

"Of course he does. He's smitten with you."

"I don't think so." Ivy shook his head. "You know, I haven't taken on another client since I got here. Chancey's the only person I've been with. But I broke the cardinal rule. I let my feelings get involved with the guy who's paying me."

"That's not a bad thing, in this situation," I insisted.

"He's literally my second chance," Ivy whispered, and his eyes got misty. "I don't know what I would do if I lost him. And I don't mean anything to him. I'm just his whore."

"That's not true," I insisted. "Ask him to be your boyfriend! I know he'll give you the answer you want."

"How can you be so sure?"

"Because he loves you, Ivy. It's plain to see when he's looking into your eyes."

The look on Ivy's face got so soft, and I saw tears welling over his eyelids. "Do you really think he loves me?"

"Of course! The evidence is all there. He stopped dealing drugs, he doesn't gamble as much, hell, he's even less of a prick. Overall, he's turning into a nice guy. I never saw him change— he didn't *want* to change— until you showed up. He's becoming a *better person*, for you!"

I purposefully avoided bringing up the fight club, because even though I thought that was Ivy's right to know, that was a conversation he and Chancey needed to have. Chancey was a bad guy... but he was turning into one of the good ones, for Ivy's sake. That meant they had something special.

"Maybe you're right. But I'm so scared," Ivy confessed. "What if he breaks my heart?"

"You never know until you try. Give him a chance. I promise it'll feel better than holding back on your feelings," I said.

Ivy chewed on his lip, and I watched his fangs pierce the top of his skin. "I'll think about it. I don't know if I'm ready. How did you know Charlie was the one for you?"

"Because he doesn't run away. He runs toward me," I said. "I didn't think I'd find anyone who puts up with my shit, but it's more than that. He pushes me to be better. Charlie gives me hope I can have a normal life. A better life, even with my bipolar. Maybe Chancey can give you the same hope."

Ivy made a sad face. "I don't know if I'm cut out for the two-kids and a picket fence life. It's nice to dream about, but I'm just too... bad."

"That's not true. I used to think the same way, but we're at the Institute to correct our behavior, right?"

Ivy gave a sour laugh. "Nothing's going to change me, precious. I always thought I'd end up dead in some alley somewhere, after a client killed me, or after overdosing. You don't live a high-stakes life like me without paying the consequences."

"Don't say that, Ivy. You deserve so much better. You deserve to be loved, and to die as an old person who's lived a full life."

Ivy made a scoffing noise. "Sounds like a fairy tale to me."

"Don't think that way. You said Chancey is your second shot. You two can build a new life together once you get out of here. Take it."

Ivy drummed his fingers against the bar. "Maybe."

Ivy gave me a wink. "But enough about me. You've got someone waiting for you in the music room, don't you?"

With a thrill, I checked my watch and realized Charlie was finally out of class. I jumped up. "You're right. I'll see you later, Ivy!"

I grabbed the bag at my feet and bolted out of the room. Oberi followed me. Her cape billowed behind her as she trotted behind me through the hallways, and people cleared the way to give her space.

I couldn't help it. When I knew Charlie was nearby, I had to run to him.

Oberi nosed me, as if she was asking if I'd really believed what I said to Ivy. And I knew I did. I didn't think this dump would ever start to change me, but it *was*. The reform school was reforming me, but not because of the consequences of the program or the strict rules.

It was because of the people. Because of my friends, and Charlie, and the teachers who cared. It'd been so hard living in Kinpago, and I hadn't even realized it— my family was great, but they didn't have the same impulses I did to react to everything. I'd never realized it before, but I'd felt inferior— the bad kid who did bad things just because she could, surrounded by people who were not just heroes, but who *wanted* to be good, because that's who they were on the inside. I felt so out of control all the time, and I didn't know how to stop it.

Here at the Institute, I was surrounded by people who were just as fucked up as I was, so my thought process didn't seem like such a sin. It felt normal. Better than that, it felt like it wasn't a life sentence to think that way. I was witnessing people turn their lives around after they'd really screwed themselves over. At the Institute, you either got better, or you got worse, and I saw what happened to the people who got worse... what kind of monsters they became.

Being bad didn't feel like a choice to me before, but it did now. It was making all the difference.

I skidded to a stop in front of the music room, and nearly fell over. I *did* fall over when Oberi failed to stop behind me, and her front smashed into my ass. I went toppling into the music room, slamming into an accordion, and Oberi neighed an apology.

"You always know how to make an entrance." Charlie stood above me, holding out a hand.

I took it, and once our skin touched, a surge of energy went through me. I launched myself upward and grabbed on to him. I squeezed him so tight my arms almost went numb. The powerful feelings rushing through me made me feel high. I placed my head on his chest and made a happy sound. "I love you."

Charlie kissed the top of my head. "I love *you*."

Charlie and I really liked saying *I love you*. It was like we couldn't stop. I figured I had to make up for a lifetime of saying it, because Charlie had never heard it before, and that was *so wrong*. How anybody couldn't love him, I wasn't sure.

He bounced me in his arms. "You should let go."

"No. I don't want to."

Charlie gave a noise of amusement. Oberi guided him to the piano bench, and Charlie sat us both down. I ended up on his lap.

I *loved* his lap. It's where I felt so safe.

Also, his dick was right there. And I loved that, too.

Oberi carried over the bag I'd dropped, and my heart leapt. How could I have forgotten? I took it from her and said, "I brought you presents!"

"Presents?" Charlie's tone was hesitant.

"Yes! Open it!"

Charlie slowly took the bag. "How much did you spend?"

"It wasn't a bipolar binge. I set myself a budget," I said. "It only cost like, five-hundred dollars."

"*Five-hundred dollars?!*" Charlie sputtered. "That was my rent back home!"

"Yes, but you're my *boyfriend* now, so you should be spoiled!"

I didn't want to overwhelm him with gifts, but at the same time, how could I *not*? He deserved them, and so much more.

Charlie pushed the bag back toward me. "You should send them back. I can't accept this."

"Nope! It's all for you." I giggled and swung my legs. "Consider it twenty-three years worth of Christmas presents from me."

"You already made me the armband," Charlie muttered.

"So twenty-two years. Go on, look inside!" I was fit to bursting with excitement.

Charlie still looked uncomfortable, but he did as I asked. His face frayed on the edge of becoming emotional as he removed items and placed them on top of the piano. I noticed he fingered each item carefully, taking in the shape and texture.

"I got you all kinds of soft new clothes, and new shoes, and a candle that smells like *me,* and food you like— fuck the guards, they don't need to know you have it— oh, and I made you this jacket," I said, pulling it out. "It took me all week to sew. Try it on!"

Charlie slipped the jacket over his shoulders. I'd guessed the right measurements. It fit perfectly. His hands roamed over the fabric, feeling it as I said, "It looks so good. Now when we go into Shade Hills for our field trip, you'll have something nice to wear."

Charlie didn't say anything, and my smile faltered. "Did I do something wrong?"

"I just... I feel bad I can't give you the same," he admitted. "No one's ever done this for me before."

I scoffed. "I have enough *stuff*. What I didn't have was you, and I do now, so that's all it takes to make me happy!"

Charlie sniffed and wiped at his eyes. I swear, it touched my cold, dark heart.

"Thanks, pidge," he said. "I don't know what to say."

"You don't have to say anything. If you're happy, I'm happy!" I wiggled on his lap, and I felt his dick begin to press against my ass.

Charlie's voice went low. "You keep doing that, we're going to have a problem."

"So?" I wiggled on his lap again, and felt him grow harder.

"We probably shouldn't. Ez is gonna be here any minute."

I let out a breath of disappointment, before I slid off his lap and started fiddling with the piano.

Charlie put his presents back in the bag. "I didn't know you felt this way."

"About what? You?" I asked. I played a medley on the piano, and it grew over the room. Oberi began to sway back and forth.

"Yeah." Charlie nodded. "Before, it was hard for me to even tell if you liked me."

"I kind of go from zero to a hundred really fast," I explained. "I've been holding back forever, so now I have to let out everything that I've been suppressing inside of me."

"What do you mean?"

"I've been in love with you for a really long time."

"Really? How long?" Charlie leaned forward, like he was obsessed with knowing the answer.

"Since the night I told you everything in the loft above the chapel. The night of the party, when we got matching tattoos." My fingers played across the keys.

Charlie stilled. "Ava, that was months ago."

"Em-hm." I pressed down harder on the keys, to make the notes really shine. "It was really hard not telling you during the Darke Games. I didn't know if we'd make it to the end, and if one of us died, I wanted you to know how I felt."

"Then what held you back?"

"I knew if we both made it out, I'd have to face my feelings," I explained. "Plus I knew once I admitted it, I'd go overboard with... all this."

I gave a sheepish shrug. "I'm not a person who refrains from affection once I care about someone. I can be over the top, and I didn't know if that would scare you off."

"That doesn't scare me off. It draws me in." Charlie moved closer. "I never knew a person could love so... deeply."

"Well, if you're going to do something, might as well do it right," I said, and I kissed him on the cheek. "With me, it's all or nothing, and you are my all."

Charlie's face glowed warm. I was ready to have a kickass makeout session right then and there, before Opal and Ezekiel walked into the room.

A smile spread across my face to see them together— even if they weren't technically *together*. They'd been hanging out a lot lately, and I dared to say they looked super cute.

Ez held a camera and waved it around. "I checked out a camera from Professor Ellender. It's really shitty, though."

Cameras didn't work well at the Institute, due to all the magic use. The ones the school had for students to use were really old, and took awful video, made worse by all the supernatural energy floating around.

"It'll have to do," I said.

Ez paused. "Ava, are you *sure* you want to do this? It's been a really long time."

My spirit twisted inside of me, but the pain wasn't greater than the longing. I wanted to start making music videos again, and I wanted them to be with Charlie.

"Yes. This is what I want," I said softly. "This is the best way to honor Monica. I don't think she would've wanted me to give it up like I did. I want to get back to it."

Ezekiel nodded before he set up the camera. I worked on testing the crappy microphone we'd found while digging around in the music room, while Charlie got situated in front of the piano. I struggled with the mic for a minute— the Institute always had the shittiest materials— before I got it to work. I gave it a couple of tests before I said, "I think we're ready."

"You can do it!" Opal gushed, giving us a tiny clap.

Ezekiel pressed record. The red light of the camera came on, and I swallowed down my nerves.

"Hey, subscribers," I said shakily. "I know it's been— um, three years, and during my last video, I told you guys I was done with my channel."

I took a deep breath. "But... I've kinda decided to start making videos again. This is Charlie." I gestured to him behind me, and he nodded. "He means a lot to me. He'll be playing piano, while I'll be singing vocals. This is a song we made together. It's called *Half a Soul*."

Charlie counted down, then began playing the opening chorus. I shook off my anxiety and began to sing.

"You were the beginning of my story
Or was it the end?
Holding us together like fragments of paper
Or ashes upon the wind

You promised me that you could fly
And I thought that so could I
Until our voices lay scattering
On the glass that had been our home

So I let you go
In this lifetime, or the next

Our worlds will never be apart
Because I swear you are my heart
And I'll always find you again."

The piano and my voice twisted together into an elaborate harmony. I didn't know what it was, but when Charlie played, the piano made a different sound. It was as if we were fated to make music together, and it only sounded *right* when we were creating it as one. Separate, both of us were good, but together— we were brilliant.

When I'd finished singing, Charlie tapered off the piano, and I waved to the camera. "Thanks for watching, guys. I'll see you next week with a new video!"

Ezekiel switched the camera off, and Opal bounced up and down. "Eek! Ava, that was *amazing*! I didn't know you could sing like that. I didn't know Charlie could play, either."

"It was really good. We can go to the library and upload this right now," Ezekiel said. "Shouldn't take too long to edit."

My stomach tumbled with nervousness at the thought of uploading a new video after so long. I wasn't sure if my subscribers would forgive me for taking such a long break, but Charlie sounded excited. "I know your fans are going to love it. Thanks for letting me be a part of this."

"Of course," I said. I couldn't have Monica, but I had Charlie. I couldn't explain it, but since losing her, doing this with him felt like the *right* thing to do.

The four of us walked to the library together, Oberi giving a tap-dance with her hooves behind us. She was so happy Charlie and I had made the video. Her mood had been amazing ever since we'd officially gotten together.

"Your song was so romantic," Opal swooned. "It speaks of true love!"

"You know Mom and Dad are going to read into it, since they know Charlie's your boyfriend now," Ezekiel teased.

I stopped directly in my tracks, and Charlie slammed into me from behind. He had to grab me to keep me upright as I hissed, "You said something?"

Ezekiel's face fell. "Oh. Was I not supposed to tell them?"

I facepalmed. *"Not yet.* I thought you and Daddy weren't even talking?"

"We're not. I mean, I told Mom, who I'm sure told Dad," Ez explained quickly. "I didn't know you wanted to keep it private."

I moaned. Charlie shifted beside me. "You wanted to keep me a secret?" He sounded hurt.

"It's not that I didn't *want* to tell them," I explained. "My parents just freak out every time I get a boyfriend. They're so overprotective. I wanted to tell them on my *own terms* this weekend."

I glared at Ezekiel, and Opal gave a giggle.

"I'm so sorry! I have a really big mouth," Ez apologized. Opal continued to laugh.

"I'm sure I'm your dad's new favorite person," Charlie grumbled.

"Let me handle it." I laid a hand on his arm, and tried not to strangle my brother. "It'll be okay once I talk to him."

I berated Ez the entire time we were in the library, and he apologized a thousand times more. After we uploaded the video, I walked down to the phone hall, to do some damage control with my parents.

I paid the guard for extra time, but before I could pick up the phone, I saw Marcus standing alone. He was talking to someone on one of the payphones, and looked awfully annoyed. He held Rishi in one arm, who dangled there limply with his tongue sticking out.

Most witches and warlocks left their cats in their cells, but Marcus always had Rishi with him. I wondered why.

Marcus saw me coming. He held up the phone with an eye roll as I approached.

A male voice came out of it— I was guessing it had to be his dad. "I'm sorry, kid. I know you won't believe me when I say it, but I know how you feel. It may seem impossible now, but we can change it, if you're willing to put in the work."

"Yeah, I get it," Marcus said, sounding bored. "Can I go?"

"Sure," his dad said, though he sounded disappointed. "Talk to you later."

Marcus hung up without a goodbye. He sank sullenly against the wall to the cold, stone floor, and muttered something under his breath. He squeezed Rishi with both arms, and the cat's eyes bugged out a little.

"What was your dad on to you about?" I asked, and I sat beside him.

"Just the same old lecture about how I need to take my antidepressants and not skip therapy and shit. Heard it all before," Marcus said. "What about you?"

The school must've notified his parents that he'd skipped out on our last therapy session since Kallie's blow up. It'd just been the three of us with Takahashi, and without Marcus, the session had been long and tense.

"I'm just here to talk to my parents, since Ez told them the news about me and Charlie being together."

"Smooth. Can't trust Ez to keep a secret."

"He means well, but you really can't." I paused for a moment before I stated cautiously, "What about you and Kallie?"

"What about us?" His tone was harsh.

"I mean... you two ran out of therapy the other day. I don't even know if you guys made up."

Kallie had been avoiding all of us since that day. I think she was embarrassed.

"We talked," Marcus said. "It wasn't a big deal."

"What about?"

"I'm not gonna tell you about it." Marcus turned his head away, and Rishi gave a mew.

"Okay, this has got to stop," I insisted. "I'm not putting up with this bullshit that we aren't friends. To be honest, it was pretty damn offensive the other day when you said we weren't."

"We aren't friends. Just leave me alone," Marcus mumbled, and he curled inward.

"Marcus, I am a pro at pushing people away, which means I'm not going to take your crap, because I know what you're trying to pull," I said flatly. "Trust me, it's not working. You want to deny that all of us are close, when it's so obvious that we *are*. What about the Villain's Club, huh? What about what we went through together in the Darke Games?"

"That was for survival," he argued, but his protests were quiet and meek.

"Big deal. The four of us still hang out every day," I said. I started counting on my fingers as I listed off all the reasons. "If you're not with

Kallie or me, you're with Charlie. You help us with our homework. We go everywhere together, even to dangerous places like the fight club. We promised to help each other figure out my prophecy, and this demigod mystery. We open up to each other in therapy. You've told us your darkest secrets, and we've told you ours. If that's not friendship, then I don't know what is."

"You guys don't *really* accept me. I'm just sticking around because I have nowhere else to go," he said. He sounded like he really believed it.

"Ancestors, that is such BS! If we didn't want you in our group, we would've kicked you out. We keep you around because we like you, dammit!"

"Really?" Marcus lifted his head.

"Yes. I wouldn't lie to you about something like that."

"I don't want to hurt my friends," Marcus said sadly. Rishi started licking his cheek.

"Marcus, I know you can't forgive yourself for what happened with Anya. But trust me, the three of us can handle whatever you throw at us, and so much more," I insisted. "We're just as strong magically as you are. You don't have to worry about hurting us, because we're all on the same level."

Marcus stroked Rishi's fur as he considered my words. "I guess we are friends," he admitted. "I care about all of you guys. Charlie, you... Kallie."

"One of us more than the rest," I pointed out.

Marcus sighed. "It doesn't matter. We can't be together, anyway."

"Why?" I wanted to reach out and comfort him, but I was afraid it'd scare him away, so I didn't.

"Because we live in two separate worlds," Marcus said. "Kallie— she told me we were bonded, when we got into that argument."

"So you know that you're her true mate."

"She says so, but how can a warlock be mated to a fae?" Marcus asked. "Even if there is a magical connection between us, it doesn't matter. I can't fit into fae culture. They *hate* witches. I'll be hanged the moment I set foot in Malovia. And it'll be the same for Kallie, if I bring her back to Octavia Falls. My people will slaughter her for being a fae. Our two races have been at war for centuries. How are we supposed to be together in a world like that? Where are we going to live, where are we going to *go*?"

"You could find somewhere else to live, somewhere that doesn't care about what you two are," I argued.

"You don't understand, because you and Charlie are Elementai. You come from the same culture. But both of us would have to give up our families and our homes to be together," Marcus argued.

"Elementai from different Houses weren't allowed to be together twenty years ago," I pointed out. "My parents are Koigni and Toaqua, Fire and Water. It was forbidden for them to be in love, until *they* worked together to change the law. Now interhouse relationships are legal among our tribe. Why couldn't the same happen with witches and fae?"

Marcus shook his head, like he didn't believe that was possible. "The Elementai are still just one race, not two different kinds of supernaturals. No matter what Kallie says, I know she wants to restore her honor and return to Malovia after she graduates. And though everyone back home hates me for what I did, I *really* want to earn forgiveness, and go back to Octavia Falls at some point. It's my home. How can we be together when our hearts are in two different places— two different countries that are across the world from each other?"

"It doesn't matter, as long as you guys are in love. If your culture doesn't accept you, so be it, but I'm sure your parents will be open to the idea, if it makes you both happy," I insisted.

"My dad doesn't like fae, and I'm sure her family probably despises witches," Marcus said. "It's not going to work. No matter how much we like each other— hell, how much I *love her*, even— all we're going to do is hurt each other. I can't ask her to give her home up just to be with me. It'd be so selfish."

He let out a scoffing sound. "Not to mention she's a princess. I can't fit into high society. I barely can handle being around normal people. She's meant to be with someone *special*, a prince, a noble of some sort with royal blood. Not a nobody from Connecticut."

"And how does she feel about all this?" I crossed my arms.

"Kallie doesn't want to lose her parents and her brother by being with me, and she knows she has a long way to go to repair that relationship after what she did. Being with me would just... get in the way."

I wasn't convinced, but it looked like these two had talked themselves out of it. "That must've been really hard."

"Of course it breaks my fucking heart, but I don't have a choice. I don't want her to lose everything because she's with me," Marcus spat. A tear slipped out of his eye, and he wiped it away with the back of his sleeve.

"I'm sorry." My heart ached for Marcus. It was so wrong he and Kallie were supposed to stay apart because their people wouldn't agree with them being together. They shouldn't have to make the choice between their families and their true mate.

Marcus staggered to his feet. "I don't want to talk about this again, okay? It just hurts. Kallie and I have come to an understanding. This is the way it has to be."

"Okay." I softly rose.

Marcus practically ran down the hallway— like if he stayed any longer, he'd break down into sobs, and he didn't want me to witness that.

I felt so sorry for Marcus— and Kallie too. But inwardly, I wasn't willing to give up on them. Someday, I was sure they'd get their happily-ever-after, despite everything that was keeping them apart. I just didn't know how long it would take for that to happen.

I dialed the rotary phone, and waited as it rang. My mother picked up, and I shouted, "Hi, Mama!"

Mama gave a soft laugh. "Hello, Ava. Your father's home. You're on speaker."

"Oh, good," I said. This should make it a lot easier, talking to both of them at once.

"How are you reacting to your new medication?" Mama asked immediately. It'd been all that was on her mind whenever she talked to me, since I'd been in the infirmary.

"I'm doing pretty well," I said. "I actually don't think I'm cycling right now. I feel pretty normal. For me, anyway."

"That's a relief. Both of us were worried when the school told us about the episode," Mama said.

"My mood is stable. I haven't felt this steady in a long time."

Even the voices in my head had started getting quieter. It was really a win-win.

"I'm supposing you have news?" Mama had a triumphant *I-told-you-so* tone in her voice. I hated when she was right— which was all the freaking time. The woman had a sensor for predicting the best outcome, no matter how unbelievable it was.

"Um, maybe," I giggled, and I twirled the phone line around my finger. "But Ez already told you!"

"Doesn't matter. I want to hear it from you," Mama teased.

"I'm seeing somebody," I said slowly, biting my lip.

"And who might that be?"

I let out another nervous sound, and squeaked, "Charlie."

Mama squealed. "Oh, that's so sweet. I thought you two looked cute together during the dance."

"*Yes*! I win the bet!" I heard Uncle Jonah's voice echo from somewhere in the background, and Auntie Imogen's excited chittering. They must've been over for lunch.

Daddy's voice came over the line as he picked up the phone. "Peanut, is he treating you well?"

"Like a princess!" I gushed. "He's amazing."

"He better, because if he isn't, I'm going to storm into that prison and—"

"*Liam*," Mama said, and Daddy let out a grumpy sound.

"He's the best!" I said. "I'm so happy! When I hug him, he's so squishy. It's like cuddling a big teddy bear."

"Squishy, huh." Daddy was *not* amused.

"Charlie's a nice boy. Let it be," Mama insisted.

"I have a right to be concerned, seeing as how he's involved with my daughter!" Daddy said.

Mama made a *tsking* noise, and I knew she was rolling her eyes.

Daddy's voice became more urgent. "Honey, *please* tell me you're at least using protection."

I grinned. "I mean, he pulls out. Sometimes."

Daddy groaned. "I'm getting too old for this bullshit," he mumbled.

I gave a laugh. "It's just a joke. We haven't even done anything like that."

Nothing that would get me pregnant, anyway.

"This really isn't something to joke about," Daddy said, though he was obviously relieved.

"Relax! Charlie is *very* adamant about safe sex. I'm sure the man won't get within six feet of me without a condom."

I spun in place. "Not that it's a thing, anyway, because it isn't. We're taking things slow. He's very polite. A true gentleman."

Daddy muttered something very quietly to Mama, but I was sure I heard, "*I might like him a little more now.*"

I bounced up and down. "Daddy, guess what?!"

"What?"

I giggled and whispered, "*I love him.*"

Daddy hitched a breath. He took his time responding before he said, "That's wonderful, peanut. You always had such a big heart—"

"That's me!"

"— But you should be careful to make good decisions."

"We won't get into trouble. Too much trouble, anyway."

"Behave yourself."

My voice took on a whining tone. "But I don't *want* to behave, I want to be evil!"

"We're all aware."

"You approve of him, don't you, Daddy?"

There was a long pause, and I really hoped he said yes. His blessing meant the world to me.

"If you're happy, that's what matters," Daddy said. "As long as he treats you well."

"He does, I promise." My heart fluttered at the acceptance of my boyfriend. "I can't wait until we're all together again. Charlie's so sweet. You'll see."

"Just slow down, okay?" Daddy sounded so worried. "I don't want you getting too attached too quickly."

My spirit twisted. *Too late for that now.* The thought of this ending badly gutted me. "I won't. I'm keeping my heart safe, I swear."

But it was a lie. I'd given Charlie my whole being— not just my heart, but my soul, too. I had a deeper connection with Charlie than I had with anybody.

And even now, part of me feared losing him.

THE VIDEO HAD GOTTEN three-thousand hits within the first twenty-four hours. I figured all my subscribers would've forgotten about me by now, but apparently, they hadn't. I guess they really had been hoping I'd get back to making music again. Some comments on the video were mean, but most were very supportive. I couldn't watch the feedback come in, as we were only allowed spotty access to the Internet in the crappy library, but from what I'd seen when I'd checked this morning, people were thrilled that I was creating content again.

On Sunday, I worked in the laundry room of the Institute in a better mood than what was usual. I hated my shifts down here, but my video launch had really lifted my spirits.

Every inmate at the Institute had a job they had to perform, to keep the prison running. Charlie worked in the noxite mines. Kallie worked in the cafeteria on Fridays, a job she despised, and Marcus swept the floors before class on Mondays.

I worked Sunday nights in the laundry room, washing all the gross sheets and uniforms. It wasn't a glamorous job, and it was boring, but at least I wasn't stuck down in the noxite mines working my ass off. I felt so bad for Charlie and Ez, being stuck down there.

Usually, there were other inmates down here with me, but one of them had gotten sick and the other had gotten hurt in a fight, so it was just me tonight. Guards lurked around, but they obviously had better things to do, as they'd checked in on me a few times during my shift and hadn't returned in hours.

I could totally ditch without being caught, but I'd get in trouble if this laundry wasn't done, so I finished up washing a round of blankets with a bored sigh. Only one more hour, and I'd be able to go back to my cell.

The only sound that could be heard was the sound of the washers, and the rain pounding on the roof of the Institute— then hushed voices as I heard someone whisper, "It didn't work! We need more power!"

That sure sounded like Professor Gael. The door to the laundry room had been propped open, and people were having a conversation outside.

Despite my better judgement, I pressed myself to the wall to listen in... like I was drawn to whatever secret discussion was happening.

"We can't keep continuing with these experiments. Eventually, parents will start to notice their children have gone missing," Professor Cusak replied with a shaking voice.

My jaw dropped. The Institute was stealing inmates to *experiment* on? Why? And who? Nobody I knew had gone missing— or maybe their absence hadn't been noticed.

"Do you think most of these wretched families care where their children have gone? Most are glad to be rid of the degenerates," Professor Mazur hissed.

All of them were angel professors. Interesting. I went to take a step closer, until a shiver traveled up my spine as I heard the Warden say, "Be patient. We merely need to find a demigod."

My stomach dropped to the floor, and my skin went ice-cold. A demigod? Why did they need one of those?

"Demigods are hard to find, my lord," Professor Cusak whimpered. "Who knows if they even still exist?"

My lord? I was listening so intently now, I was straining my ears.

"They exist," the Warden replied. "They're merely in hiding, and they're here. We'll force them out, and once we have them, our experiment will finally bear fruit."

"What do you want us to do, my lord?" Professor Mazur asked.

"I want a list of the most powerful students in your classes. We'll go through them one by one, determine which ones are the strongest, which ones could be demigods," the Warden replied. "We'll proceed from there."

"And what about their families? The last girl's mother was particularly difficult to convince," Gael said.

"Accidents happen all the time at the Institute," the Warden replied smugly. "And like Mazur said— most won't even care their children have gone missing. It's all about taking the right students at the right moment."

"Yes, my lord." There was the sound of flowing capes, like the three teachers were *bowing* to the Warden, before I heard their footsteps shuffle away.

I booked my ass to the other side of the laundry room as quickly as possible, to grab my stuff. I didn't even care if I got in trouble for skipping work. I had to get out of here.

As I gathered my bag, my mind spun a hundred miles an hour. There were so many angel professors at the school. Were they all working for the Warden? And why?

Experiments had been performed on inmates at the Institute for years. It was part of the prison's history. But when we'd come here, the people in charge had insisted that wasn't the case. These creepy *experiments* no longer happened here.

Apparently, we'd been lied to. I flung my bag over my shoulder, but stopped in my tracks when I saw the Warden standing in the doorway to the laundry room, which was now open. He had the worst smile on his face, taunting me.

He'd known I was listening in. It was almost like he *wanted* me to overhear.

Did the Warden know I was looking for Forevermore, and what the Elves had left behind? That seemed like my worst nightmare.

"You know better than to eavesdrop, Miss Mitoh," the Warden said. "It isn't polite."

My throat ran dry. "I heard nothing."

He raised an eyebrow. "I'm sure. And I'm also sure you're aware that you're very alone in here. With me, I might add."

I felt my lungs seize up in fear. I went to move past him, but froze at the wrong moment. The Warden grabbed my arm before I could leave. His touch made my entire body go rigid.

"Your research in your free time is quite interesting. Not all of us have the time to go looking for missing cities. I wish I did— a pastime of mine I had to give up for other hobbies, I'm afraid."

Oh *fuck*, he knew. He definitely knew. I felt my face drain of color as he leaned in. "But I'm sure you'll find it. If anyone could, it's certainly you."

"I'm not looking for anything," I spat. "Let me go."

I wanted to conjure Fire, or Water, to protect myself, but my magic refused to rise to my command. I was too frightened.

The Warden smirked. "Mister Wahkin's an interesting choice. Very domineering, wouldn't you agree?"

My throat tightened. This was *exactly* what I'd been worried about — people at the prison finding out I loved someone, and then hurting them to get what they wanted from me.

"We're not involved," I lied. I tried to take a step back, but the Warden held me in place.

"Oh, but you are, Miss Mitoh." The Warden gave me a sinister, gloating smile that made me want to slap it off. "Because you don't need someone who's going to set you loose, do you? You need someone who can control your darkest impulses and rein you in. That's what you want, isn't it? To be contained."

I gritted my teeth together as I growled my next words. "If Charlie's keeping me under control, you'd damn well better be ready when he lets me out of my cage."

I ripped my arm away from the Warden. He grinned, like he knew he'd broken me, before letting me walk away.

The Warden acted like Charlie had me on a leash. But maybe he did. Maybe I was just like Mad Dog... a psychopathic lunatic who was waiting for the wrong moment to go off.

I was so scared that I wanted to cry. *Demigods.* They wanted *demigods.* And by the sound of things, I knew that the inmates who were taken for these experiments didn't come back alive.

The Warden couldn't find out what Charlie, Kallie, Marcus and I were. Otherwise, we'd be used for these strange experiments... which I didn't even know the purpose of yet.

Although I wasn't sure he didn't already suspect us. The Warden was watching us closely, and if we weren't careful, we'd disappear.

To where, I didn't know— and I didn't want to find out.

FIFTEEN

"This is insane!" I seethed.

My hands fisted at my sides as I paced back and forth in the Lair. Ava had gathered us together before breakfast and told us we had to meet here— that it was urgent. But holy fucking shit, I hadn't expected this!

The ground quivered beneath me as I tried to keep my Earth magic together. Kallie had conjured couches with her illusion power, but I couldn't sit still after what Ava had told us.

"The Warden can't seriously think he'll get away with experimenting on students," I demanded.

"He *is* getting away with it." Ava sounded pissed, too, but not like I was. She'd had more time to process it since she'd overheard the Warden talking to our angel professors. Oberi nickered at Ava's side, like she agreed with her.

"How many professors do you think are in on it?" Marcus asked in a shaky tone. "All of them?"

"I doubt it," Ava said. "I can tell some of our professors actually care about us, but at the same time, I really don't know who we can trust."

"You know what we have to do," Kallie stated.

"Yes," Ava replied confidently. "We must avoid drawing attention to ourselves at all costs."

"*What?!*" Kallie snapped. "I meant we have to leave!"

"We can't," Ava stated firmly.

"You want to *stay?*" I balked. "You just said the Warden is experimenting on kids in search of demigods. That's *us*, pidge! We have to get as far away from here as we can, before they find out what we are."

Ava huffed. "And how do you expect to do that? Marcus and Kallie tried breaking out last semester, and got caught. No one's *ever* broken out of the Institute. The Darke Games was our only way out, and we threw that away."

"There *has* to be a way out," I insisted. "What about your dad? He's the one who sent us here. Surely he can get us out."

"I talked to him already. I called him last night as soon as I left the laundry room— cost me a fortune, too." She huffed.

"He must have an idea," I insisted. *No way* was he going to let Ava stay here after he found out about this.

"He's working on it," she said in a whimper.

"*Working on it?!*" My nostrils flared. "That's not good enough. The man is a chief of the Hawkei tribe, for fuck's sake. What is there to work on?"

"Charlie, please sit down," Ava begged. "I felt the same way you did when I heard the Warden, but Daddy helped me see things rationally."

For the ancestors' sake, how could Ava see *anything* rationally right now? It's like we'd totally reversed our roles in the relationship. Last semester, *I'd* been the one to demand we play along, but that was only to keep her safe.

Now she was in danger— more than I could ever imagine.

I forced my pride downward and plopped into one of the couches Kallie had conjured. I knew it'd disappear as soon as we left the Lair, but it was the only thing that felt solid under me right now.

"Fine, I'll bite," I said. "What did your father say?"

"Daddy would get us out in a heartbeat if he could, but he no longer has any control over our sentence," Ava explained. "As inmates, we belong to the United Supernatural Union now, and without proof of what I overheard, Daddy's hands are tied. Even *he* can't overrule international law. But he believes me, and he's going to do everything he can to find proof of the experiments and get us out of here. *All* of us, because ancestors know I'm not leaving Kallie or Marcus behind."

Marcus cleared his throat, like he'd gotten a little choked up.

"We should tell everyone else's parents, too," Ava suggested. "Kallie's dad is the king of Malovia, and Marcus' mom is a detective. They can help."

"No way," Marcus said immediately. "I'd bet *anything* the Warden has the phone lines tapped. I won't put my family at risk by contacting them. Chances are, you've already put us in danger by telling your dad."

"I was careful with my words," Ava assured us. "I didn't tell him anything the Warden doesn't already know— didn't mention demigods or anything. Daddy gave me strict instructions that until he finds proof, I can't stir the pot. We have to stay put until my parents figure out how to prove what the Warden is doing here, so they can get us out."

"I'm not talking to my dad," Kallie said with a huff. "I can get out by myself, without *his* help."

"Kallie, this is more important than a personal grudge with your family," I growled. Having a king on our side would sure help us right now, but Kallie refused to talk to him.

"We can't stay put!" Kallie burst. "That puts us at risk."

"If we try to break out, we'll be caught!" Ava argued. "*That* puts us at risk even more. Think about it. Which kids are disappearing? Which ones don't have family who care enough to ask where they've gone?"

It hit me immediately. "The kids in Cellblock 9."

"Exactly," Ava stated. "I bet there *is* no Cellblock 9. It must be a code for the experiments."

I thought of all the people I'd seen being dragged away to Cellblock 9, never to be heard of again. I should've felt bad for getting Digger sent there, but I didn't— not after the way he treated Ava.

"If we get caught trying to escape, they'll take us straight to Cellblock 9, and experiment on us," Ava pointed out. "It's too risky."

"Fuck, you're right," Marcus groaned.

"Whatever experiments they're doing there will expose us as demigods," Ava added.

Marcus scoffed and joked, "I guess I'm safe then."

The three of us gave a collective sigh. Even Rishi, who sat in Marcus' lap, growled.

"You know that's a lie, man," I said.

"I admit I did some stuff above my pay grade during the Darke Games, but I'm not as powerful as any of you," Marcus argued. "I did that stuff to survive. I can't replicate it now."

"You're only shit at magic because you think you are," Kallie told him, obviously annoyed he didn't see his own potential.

"You have power from all five of your coven's Casts," Ava reminded Marcus. "Of *course* you're a demigod. The Warden probably suspects it, too."

"I wouldn't be surprised if that's why you ended up here in the first place," I added.

"I ended up here because—" Marcus started, but I cut him off.

"We all know the story," I said. "We also know it was an accident, and that it happened within your own coven. They could've sentenced you within their own criminal justice system, but they didn't. They sent you *here*, because they're afraid of you and wanted you far away from Octavia Falls. I bet the Warden wanted you here, after he learned what you did."

"It's not even a question," Ava said. "The Warden told me during the Villain's Ball that he's watching us. He already suspects something after our performance in the Darke Games. The last thing we want to do is confirm his suspicions. That means no showing off in class, too."

Marcus gulped. "What do you think he wants a demigod for?"

"He practically told me he's looking for Forevermore," Ava said. "We know the portal was made for demigods. He needs one to lead him to the city."

"And there's *nothing* we can do?" Kallie asked.

"I told you, my dad's working on it, but I have no idea how long it'll take him to find proof," Ava replied. "The Warden is *very* smart. All we can do is stay alive until Daddy figures something out, or until our sentence is up."

"This is fucked up," Kallie huffed.

My hands curled into fists. "You can say that again."

"I'm with Ava," Marcus piped up. "I want to stay here, where it's safer."

"Of course you do, you big chicken," Kallie grumbled.

Marcus sighed. "Unfortunately, if we don't want to draw any suspicion to ourselves, Kallie and I have to get to class," he said. "We don't want an infraction for skipping."

Class was the last thing on my mind. I couldn't give a damn about school right now, not when our necks were on the line.

"Ugh, you're right. Fuck the rules." Kallie stomped her foot and got to her feet, but she started toward the entrance to the Lair anyway. The sound of Marcus' footsteps followed behind her, and Rishi meowed lightly.

Before they left, Kallie turned back to add, "Those illusions aren't going to last all day."

I got to my feet a moment before Kallie's illusion vanished. I felt for the chair I'd just been sitting in, but it was gone. The sounds of Kallie's angry curses and Marcus' loud footsteps faded as they left for class.

I turned to Ava, still fuming. "What does Oberi think of this?"

I heard the light bristle of Ava's fingers running through Oberi's mane. "She's on my side."

"How can you be so sure?"

"I just do. Oberi always does whatever's going to keep us safe."

I blew a breath. "You think *this* is going to keep you safe, pidge? You're a freaking demigod. The Warden wants you. The Institute is the *last* place you should be!"

"You don't think I know that?!" she snapped. "It's not like I *want* to stay. I'm fucking *scared*, Charlie. I thought you would understand."

"You think I don't understand what it's like to be scared? I've known nothing but fear my whole life, and I know when to cower and when to fucking run."

"I'm telling you, there's nowhere *to* run," she insisted.

"That's not what you said last semester," I reminded her. "You're not even entertaining the idea of breaking out. Maybe if you gave it a chance, we could come up with a plan. You said it yourself that we're demigods. The Institute wasn't built for people like us. I bet it can't hold us if we really try."

"Maybe not, but we haven't even scratched the surface of our powers," Ava pointed out. "We can't harness our demigod abilities to break out if we don't know how to use them."

She reached out for me, but I yanked away. That seemed to piss her off, and her tone became sour. "You don't seem to understand that getting caught trying to escape is worse than staying."

"I *do* understand," I insisted. "You don't understand what *I'm* saying."

"I don't get you!" she cried. "Last semester, you were willing to bend over and get fucked in the ass by the school for no good reason. Now that I agree with you, you're flipping sides on wanting to leave."

"Things have changed," I insisted.

"What do you mean? The prophecy?" Ava demanded.

I blew a breath. "Screw the prophecy. All I care about is keeping you safe— and that means getting you far away from the Warden. We're smarter than he is. We don't *have* to get caught, if we're careful."

"And what if we're not?" she demanded. "What if we're not careful enough?"

"Exactly!" I fumed. "What if we're not good enough at hiding our powers? What if one of us lashes out while we live out our sentence?"

Hell, all I wanted was to get Ava as far away from here as possible. Playing it cool simply wasn't an option. I had to hit her where it hurt, for her to see the danger she was in.

I gritted my teeth before delivering the blow. "What if you have another episode and can't control your powers? What then?"

That royally pissed her off. "Don't you *dare* use my diagnosis against me!"

Ava shoved me, and I stumbled back a step. Oberi shook her head so fast that embers from her mane landed on my skin. They were only hot for a second before they fizzled out.

"You promised to help me with the prophecy!" she cried. "Where in *your* scenario does that fit in? Because we sure as hell aren't breaking out just to stay on Darke Island, where the Warden will hunt us down for sure."

"The prophecy isn't worth your life!" I yelled.

Ava drew shallow, wavered breaths. "So you'll break your promise?"

"I'll break my promise to save you, yes," I growled. "That's something you can *always* count on."

"I can't count on anything if you're always breaking promises!" Ava snapped.

I pressed the heel of my hand to my forehead, as a headache started to form. "Ancestors, pidge! Why can't you see that all I want to do is save you?!"

"Maybe I don't *need* you to save me!"

"*Bullshit*! Go suck a dick, Ava!"

I whirled around to make a dramatic exit. I made it a step away from the cave entrance when Ava grabbed my wrist and spun me back around. Her hot, angry breath swept across my collar bone, and her fingers fumbled with the button on my pants.

I was so shocked that I didn't push her away. She undid the button, and my pants loosened around my hips.

"Uh... what are you doing?" I demanded.

Ava placed her hands firmly on my shoulders and shoved me back a step, until my back was pressed against the stone wall. She dropped to her knees. "Exactly what you told me to do, you prick."

My whole body shivered as her warm breath seeped through the layers of fabric between us. Hell, she wanted to *blow me* right here— in the middle of our argument?! Oberi was *right there—*

I heard Oberi slip through the entrance to the Lair, as if giving us privacy. She was *encouraging* this.

Ava reached up for my waistband. She paused momentarily, then impatiently asked, "Or did you want me to stop?"

My dick became rock hard, and my voice quivered. "Well... I *did* ask for it."

There was nothing romantic about it. Ava and I were both pissed, but hell... that made it that much *better*. The raw passion was unmatched as she yanked my pants down to my ankles and wrapped her fingers around the base of my cock. She didn't hesitate a moment after gaining my consent.

She slipped the tip of my cock into her mouth. Her warm tongue — blazing with the anger of her Fire— roamed over me. Her lips seemed to work in perfect sync with her hand, pumping faster and faster. She skimmed her teeth against me, and I squirmed under her touch.

She pulled back for a mere moment. Even though we were pissed at each other, she still cared enough to make sure I was okay. Before she could say anything, I shoved my fingers into her hair and guided her lips back to my dick. She pulled it into her mouth again and moaned.

Everything we'd been fighting about fell from my mind. All that seemed to matter was this moment. All I could process was her soft mouth and her fingers on me. I began to sway on my feet as my blood rushed to my dick. A primal instinct to please her— and to be pleased *by* her— overcame me.

My head lolled backward into the cool stone of the wall. I shoved my fingers deeper into her hair and thrust upward with my hips. She opened her mouth wider, and I went in deeper. My moans mingled with Ava's and echoed off the walls of the Lair in a beautiful symphony.

I pulled on the strands of her hair. She must've liked it, because she increased her speed as my dick moved in and out of her mouth. Fuck, how it felt to be inside of her— there simply weren't words for such a pleasure.

"I love you, pidge," I gasped. "I hate you, but I fucking *love* you."

"Mm..." she moaned as she sucked hard on the tip. She pulled it out of her mouth for a moment to say, "I hate you, too."

Then she was on me again, pumping me until I couldn't take it any longer. Tingles spread throughout my body as if my skin had turned to sunlight, until the glorious sensation burst through my cock.

She rolled her tongue over me again and again as I emptied into her. She sucked one last time, before audibly swallowing.

I slumped against the wall of the Lair, my head spinning. I barely had half a mind to pull my pants back on, but I managed. I sank to the ground and wrapped an arm around Ava's shoulder. She sat next to me and leaned against my chest, listening to my heart beat. The fight we'd just had seemed like a distant memory as we melted together.

"That was so hot," Ava said dreamily, like she was riding the same high I was.

I expected her to climb on top of me and ask for something in return, but she simply snuggled close. It took me a few moments to realize she wasn't going to move. I didn't know why I thought it so strange, but then it hit me.

Ava had done this for *me*. Never before had anyone considered whether *I* enjoyed it. And that made it all the more special, because for the first time in my life, someone actually cared about my pleasure, not just their own. Ava wanted to make me feel good, just to show me she loved me.

Hell if that didn't make a tough guy like me crumble inside.

"Holy fuck, pidge," I said once I'd caught my breath. "What made you want to do that?"

She snickered as she cuddled in closer. "You told me to suck a dick. I got horny."

I kissed the top of her head and inhaled her delicious scent. "Mm... I suppose I should say stuff like that more often."

"You should," she teased. "I've been wanting to do that for a while now."

"You seemed to know what you were doing," I remarked.

She shrugged. "Ivy gave me some tips."

I smirked. "That was one hell of a first time."

"I tend to be *very* good when I put my mind to something," she stated sternly, as if daring me to question what she was capable of.

I couldn't, because I knew my pidge far too well. Whatever Ava wanted, she got. She already had my soul. I knew then that if I wanted to protect her, I had to follow her to the end.

I worried it'd be straight to the Warden.

I COULDN'T STOP THINKING about what had happened the rest of the day. Ava must've been feeling pretty damn good about it, too, because Ezekiel mentioned her mood shift the following day in the mines.

"Has my sister been acting weird lately?" he asked.

We stood in a narrow tunnel. It was a new section of the noxite mines— only discovered this semester, according to our professor. Sound echoed down the tunnel for what seemed like a mile, and I figured it must've formed naturally. Only a couple of us had been assigned down here— me, Ez, and Chancey on a team, as well as another mining team twenty yards down. Ez had been working outside the mines for weeks now, but they'd assigned him down here when they discovered the new tunnel. Oberi was with Ava today.

"No, why?" I said innocently. I brought my ax down onto the rock, and the impact sent vibrations up the handle. Pieces of rock crumbled from the wall and knocked against each other. A small piece rolled over my foot.

"I know how she gets," Ez said. "She's on new meds, and it's important they help balance her mood. If she's riding a high one week, I know she's about to crash the next."

"She's okay," I assured him.

Chancey stepped up behind me to haul pieces of rock into a cart. "Yeah, there's only one thing Ava-Marie is riding, and it's Charlie."

Ez groaned. "Don't say stuff like that."

"Why not?" I teased with a huge smile on my face. "He's not wrong."

"I asked about her mood, not her sex life," Ez complained. "I'm her brother. I don't want to hear about shit like that."

"If Chancey's around, *everyone's* sex life is on the table," I cracked.

Chancey laughed along. "If there's a table around, *my* sex life is on it."

"Fair enough," I said. "But seriously, don't let me hear you talking about Ava's sex life. You won't be able to breathe long enough to keep laughing about it."

Chancey bent down to pick up another rock. "Not down here in the mines, baby. Try your Air magic on me. I dare you."

"Back to work!" a guard shouted down the narrow tunnel.

I gripped my ax tighter and turned back to the wall. "Another day, perhaps."

"Told ya you couldn't," Chancey mumbled. His cart must've been full, because he walked off, the wheels squealing as he went.

Ez's ax clanged against the wall. "I thought Chancey wasn't taking bets anymore."

"Technically, that wasn't a bet," I pointed out. "It was a dare. I'd take it if the guards weren't around."

Ez scoffed as he swung his ax again. "No point in humiliating your-self. No one can use their magic with this much noxite around."

"Right," I agreed flatly. I didn't get why everyone always said that. Sure, magic was a hell of a lot weaker down here in the mines, but it wasn't impossible to use.

Unless... it was just me.

I was a demigod after all, or so I'd been told—

I snapped out of my thoughts as a rumbling sensation trembled the ground beneath me, vibrating through my Earth magic. The hairs on the back of my neck stood up, and I heard a crack above us. Ez groaned in the way he always did when he was about to swing his ax. One more blow, and this tunnel was done for.

"Ez, no!" I shouted, but it was too late.

His ax clanged against the side of the tunnel, and the structural integrity faltered. I reacted without thinking about it. A blast of Air shot out of my hands, sending the two of us flying apart from each other. The deafening sound of rock falling over rock filled the tunnel as I flew back-ward, and I felt the air in the tunnel shift, then become blocked.

I landed flat on my back. Dirt rained down on my face and into my eyes, burning them. I inhaled a deep breath and coughed.

"Charlie! Charlie!"

Several voices called my name, but they sounded muffled and far off.

"Fuck, he's dead!"

I finally caught my breath and shouted, "I'm fine! Ez, you all right?"

"We're okay!" he called back.

My shoulders sagged in relief. One split-second had made all the difference.

"Fuck, that was close!" Chancey cried. "Can you get through?"

I got to my feet, but my knees shook. I'd used up most of my energy in the blast of Air that had shot Ez back from the cave-in. The noxite in the mines drew everything else out of me.

I stumbled forward, feeling out in front of me. My hands landed on sharp rocks, most of them bigger than my head. Panic set in as I felt upward, moving higher and higher until I couldn't reach any further. My head spun as I inhaled dust. I tried to work my magic to find holes in the rock, but my powers were useless.

So much for being a demigod. There was no way in hell I was moving this rock with all the noxite inside of it.

"I can't find a way through," I called through the barrier. "Do you see anything?"

"We don't see nothing!"

I listened carefully to Chancey's reply, in case the sound came through any spaces large enough to crawl through, but it was completely muffled.

I was trapped.

I tried to think fast for a solution, but without my magic, I felt disoriented. "Any chance we can move the rock?"

"There's so much," Ez said. "It could take days!"

"Then you best get started," a guard growled at them.

I heard rocks tumbling, and Ez swore. He launched into a coughing fit, and my guts sank. He'd already worked too hard today. The dust billowing through the cave surely wasn't helping his condition. I knew the guards would push him beyond his limits.

"Guys, no!" I insisted. "It's not safe. This whole thing could come down on you. By the time you get through, I could've starved to death."

"No," Chancey argued. "We're going to get you out of there."

"I'll find another way out. This tunnel has to go somewhere."

"You don't know what's down there!" Ez protested. "You can't navigate unknown tunnels on your own!"

"Yes, I can. I'm blind. I navigate in the dark all the time. Take it easy, Ez. I'll get out."

I wasn't going to let him work himself to death for me, so I turned and started down the tunnel. The sound of Chancey's protests followed me, but they were so muffled that they faded quickly.

These mines were a maze of tunnels. There was more than one way out of this one. I just knew it.

I placed my hands on the tunnel wall to guide me forward. I kept telling myself the way out was only ten more paces away. If I went back now, I'd miss the exit straight ahead. But again and again, the ten paces came, and no exit appeared.

My head started to clear the longer I walked. The air chilled, and the effect of the noxite seemed to wear off. I must've been traveling deeper into the earth, but my magic wasn't back at full-force for me to feel how deep underground I was.

I swallowed down any panic I felt and focused only on the thought of getting out of here— back to Oberi, and back to Ava. It kept me moving forward.

I felt like I'd been walking for an hour before my magic came back to me. I could feel the air around me with more precision, though all I sensed was the tunnel ahead— no side tunnels that might lead me back to the main entrance.

"Maybe I'll find an exit far away from the Institute," I said to myself, mostly to help keep myself sane. "Maybe it'll be our way to escape."

"Hello?" a male voice called from further down the tunnel. Someone had found a way around! They'd come to rescue me!

My heart skipped a beat. "Hello? Yes! It's me, Charlie! Who's there?"

Footsteps approached and slowed beside me. The air in front of me warmed my arm, as if the person was carrying a lantern lit by a flame.

"Charlie?" the person asked. I couldn't place their voice, but there were tons of students who worked in the mines. I didn't know them all personally. He sounded young— around my age— so I knew it wasn't a professor.

"How close are we to the surface?" I asked. "I feel like I've been walking forever."

"You're a long way from the main entrance," the stranger replied. He had a bit of an accent I couldn't place.

"That's what happens when a cave-in traps you down here," I chuckled, but nausea swirled in my gut. I was just relieved to hear another voice. "How'd you get this far down? There must be a connecting tunnel nearby."

"A connecting tunnel to the surface?" he said slowly, as if choosing his words carefully.

"That's where everyone's waiting for us, isn't it?" I asked.

He cleared his throat. "Absolutely. Let's get you back up there."

"Do we know each other?" I asked, since I was curious. "Sorry, I'm not always great with voices."

"Oh, we haven't met," he said kindly. "Call me Eddie."

I chuckled nervously. "I know a guy named Eddie— Edwin, actually. Kicked his ass in these mines a few months back, actually."

Eddie laughed. "Well, I can assure you, it wasn't me. Would you like me to guide you?"

It was awfully nice of him to ask. Being blind, people often assumed I wanted them to hold my hand, but I just wanted to be asked first.

"Yes, thank you." I reached out, and he took my arm to help me through the tunnels.

"What do you know about these mines, Charlie?" Eddie asked. I figured it was just to make small talk.

"I know they're filled with noxite. That's about it. Hence, why I got lost. You know much about them?"

Eddie chuckled under his breath. "A bit."

"You've been down here a long time, huh?" I asked. He didn't sound frightened at all, as if he'd grown comfortable with the cave system. He must've been a senior at the Institute, which was why we'd never met.

"Yeah, just a while," Eddie said.

It wasn't long before Eddie turned down another tunnel. I wasn't sure I'd have found it by myself, to be honest. The entrance was pretty small, but we both fit.

Eddie and I made small talk, so the walk didn't seem as long. He mostly asked me about which classes I was taking at the Institute. I told him that I'd been sentenced because my girlfriend stole a boat. He thought that was ironic and a little hilarious.

"Almost there, Charlie," Eddie said. "See? I told you it wouldn't take long."

"I guess not." I actually really liked talking to Eddie. He wasn't like the other kids at the Institute. He was really nice.

The sun touched my skin as we exited the caves, and Eddie let go of my arm. "The bus is just ahead. Be careful in the mines, Charlie. I don't want to have to rescue you again."

I laughed. "Not unless there's another cave-in. Thanks for helping me out."

"No problem," Eddie said kindly. "I suspect I'll see you around."

The sound of a diesel engine starting up met my ears, followed by angered voices.

"He's still down there!" Ez shouted.

"We can't leave without him!" Chancey demanded.

"Shit, those are my friends," I told Eddie. "Come on."

I started hurrying toward the sound of the bus. "It's okay, guys! I'm here!"

Ez gasped. "Ancestors, Charlie! I can't believe you're back. They had us moving rocks for hours!"

I could hear it in Ez's shallow breaths that he'd overworked himself. Fuck the guards. That's why I'd left the cave-in site in the first place.

"We carved out a crawl space, but you were gone," Chancey explained. "They ordered us back to the bus."

"And you'll get on it. Now!" one of the guards growled.

Someone grabbed me by the collar and shoved me forward. "Now that you're back, we can return to the Institute."

Hell, they'd been searching for me for hours and didn't give a damn that I was alive. All they cared about was protocol.

The guards shoved us onto the bus, and the doors squeaked shut. I ended up in a seat next to Ez. His arm touched mine. I noticed he was really sweaty.

"How'd you get out?" he asked in a low whisper.

"Eddie helped me out," I told them.

"I did not!" a growl came from across the aisle.

"Not you, dipshit!" I snapped at Edwin. "The *other* Eddie."

"Um... what other Eddie?" Chancey asked. "No one else was down in the mines, Charlie. We've all been at the cave-in this whole time."

I scrunched up my brow. "But he..."

Technically, Eddie had never *said* he was from the Institute. He never said he wasn't, either, and I had assumed. Maybe he lived in Shade Hills.

Why was he down there in the first place, then?

"Never mind," I said.

Chancey clapped me on the shoulder. "Well, you're back now, and that's all that matters. You still up for your fight against Deuce tonight?"

My stomach dropped. Hell, that was tonight. I'd almost forgotten about it. This was the biggest fight of the semester— the club's two best fighters pitted against one another. I hadn't lost a fight— and neither had Deuce. I couldn't miss it.

I was fatigued and dehydrated, but I had no choice. "Yeah, I'm gonna fight."

THE CROWD CHEERED WILDLY from outside the locker room. I'd spent the better part of the afternoon trying to pump up my strength after my mishap in the mines. I was feeling much better after I ate, but nerves knotted in my stomach. I'd never let Chancey see it, though.

"That's it," he encouraged as I punched the air with my fists. "Work up that anger. You've got this. Deuce is going down."

"No fucking kidding," I said. Deuce was a freaking asshole, on par with Mad Dog. He'd messed with the Villain's Club one too many times. I'd take pride in knocking him out and sending him to the medical tent.

So why was I so nervous about this fight?

"You're gonna have to swing faster than that, Bandit," Chancey said. "You're going up against a vampire."

"Yeah," I grumbled. "You don't have to remind me."

I'd won all of my fights so far, but I hadn't been up against a vampire yet. The one time I'd kicked a vampire's ass, I'd used my Air magic— when I'd sent Mad Dog flying into the lake my first week here. But I wasn't allowed to use my powers in the ring. It was more entertaining for the guards to witness the hand-to-hand brawls that drew blood.

But I'd never been paired with a vampire. The bet was too easy to make. With supernatural strength and speed, I'd easily be crushed. I had no doubt all bets were on Deuce.

No. I couldn't think that way. Captain pit me against Deuce for a reason. He must've believed I had at least a *chance* at beating him. Otherwise, the show wasn't worth it.

"Bandit!" Captain called into the locker room. "You're up!"

"You've got this," Chancey encouraged. "I've seen you take down every other supernatural out there. You can beat a vampire."

I swallowed. I *had* beat shifters, who also had enhanced strength, and were just as strong as vampires. I could beat Deuce, but I had to be smart about it.

I cracked my knuckles. "You're right. He's going down. I hope you bet on me."

Chancey laughed loudly. "Oh, I bet all right."

I let Chancey's comment slide as I followed Captain out of the locker room. The sound of the roaring crowd filled my ears as I walked toward the ring. I lifted my hands in the air and joined in on their cheers.

"*Blind Bandit! Blind Bandit!*" a section of the crowd chanted.

I yanked a blindfold from where I'd tucked it into my waistband. I lifted it above my head and waved it around. The crowd loved it. They went fucking nuts, until my ears rang.

Captain stopped me next to the ring, and I spun around, showing off the blindfold to the crowd. I put on a show about tying it over my eyes. It made no difference to me, but they loved the act.

"Ladies and gentlemen, shifters and sorceresses, witches and warlocks, mermaids and mermen..." an announcer called over the speaker. "The event you've all been waiting for. The fight of the night! Welcome to the ring your favorite resident vampire— Deuce!"

The crowd cheered loudly, and I heard Deuce's heavy footsteps as he climbed into the ring.

"Does this vampire have what it takes to defeat our undefeated champion? Well, tonight you'll find out. Give it up for the Blind Bandit!"

Screams filled the room and echoed off the walls as I stepped into the ring. I bounced on my toes and did my best to block out the noise. I honed in my senses on Deuce— using the sound of his footsteps to determine his position in the ring, and my Air magic to sense the quick movement of his fists.

A bell sounded, and the fight was on. Deuce came at me instantly, not wasting a second. I was prepared for a quick attack and threw my fist out before he started moving. He was moving so fast that his chest slammed into my knuckles. Pain radiated up my arm. It hurt like hell, but I didn't even wince. I was so pumped for this fight that it almost felt *good.*

Deuce stumbled back a step, obviously startled by my quick reaction. He coughed a few times, then snarled, "If you think you can beat me, you're delusional, Wahkin."

I chuckled. "The name's Blind Bandit. Stop talking and fight."

Air swept by Deuce, and I knew instantly that a fist was coming my way. I threw up an arm to block him, but he moved faster than me. Before I could block him, his fist slammed into my cheek. I stumbled sideways and was very alert to the fact that the crowd was booing. It took me a second to right myself, and I wondered why Deuce wasn't initiating a second attack. His footsteps moved around the ring deliberately as we began to circle one another. He was making a show of it.

"You're weak, Wahkin," Deuce taunted. "I'm going to rip you apart."

"What are you waiting for?"

I was sick of the trash talk. I wanted to fight. I wanted to *beat him.*

Deuce came at me, and I spun out of the way. My plan was to use his speed and strength against him. As he swept past me, I thrust my hands into his back and sent him stumbling forward into the ropes surrounding the ring. They *twanged* as his body ricocheted back at me. I went to grab him, but he recovered quickly and ducked out of my reach.

His footsteps moved quicker as he circled me, and his breathing rate increased. It was obvious I'd embarrassed him by dodging his attack. Good. If I could throw him off his game, I had a chance at winning.

Deuce jumped for me. I wasn't fast enough, and his foot sank into my gut. I gasped for breath, but I didn't get another inhale before his foot connected with my abdomen again. On the third kick, I grabbed for his foot, but he was so fast that I couldn't get my hands around it.

I quickly calculated in my head that I had two options. I could run away, or engage. There was a reason I was undefeated, and that was because I never ran away.

I reached for Deuce again and caught his leg before it could sink into my gut. A wild rage surged through me as I struggled for breath. Deuce paused for a second, like he was shocked I managed to catch him. I yanked downward. The force would've sent anyone else spiraling to their ass, but Deuce didn't move an inch.

He let out a deep belly laugh. At this point, he found it humorous.

He was humiliating me in front of everyone. I wasn't about to lose to this jerk.

Rage built up inside of me, and a sensation that felt like Ava's Fire swept through my hands and up my arms. I thought it might be magic swelling with my anger, so I quickly pushed it aside before I could be disqualified.

As Deuce continued laughing, I drew my hand back. Gathering up all the strength I could muster, I thrust my palm straight into his chest. Air swept by me so fast, I could only assume I'd knocked him off his feet. A *thud* sounded from the other end of the ring as he landed hard on his back. The crowd gasped.

Holy fuck. I didn't know how I'd done that. It was like I'd had supernatural strength *myself*. I must've accidentally accelerated the blow with my Air magic without realizing it.

... But if that was true, why hadn't it felt like it always did?

"*Blind Bandit! Blind Bandit!*" the crowd cheered.

Holy hell. They wanted *me*. I could actually win this thing.

Deuce jumped to his feet so fast the ring shook beneath my feet. "I'm done playing," he growled. It was clear he was *pissed* the crowd had taken my side. "You're dead, Wahkin."

I threw my hands upward to block the blow that I knew was coming, but I wasn't fast enough. Deuce jumped on top of me, and we crashed to the ground. Once he was on top of me, I put my fists up to block, but there was no hope. I was exhausted from getting out of the cave-in earlier, and so, he had the advantage.

His heavy fists landed on my face, and pain shot out through my cheek. Blow after blow came, until I heard the crunch of bone and my ears rang. His vampire speed was too much for me to deal with. It was like I was fighting in slow motion, and he was on fast-forward. One hit landed as soon as another left my cheek.

I slipped into unconsciousness for a moment. When I came back, I was barely hanging on. I thought I heard a whistle blow, but I couldn't be sure. All I was certain of was the fists landing harshly on my face, and the spittle flying from his mouth as Deuce spat offensive names at me.

"Stop!" Captain screamed from somewhere in the distance. I was so disoriented that I couldn't tell where his voice was coming from. "Cut it out! You've already won!"

The words sent an icy chill over my entire form as the crowd groaned in disappointment. I almost didn't even care that I was getting the shit kicked out of me. All I knew was that I'd lost.

Deuce was dragged off of me. Captain raised his fist into the air, and my mouth poured blood. I was barely aware of Chancey dragging me out of the ring, my body leaving a bloody smear on the ground, but it hardly mattered.

I'd gotten my ass kicked. If I couldn't stand up to a vampire, I couldn't fight the Warden— because even if we got away, he'd find us.

The horrifying reality hit me. If I lost a fight in the ring, then I could lose a fight in the real world, where it counted.

I could lose Ava.

Whether we stayed at the Institute or not didn't matter, because we were totally fucked.

ava-marie

SIXTEEN

I felt something was wrong with Charlie the minute I awoke on Tuesday morning.

I was a *sleep-in-until-noon* kind of person, but once the lock on my cell clicked open at six a.m., I was up. Oberi lay at the edge of my bed, quivering. The husky whimpered, indicating something was very wrong.

"Fuck." I started throwing clothes on. Oberi scratched at the door, letting out loud whines. I tried mentally checking in with Charlie, but he didn't give any response, and ancestors, it scared me.

"Charlie?" I bolted to his cell and flung open the door, but he wasn't in there. It didn't look like he'd been here all night.

My heart dropped. The fight club. Oberi barked and began leading the way down the hall. I wasn't sure where he was going, but I trusted that he would lead me to Charlie.

I couldn't stop thinking about all the horrible possibilities. He wasn't dead— that much I was almost certain of— but he was badly hurt.

Oberi led me to the angel cellblock. I started shoving people aside who got in my way. Cries of *savage* rang out, but I didn't even hear them. Oberi put his paw on a cell door. Outside of it was a thin trail of blood.

My guts tumbled as I pushed open the door. I gasped, and my hand flew over my mouth as I witnessed the scene. I stumbled backward so hard, I nearly fell over. Chancey looked up and gave me an apologetic glance, but no *sorry* could make up for this.

Charlie sat in Chancey's desk chair. I wouldn't have been able to recognize him if it wasn't for our bond, because his face was so badly beaten. His entire face was massed with purple bruises, and he had two black eyes, both of which were swollen shut. There were so many cuts on his face from where the skin had split open, it looked like someone had taken a knife and cut into it. His nose was broken, and red streaked from his face and all the way down his neck. His head lolled, like he was still trying to come around.

Chancey was trying to dot the blood away with a cloth, but I shoved him out of the way. I checked Charlie's mouth and found teeth missing. Blood was still pooling against his tongue.

"Who the fuck did this?!" I seethed. At the sight of Charlie beaten like that, I was ready to kill.

"Deuce. He whacked him so hard he almost got his sight back," Chancey replied.

"Shut the hell up, Chancey," Charlie replied in a slur. He tried to push him away, and failed. He was barely conscious.

"Why'd you bring him back here, instead of the medical tent beside the ring?" I hissed. "Don't you have people who'll heal the fighters?"

Chancey blinked slowly. "If they're too badly roughed up— some guys they don't see the point in trying to help, ya know? They woulda just taken him out back."

I felt bile rise in my throat at the thought of the guards dumping Charlie somewhere in the back of the prison, leaving him for dead. "He looks like shit."

"He'll pull through," Chancey said nervously.

"He has a fucking concussion!" I shouted. "He needs to go to the infirmary!"

"I did what I could to clean him up, but if we take him to the nurses, they're gonna ask questions," Chancey insisted.

"I couldn't fucking give a damn. Help me." I hauled one of Charlie's arms over my shoulders, and Chancey took the other. We walked Charlie to the infirmary, but it was more like dragging him. People whispered and looked our way, pointing at the blood trail Charlie left on the floor.

Lady Helga immediately stopped what she was doing once she saw Charlie dangling between the two of us. She and a couple of other nurses hurried over with a gurney. "Lay him here, please."

We put Charlie on the gurney. His fingers slipped from my hand as he was wheeled away, and it felt like the action ripped my arm from its socket.

"Will he be okay?" I asked.

"We'll take good care of him, Miss Mitoh. We promise."

Lady Helga hurried off to take Charlie to a private room— which I knew was bad. The infirmary was set up with a bunch of single beds tucked close together, with little privacy. If Charlie was getting his own recovery space, it meant Deuce had really hurt him.

Oberi growled and snapped his jaws beside me, feeling my rage. My knuckles cracked as I bunched them into fists, and I swear I saw red.

"Ava," Chancey started, like he could already read my mind.

"Don't," I snapped, cutting him off. "I swear to the ancestors, Chancey, I'll stick your wings up your ass and send you crawling back to whatever hell hole you came from. Don't interfere."

I whirled on my heel and marched down the hallway with Oberi beside me. Chancey didn't stop me, but ran after me anyway.

All the advice Daddy had given me about lying low completely flew out of my mind as I ran through the prison, looking for Deuce. It was still early morning, so there weren't a lot of people up, but I wasn't going to quit until I found him.

Then I heard a mocking laugh emit from the Villain's Den, and I pivoted on my heel, finding my prey.

Marcus and Kallie were on the other side of the room, playing a foosball game before breakfast. They noticed me striding toward Deuce and stopped their game. They moved to back me up, though I don't think either of them were stupid enough to try and stop me. Oberi changed into a Fire unicorn, her fiery mane exploding into bright red flames as we drew closer.

Deuce leaned against one of the arcade games with his vampire buddies. I noticed Charlie had gotten in a few good hits on him before Deuce had beaten his ass.

I didn't care that Deuce was a gang leader, that he was a super strong and super fast vampire, or that he'd just beaten the hell out of my boyfriend. All I cared about was delivering a message. I launched myself on him and put my hands around his neck. Flames began licking around my fingers as I slammed Deuce into the wall, and his eyes widened as he felt the intensity of my heat creeping up his stone-hard skin.

"You'd better take your hands off me, psycho!" Deuce snarled.

"You or anyone else tries to stop me, I'll ignite your body into flames!" I screamed. I increased the intensity of my Fire until it was rippling up and down my arms, and all along Deuce's body. Deuce yelped. His gang held back, not sure of what to do. Oberi pounded her hoof into the floor and lowered her horn, like she was ready to drive it through Deuce's heart like a wooden stake.

"You got a lot of nerve, coming after a vampire who just turned Wahkin's face into mush," Deuce seethed.

"Yeah, but you know what? I've got the one thing vampires are afraid of. *Fire*, jackass," I growled. "And I will burn you into fucking oblivion if you touch Charlie again, do you understand?"

His gang members posed around him, ready to move on his say-so. Deuce's eyes roamed the room and locked on my friends.

He didn't want to take on all of us at once, so Deuce simply sneered, "Your boyfriend lost the fight. It's just business. That's all there is to it."

"Ava, you're drawing attention," Marcus said nervously. "Let him go."

Reality, and the risk I was taking, suddenly took over my rampaging emotions. I had the good sense to stop what I was doing, because I knew with the Warden watching, I couldn't do anything reckless, or I'd put all of us in danger.

That was the only reason I didn't kill this fucker.

I took my hands off his neck. "It better be."

Deuce and his little vampire bitch gang ran away. I was still heaving for breath, while Oberi gave a harsh snort beside me.

Kallie grabbed my arm and shook it. "What were you thinking?" she hissed. "That was entirely reckless!"

"He hurt Charlie. Badly," I spat back at her. "He's in the infirmary right now because of him!"

"But that's Charlie's choice! He *wanted* to be in the fight club!" Kallie argued.

"Big deal. Would you let someone get away with breaking Marcus' skull open?" I blurted.

Kallie paled, but before she could say anything more, Marcus stepped in.

"Ava, you were really close to losing control, like I did," Marcus said quietly. "What if you had? You would've killed everyone in this room."

I felt guilty— but not enough to make me regret my decision. I crossed my arms and turned away from all of them. "I won't do it again. He just had to know."

Chancey shrugged. "It'll be okay. They'll give Charlie time to recover. The guards won't make him fight for a long time—"

"He's not fighting again!" I snapped. "He's done!"

Chancey stared at me. "That's not how the fight club works. You don't decide when you get to quit. They do."

I huffed, but Marcus said, "That isn't important right now. What's important is helping Charlie recover."

"We should also avoid telling him about this little *incident*," Kallie added. "Because I think if he knew Ava threatened Deuce, he'd lose his shit."

There was a mumble of agreement throughout the group. My friends dragged me down to the cafeteria and tried to force some food into me, but I didn't eat it. I didn't want to eat without Charlie. I was too pissed, anyway.

I went to class, because obviously I had no choice. I wanted to go to the infirmary and stay by Charlie's side, but that wasn't allowed. I was thinking that the guards would come by any minute, to drag me to the Warden for my punishment, but no one showed.

Deuce was a gang leader— he wouldn't snitch. He'd get back at me another way, but I wasn't afraid. I was waiting for an opportunity at this point to put him in his grave.

Thoughtless as that was. Charlie was right. Lying low wasn't my strong suit. I didn't think I'd be able to control myself long enough for my dad to gather enough evidence to get us out of here.

Maybe we *should've* agreed to break out. At least then, Charlie wouldn't have gotten the shit kicked out of him.

Two days passed, and I didn't hear a word from the infirmary about Charlie. My stomach was in knots the entire time, but when I reached out across our bond, he recoiled away from me instead of pressing in, purposefully creating distance, and it hurt.

He was definitely awake and fully conscious by now. He just didn't want to contact me. Was he ashamed that he lost the fight? I didn't care about that. I just wanted to make sure he was okay.

I walked to Elementai Magic alone with Oberi, feeling quite lonely. I kept my head down, but Oberi let out a whinny as we walked into the usual grassy area in the prison yard where the class was held. Her hooves pounded on the dirt, and my head lifted. Charlie stood with the rest of the class. His face was a little less swollen, and he was more recognizable, though both of his black eyes appeared to be healing slowly. Oberi rubbed her head against Charlie's chest, and he stroked her shoulder tentatively.

"Hey," I said quietly. My hand reached out to touch his arm, but Charlie flinched. I blinked away tears as I pulled back. "Are you okay?"

"I'm alive," Charlie said bluntly. "I don't want to talk about it."

"I don't care that you lost the fight—"

"I *don't* want to talk, Ava." He seemed bitter. He put his arm around Oberi's shoulders, and the unicorn nickered.

I bit my lip. "Okay."

I stepped away. He obviously wanted space to heal his bruised ego. Anything I could say would only hurt his feelings right now.

"We'll be practicing today," Professor Summers announced as she entered the circle with her red river hog Familiar. "Feel free to take some time to work on anything you've been struggling with."

I rolled my eyes. All we *ever* did in this class was practice, with very little direction. It was like all Professor Summers knew how to do was teach the basics of elemental magic.

Charlie and I worked on our magic on opposite sides of the area. He moved around Earth mounds and Air columns, while I conjured Fire and Water balls. The other Elementai around us conjured other kinds of weather magic, while their Familiars watched.

Ezekiel was across from us, sitting in the grass with a bowl of water in front of him. Ez *hated* this class. I had tried to help him, but all my advice had gone over his head. It was like no matter how much instruction we gave him, it didn't help him to master Toaqua magic.

"Dammit!" Ez cried, clearly frustrated. He tried to make water rise out of the bowl, but it just wouldn't budge. He smacked the bowl, and the water spilled over onto the dirt.

I immediately skirted to his side, wanting to fix the problem. "How can I help?"

"It won't move," he snapped. "There must be something wrong with it."

I moved my hand, and the water that he'd tipped over rose from the ground. I flowed the water from one of my palms to the other as I directed it. My brother's expression only got more burning as I returned the water to the bowl. "It's fine, Ez. Maybe it's because you're not feeling well," I hinted.

Ez's face was flushed, and he'd been coughing all day. He also hadn't touched breakfast, which was so unlike him.

"I just have the flu. It's no big deal," he grumbled.

I frowned. "Ez, you just had a bad cold not two weeks ago. Are you not over it?"

"Leave me alone, okay! I just suck at magic, and I don't have a Familiar to help me." He crossed his arms. "I'm probably not even going to *get* one until I get out of here."

Guilt ballooned in my gut, but I pushed it aside, because it wasn't going to help him learn magic. "Water magic is flowing. It won't work if you resist it. Try again."

Ez huffed. He hovered his hand over the bowl, but his magic only created ripples in the liquid.

I felt a shiver cross over my skin as Charlie knelt beside me. "Still having trouble?"

"I don't know what to do," Ez moaned. He sounded near tears. "The water just won't listen to me."

"It can't be too hard," Charlie said with a shrug. "Try moving *with* the water instead of telling it what to do, like I do with Air."

Charlie maneuvered his hand in a complicated fashion, to demonstrate. My jaw dropped open as I saw the water in the basin form into a tiny ball and rise into the air. I felt a small bit of energy drain out from my core— like I'd cast the spell myself.

"Holy hell, Charlie," I gasped. "You're directing Water!"

"What?" Charlie asked. The Water ball immediately dropped and splashed back into the basin. "No, that's impossible!"

"Do it again," Ezekiel said, like he couldn't believe his eyes. Charlie hovered his hand over the bowl, but I grabbed his wrist.

"Stop," I told him. "We're not supposed to draw attention to ourselves, remember?"

Charlie hesitated, and I looked around. No one else had noticed what Charlie just did. Ez and I moved in closer around him, to block him out from the rest of the class and Professor Summers.

"Now try," I whispered. Charlie repeated the action. The water formed into a ball again at his command. He reached out to touch it with quivering fingers as Oberi stood nearby, bobbing her head like she approved. Both Ez and I gaped in awe.

As Charlie replaced the water back into the bowl, he said, "I have an idea. I wonder if—"

He snapped his fingers, and again, I felt a small bit of energy retreat from my body and flood into him. A little flame, no bigger than my pinkie, hovered above Charlie's hand.

"Fuck," Ezekiel said in a mystified way, like he couldn't believe it.

"Fuck indeed." There were so many mysteries to Charlie and me— there seemed to be no end to them.

Charlie shook out his hand, and the tiny flame vanished. "How can I do that? My parents were Yapluma and Nivita. I shouldn't have any ability to direct Fire or Water."

"It has to be because of our bond," I mused. "I don't see any other way how you could direct elemental energy that wasn't in your ancestry unless it was connected to me. You have to be pulling magic from me, in some way. I could feel the power leave my body as you were directing the water droplets."

"Let's try it the other way around," Charlie said in excitement. "See if you can move Air or Earth."

I was thrilled of the thought of whipping out tornadoes and causing earthquakes, but when I attempted to move a tiny pebble on the ground, like Charlie had shown me, or cast a little gust of wind through the air, neither attempt worked. I tried pulling from Charlie's energy, like I pulled from Oberi, but it didn't seem to work in the same way.

By the end of class, I hadn't moved a single leaf or rock, though Charlie had been able to conjure miniature fireballs and move water droplets with relative ease— not anything near what I could do, but impressive anyway.

We had to stop, before someone noticed what we were doing, but the fact that Charlie could do anything with Fire or Water at all was incredible.

"This is amazing, Charlie!" I gushed as we walked back into the prison. "Just think of all the badass things we're going to be able to accomplish!"

"Great for you guys," Ezekiel said glumly. He'd ceased to be amazed at what Charlie could do, and was clearly depressed.

"You'll get it," I insisted. "You just need more practice."

"It's hopeless. I'm a useless Toaqua," Ez mumbled. "Charlie doesn't even have Toaqua blood, and even he can direct Water better than I can."

"It's only because of our bond," I told him.

Ez scoffed. "Yeah, okay. You got all the talent, and didn't leave anything for the rest of us."

My mouth dropped open. "Ez."

He didn't respond, and stomped into the Villain's Den. He flung himself into a chair by a table and hunched over it.

I wasn't willing to let this go, so I followed him. I sat in the chair beside Ez. "Talk to me."

"Go away." He turned his back to me, but I got up and sat in the other chair, so he had to face me. He let out an aggravated huff.

"You're clearly in a mood. I'm not leaving until you tell me what this is about," I said.

"I don't want to be bothered by Ava-Marie and the Fuck-Around Gang," Ezekiel growled.

"That's an *amazing* band name," Charlie added unhelpfully. "Too bad we already picked the Villain's Club."

I sent a note of irritation through our bond. Charlie got the hint, and Oberi led him away, to his next class.

I leaned in closer and lowered my voice. "Ez, what's wrong? You're never short like this. I know you're upset about your magic, but this runs deeper."

He held back a moment, then his anger faded away into hurt. "It's Dad. We can't talk anymore without it becoming an argument."

"It was like that between me and him for a time, too. It'll pass."

"This is different. He sent you here because of the prophecy, because he had no other choice," Ezekiel said lowly. "He actually thinks I'm some kind of psychopath for what I did, like I belong in here."

"He doesn't think that. He's just being tough," I argued.

"You don't get it because Dad thinks the sun shines out your ass," Ezekiel said harshly. "It's not like that for the rest of us. You can do or say whatever and he'll just let it slide."

His comment bit. Was my brother *jealous* of me?

"It's because he doesn't want to push me over the edge," I said quietly. "He's worried about what I'll do. He knows the rest of you guys aren't as crazy as I am."

Ezekiel knew he'd gone too far, because he sighed. "I know it's not your fault. I just wish he'd *talk* to me, instead of laying on the guilt trip. It's not like I *want* to be here."

"Maybe you should tell Daddy the truth," I said. "He wouldn't be mad at you for what you did if he knew you were defending me."

"*No*, Ava. I'm not going to sell you out. What pisses me off is that Dad should know me better than that. He acts like I just popped off for no reason. You should've seen him when I was arrested. He was so angry he didn't even bother to ask *why*."

"You could explain how you feel."

"I've tried!" Ez burst. "But it's near impossible, because he doesn't want to listen."

"I don't know how to fix what's between you and Daddy," I began.

"But Ez, you *do* need to talk to him about one thing. And it needs to be soon."

"Not this again," he spat.

My tone softened. "Ez, you've been sick all semester."

"So? It doesn't mean anything."

"Yes it does. You need to get tested—"

"Ancestors, I don't want to, okay?" Ezekiel jumped up and shoved the table back. "Just leave me alone."

He strode off with hunched shoulders. I got up to head after him, but before I could, Opal stepped in the doorway. She put up a hand, to block me from going further.

Opal had been hiding behind the wall, and she'd overheard the whole thing. She was so quiet I hadn't even noticed her when we were coming in.

"Don't be upset about Ez. He's just not ready," Opal said.

Worry knotted inside of me. "He needs to face the facts. I'm terrified he'll keep refusing the care he needs, and then something horrible will happen, because he's not doing what he needs to in order to stay alive."

Opal's eyes dropped to the floor. "I know. I've been pushing pain pills into him all semester, just to keep him going."

I gaped. "You've been stealing from the prison pharmacy?"

Opal shrugged. "Not really. One of the nurses likes me, so she'll give me extra pills when it's time to take my dose, if no one's looking. I usually pass them on to Ez. He hasn't told anyone, because, well... he can't really get by without them."

I wondered what Opal needed pain pills for, but that wasn't what we were talking about, so I didn't ask. "He needs a prescription. Along with a treatment plan, and a host of other things."

"I know, but you can't force him to acknowledge what he already knows is the truth," Opal replied. "One day, he won't have a choice but to accept what's real. Then he's going to need all of us. Let him have his ignorance if it makes him feel better, for a little bit longer."

"Combined Magical Suppression Syndrome can be a fatal illness. He's playing with fire by ignoring it for this long. My dad has almost died *so* many times from it."

"Ez knows," Opal said softly. "But regardless of the facts, his body is his, just like your body is yours, and mine is mine. It's his choice of what he wants to do with it— even if he wants to destroy it. You can't force him to get tested and treated without his consent. It's not right."

My shoulders dropped, because that got to me. "I know, Opal. It's just so hard watching someone you love waste away."

"He'll come around," Opal said. "Let me talk to him."

Opal bustled off in the way Ezekiel had gone, and I sighed in aggravation. With Charlie acting distant and my brother being frustrated, I really wasn't in the mood to be social right now. I went back to my dorm and started digging through the journal my aunt Maddie had left me, looking for more clues on the prophecy.

I wasn't as obsessive about reading it anymore as I had been last semester. The information inside still ceased to make any sense, so I felt like the journal was a dead-end on finding answers. Our goal right now was finding Forevermore, and getting through the portal that led to it. The journal didn't have any information on either, so I'd hardly been reading it lately, but was messing around with it now on the off-chance there was something I'd missed.

I was shuffling through pages when my fingertips skimmed something odd. I flipped to the inside of the back cover, and noticed for the first time there was a bump in the backing of the journal— as well as an oddly stitched line near the spine, as if the cover was a sleeve for a secret page.

Heart pounding, I began to pull apart the stitching that kept the inside cover of the journal attached to the spine. When I had gotten the entire thread undone, the leather popped open. A singular journal page slipped out, falling onto my lap.

My mouth ran dry. My aunt would've told me about this if she remembered. She must've sewn it in during a prophetic trance. That's the only way she wouldn't recall she did this.

I wanted to call and confirm, but held back, just in case Marcus was right and the phone lines were being tapped. With shaking fingers, I unfolded the hidden journal page. I felt my breath catch in my throat as I saw drawings of seven keys on the page. Each of them were different, all various sizes and shapes, with different designs etched into the metal — but I got the feeling they were all very important.

The largest key on the page got my attention. It was a copper key edged with green patina, the handle forming a heart around a crown.

My hand immediately flew to the key around my neck. It was the necklace Daddy had given my mother on their wedding day, which she'd passed on to me before I left for the Institute. I never took it off. I fumbled to loosen the clasp, and the key dropped from my neck, landing on the journal page.

It was an exact copy of the key Maddie had drawn.

There were no words on the page, no further instruction, but my heart began to pound as I realized the possibility of what this meant. The strange Elven gate Charlie and I had come across during the Darke Games had odd keyholes that had been scattered around it amongst the runes inscribed on the stone. I put together the information we had, and came to a conclusion.

These were the keys to Forevermore. That's why no one else had found the city before— because they didn't have these keys, and therefore, couldn't open up the portal. By a stroke of luck, I already had one key. All we had to do was locate six others, and I bet once we did that, the Elven gate would open, creating a portal to the lost city that we could venture through.

We were *so* close to getting answers. For the first time, it looked like Forevermore was within our reach.

charlie

SEVENTEEN

"I'm not gonna lie, you look like shit," Marcus said when I met up with him and Kallie in the Villain's Den after class.

"But we're glad you're out of the infirmary," Kallie quickly added.

"Ow!" Marcus cried. I could only guess Kallie had slugged him.

"You should've seen the other guy," I joked. Making light of the situation was the only way to handle it, because I was devastated otherwise. I touched one of the tender cuts on my face, and though it stung, it felt a hell of a lot better than before.

Oberi sighed and laid his chin on my knee. He got that way whenever someone brought up the fight club. Rishi tried to get him to play and kept running into my leg as he jumped at Oberi, but Oberi ignored him.

"I actually saw Deuce earlier, and he looked fine— *ow!* Would you stop that?" Marcus snapped.

Kallie blew a breath. "You never learn."

I frowned. Marcus *really* wasn't helping.

A pair of footsteps rushed into the Villain's Den— a woman's, judging by the click of the heels. She breezed up to our table, and Ava's raspberry scent surrounded me. I instantly noticed her unease through our bond, which I'd been trying to block earlier today. I didn't want her to know how much the fight had really affected me. Now, though, I let her through, and my heart lurched.

Before I could ask what was wrong, Ava said, "The Lair. Now."

I stilled for a beat, but Ava was already walking away. Oberi perked up and followed behind her. None of us said a thing as we scrambled out of our seats and followed behind her.

Getting to the Lair was easy now, since we'd been there so many times. Whatever Ava had to tell us must've been really important, because she didn't say anything until we were safely inside where no one could hear us.

Kallie cast a privacy illusion around the Lair, as she always did. "It's safe to talk," she announced once the spell had settled.

"You guys are *not* going to believe what I found." Ava spoke fast, and she paced around the Lair frantically, her shoes padding sharply on the stone.

"What's that?" Kallie asked.

I heard the sound of paper unfurling. "I found *this* in the journal Aunt Maddie left me, sewn into the leather binding. These seven keys have something to do with the prophecy, and I already have one of them."

"Seven keys?" I asked.

Ava explained. "It's a drawing of seven keys, all different sizes and shapes. It's a clue to the prophecy. I'm sure of it; otherwise, it wouldn't have been in that journal."

"Can I see?" Kallie asked.

The paper rustled as Ava handed it over. "Charlie, you remember the stone gate we found— the portal to Forevermore— had seven keyholes, right?"

"Yeah, I remember." My stomach sank. I wasn't sure what any of this meant, but another clue was another step toward Ava's demise.

"These keys *must* be the ones that will get us through the portal—" Ava said, but Kallie's gasp cut her off.

"Oh, my gods," Kallie said breathlessly. "You said you have one of the keys already?"

"Yeah," Ava replied. "My mom gave it to me before I came to the Institute."

"Well, you can check another off the list, because I have one, too," Kallie said. The fabric of her shirt rustled, and I heard metal fall against the buttons of her uniform.

"Hold up," Marcus said in a croaky tone. "I recognize this one."

Something clinked to the ground like it'd come out of nowhere, and I assumed Marcus had conjured it. He cleared his throat as he bent to snatch it up.

Aw, fuck. This wasn't just a *clue*. It was the whole freaking key to the prophecy— no pun intended.

"We already have *three* of the keys?" I asked, trying not to let my unease show.

"Ancestors, we're so close!" Ava cried.

Each of them started showing off their keys to one another, and Ava passed me one. I ran my fingers over the cool metal, detailing the large key in my hands.

"Where'd you all get these?" I asked curiously.

"My parents," they all answered in unison. A silent beat passed, as we all thought it was strange.

"Could our parents *know* about this?" Kallie questioned.

"Mine sure as hell don't," Marcus said. "My mom gave it to my dad as a present a long time ago. My dad told me this key held a protection enchantment. He gave it to me right before I came to the Institute, to keep me protected here."

"Mine was a wedding gift from my dad to my mom," Ava said. "There was a whole story about how he found it the day he proposed. If my parents knew it had to do with Forevermore, they would've told me. Where'd you get yours, Kallie?"

"My mom had it for ages," she explained. "I always admired it as a kid. She said it came from one of her professors at Arcanea University."

"That's only three out of the seven," I said with relief. I assumed we needed all seven to open the door.

"Yeah, but isn't it *weird* that we all have one?" Ava pointed out. "What about you, Charlie? Do you have a key?"

"No," I said a bit too bluntly. Even if I had one, I wouldn't hand it over.

"It *does* seem like too much of a coincidence," Marcus mused.

"So does the fact that we're all demigods," Kallie added.

Ava drew a breath, like she was thinking hard. "It's like we were drawn here for a reason. The inscription on the door mentions demigods, and we know the Warden is looking for demigods to lead him to Forevermore. What if we're all here to bring the keys back to the island? That must be what the Warden is truly after."

"You think there's a spell calling the keys to the island?" Kallie asked. "And because we're demigods, we were somehow... I don't know... *sent* to deliver them?"

"Not a *spell*," Ava emphasized. "Destiny!"

Fuck destiny. I didn't give a damn— not if it hurt Ava.

"You don't think there could be four other demigods on Darke Island with keys, do you?" I asked through a dry mouth. That put us *way* too close to fulfilling this prophecy.

"There could be." Ava sounded excited, which twisted my gut. "Think about it. There are seven major supernatural races— elementals, fae, witches, vampires, mermaids, angels, and Astromancers."

"Seven races, seven keys," Marcus whispered.

"Exactly," Ava stated. "Charlie and I are both Elementai, so we would share a key."

"So all we have to do is find the other four demigods with keys," Kallie said. "Astromancers are rare at the Institute, so that shouldn't be hard."

My hands curled into fists, but I forced my voice to remain steady. "You're making assumptions. We don't even know if these keys fit the doorway."

Apparently, my voice wasn't as steady as I thought, because Ava blew a breath. "Why are you being so pessimistic? It's a logical assumption."

"Because like I said, it's an *assumption*," I said harshly.

"Then we'll have to test that assumption out by going to the gate," Kallie shot back, sounding a bit annoyed.

If only they knew why I was against this... but Maddie warned me not to tell Ava. How could I explain to Ava that I was the one prophesied to bring her down, the one who was fated to bring her a fate worse than death?

She couldn't love me. Not after that.

"How do you suggest we do that?" I challenged. "Now you guys *want* to escape?"

"No, because that's impossible," Ava stated bluntly. "But there *is* a way we can test it without escaping."

"How?" I asked skeptically.

"Our field trip into Shade Hills is in a couple of weeks, and we're all getting good enough grades to go," Ava reminded us. "We can sneak off and be back before they notice."

"If we could sneak off, why not just escape?" I asked.

"Because we'll have noxite bracelets on, ones that have trackers inside," she reminded me. "They're impossible to get off, and we'd never get off the island. They'd find us if we were gone too long. And no way in hell am I leaving Oberi behind. She's not permitted on the trip. A few minutes is all I'm willing to risk."

"So we create a distraction, visit the doorway to test the keys, and return before anyone knows we're missing?" Marcus asked. "I like it. I'm in."

"Me, too," Kallie agreed. "Getting our keys close to that door might have some sort of magical reaction— something that could lead us to the other four keys."

"Another assumption," I growled. "You don't know the other keys are here. Do you see any other demigods around?"

"Even if there aren't other demigods, the keys are being called here," Ava argued. "They *have* to be, or we wouldn't have three keys already. That's how magic works— in unnatural, mysterious ways that are too obvious to be coincidence. That means the other keys are already here, or they'll be here soon. I don't know why you're so against this."

"Because I don't want anyone to get hurt," I insisted.

"It's a prophecy about the fate of the world, Charlie!" Ava cried. "People are going to die, and it's our duty to save as many people as we can by *fulfilling* the prophecy."

Hell, how could I keep pretending I was willing to help her when it was the furthest thing from the truth? That damn prophecy was all she seemed to care about. She didn't know what it truly meant.

I wished so badly that I could tell her, but I knew my pidge. It'd do nothing to stop her, and would only push her toward it further.

Kallie took Ava's key from my hand. "So it's settled. Charlie doesn't have a key, so it doesn't matter if he comes or not."

I frowned. They were going to do this with or without me. I was going to have to get creative if I wanted to stop this.

"Fine. I'm in," I said.

"I knew you would come!" Ava piped happily. If only she knew I wasn't on her side— not the way she thought I was.

"Kallie, we should probably get going," Marcus suggested. "We have that study session with Ivy and Opal."

"Right," she agreed. "We'll catch you guys later."

"Bye," Ava and I said together.

Ava waited until Marcus and Kallie left before saying, "I'm sick of them acting like they're not together. They're supposedly mad at each other, and I still see them hanging out all the time."

"Maybe they can't help it," I suggested. "Because they're mates, I mean."

"I guess that kind of bond would be hard to ignore..."

Ava trailed off. I sensed she was talking about us.

I cleared my throat. "We should probably get back, too. We don't want anyone coming to look for us out here."

"You're probably right," she agreed. She took my hand and led me out of the Lair. Oberi followed.

Ava must've been excited that I'd agreed to go along with her plan to test out the keys, because she walked with a bounce to her step, like she feared nothing— not even the Warden. As we stepped out of the Lair and into the forest, I felt a few water droplets hit the top of my head.

"What was that for?" I asked.

Ava laughed under her breath. "I'm not doing that. It's raining!"

She sounded delighted. She let go of my hand and pranced on ahead. Oberi barked and hurried after her. Big, heavy raindrops splattered the top of my head and started coming down faster.

"Can't you make it stop?" I asked.

Ava's laughter filled the forest. "I *love* the rain! Isn't it great?"

She sang a note, the kind a kid would make when they turned their head to the sky and tried to catch the raindrops in their mouth. She spun around me, then accidentally ran into me and stumbled to the side. I caught her, and my breath hitched as I held her in my arms. Her delight was infectious. It bled through our bond, and I couldn't shy away from it even if I wanted to.

Laughter bubbled up in my throat. "Pidge, what are you doing?"

"I'm dancing in the rain!" she cried. "I used to do this all the time as a kid. It was my favorite. Come on, Charlie. Dance with me!"

Ava grabbed my hands, and we twirled around. I wanted to resist, but it meant the world to me to see her happy. For a second, I felt like I could actually forget the prophecy, because in this moment, Ava was safe, loved, and carefree. The least I could do was let her enjoy it.

I succumbed to her joy. My magic felt for the trees around me, and we wove through the forest in a blissful dance. As the sprinkles turned to a downpour, it became easy to understand why she loved dancing in the rain so much. There was something spiritual about it, as if the rain was a blessing from the Great Spirit himself— a blessing that could cleanse our worries and refresh our spirits.

Oberi barked happily and pranced around trees. His jaws snapped, like he was trying to catch the raindrops as they fell.

Ava spun me around faster, until I lost my footing and tumbled to the ground. Ava came crashing down on top of me, and we landed together on a soft bed of moss. Her wet hair draped downward and tickled the tip of my nose. I laughed and pulled her close to me.

Her lips pressed into mine passionately, and my hand trailed down to her ass. She snickered as I grabbed it, obviously enjoying it. Oberi paid no attention to us, as he continued running around trying to catch raindrops in his mouth, barking with glee.

As she came up for breath, I joked, "Ava, you're so wet."

"Oh, no," she said innocently. "What will we do about it?"

"We'll have to take our clothes off, so they can dry," I teased.

She kissed me again, then whispered, "Ah, my favorite rainy-day activity."

Our lips moved over one another, and my tongue slid inside her mouth. Water trickled down our faces. My mind raced with all the things I could do to her— good and bad. This prophecy shit was so depressing. I wanted all the good we could get together.

Ava's hands plunged into my hair, and mine moved to the buttons on her blouse. I waited to see if she'd protest, but she just tugged my hair harder, as if begging me to do it.

Our hands did the talking as I slowly undressed her. I undid the buttons on her uniform, then slid the soaked blouse off her shoulders. My fingers trailed over her wet skin and across the key hanging from her neck— the one that could open the door to Forevermore.

I didn't want to think about that, so I put my mind— and my hands— on other things. I cupped her breasts. She straddled me and arched her back, welcoming my touch. I squeezed her breasts, and my dick hardened.

Ava seemed to think I was taking too long, because she reached behind herself and undid the clasp of her bra. The wet fabric fell away, and I gasped in pleasure as my hands moved over the swell of her breasts.

"It's a bit chilly out here, huh?" I teased as my fingers touched her hard nipples.

"Just a bit," she snickered. Playfully, she brought Fire to her skin, until she was so warm that I drew away. Raindrops sizzled as they hit her body.

"Anyone tell you you're fucking hot?" I asked.

"Hot *and* wet? My two favorite things!"

I loved how playful she was being right now, and I didn't want it to end. She let her Fire subside, and I wrapped my arms around her waist and rolled us over. I tossed her onto the ground below me, and she gasped— like she was excited about whatever came next.

Rain pounded against my back as I leaned over her. I ran my hand up her thigh but hesitated at the hem of her skirt.

"You don't have to ask, Charlie," she assured me.

"Really? I thought—"

"I'll be okay," she promised. "Unless I say otherwise, you have an open invitation. Take it off."

Hell, I wanted nothing more than to get her naked. I yanked her skirt down her legs, then placed my fingers beneath the band of her thong. I tried to pull those down, but her legs were so wet that they tangled.

"How do you... get these..." I struggled with the fabric until I heard a tear. I shrugged and tossed the underwear aside. "I guess that works."

Ava got to her knees, laughing. Her fingers skimmed my waist as she grabbed for the hem of my shirt. I shivered beneath her soft touch. "Your turn," she announced.

I couldn't get my clothes off fast enough. I yanked my shirt over my head, then kicked my shoes off and tossed my soaked trousers and boxer shorts aside. We were both on our knees facing each other.

I went as still as a statue when it hit me that Ava and I were totally naked in front of each other for the first time— and in the fucking pouring rain, no less. Though the rain was cold on my skin, my whole body seemed to be burning. The forest fell silent, apart from the raindrops hitting the leaves above us. I couldn't tell what Ava was thinking.

"I, uh... hope you like what you see," I said.

She reached out for me, and her fingers began to trace the valleys of my chest, following the same path as the raindrops. She was gentle with me, like she admired me.

She drew a deep breath. "I *love* what I see."

Another shiver rocked through me as her fingers fell lower. She nearly touched the tip of my cock, but she was teasing me. And it was driving me fucking nuts.

"I wish I could see you," I whispered. I bet she appeared extravagant, and it was a cruel curse that I couldn't witness it.

"You can." She took my hands and placed them on her body.

Hell, she felt amazing. I began to explore her body at will, roaming my hands over her shoulders, down to her breasts, and to her ass. Ava gasped as I pulled her close to me and cupped her ass in my hands. She turned her face skyward as I buried my face into her neck. The moment was intimate like I'd never felt before, and I longed to weep into her— to *be* with her like I never had before.

Gently, I laid her back on the ground, and I climbed on top of her. Our naked, slick bodies pressed together, and tingles ran up and down my skin. I was fully aware of where my dick lay between her legs. All I wanted was to move my hips to the rhythm of the moment, to take the intimacy further and pleasure her in other ways. But Ava shifted beneath me, and I sensed unease through our bond.

She wasn't ready for that.

I drew away from her and got to my knees. She may not be ready for *that*, but there were other things I knew she'd enjoy.

I ducked my head and waited for her response. She spread her legs further, and I took it as an invitation. My tongue grazed over her sensitive areas. I let the sweet taste of her fill my mouth, and I went wild inside. Ava grabbed one of my hands and squeezed tightly, begging for more. With the other hand, I gingerly touched her.

As her passion intensified, so did her magic. I felt some of it spill over to me through the bond, and I experimented with the water droplets. They trailed over her skin to my command, moving over her nipples in a way that must've driven her crazy, because she gasped.

She began to moan as my fingers played with her and my tongue pleasured her clit. Her breaths grew shallow, and she arched her back as I dove my fingers in deeper. Her body stiffened, and I sucked her most sensitive area harder as I felt her topple over the edge.

"*Fuck!*" she cried out into the forest as she reached her peak.

Her euphoria came through the bond, and my head spun at the high. It was as if I had come myself. The feeling was so intense. It made me want more, and more.

I licked her several more times, then smiled in triumph as her hand became limp in mine. "How was that?"

Her body felt boneless underneath my hands. "Ah-mazing," she breathed.

I lay on the forest floor next to her, enjoying the warmth of her skin on mine and the contrasting cool of the rain coming down on us. She lay in my arms for several minutes, enjoying the euphoria that came post-orgasm. Eventually, she pulled away.

"Your turn," she announced.

"My turn?" I'd have been fine with leaving things at that. Pleasuring Ava was hot enough as it was. But she wanted to reciprocate, and I sure as hell wasn't going to argue.

Ava pushed me onto my back, onto the bed of moss, and I closed my eyes as raindrops splattered on my face. It was actually quite pleasant, and I got why she liked it— though that might've had something to do with the fact that her hand was curled around my dick.

Ava went down on me. My heart hammered in exhilaration as she moved her mouth over my cock. I couldn't help but shove my hands into her wet hair. There was something purely sexual about feeling the motions of her head as she moved. My fingers trailed down as far as I could reach— to the back of her neck— and I touched the chain of her key necklace.

She moaned and sucked me harder, and I went spiraling into an orgasm. My whole body quivered as euphoria washed over me. Hell, she was incredible.

Ava swallowed. I practically melted into the forest floor as she came to curl into my arms once more. The rain had let up a little, but I didn't mind it. We could've been curled up on a king bed in a penthouse suite, for all I knew. All that mattered was Ava.

"You like that, huh?" I asked.

"You taste good," she admitted in a blissful whisper. "I think it's sexy."

I pulled her tighter. "I think *you're* sexy."

"You, too." She relaxed into me. We continued to let the rain pelt our naked bodies, moisture dotting over our skin. I ran my fingers over her hips and made trails in the water, feeling like life couldn't get any more perfect than this.

We must've stayed that way for another twenty minutes before the rain let up. Oberi came scampering back into our little corner of the woods, his paws making squishing noises in muddy puddles.

"Oberi, you're filthy!" Ava cried. Oberi shook out his fur, and I felt a bit of mud splash my face. He must've found a puddle and rolled in it.

"Bad dog," I scolded. Oberi barked, and I heard his paw hit mud. A chunk of dirt smacked my nose, and I scowled as I wiped it off.

"We should probably get dressed and head back," Ava suggested. "We've been gone a long time."

I didn't want to leave. This little moss bed was a perfect, private little slice of the Institute. Here, I could forget that we were locked up.

But Ava was right. We had to get back, before people started to wonder where we were. Though our clothes were wet, we pulled them back and headed back to the Institute. I clenched my fists and held my breath the entire way, hoping Ava was too happy to notice what I'd done.

"That was fun," Ava remarked when we got back to the building. "We should do it again sometime."

I smiled. "Definitely."

Ava stood on her toes and kissed my cheek, before we went our separate ways. Oberi followed her. It wasn't until I could no longer hear the click of her heels or the scratch of Oberi's paws that I finally dropped my shoulders. She hadn't noticed the key missing from around her neck— or the fact that I'd been clutching it the whole way back.

I placed my hands in my pockets and deposited the key there. I hated that I had to deceive her, but it was what had to be done. It was the only way to save her from the prophecy.

Now all I had to do was destroy the key.

ava-marie

EIGHTEEN

My head buzzed, and my whole body was warm with the aftereffect of mine and Charlie's exploration of each other's bodies in the woods. I'd never been authentic with somebody else like that. What had happened with John was in the forest, but this was so different. It was like the rain falling from above washed my fears away. I could be vulnerable without the worry of having something being taken from me, be open to Charlie while knowing I wasn't being manipulated or used. I was entranced by the thought of the rain dripping across Charlie's skin, down his broad shoulders and abs, and across his perfect dick.

And the sight of his nice, supple ass as he went down on me underneath the rain clouds. I smiled with the memory as I washed the moss and mud out of my hair in the showers that evening. Everything had been so magical. I was still humming with the pleasure of it as I dried off my hair in my cell, wishing I could go back in time and relive the moment all over again.

My hands froze when I realized something was missing. My key. It wasn't around my neck.

My heart stuttered. Maybe I had taken it off in the shower and forgotten about it. I rushed back to the communal showers, but the key wasn't anywhere in sight. I felt my eyes begin to water, and panic grew hot in my throat. I ran back to my cell and began throwing things aside, desperately searching for my key.

It wasn't anywhere. Where had it gone? Had I misplaced it somewhere in the Lair? I could've sworn I had it on me when I left. But if it wasn't there, and it wasn't *here*, where else could it be?

I needed that key. It was priceless. It wasn't just a precious item that could help us with the prophecy and open the gate to Forevermore. It was a family heirloom, a symbol of Daddy's love for Mama. I couldn't lose it. It meant *everything* to me.

I didn't sleep. I tore my cell apart that night, looking for my key. By morning, my stuff was in a heap around my room, and I was a crying mess. I didn't know *where* it could be.

There was a knock on my door. "Ava? What's wrong?"

Charlie had heard my wailing. He stepped into my cell. His face twisted into concern. I staggered to my feet and wiped my face with my sleeve, which didn't do much good, because I was still crying.

"I'm so upset," I sobbed. "My key is missing!"

"Missing?" He stilled. "You mean, it's gone?"

"Yes!" I tried taking deep breaths, but it was like gulping air. "If that key is lost, we're *so* screwed!"

"It'll be okay. We'll find it," Charlie said soothingly as he stroked my arms.

His attempts to calm me weren't working. My body shook against his hold. "But what if we *don't*? I'll fail to fulfill the prophecy. The world will be doomed because I was stupid enough to misplace my key! This is all *my* fault."

I cried into Charlie's front. He wrapped his arms around me and rocked me from side to side. "I promise it'll be all right," he said, but his voice wavered.

There was a whinny from the hallway. I pulled away from Charlie's arms and stuck my head out the door, wiping snot from my nose— I was an ugly crier.

My spirits lifted when I saw Oberi trotting down the hallway. Around her horn was my key, suspended on the chain. She slid to a halt, and I immediately removed the key from her horn, fastening it around my neck again.

"Oberi! Thank goodness," I wept. "She found my key!"

Charlie stiffened. "What?"

"It's around her horn. It must've fallen off when we were messing around in the woods, and she went back to look for it," I said in relief. "Good job, Oberi!"

Oberi nickered. I flung my arms around her neck and gave her a hug. "Ancestors, I'm *never* taking this thing off again! That was too close! Right, girl?"

Oberi gave a hot snort that blew Charlie's hair back. He frowned.

"It was fortunate Oberi managed to find it. We might not have located it if we went back to the woods," I said, stroking her fiery mane back. "It was so lucky."

Charlie sighed, and his shoulders sagged. "Yeah. Real *lucky*."

Oberi swished her tail, and it smacked Charlie in the face. I clutched the key, promising myself I'd never lose it again. I couldn't be careless like that. It wasn't okay to mess up when the world was counting on me.

From now on, no more mistakes.

A COUPLE OF WEEKS LATER, Kallie, Marcus, Charlie and I gathered in the Lair. We had gotten together to review the plan for getting to the Elven gate, before we headed to Shade Hills on our field trip.

"Are we all in agreement?" I said. "We act casual for as long as we can, and then, once we get an opening, we sneak into the woods so we can test our keys on that gate. Then we rush back, so we can rejoin the group again and no one notices our absence."

Marcus and Kallie gave remarks of agreement. Charlie remained silent.

Oberi was giving Rishi pony rides around the cave. Rishi meowed as Oberi pranced up and down in her unicorn form, tossing her head joyously.

"Do you think we *should* be doing this?" Marcus asked. "Running off during a field trip to Shade Hills is a huge infraction. It's enough to get us tossed into Cellblock 9, if the guards realize we're missing."

"We don't have a choice," I said. "If we're sneaky enough, we won't get caught."

Charlie brushed back his hair, which was falling into his eyes again. I could tell it was irritating him.

I touched Charlie's locks. "Your hair is getting a little long," I said. "Let me cut it."

"How? We aren't allowed scissors, and I'm not going to the prison barber," Charlie said.

Most inmates were forced to get their hair cut by the guards when it got too long. They always did a horrible hack job.

Kallie conjured a pair of hair cutting scissors with a hairdressing cloth, and handed them to me. "Here you go."

"How can you do *that* and not conjure something to get us out of here?" Marcus complained.

"Come to think of it, you did conjure swords for us to use in McCauley's class last semester," I added.

"I *can* conjure almost anything, but that doesn't mean I should," Kallie said. "McCauley's class was different. Fae are allowed to make any illusion under teacher supervision. But any fae that conjure stuff they aren't supposed to have *outside* of class, like knives or weapons, and who get caught, are forced to wear noxite tracker cuffs twenty-four-seven until they graduate. If I get caught conjuring something that's contraband, my powers will be useless, because I'll instantly get booked."

"So don't get caught." I shrugged.

Kallie scoffed. "Yeah, like I want to take that chance. Fuck up once, my magic is taken away until I get out of here. No thanks."

"What about a portal?" Marcus offered. "You can make those, can't you?"

"Of course I can, but they're still hard to create," Kallie argued. "A lot of fae never master them. It's opening up a door in two different spots of reality, which is really hard, and it gets harder the farther away the destination is."

"Just make one and get us out of here," Marcus suggested.

"You *really* think the Warden hasn't thought of that," Kallie asked flatly. "The fae guards have put up wards around the prison to make portals ineffective, so they won't work anyway. Not to mention the wards can *also* identify who cast the portal right away. I don't want to get myself an instant trip down to Cellblock 9."

"Now who's being a chicken?" Marcus asked.

"Shut up, Marcus! At least I *can* cast a spell."

While they were bickering, I shook my head and steered Charlie toward a chair. I looped the cape around his shoulders, and started trimming Charlie's hair. The black tendrils drifted to the floor.

"What made you study cosmetology in high school?" Charlie asked.

"I don't know. I was always so interested in how things looked. I wanted to push the boundaries of style. See how shocking I could be, what I could create and get away with."

"Typical Ava answer."

"I was very good at it. But hair and makeup always seemed like a hobby, never my calling."

I observed the shape of his face carefully, and sculpted his haircut to complement his features. "You know, I never noticed, but your ears are slightly pointed. It's kind of cute."

"Really? Guess I didn't know."

I bit my lip and checked the length. "I don't want to cut it *too* short," I said. "You look nice when it's slicked back."

"If it gets any longer he'll look shaggy, like Marcus," Kallie added.

"Hey!" Marcus complained. He tugged self-consciously at the end of his hair, which was close to his shoulders by now.

"My hair used to be all the way past my hip bones," I said proudly. "I'd like to get it that long again."

"Why'd you cut it?" Charlie asked.

I snipped off a couple of stray pieces. "In Hawkei culture, our hair is thought to be part of our spirit. Many of us grow it long, to show our inner strength. But when someone we love dies, we cut our hair in mourning, to show that our spirit has been wounded, and how deeply we've been hurt. It's a symbol of what we've lost."

I shrugged. "But then the hair regrows, showing that we've been reborn after the loss."

"You cut your hair when Monica died, didn't you?" Charlie asked.

I didn't clearly reply. Instead, I said, "When I was sad, Daddy used to tell me our tribe would braid our hair, to trap the sadness inside, and then the wind would come and blow all our troubles away as it rushed through our braids. I remember I braided my hair almost every day after she passed. I'd stand outside on stormy days and just wish that all the pain would get carried away with the wind."

"Did it make you feel less sad?"

"A bit." I finished up and brushed loose hair off his shoulders. "Your hair is important. It's part of your spirit, which means you shouldn't let just anyone touch it. Don't let anyone cut your hair but me, okay?"

"Okay." Charlie ran a hand through his new haircut tentatively. Then he scowled.

"What's wrong?"

"I don't know anything about our culture. I'm so far behind," he said in frustration. "I'm too old to learn all this stuff. I know nothing about our tribe."

"You're never too old to learn where you come from." I kissed his cheek. "Plus, you have me."

"Ugh," Kallie complained. "You two are gross. Marcus and I already figured out you two have *broken-in* the Lair."

I hissed with laughter, thinking back to the delicious blow-job I'd given Charlie. "Maybe."

"No time for that," Marcus said as he checked his watch. "The bus for Shade Hills leaves in fifteen minutes. We'd better get going."

We had to leave Oberi and Rishi behind in our dorms, per Institute rules. It was a good way of preventing people from trying to escape during the field trip— forcing them to leave their pets and their Familiars behind. No witch would leave their cat, and no Elementai would abandon their Familiar, either.

Oberi insisted on remaining a unicorn, until she realized that Charlie and I couldn't stuff her through my dorm room door, despite trying. She changed into a husky and hopped on my bed with a grumble. Oberi whimpered, and Rishi let out a soft yowl as we left them behind in my dorm. I felt *so bad*, as I knew Oberi wanted a chance to play outside Institute grounds, but we didn't have a choice.

Dozens of prisoners were already waiting at the bus stop in front of the prison, excited at the prospect of getting out for the day. Most people had been stuck inside the Institute for a year or more, and were thrilled at the opportunity just to get some space, even supervised. Field trips into town were rare, and not everyone got to go every time, so for once, I was glad for my good behavior.

We were fitted with the noxite tracker cuffs, which definitely put a damper on my mood. I could feel the poison sucking away at my magic. I knew if anyone here tried to escape, they'd have a rough time of it with these cuffs on. Slipping away to go check on the gate in the middle of the woods was going to be a long shot, but we had to try.

We were ordered to loop our prison ID cards around our neck with the lanyards they handed out, and told we had to keep them on at all times. Anyone who took theirs off would get an immediate infraction, and a trip back to the Institute.

Charlie put the lanyard on. A giggle rose past my lips as I read his ID tag. "Charles? Your full name is *Charles*?"

"It's the formal name for Charlie, yes," he replied tiredly, like he'd known I'd figure this out eventually and hadn't been looking forward to it.

I snorted. "Charles. It's so *fancy*. Lord Charles. No, *Prince* Charles!"

"I don't know what my parents were thinking when they named me that. I'm not a stuck-up guy," he argued.

"Of course not, *Charles*," I replied in a snooty tone. He sighed.

I teased Charlie all the way to Shade Hills. When we disembarked the bus, I looked around. We hadn't had much of a chance to observe Shade Hills during the Darke Games, but now that we were here, I could take in the sights. Shade Hills was overcast and cloudy, with a lot of abandoned shops along the twisted and winding cobblestone roads, but it was also quirky. The windows we passed advertised all kinds of unusual items. We walked by a botany shop that exclusively sold poisonous, man-eating plants, and a bookstore that only contained banned books. I wanted to go in there, but a guard cut me off before I could enter, so I was forced to stay with the other inmates.

We moved as a massive group through Shade Hills, the guards surrounding us so we didn't have a chance to walk off. We weren't allowed to have any money at the Institute, but the guards had permitted us to bring a couple of small bills, for approved trinkets and treats in Shade Hills.

Cursed Collectibles was the first shop we entered. It was a witch store, but instead of being full of the usual things witches would want like wands, crystals, and herbs, the shelves were packed with cursed objects, skulls, haunted cauldrons, mummified cat remains, possessed Ouija boards, and magical artifacts. It was dark in here, and smelled musty. The necromancer running the shop was balding, and he had a crooked, toothless smile that I really didn't like. A bone parrot sat on his shoulder, squawking and flapping its skeleton wings.

"Couldn't let him go after he died," the necromancer croaked to me when I passed, and he stroked the parrot's beak. "Now he's with me forever."

Totally gross. A couple of people bought things, but me? No thanks. The last thing I wanted was to bring a cursed object back to my cell, where I'd certainly receive bad side effects, if not bring back a fully-fledged ghost. My cell was too small to even share it with the dead. As the group left, we had to pull Marcus away from the artistic section of the shop, which was full of magical paints that would change colors as you put them on the canvas.

"Why would you even want to tamper with that? The sign said the paint has *demon blood* in it. You're asking to summon something you don't want to play with," Kallie protested as we left.

"I'm part necromancer. It doesn't bother me," he said.

"I'm not helping you exorcise a demon once it possesses your ass," Kallie grumbled. Marcus shrugged, like he didn't see what the big deal was.

Our next stop was a pet shop for Elementai named *Precarious Pets*. I usually didn't like pet stores that sold animals, as I thought they could be cruel, but this one was very unique. It was full of creatures in cages and stalls that could potentially bond with Elementai. There was a ram with fire horns and pitch-black eyes, a bear with tentacles for a face, a twelve-foot long basilisk that had crocodile legs, and a giant spider with a gibbon's head (and a hundred black eyes). Every creature in here seemed to be sort of dark and twisted— evil, in a way.

I was firm on the standing that Familiars needed to roam free, in order to find their Elementai at the right time. But on the other hand, I was glad these creatures were locked up. They seemed deadlier and more dangerous than the average Familiar.

Charlie and I bought a couple of dog treats to take back to Oberi, along with a fancy rhinestone halter she could wear in her unicorn form. Opal and Ezekiel hopped between each aisle, taking in all the creatures with wonder.

"This one is really neat!" Opal said as she leaned closer to a cage. It held an animal that had the head of a cobra and the body of a cat. The cobra lunged its fangs at her, and Ez yanked Opal back. She fell against his chest, and he pulled her away from the cage, naturally wrapping his arms around her. He didn't seem to realize what he was doing, but Opal's cheeks blushed pink.

"Not *that* one," he said. "But maybe I can find a Familiar here!"

Ez let her go and hurried from cage to cage, looking for his Familiar, but didn't bond with any of them. He was forced to leave the shop disappointed— unlike one student, who squealed with joy when he realized he'd bonded with a purple toad with a forked tongue that leaked poison.

"Darn." Ez sighed. "I just don't have any luck, do I?"

"You didn't want any of those, anyway," Opal said brightly. "Your Familiar will be *better*."

"You think so?"

"Yes— better than better— the *best!*" Opal cheered, and Ez smiled.

As Opal and Ez chatted on about what his Familiar could be, we went further into town. I didn't think the downtown area could, you know, get *worse* than any other part of the village, but apparently, I was wrong. Shade Hills became... well... *shadier* the further in we went, with more and more shops that sold paraphernalia that would be illegal anywhere else but on the island.

There was a blood bar for vampires called *Last Drop*, but the guards wouldn't let us go in. The vampires loudly complained as we passed by, whining they wanted a drink.

"I just want one damn cup of *real* blood, for fuck's sake," I heard Ivy say. "The synthetic shit they give us at the prison is garbage."

"You can take a drink from *me*," Chancey said. "I wouldn't mind."

Ivy audibly swooned. "Oh, Chance, baby, what an *honor*! I'd be delighted, sweetie peach."

And Kallie said *we* were bad. Ancestors.

"No drinking from inmates, or I'll give you an infraction!" a guard barked. Ivy flipped him off.

There was a strip club that was run by sirens next to the blood bar. The guards wouldn't let us go in there, either. Instead, they ferried us toward a small aquarium, where a couple of bored-looking mermaids led us on a tour. The fish inside the aquarium were unlike any sea creatures I'd ever seen— and I was half-Toaqua. There was a giant squid in a dark tank who had tentacles that glowed, and an ugly, massive fish that had pointed fangs and a glowing feeler sticking out of its head. A shark with two heads swam beside a massive eel with crab-like pinchers. An eyeless worm that had a circular mouth, which we were informed was for sucking blood out of its prey, was beside the tank of a sea urchin that had points which oozed purple venom. It was interesting to observe them, if not a bit creepy.

We stopped in a small cafe called *The Buttered Bluebell* for lunch. The food was made by faeries, who charmed the food with different illusions. The place looked like a cute little tea shop, with mismatching furniture and doilies on every surface. The shelves were stock full of flowers growing in pots, while illusions of pink butterflies flew over our heads.

I wasn't supposed to have magical food, as per my meds, so the staff was forced to make me cucumber tea sandwiches from scratch. Charlie was going to share my food, until I convinced him to try a turkey craisin croissant that made it feel like you were getting a back massage. He sagged under the relaxation of the illusion, while Marcus' eyes grew wide as he painted the air after consuming a lemon tart, colors bleeding from his fingers.

Kallie's eyes gleamed at a pink fae cupcake in the display, which had a little sign by it that said it helped strengthen a fae's wings. She'd spent all her money already, so she turned to Marcus.

"Marcus, give me five dollars," she asked, holding her hand out.

He didn't hesitate. He dug in his pocket and handed her the money. As she skipped off, I'm pretty sure I heard Marcus whisper, *so hot.*

"You're one of those guys that has a fetish for women that boss you around, aren't you?" I asked Marcus.

Marcus blushed and mumbled something incoherent. Charlie smiled.

"Marcus, do you get off on being told what to do?" I teased.

"He wants to be bullied by Kallie." Charlie snickered.

"Might as well be lingerie for him." I laughed, and Charlie joined in.

Marcus scowled. "Shut up, guys. I'm not a weirdo who— who wants a blonde to put her heels on and walk on his chest, or whatever."

"That description was way too accurate to *not* be a fantasy," Charlie pointed out.

Marcus flushed and stormed away, to the other side of the restaurant. Charlie and I were still chortling.

"He's certainly got a type, doesn't he?" I asked.

Charlie wrapped an arm around my waist and drew me close. "Nothing wrong with enjoying the presence of a strong, independent woman."

That made me glow inside, so I wrapped my arms around Charlie's middle and squeezed, loving the fuzzy feelings. Charlie ducked to give me a kiss, and a couple of people around us complained.

"Hey, arms-length apart," a guard growled, yanking Charlie off of me. "No physical contact. Institute rules."

Annoyance flickered as the guard strolled away. Ancestors, I got this was a prison and all, but we were consenting adults. We were too old to be playing the *leave-room-for-the-Great-Spirit* game. This wasn't a middle school dance.

Kallie strode up to us, nibbling on the cupcake. Her face appeared concerned. "Hey, do you guys think I'm a little too mean to Marcus?"

"Yes, but also, no," Charlie replied.

"What does that mean?" Kallie blinked.

"He likes it, I'm sure," I said. Both Charlie and I let out a snicker.

"How?" Kallie began rambling. "I mean, I get we have this *dynamic*, but maybe he doesn't know I'm just playing around? I don't want to hurt his feelings. He just ran off a minute ago. I'm worried he's taking my teasing too hard."

"Something's hard, I'll bet!" I added, and Charlie howled.

"I don't know what's wrong with you two." Kallie's eyes narrowed. "This is serious."

"Don't think too much about it," I said casually. "I'm sure he knows you're just playing around."

Kallie took a bite and said, "Okay."

Marcus sulked for the next hour. I kept looking for openings where we could slip away, but this field trip was far too organized. There were guards everywhere, circling the group and preventing us from sneaking out. I was wondering if we'd ever get our shot to take off.

We'd been shuffled along to a museum in the middle of town, which was run by angels. I usually *loved* historical stuff like this, but it was clear the guides running the museum were trying to convert us to the angel religion instead of teaching us about their culture as they rambled on about religious stories of their golden idols. I was sure this was a mandated part of the trip, ordered by the Warden. The four of us stood at the back of the group and hushed whispers to each other as the sermon went on.

"This isn't working. We need a distraction," Kallie insisted. "There's only a couple of hours left in the trip. If we don't go now, we won't be able to leave and come back without them noticing we're gone."

"Maybe one of us should stay behind, to cause a diversion?" Marcus asked.

His words were cut off by a crashing sound at the front. Mad Dog was wrestling with a plethora of guards. He'd tried to steal one of the gold idols on display, and now, all the guards were trying to restrain him. Even with the noxite cuff, Mad Dog still appeared pretty strong. The rest of the guards ran forward, to help the others attempting to put him in handcuffs. All the other inmates were watching the fight with interest.

"That's our cue," Charlie said.

While the guards were busy trying to control Mad Dog, we ran off. We left the museum and dipped into a back alley of Shade Hills. We ripped off our ID tags, shoving them into our pockets. We took off into the woods at a run. I grabbed Charlie's hand and hauled him behind me, to lead him around trees.

We ran until we could no longer hear the noises of the town. We stopped to gather our breath, and Kallie said, "Do you guys know the way?"

"I don't," Charlie said. "I couldn't lead you to it if I tried."

"I wasn't expecting you to get us there, Charlie. You can't see where we are," I said. "I'm sure I can find it. Follow me."

We wound our way through the woods in the direction of the gate— at least, what I *thought* was the direction of the gate. We walked for a half hour, and didn't get anywhere. I turned in place, wondering why we hadn't found it by now.

"Ava, do you know where this place is?" Marcus asked scathingly.

"Of course I do," I snapped. "It's just... hard to find."

"Darke Island is pretty big," Charlie said. "I don't think we covered it all during the Darke Games. We could be wasting our time out here."

Frustration rolled inside of me. What was *with* him? He wanted to give up so easily. He was supposed to be helping me out, not throwing in the towel.

Kallie changed into a wolf and put her nose to the ground, like she could smell it out. The attempt must've been unsuccessful, because she changed back. "I have no idea," she said, throwing her hands up.

My stomach rolled nervously. "Let's walk this way," I suggested. "I'm sure it's close."

I wasn't sure if I was leading us in the right direction or not. I hoped I wasn't getting us lost, because if we couldn't find our way back to Shade Hills, we'd be in real trouble.

"What's that itching?" Marcus asked, and he scratched at his arms like he had a rash.

"I don't feel anything," Charlie said crossly.

"It's bad!" Marcus insisted. "There's something crawling across my skin! And there's this *buzzing* too. Can't you hear it?"

"No," Charlie snapped. I could feel his grumpiness through our bond. He'd crossed into a bad mood.

"Wait a minute," Kallie said. "I can feel it, too."

I paused to pay attention. There was a strange feeling tingling across my skin— and the faintest buzzing in my ears, calling me toward the unknown.

The gate. It was calling to us as demigods.

"Come on!" I increased my pace, and the others followed.

Relief— and awe— entered my veins as we reached the clearing where the gate was set. Now that we had more time and weren't constrained under the pressure of the Darke Games, I could appreciate the majesty of the beautiful structure. The curved stone gate rose up to the sky, ascending to the treetops. The beautiful Elven runes were carved in a cursive, twirling fashion around the gate's edge, creating an intricate design. The massive wooden door in the middle of the gate appeared like it'd barely been touched by time, save for the ivy vines crawling up the bottom of it. The seven keyholes in the door stood out sharply in the sunlight, uniform and expertly crafted.

"This is it," I whispered.

Kallie and Marcus came beside me, craning their necks back to take in the majesty of the beautiful stone gate.

"Cool. We're here." Charlie crossed his arms. "Let's do what we came for, so we can go."

I frowned. This place was *special*. It was where we'd had our first kiss. Why was he ruining it?

Kallie, Marcus and I took out our keys. We tried fitting them into the various key holes in the wooden door. Most didn't fit, but my mouth fell open when my key slid into the first slot on the left. Kallie's key fit beside mine, and Marcus' key slid into the keyhole next to hers.

The three of us gasped as they keys began to glow. They shone with a white light that was almost blinding. When I touched my key, I found it was warm underneath my palm.

"Charlie, come here," I said. I put his hand on the key, but he jerked his fingers back when he felt how warm it was. It wasn't hot enough to burn him. He more acted like... I don't know. Like he hadn't been expecting the keys to react, and they did.

"These keys definitely fit this door," Kallie insisted. "They were made for it."

"This has to be a portal to Forevermore. There's nothing else behind this gate," Marcus insisted.

"So our original theory is right. We just need four more keys, and then the portal to Forevermore will open," I said.

There was triumph in my voice. We were getting *so close*. And if these keys were being drawn to Darke Island, like I predicted, it was only a matter of time before we found them all.

Charlie scoffed. "We know now that the keys fit the door. We don't know if it's really a portal to Forevermore."

I yanked my key out of the keyhole and looped it back around my neck. "What other clues do we need? Our theory matches up!"

"Your *theory*," Charlie emphasized. "We don't have any proof. That door could lead to *anywhere*. It could let out someone— or something— we don't want to tamper with."

"The runes say that the door leads to Forevermore, pretty much," Marcus offered. "*I* even think it's safe to open."

"Then you're being an idiot," Charlie shot at him.

Marcus blanched, and Kallie stepped in to defend him. "Don't be like that," she said. "Opening this door might mean avoiding another Great Supernatural War— which is what we're trying to *prevent*, right?"

"You don't know what's behind it," Charlie growled. "What if opening that door is what *starts* the war?"

Charlie seemed firm in his viewpoint— but so was I.

"Look. Whatever's behind that door, it links to my prophecy. My destiny," I insisted. "Which means I have to open it, no matter what."

"This isn't a game, Ava!" Charlie shouted. "The prophecy says that *a discovery of the ancient ones on the island of shadow will change the course of our universe.* That sure sounds like opening that Elven gate— and if it is, do the four of us really have the right to change the course of the entire *universe*? What if it screws things up?"

My insides did loops. "Whatever the prophecy means, this door has to be opened," I insisted. "Marcus, Kallie and I wouldn't have keys if that wasn't the case. It's too much of a coincidence. Fate has led us here. We just have to have faith that opening the door is the right move."

Charlie huffed. "Well, I guess it doesn't matter anyway, because we don't have the other keys," Charlie said, and he crossed his arms. "Good luck finding them."

My heart dropped right out of my chest and landed on the ground. He didn't want to help me. If anything, he had me convinced that coming here today was a bad idea.

Marcus shifted anxiously. "We should get back, guys. Before the guards realize we're gone."

Kallie's look grew mischievous. "You know... we're free now... we could just... wander our way off of Darke Island, if we wanted to. There's no wards stopping portals out here."

"We're not leaving Oberi," Charlie and I both said at the same time.

"And I'm not leaving Rishi," Marcus said firmly. "Kallie, let's go. We still have trackers on us. You won't make it on your own."

Kallie rolled her eyes and groaned. "Fine. Gods, you people are lame."

We made our way back to Shade Hills— me, a little depressed. We had some answers, but to me, they were useless if Charlie wasn't beside me.

Charlie must've noticed how sad I felt, because he squeezed my hand. "I'm sorry," he started. "I just... don't want you to get hurt."

"I'm *going* to get hurt, Charlie. That's the promise of being a chosen one," I told him. "But it won't be as bad if you're not fighting me on every single thing."

"I want to protect you."

"I don't need a protector. I need a partner," I said. "Can't you do that for me?"

Charlie got quiet. I was ready for this field trip to be over. I just wanted to get back to Oberi, so I could cuddle him and bury my face in his fur. He'd make me feel better right now, because obviously, Charlie didn't see my side of things.

When we entered the alleyway we'd left the museum from, a guard immediately jumped out at us, raising a noxite gun. The four of us put our hands up, and I scowled. Great. So much for not getting caught.

"Where have you four been?" the guard snarled. "Your trackers went off the moment you left! We've been looking for you for over an hour!"

"We just— uh— snuck off to smoke some weed," Kallie blurted, like it was the first thing that popped into her head.

Marcus facepalmed, and the guard's face twisted into a snarl. "You're lucky the Warden's in an awful mood. I don't want to be the one to deliver more bad news to him. Get the hell back on the bus, before I change my mind."

We didn't argue. The four of us hurried onto the bus that was parked in the street, and took seats near the back. Ez gave me a curious look, asking why I'd wandered off, but I shook my head to tell him to ask me later. Marcus leaned his head in as the bus started down the road.

"He didn't give us an infraction. That's crazy!" Marcus hushed under his breath. "Why wouldn't he report us?"

"I don't know, but it's pretty obvious he only let us go because he doesn't want to face the Warden," Kallie whispered back.

"Why?" I asked. "Why is the Warden so pissed off? What's frustrating him?"

"Probably the same thing that's frustrating us," Kallie said, with a glance at Charlie. He didn't say anything, and I felt my chest twist.

Charlie didn't want to do this with me— didn't want to help me work out the prophecy. But he was my bonded partner. I couldn't do it without him.

Yet by the looks of things, it seemed he'd already made up his mind.

charlie

NINETEEN

Damn those keys. I'd be lying if I said I hadn't been holding my breath the whole time, hoping those keys wouldn't fit that door. But they had, which meant Ava-Marie was right. The door led to Forevermore, and she nearly had half the keys needed to open it.

I'd tried to destroy Ava's key the night I'd stolen it. It was made of metal, an element of the Earth, which meant I should've been able to manipulate it— at least to some degree. But no matter how hard I tried to change the shape of the key, or to disintegrate it into nothing, it didn't work. I was no match for the magic inside of it. I'd resolved to try other methods later, until Oberi showed up, taken the key out of my dorm, and handed it back to Ava.

Traitor.

Oberi had been avoiding me. He was mad I'd tried to sabotage Ava again.

Whatever. He could be mad. I was pissed he'd given the key back. He knew what fulfilling this prophecy meant. I didn't get why he didn't seem to care. Didn't he want to protect her, too?

The only solace I found was in the fact that Ava hadn't figured out where the other keys were yet. She didn't even have a clue, thank the ancestors.

"I bet Ivy's a demigod, and he has the vampire key," Ava mused one day when we were hanging out in the Lair. She sat on a rug Kallie had conjured, using sticks to doodle things in the dirt with Marcus. "Out of everyone on campus, it *has* to be him."

"Why do you say that?" Marcus asked. "Is he good? I don't have any classes with him. I haven't seen his magic yet."

"I haven't much, either," Ava admitted. "He just has this... *flair*. You know?"

"What do we do? Ask him if he has a key to a lost Elven city?" Kallie asked sarcastically. She sat on the rug next to Ava, painting her nails. "What do you think of this color?"

"Ooh, I *love* it," Ava gushed.

I threw a ball across the Lair, and Oberi chased after it, panting loudly. A squeal sounded, and Oberi barked as he tripped over Rishi. The ball made a *thwacking* noise as it hit against the wall.

Ancestors, I wished they'd stop talking about those keys. I wanted to convince them it was no use searching for them, but Ava wouldn't listen. I kept my mouth shut.

"There has to be *some* way to bring it up without giving anything away," Ava mused.

"Ivy's half-blood, though," Kallie pointed out. "Can half-bloods *be* demigods?"

"I don't know," Ava said nonchalantly as she scratched her stick through the dirt. "Either way, I'm thinking of letting Ivy in on things. He has some really creative ideas, and he's running that secret nightclub. He's bound to overhear tons of stuff down there."

"No," I said too quickly. Oberi shoved the ball into my hands, which was wet with slobber.

Ava's scratching stopped. "Why not?"

"We can't tell anyone," I said. "It's too dangerous. What if the Warden overhears?"

Truth was, I didn't want Ava finding any more clues. Involving others might actually lead us somewhere.

"We'll think about it," Ava stated firmly, but it sounded like she'd already made up her mind. She was just waiting for the rest of us to agree with her.

"I've been thinking..." Marcus started. "What if whoever has the other keys *aren't* our allies?"

"You mean someone like Mad Dog or Deuce?" I asked as I threw the ball for Oberi.

"Well, they're both pretty strong supernaturals," Marcus pointed out.

"No. I refuse to believe it," Ava said. "Fate led us here. No way would the Great Spirit hand over one of our keys to one of *them*."

Freaking *fate*. Ava wouldn't shut up about it lately.

"What about a professor?" Marcus thought aloud.

"Mm..." Ava thought.

"Hemlock, maybe?" Kallie theorized.

"No. I think she would've at least *hinted* to something if she was," Ava said. "She spoke to me about demigods, and I didn't get the sense that she was talking about herself."

"I wonder if she knows anything—" Marcus cut off as Ava gasped.

I stilled as Oberi nudged me with his nose. "What is it?"

"I think there's something under here!" Ava exclaimed.

She began scratching the dirt away, and Marcus joined in, their sticks grinding into the ground below. Kallie coughed. Dirt filled the air, and I sneezed.

"Ancestors," I groaned. "Let me."

I swirled my hands around, and the dirt below us followed my command. I could feel the bedrock was only an inch or so down. I swept the thick layer of dirt away with my magic, piling it into a corner of the room.

Marcus, Ava, and Kallie rose to their feet, and their slow footsteps sounded as they backpedaled several steps away from me.

"What are you doing?" I asked.

Ava drew a deep breath. "Ancestors, Charlie! I wish you could see it."

"See what?" I questioned. It was obvious in their shocked silence that Ava *had* found something beneath the dirt. Even Rishi and Oberi had quieted to take it in.

"It's Elven runes!" Ava cried in excitement. "The whole floor is covered in them!"

"I wonder how old these paintings are," Marcus mused.

Gingerly, I made my way over to my friends. I didn't want to ruin whatever message lay beneath my feet— but then I realized maybe I *should*. If it was another message about Forevermore, I wanted nothing to do with it.

"Can you translate it?" I asked Ava.

"Some of it's familiar," she said thoughtfully. She began moving around the room, as if trying to inspect the runes from every angle. "This rune here— that's the symbol for Forevermore. I've seen it a bunch of times. And that one— it's on the gate in the forest. That's the rune for *demigods*."

My stomach sank. Fuck, it *was* a message about Forevermore. I began to panic, but I quickly forced myself to calm down. Maybe it wasn't anything more than we already knew.

"Anything else?" I asked.

"I've been studying enough Elvish that I can decode some of it, but I'll need the book Hemlock gave me to translate it all," Ava said.

A piece of paper rustled in Marcus' hands. He must've conjured it, because he didn't have it with him earlier. "Here," he told Ava. "I've got something you can start writing the translations on."

Ava began humming while she translated the runes she recognized. Kallie and Marcus walked around the room to look at the runes.

Kallie snickered. "That one looks like a... well, you know."

"I *don't* know," Marcus said dryly.

Kallie sounded disappointed in him. "A dick. A penis. A cock. Take your pick."

"It does not," he argued. "These are a *work of art*."

"A dick can be a work of art, too," Kallie pointed out.

I slumped against the wall, because there was nothing I could do to help— or to stop them. Oberi had stopped playing catch with me and sat over by Ava, happily slapping his tail against the ground.

After what felt like hours, Ava finally announced, "I translated a passage. It's probably the only one I can do for now. The others are too complicated."

Marcus and Kallie quieted, and we all turned our attention to Ava.

"What does it say?" I asked.

"It's not an *exact* translation," she admitted. "But the gist of it is an overview of demigod powers."

I perked up a little. So, it wasn't necessarily about the prophecy. Learning more about our powers was useful in other aspects, too. "Did you learn anything new?"

"Yeah. It says here that demigods are able to overpower supernatural restraints," she said.

I thought about it a moment. "Supernatural restraints... like noxite?"

"Exactly," she replied brightly. "It doesn't specifically mention noxite. I'm not even sure the Elves had a symbol for it. I never saw any mention of noxite anywhere in my book. But *supernatural restraints* must mean noxite, right?"

"This could be a game-changer for us!" Kallie cried.

"Yeah, we could actually escape," Marcus pointed out.

My heart surged for a second before Ava said, "I'm not sure I'd go *that* far. *Overpower* isn't an exact translation. Magic like noxite will still weaken a demigod, but because they're so powerful, it won't be as effective as on a regular supernatural."

"That makes sense," I said thoughtfully.

"What does?" Ava asked.

"Down in the mines, people talk about how tired they get from the noxite exposure," I explained. "My magic takes a bit of a hit too, but I'm still able to use it."

"How far do you think we could take this?" Kallie wondered aloud. "I mean, could we blast through the effects of a noxite bracelet? Could we get through the fences?"

I got thrilled over the idea— the first thing I'd been excited about in a while. This gave us a huge advantage inside the prison— against the guards, the Warden, and even other students. It could be our ticket out of here.

"Damn," Marcus muttered. "I wish we would've tested it out on our field trip."

"We can still test it out," I said.

Kallie scoffed. "I'm not trying to jump the fence again."

I smirked. "There are other ways to experiment with noxite."

"Charlie, no," Ava protested immediately, sensing where I was going with it.

"Hey, pidge, you said you wanted my help," I said nonchalantly. "Did you mean it, or not?"

Ava fell silent, then gingerly said, "What were you thinking?"

I smiled. "Leave that to me, baby girl."

I STAYED on high alert the following day, waiting for my opportunity. Ava was wholly against this. She didn't want me playing with noxite.

But screw it. I didn't want her messing with the prophecy, and she damn well didn't listen to me. I wondered if I was doing this just to spite her, but I pushed the thought aside. *Someone* had to take one for the team and figure this out.

Not all the guards carried fully-dosed noxite guns. They were *supposed* to be diluted, so they just slowed us down, not totally knocked us out. They didn't want us missing shifts at the mines if they could help it. But I'd overheard some of the guards during fight club training. They'd bragged about their full-powered guns and how they just *loved* to test them out on students. I just had to find one of the jerks.

"Where's Ava?" Ez asked with a full mouth as I sat beside him at lunch. The cafeteria was alive with chatter.

"Sulking, because we got into another argument," I teased. "What else?"

"What happened?" he asked hoarsely.

"Nothing. Ancestors, you worry too much." I took a bite of a dinner roll. "You act like she's *your* little sister, not the other way around."

"Someone has to look out for her," he said.

I swallowed. "Oberi's with her."

Footsteps approached. At first, I thought it might be Marcus, but then a heavy hand landed on my shoulder. The hand was cold, with a firm grip. Definitely a vampire.

"I've got a message from the Captain," a gruff voice growled in my ear. He sounded older, like one of the guards. And he worked for

Captain, which meant I'd found my man. "You fight this weekend— no exceptions."

I hadn't entered a fight since Deuce kicked my ass weeks ago. I was ready to get back into the ring and reclaim my title. But I wanted a noxite dart in my ass even more.

"Tell him I refuse," I snapped.

Ez gasped from beside me. He didn't know about fight club, but he sure as hell knew you didn't talk to a guard like that.

"What did you just say?" the guard snarled.

I turned to him. "You heard me. I'm not doing it."

"You don't have a choice." The guard tried to keep his voice down, but the irritation was clear in his tone.

I stood and puffed out my chest. Damn, it felt good to stand up to one of these jerks. "Who's gonna stop me? You?"

His gun clinked against his belt as he grabbed for it. "If I have to. You really want to make a scene, Bandit?"

I leaned toward him and hissed, "If it keeps me out of the ring. I'll fight when I say I *want* to fight."

"You'll fight when you're told," he hissed back.

"You want to see a fight?" I challenged. "Be my guest."

I swung a fist, and it cracked against the guards' jaw. Pain radiated through my knuckles, and adrenaline shot through my veins. I could practically dance across the cafeteria, it felt so good.

If anyone actually believed the crap I just spewed, they didn't know me at all. I *loved* the fight.

Gasps traveled around the cafeteria, but I didn't care. I was just glad Ava wasn't here to see it, or she'd make a big deal out of it.

"Get down on the ground!" the guard shouted. The cafeteria quieted.

I chuckled under my breath. He was trying to let me down easy, since I was in the fight club.

"Or what?" I challenged, shoving him. I'd probably get an infraction for it, but I didn't care. I needed this brawl. "You'll shoot me?"

The guard laughed in satisfaction. "You asked for it, kid," he sneered.

A *click* sounded, and a sharp pain entered my thigh. I immediately felt my energy siphon out of me, and I collapsed to the ground.

"Charlie!" Ezekiel cried. The guard snapped at him, and he backed away.

I'd only collapsed for show. I paid close attention to the sensations spreading through my body. Tingles radiated from the injection site, and fatigue washed over me. A full dose would knock any supernatural out, but not me. I was weak, but conscious for the whole thing.

"Get him on a stretcher," the guard growled to a couple of other guards.

Two pairs of hands landed on me, and they lifted me onto a stretcher. Ez was nearly sobbing beside me.

"Take him to the infirmary," the guard instructed.

"You sure?" one of them asked.

"He's learned his lesson," the guard replied spitefully.

I resisted a prideful smirk. He'd probably bet on me for the next fight, and didn't want to report me to the Warden.

They lifted me, and the sounds of the cafeteria drifted away as they carried me through the halls. Noxite continued to work through my system, and if I didn't know better, I'd have thought I was in the mines. My magic went from feeling like a strong buzz inside my body to a low hum. I didn't like how it felt— like my strength was being stolen from me.

"Noxite dart to the thigh," one of the guards told the nurse.

"Set him right here," she said. "He should be back on his feet in twenty-four hours."

The guards transferred me onto a bed, then left. The nurse assumed I was knocked out and didn't say anything to me. I waited until her footsteps faded and I heard no one else around before I tested my magic out.

A breeze passed through the room. I pushed to see how far I could go, until I created a whirlwind in my palm. I levitated myself off the bed a few inches, but I couldn't go much further than that.

Ava's theory was right— demigods *were* stronger than noxite, but it still limited us.

I kept trying different things with my magic. I was working on blooming a flower in a vase across the room when I heard a noise and drew back my magic. Several pairs of footsteps came racing over to me, so fast I couldn't count how many people there were.

"Charlie!" Ava cried. She flung herself onto me. Since I didn't know who was with her, I didn't react. Oberi jumped on top of me, and I had to hold back a grunt as his paws sank into my gut. He licked the side of my face.

"Is he conscious?" Marcus asked.

"He better be," Kallie replied. She slapped my shoulder lightly. "Charlie, it's okay. It's just us."

I sighed. "Ava's theory is right."

"I can't believe you got yourself shot!" Ava hissed, though she sounded slightly relieved.

"What are your side effects?" Marcus asked.

"Yeah, I'm super curious," Kallie added as she leaned on the bed a little. "Marcus and I were shot when we tried to escape last semester, but the formula was diluted. What's a full dose like?"

I drew a breath, wondering how to explain it to them. It was an odd sensation I couldn't quite put into words. "You know when a furnace is running, and you don't really notice it's going until it turns off? And suddenly you realize the whole room was making noise?"

"Yeah," Ava and Kallie said together.

Marcus was oblivious. "You guys notice that kind of thing?"

I ignored him and continued. "It's kind of like that, but like the furnace is just malfunctioning, not totally turned off. I can still use my magic."

"Show us," Ava said, sounding intrigued.

I called upon my Air power, and a breeze swept through the room. "I think if I keep practicing, I can do better. Noxite won't stop us."

"This is good," Ava said thoughtfully. "I don't know how we're going to use it yet, though."

Marcus shifted, and his shirt brushed against my arm. "It's worth keeping in our back pocket for when we need it."

"Agreed," Ava replied. "I'll bet the Warden knows noxite doesn't work on demigods. It's probably why it's all around the Institute in the first place. If he suspects any of us are immune, he'll find a reason to send us to Cellblock 9. We have to be extra careful with this."

Kallie scoffed. "I'd rather suck a dragon dick than get caught."

Marcus stiffened beside me, and Ava snickered.

"We'll be discreet," I said. "I can swipe some noxite from the mines for us to practice pushing our powers with in private."

"As long as we aren't caught, then I'll push whatever limits I have to," Kallie said.

"Same," Ava added.

Marcus hesitated a moment, then added, "Eh, it's magic. What's another challenge?"

We were all on board with testing our noxite limits. We talked a while longer, until we heard a nurse passing through the ward. I went back to pretending I was unconscious, while the nurse told the others they'd overstayed their welcome.

"Charlie and I are bonded," Ava argued. "Elementai are permitted to have their Familiar with them in the infirmary. Seeing as Charlie and I share a Familiar, I believe it's my *right* to stay."

The nurse sounded skeptical, but she let Ava stick around. Soon, the two of us were alone in the ward, with Oberi curled up at my feet.

Ava squeezed my hand. "I'm going to stay here all night."

"I'm not hurt," I assured her. "It's all right."

"It's not," she insisted. "Noxite or not, you got shot."

Ava kept pushing it until I agreed. I didn't think she was worried about the noxite. The fear pulsing through our bond was stronger than that. It was like she was afraid someone like Deuce or Mad Dog might show up and try to hurt me while I was vulnerable. It was nice of her to care, but I was the one who was supposed to be protecting her, not the other way around.

Ava and I talked for hours, mostly about music. She sang a song to me that she'd written in class earlier that day, and I helped her tweak the lyrics in the chorus that she was struggling with. We were working on another song when I realized the nurses hadn't come to check on us in a while.

"What time is it?" I asked.

"Almost midnight," she replied. "Why?"

"The nurses must've forgotten about you," I remarked. "The dorms are already locked down for the night."

"I'd rather be here with you," she said softly.

"You should get some sleep."

She pulled the sheets back and crawled into bed with me. Oberi shifted at my feet, but he was asleep. Ava laid her head on my chest. "Can I sleep right here?"

I squeezed her tightly to me. Her raspberry scent surrounded me. Ancestors, I wished we could fall asleep like this every night. "Right here is perfect."

The moment I pressed a kiss to the top of her head, a gust of wind swept through the empty infirmary. Oberi perked up immediately, and Ava gasped.

I froze. "That wasn't me."

Ava shot upright to a sitting position. "Charlie, it's... *ancestors.*"

She trailed off, like she couldn't find the words. Amazement filled her voice.

"What is it?" I sat up next to her. A magical energy sizzled in the air that felt welcoming and warm. The magical buzz swirled around me, melting away all tension in my body and filling me with peace.

"It's an *ancestor!*" she cried in excitement. "It's a spirit of a *beautiful* whale, dancing above us like a watercolor painting."

The spirit swooped downward, and her energy touched my skin— as if she'd passed through me. When our spirits touched, an image formed in my mind of what Ava had described... a massive whale of so many colors, bleeding together into light. It was like when I'd witnessed my ancestors last semester. They'd reached out to touch me after Ava had summoned them in the Lair. Absolutely breathtaking.

"She's... transforming... into a woman." Ava's words slowed as she took in the wonder of the magic.

Even without seeing her, I could sense we were in the presence of a great supernatural being. Her energy surrounded me and felt warm and kind, like a motherly hug. I'd never felt magic so strong before— save for one time, at the Villain's Ball, when Ava had been talking to the deity known as Coyote Spirit.

Then the ancestor reached out to touch me again. I stiffened as the image of a woman broke into my mind. It'd been so long since I could see that I had no visual memories of what people *looked like.* But this woman was different. She had long, dark hair, kind eyes, and a gentle smile. I instantly felt warm against her in the light of her presence.

Ava grabbed my arm. "*Whale Spirit!* Charlie, it's the Elementai Goddess of Water— the Goddess of Toaqua and part of the Great Spirit."

My jaw hung slack. I could hardly wrap my head around it. "She's here for us...?"

"*It is nice to see you again, Ava-Marie,*" Whale Spirit said in a melodic voice.

"Again?" Ava asked. "But we've never met."

"*We have, you just didn't see me,*" Whale Spirit said kindly. "*I was there in the hospital when your father was healed, the night he nearly died. You remember, don't you, Ava?*"

She gasped. "That was you?"

Whale Spirit didn't answer directly. Instead, she said, "*I have been beside you always, along with Coyote. From your birth, gods and goddesses on the side of the light and the dark have been warring over you, attempting to control your path. Some have even sought to take your life. Do you remember when you were a young girl, and you went missing in the forest?*"

I hadn't heard this story before, but to Ava, it seemed to make sense. "Yes! I was so little— one moment I was in my house, and the next, I was in the woods. A monster attacked me, but something saved me!"

"*A dark entity, sent by an evil god, teleported you into the forest in order to take your life,*" Whale Spirit said gently. "*But Coyote and I sent your spirit guides to protect you, and they defeated the creature while you ran away.*"

"The animal that saved me... it must've been a bear," Ava choked out. "It was my grandfather's spirit!"

"*Precisely, dear.*" Whale Spirit had reached out to stroke Ava's hair. I felt the chill from her hand emitting near my skin. "*You are very important to the magical world— you always have been. Ever since, deities in the spiritual realm have been fighting over your existence, and trying to control you. I am here to say that you must not listen, and must forge your own path. Be very careful, for there are mortals and gods alike that seek to bring about your end.*"

Ava's voice wavered. "What do I need to know?"

"*I am here to deliver a message,*" Whale Spirit announced. "*You are closer than you believe to your goal. The directions are already in your hands.*"

My stomach dropped. This was about the prophecy.

"What directions?" Ava asked. "To Forevermore?"

"*You must go into the noxite mines for the answers you seek,*" Whale Spirit said. "*But be warned. Reaching your destination will not be easy. There will be traps along the way. But should demigods as yourselves work together as one, you will conquer these obstacles and uncover the truth.*"

"The mines..." Ava mused to herself, before turning to me. "Charlie, that must be where the next key is! That means—"

Ava cut off as the magic filling the room dissipated. Whale Spirit was gone.

"Wait, no!" Ava cried. "Come back. I have questions!"

The room remained silent. It took me a few moments to gather my breath. The last thing I wanted to do was find another key to that damned portal.

"We can't go down into the mines," I stated bluntly.

"We have to," Ava argued. "You heard Whale Spirit! That's where the next key is!"

"Yeah, I heard that she said there were *traps* down there. I can't stand to see you get hurt."

"I won't. I'm *meant* to do this."

"But there's noxite in the mines," I argued.

"What does that matter?" Ava asked. "You just proved that noxite has minimal effects on us."

Hell. I'd fucked myself over on that one.

"But the mines are huge." I was grasping at straws. "How are we supposed to find a single key hidden inside a full cave system?"

Ava thought for a moment. "Whale Spirit said we had the directions. I'll bet you anything she's talking about the runes we found in the Lair."

I swallowed. "Do you think you can translate them all?"

"I have to try," she said. "I'll talk to Hemlock and see if she can help me decipher the runes I don't know. As far as traps go, I know an expert."

I took Ava's hands. I wasn't sure how much closer to the prophecy I could get without telling her what Maddie said lay on the other side. Just thinking about getting one step closer tore me to shreds. "Pidge, this is…"

Fucking crazy, I wanted to say.

Instead, she finished my sentence for me. "Dangerous, I know. But I wouldn't be here if I was scared of danger."

She sat up straighter and spoke firmly. "I don't care what traps lie between us and whatever's down in those mines. Before the semester is over, we're going down there. One way or another, we're getting the next key."

"Pidge…" I didn't know how to stop her, but I *had* to. I was putting my foot down. "You can't. I won't allow it."

"What?" she squeaked. *"You won't allow it?* You're not my father. And even *he* couldn't stop me."

"I *do* hold half of our soul, though," I reminded her. "I think I get some say in what you do with your half of it."

Ava placed her hand on the side of my face, and her tone softened. "Oh, Charlie. The last thing I want is for you to worry about me— about *us.* But you heard what Whale Spirit said. I'm important to the magical world, and you're a part of me, which means you're important, too."

"What if I don't want to be important?" I whispered.

Ava lowered her head onto my chest again. "Don't you realize, Charlie? You already *are.* You are more important to me than you can ever imagine."

I squeezed her tightly. I was glad she was lying on my chest, because I didn't want her to see the tears pricking at my eyes. No one had ever told me I was important to them before. A brand new emotion settled into my heart. It was so warm and comforting. I felt as if I could lie here for days, just soaking up Ava's warmth. Her words, and her body pressed close to mine, made me feel *loved.* I never knew what such a thing could feel like until now.

"And that's why I have to fulfill this prophecy," she said. "Because if I save the supernatural world… I save you."

I swore my heart grew three sizes. How the hell could she care about me that much?

I knew the answer before I finished asking the question— because I knew exactly what it felt like to care about someone that dearly. It was the same way I cared about her. I was desperately in love— in a way that had shifted my entire world.

I kissed the top of her head. "You have no idea how much it means to hear that."

Ava yawned and snuggled into me deeper. Hell, it didn't matter that we were in prison or the center of a dangerous prophecy. This moment was perfect. I'd do anything for this incredible woman.

Which was why I couldn't keep protesting. The more I pushed, the more Ava pushed back. She was going after answers one way or another — with or without me. And so I had to follow her.

I just hoped I could save her from herself.

ava-marie

TWENTY

We had an objective. The four of us needed to get into the noxite mines, and begin our search there for the next key. But first, I had to interpret the instructions on the floor of the Lair.

I'd spoken to Hemlock about the Elven runes I didn't know, which was difficult, because I had to play it off as research and not give away that we were trying to gain clues for a secret exploration. With her help, I'd managed to cobble together the phrases that were carved into the stone floor.

There will be trials.
A ghostly summoning
A riddle in the dark
A temptation by illusion
A flooding of water
And a door that will only open
With the blood of one that is mine.

They were obviously steps to get to the next key. As far as I could tell, they were warnings about booby traps set up to protect the key. But I didn't understand what these clues meant just yet.

My grandfather was a great explorer. He had so much experience crawling around in caves and looking for ancient civilizations. If anyone could help us understand what these instructions meant, it was him.

On Saturday morning, I hurried to the phones and dialed my grandparents' number. The elegant voice of my Grandmother Eleanor drifted over the line as she picked up the phone.

"Ava, darling, so nice of you to say hello," she said fairly. "I do wish they'd get rid of that dreadful message at the beginning. *You are receiving a phone call from a student at the Darke Institute for Supernaturals Offenders.* Huh." She huffed. "As if I do not *know* who's calling. Do I look like an imbecile who cannot read a telephone number?"

I laughed. "No one ever mistook you for one."

"It must be important," my grandmother stated. "Your grandfather and I were just about to pay another visit to the heart doctor. The Great Spirit himself knows he needs to watch his cholesterol."

"The Great Spirit *herself*, grandmother," I reminded her. "You know how I feel about it."

"Ava, please, enough of this *God is a woman* nonsense," Grandmother Eleanor said. "If God was a woman, he would've gotten it right the first time."

I heard Grandpa choke in the background, as if he considered what she said heresy, or something of a similar effect. My grandmother said, "Here's your grandfather. Oh, Elliot, did you stain your shirt *again*? It's hardly ten o'clock in the morning!"

Grandpa took the phone from her. "Ava, what a wonderful surprise! What do you need?"

I had to ponder how to ask the question, as I needed to be careful what I exposed. "I've actually been studying Elven culture," I told him. "It's fascinating."

"Is it now?" Grandpa's voice was tinged with excitement. He was always tickled pink whenever I brought up anthropology. "You know, the Elves were an incredible people. They were phenomenal fighters, had amazing voices, and were extremely talented at music—"

"Yes, I'm definitely learning all about them," I said, because

Grandpa would go on a tangent if I didn't cut him off now, and I only had five minutes to talk. "The thing is, I think I'm on to something."

"Ooh. What did you find?" Grandpa asked.

"Just a book in the library," I lied, because I didn't know who might be listening in. "It said something about booby traps. Did the Elves ever set any up?"

"Oh, absolutely!" Grandpa said. "The Elves were the heads of the criminal underworld, way back in the day. They often placed traps to protect their stolen goods, and the lairs that they hid in."

That probably meant whoever placed the traps long ago had been damn good at making them. This wasn't going to be easy.

"So, I found evidence of traps Elves might have placed on Darke Island," I said. "Do you think you can help me interpret what they are?"

"Let's hear it," Grandpa said in a jolly way. "I'm sure we can work it out."

I told him about the phrases I'd found written into the stone—though I fabricated that I'd researched about them in a book instead. I could hear Grandpa scratch his stubble as he said, "This certainly wasn't in any book I've ever read about the Elves, and I've read a lot of them. Written a few, myself."

"Yes, we are all aware of your academic achievements, Elliot," Grandmother Eleanor said tiredly from across the room.

"Those bastards at the Supernatural Anthropology Society *knew* I deserved that award!" he shot back sourly. "Instead they give the prize to Professor Woolly for his essay on magical mushrooms. *Mushrooms*, dammit! I didn't survive the Hawkei Civil War to write my manifesto on supernatural races, only to be beaten out by fungi."

"Grandpa, focus." I pulled his attention back. "What does this all mean?"

Grandpa made a musing sound. "These riddles could mean anything," he began. "*But*, what's important for you to know is that to get around them, booby traps always leave clues as to how to escape. Difficult to find when you're currently trying to escape one, but there is *always* a way out. I've found that often enough when I've had to squeeze my way out of being impaled on spikes in ancient temples, you know."

My grandmother scoffed, and I smiled. Daddy had gone on an expedition with my grandpa once, and had ranted often how he'd nearly been flattened by rolling boulders and charred by fire traps while my grandfather was aimlessly poking around. I thought Grandpa had avoided all those traps by dumb luck, but maybe he really did know what he was doing.

"Are Elven traps unavoidable once you set them off?" I asked.

"Well, when people place booby traps, they do so in order to prevent the wrong people from finding the treasure within," Grandpa said wisely. "Which means the only people who will be able to pass the tasks are either the ones who set the traps, or the ones whom the trap makers *intended* to get through the traps in the first place."

"What else would an explorer look out for, while journeying through Elven ruins?" I asked, taking mental notes.

"Well, when wandering through any place you're unsure of, you have to use your surroundings. Try analyzing and evaluating the space before you walk in. Use *all* your senses, and not just your eyes— they can be deceiving. When in doubt, think as the trap makers would— in this situation, as the Elves do. Does that help?"

"Yes, more than you realize," I said excitedly.

"A paper you're writing, is it?" he asked.

"Yes," I said, but my heart sank. I hated lying to anyone in my family, but Grandpa was especially hard, because he was just so gullible, and that made it even worse.

"I'm so *proud* of you that you're following in my footsteps! You're going to make a wonderful anthropologist someday," he gruffed.

"It's your fault." I laughed. I'd had the exploring bug ever since he'd given me my first headlamp at five years old.

"Of course it is. Someone has to keep up the work after I'm gone," Grandpa said warmly. "Who better than my granddaughter?"

I didn't like talking about Grandpa dying. It hurt. The phone pinged, telling me my five minutes were up. "Thank you so much, Grandpa. This is really going to aid my research."

"Anytime, Ava. You know my wealth of knowledge is at your disposal," Grandpa said.

"Hmph. More like your endless foolishness," Grandmother quipped.

"I'm writing a letter!" Grandpa raged. "Let's see what the society board thinks about *me* after I tell them exactly what I think of the situation!"

I hung up the phone with a giggle. I skipped down to lunch— because I was in a good mood due to making so much progress, so why not? Before I entered the cafeteria, I heard someone shout my name.

"Ava!" Ivy came tearing up the hallway. He grabbed my hands and began jumping up and down. "I did it, I *did* it!"

"Did what?" I didn't know what was going on, but I began bouncing with him anyway, because his enthusiasm was contagious.

"I asked Chancey to be my boyfriend, and he said *yes!*" Ivy gushed. "I just took charge, and told him how I feel. And he said he felt the same way!"

"That's amazing, Ivy!" I gave him a tight hug. "I'm so happy for you."

"Isn't it the greatest?" Tears beaded in Ivy's eyes. "We're going for a walk around the prison yard tonight. I just can't wait."

"I knew it was all going to work out. See, I told you!" I squeezed his arms.

A grin spanned across Ivy's face. "I'm just glad the *both* of us got our man. I've wanted Chancey and I to have what you and Charlie do for so long, and now, it's finally coming true. Thank you *so much*, Ava."

My spirit fell into my stomach as I watched Ivy twirl away. Chancey and Ivy seemed closer than ever, but when it came to Charlie and I, we just seemed so far away. This prophecy was pushing us apart, and I hated it.

I slid beside Charlie in the cafeteria. Kallie and Marcus, who were sitting across from us, leaned inward. Oberi panted under the table while Rishi batted at my shoelaces.

I nudged Charlie, but he didn't say anything— just remained stiff. I bit my lip, wondering if I should tell them what I knew. If it made Charlie upset, I didn't want to have anything to do with it.

But this was prophecy stuff. And I knew we couldn't avoid this forever.

"Did you find out anything?" Marcus asked.

I bobbed my head. "Yes! My grandpa gave me really good information."

I launched into an explanation of the phone call. By the end, Kallie was twirling her braid around her finger.

"The clues are definitely trials to get to the key, and according to your grandpa, only the right person can get through them," Kallie mused. "Interesting."

"Yeah, which means maybe we shouldn't try," Marcus said nervously. "We'll get killed if we try to get through those traps."

"Don't you get it? The trials were set up for *demigods*. That's who the Elves wanted to find the keys to Forevermore!" I said. "We're the perfect people to get through those traps, because we're the only people who *can* get past them. They're basically designed for us. What better hint do we need that we're on the right path?"

"How are we going to get into the mines? Charlie's the only one who's got clearance, and it's off campus. We can't get there unless the bus takes us," Marcus said.

A guard came to the front of the room, calling everyone to attention. "Listen up!" he barked, and the cafeteria immediately fell silent. "The Warden wants to increase noxite production down in the mines, and the current output isn't enough. We're taking volunteers for prisoners who are willing to perform extra work down in the mines. You'll be compensated with points from Commissary, as well as the potential to have infractions wiped off your record. Anyone interested should sign up on the sheet at the front of the cafeteria."

The guard went to stand behind a table by the head of the room, and my heart started. This was our chance.

"Why does the Warden want to increase production down in the noxite mines? What's he looking for?" Marcus whispered.

"It's obvious, isn't it?" I asked. "He *knows* there's a key down there, just like we do. And now he's excavating the caves, trying to find it."

"Which means we need to find it first," Kallie said. "We should volunteer, so we can get down in those mines as soon as possible."

"Exactly," I said.

Charlie made a sharp sound. "No, Ava. That's no job for a girl."

"What, do you think Kallie and I can't handle it?" I snapped.

"That's not what I meant. But it's horrible down there. There's a reason they only schedule boys for the mines, and let girls work in the mining office. It's worse than hard work. I don't want you going through that," Charlie said.

"Well, we don't have a choice, so we'll have to suck it up," Kallie replied. "I'm sure we can mine better than limp noodle over here." She jerked a thumb at Marcus.

"I'm not even offended," Marcus stated. "I know I've got weak arms."

Charlie grumbled, but I said, "This is the only way to get down in those mines. We have to do this."

Kallie, Marcus and I went to the table, and put our names down on the sheet to volunteer to work down in the mines. We were the only ones that did— nobody wanted to sign up for the worst job at the prison, even if you got extra privileges because of it.

"Doesn't it look a bit suspicious that we're voluntarily going down there?" Marcus asked as we walked away.

"Yeah, but what choice do we have?" Kallie asked. "We need to get down in those mines."

My insides tumbled with nervousness. I could tell Charlie was discontent with our plan just by the way he was acting.

He barely spoke to me for the rest of the day.

"Are you mad?" I whispered. I was sitting on his lap at the end of the day, on the balcony overlooking the prison yard. Oberi spun around in circles beside us, trying to catch his tail. "You seemed really bothered about our plan this morning."

Charlie's face twisted. "Of course I'm not mad at you. I'm just worried this is going to go wrong. I have a... bad feeling about this."

"What's so bad about finding another key? It'll get us a step closer to our goal," I said.

"And what if it rips us apart?" Charlie asked. "I won't lose you, pidge. Not for anything."

Oberi whimpered, and I brushed back Charlie's hair. "What could separate us? We're bonded, we share a Familiar, we even share a soul. Far as I'm concerned, I don't see anything that could make us want to walk away from each other— even if a prophecy is involved."

Charlie didn't answer, just held me tighter. I curled up on his lap and nestled my head against his chest.

Charlie didn't understand— I'd already made my decision weeks ago, after I'd told him I loved him.

I knew Charlie would burn down the world for me, so I'd do the same for him. If it came down to saving the supernatural races, or saving Charlie, I already knew who I'd pick... and it'd be Charlie every time.

I didn't care if it was selfish, or wrong. And the ancestors had made a mistake. They had picked the wrong person to be a hero. How could they expect a *villain* to save the world? I had a dark side— no, more than that, I was evil. I made bad choices, half of the time because I didn't know any better, and the other half just because it felt *so good* to be bad. I couldn't help it if they'd chosen the wrong girl.

I was a villain, and when we loved, we loved *hard*. Charlie was my everything, and I couldn't see myself sacrificing him for the world's sake, even if it came down to it. I wasn't my mother— I wasn't a chosen one who could give up the one she loved for the sake of other people. I wasn't that kind, that noble. I was a person who protected the people she loved with a ferocity hell itself was afraid of, damn the consequences.

Charlie was the world I wanted to save, because he was *my world*. I'd cease to fulfill the prophecy if that's what kept him safe. If I had to turn my back on the magical world, abandon my destiny and disappoint my ancestors, then so be it.

I would remain by Charlie's side, even if I had to watch this world end. No matter what happened, I wasn't going anywhere.

EARLY THE NEXT WEEK, we boarded the bus with Charlie for his Work-Study class, and were driven off the prison yard in the direction of the noxite mines. My thoughts tumbled with excitement, wondering what we'd find there— if anything at all. The next key seemed to be within reach, but at the same time, I had a feeling in my gut that we might not find what we were looking for.

I yanked at the nylon fabric on my leg with a scowl. We were given these *dreadful* blue mining uniforms, and clunky-ass boots with helmets that had a light attached. They were ugly as hell, and nothing like my exploring gear. We were practically going into this without any supplies. I didn't even have my journal.

Charlie sat beside me in silence. I touched his hand, and he grabbed it, but he didn't say a word more. His thumb rubbed the back of my hand as the bus pulled into the proximity of the noxite mines.

I looked out the window. The mines were more or less pits into hell, cave entrances that wound down into the earth. Once we got off the bus, I began coughing. The air was thick with dust and debris, and the area stung with the sharp tinge of noxite. There were already some prisoners here from the morning shift, loading noxite into mining carts and pushing them into a nearby warehouse to sort and pack.

Ezekiel began wheezing once he got off the bus. He already looked sick. Opal began walking in the direction of the mining office where she worked, but when she noticed Ez wheezing, she turned around. She started rubbing his back, and he gave her a grateful smile.

Thank the ancestors, they actually allowed Oberi and Rishi to come with us. We'd snuck them onto the bus, and the guards didn't give us shit when they saw us disembark with our animals— just told us to keep them the hell out of the way while we worked. We were given equipment, and shepherded into the darkness of the caves, where the guards took us about a mile in. Tiny lights lined the walls and provided the only illumination as the hallways grew thinner and thinner. The chill from the mines crept into my bones the further we went in. The buzzing of the noxite around me made me feel sick, even though I knew my powers could resist it. I pressed closer to Charlie, and he put an arm around me as they led us further in.

Once we reached the end of the cave, we were told to get to work. The four of us hacked away at the stone, yanking off noxite with our pick-axes. Within a few minutes, my arms were already sore, and my lungs contracted as I breathed in grime.

Charlie was right. This was hard work, and it was made worse by the close confinement of the mines, and the little light besides. Oberi and Rishi scratched at the stone with their little nails, but didn't do much besides scrape some dust off. Oberi let out a low whine, and I gave his head a pat.

It was even worse because it looked like the Institute chose the worst prisoners to work down here. The rest of our crew was all brawny men, and, as I noticed, were the type who'd been sentenced here on murder charges, or something equally heinous. The work was made more aggravating just by being in close quarters with these fucks, who seemed to get irritated by our mere presence.

"What are you looking at?" a prisoner sneered at Charlie, whose head had been turned in his direction.

"Nothing, obviously," Charlie shot back. The prisoner reddened when he realized his stupid mistake, and walked away to work on a different part of the mines.

Kallie shuffled closer to whisper, her back turned to the guard watching us. "How are we going to get away? The sooner we leave, the more time we have to explore the rest of the caves."

"I could cause another cave-in," Charlie suggested.

"That wouldn't be safe. If you did, we wouldn't be sure if we could dig our way out, even with your Nivita magic," I pointed out. "The last cave-in almost killed you and a couple others. We don't know how stable the tunnels are, and caving them in at the wrong place could topple the whole system."

"We have bigger problems than getting away. What happens once they realize we're gone?" Marcus asked, wiping sweat off his brow. He was already worn out from mining. He hit the rocks with all the force of a teddy bear.

"I can cast an illusion. Duplicates of us to work in the mines while we're gone," Kallie suggested. "As long as the guards don't get too close, they'll think it's us."

"Isn't that really hard magic?" Marcus asked. "Most fae can't duplicate themselves without getting sick, let alone three other people, and the noxite down here weakens our powers."

"It is difficult, but I can pull it off," Kallie said confidently. "But it won't last forever— only a couple of hours."

"We're slated to be down here for the next four hours. We have to be back by the time our shift is over, or we're in big trouble," Charlie said.

"We just need a diversion," Kallie said, casting her head over her shoulder like she'd been looking for one.

Ezekiel came back with another empty cart. He'd been given the job of loading the noxite into the carts instead of working in the mines directly, as Charlie had promised me, but his face was still red with exhaustion. He began loading the noxite fragments into the cart wearily, a hand placed on one side of the cart like he feared he was going to tip over and needed it to stay upright.

I placed a gentle hand on his shoulder. "Ez, you okay?"

He gave a double-take. He hadn't seen me board the bus, or come down here to work. "Ava, what are you doing here?" he hissed. "It's not a place for you."

"We're here because of my prophecy," I hushed, and he tilted his head. "There's something we need down in the mines, but we have to get away to go find it. We can't do that with the guards watching us like hawks."

Ezekiel glanced back at the guards and hushed, "Leave it to me. Opal and I will cause a distraction. It'll leave you guys time to go."

"If we hurry, we might be able to find it and get back before the guards even realize we're gone," Marcus added, and Ez nodded.

I gave him a grateful smile. "Thanks, Ez. You're a real lifesaver."

"Don't thank me. You're the one trying to save the world. I just want to help," he offered.

Ezekiel pushed the cart back out of the mine. After he'd been gone for ten minutes, Kallie whispered, "How do we know when he's caused a—?"

There was the sound of a loud explosion, one that shook the mine and caused dirt to fall from the cave ceiling. It was so strong that it almost knocked me over, until Charlie caught me. Marcus, unfortunately, went face-first into the wall and smashed his nose. Kallie helped him up as he groaned, holding his face as blood trickled between his fingers. The rest of the prisoners were on the ground.

A radio attached to the guard's hip buzzed with an urgent voice. *"The office is on fire, and spreading to the warehouse! We need all staff available to put it out!"*

The guard picked up his radio. "Be there straight away."

He shoved the radio back onto the holster on his hip, and pointed at us. "You degenerates better not go anywhere, or I'll make you pay for it once I find you," he growled.

"Wouldn't dream of it," Charlie replied sarcastically. The guard huffed, and hurried back with the rest of his cronies to the entrance of the mine.

The other prisoners working with us instantly took their chance to take off down different tunnels, but I knew they wouldn't get far. They'd be arrested the minute they left the cave entrance, with how many guards were at the head of it trying to put the fire out. Idiots.

But we were different. We were going further in.

Kallie cast the illusion spell. I blinked as I saw copies of her, Marcus, Charlie and myself formulate before our very eyes. The duplicates were identical to us, not a piece of hair out of place. It was so weird, seeing a magical twin of yourself moving around in the real world. The duplicates knelt down to grab our pick-axes, and began chipping away at the noxite.

Kallie bent over her middle, in terrible pain. Her face twisted up, teeth clenched like casting the spell had been difficult. She let out a gasp, but her illusion didn't waver.

Marcus immediately came to her side. "Kallie, are you okay?" he asked, placing a hand on her back.

"I'm fine," she ground out. "We need to get moving. Those guards won't be gone forever, and this spell won't last more than a couple of hours."

I watched the eerie sight of our clones hacking away at the noxite stone, before Charlie grabbed my arm. "Come on."

He waved his hand, and his Earth magic began shifting the dirt and stone that made the tunnel's end. We walked forward, and Charlie continued to move the dirt around us until we came to an entirely different tunnel. Charlie sealed up the dirt behind us, so the guards couldn't follow our footprints or see where we'd gone.

"Very impressive," I said as the four of us clicked our headlamps on. Oberi barked, and Rishi let out a low mew.

"I stole a noxite cuff from a guard and have been practicing magic with it on," Charlie said. "It gets stronger the more I work at it."

"How do you think your brother and Opal started the fire?" Kallie asked as we continued down the dark tunnel. Marcus rustled in his pocket, taking out a map of the noxite tunnels underneath Darke Island that we'd grabbed from the library before we left.

"Opal must've used her siren scream to explode the furnace in the office," I said. "We owe her one."

We wandered down the tunnel, until eventually, the noxite in the walls faded completely. I knew there was no more noxite around us once the buzzing in my ears had stopped. The fatigue from being around the poisonous compound drained away, leaving me energized again.

The tunnels here didn't look like they'd been excavated— instead, they were smooth and uniform, domed arches rising over our heads like expert carvers had sculpted them in ages past.

"The noxite must be close to the surface," Marcus mused. "These tunnels that we're going into must've been built by the Elves centuries ago."

"Are we *sure* the Elves built these tunnels?" Charlie asked, but his words cut off as he slammed into me from behind. Charlie rubbed his stomach as he backed away.

"Ava, watch where you're going. You know I can't see," Charlie complained.

I didn't answer, my eyes fixated on carvings in the stone beside us. Kallie and Marcus had fallen silent, but Charlie continued ranting. "This was a stupid idea. These tunnels are so old, they could collapse on us at any moment. We should turn around—"

Charlie stopped talking as I took his hand and ran it over the embellishments in the wall. He frowned as his fingers moved across the stone, realizing what they were.

Elven runes. Hundreds of them were carved into the walls, leading the way down into the depths of the Earth.

The next key was so close— it could just be a few more steps away. All we had to do was get past the traps that the Elves had hidden in the tunnels.

Life was nothing without a little risk. And in my opinion, I loved the thrill of putting my life on the line. I didn't mind if things got a little dangerous.

Maybe even deadly.

charlie
TWENTY-ONE

I didn't know if it was by sheer luck or divine guidance, but somehow, we'd ended up in the right tunnel. These runes proved it. We were deep within the caves now, perhaps even further than I'd traveled when I'd been trapped by the cave-in. We must've been the first ones down here in a century.

"What do the runes say?" I asked Ava.

"They're instructions," she answered. "Like the ones we found in the Criminal Lair. That must mean we're in the right place!"

"So it's the riddle again?" Kallie questioned.

"Just the first part," Ava replied. "It says: *A ghostly summoning.* Then just *Forevermore* over and over."

"A... ghostly..." Marcus trailed off, like it made him faint to think about.

"It'll be okay," Ava said quickly. "My grandpa said all booby traps have a way out, in case the person who built them accidentally trips them. This must be the first one."

"A trap? By ghosts?" Marcus' voice rose a few pitches. "That sounds a lot like possession."

"So what?" Ava said casually, like it didn't scare her. "You guys have been possessed before."

"And we had resources to brew a potion that would exercise the demon!" Marcus cried. "How are we going to—?"

Kallie cut Marcus off. She grabbed his arms and began shaking him. "Get a hold of yourself! You're a member of the fucking Miriamic Coven. Your people talk to ghosts all the time. Look at the tattoo on your arm and tell me you're not a fucking Seer!"

"Well, I-I am," Marcus stammered. "But I've never—"

"I don't care what you've never done!" Kallie barked, though she was trying to be encouraging. "You are Marcus *Fucking* Taylor, and you can handle a damn ghost! You need to start believing that you're capable—"

Kallie's voice stopped dead as a cold breeze swept through the tunnel. We all stilled, and a shiver traveled down my spine. We were so deep within the caves that there shouldn't be airflow this far down.

Ava leaned into me and shivered, while Marcus ducked behind me, as if using me as a human shield. A moan echoed down the tunnel, and my friends gave a collective gasp. Beside me, Oberi barked, and Rishi hissed.

"What is it?!" I demanded.

I barely got the question out before I felt a cold chill sweep through me. It wasn't like the chilly air, which only touched my skin. This permeated every inch of my body and ached in my bones, as if a spirit had just passed through me.

"Ancestors, it's *ghosts*!" Ava cried.

"Ghosts of the Elves!" Kallie screamed. "Hundreds of them!"

The moans grew louder as the ghosts began to surround us. My heart hammered, and I asked in a shaky tone, "They can't hurt us, right?"

"Well, actually— *oof*!" Marcus started, but he cut off when a pair of hands shoved me, and I stumbled backward into him.

"Ancestors, Kallie!" I screamed. She was the only one who wasn't near me. It had to be her.

"I didn't do it!" she cried from several feet away.

I felt the blood drain from my face. I realized I'd just been shoved by a freaking *ghost*.

"How do we— ow!" Kallie yelped. "Fuck, they left a *bruise*."

"They're just trying to scare us," Ava insisted, though she sounded frightened. "We can't turn back now. Come on!"

Ava grabbed my hand and yanked me forward. We burst out into a run— *in the direction of the ghosts*. Was she fucking insane?

Hell, we all were, just for being down here in the first place.

Rishi yowled, and Oberi continued to bark as we rushed down the tunnel. Shiver after shiver traveled down my spine as spirits of the Elves passed through me. Hands as cold as ice landed on me, taking physical form for the briefest of moments. I tried to shove them aside, but I couldn't barrel my way through spirits. One moment their hands were solid, and the next, they passed straight through me. They could touch us, but we couldn't touch them. The ghostly moans of the forgotten Elves resonated throughout the cave, like some kind of death anthem. It only made the situation that much more terrifying.

Kallie wasn't lying about the bruises. I'd taken plenty of hits this semester, but I'd only been up against one guy at a time. These attacks from the ghosts came from all angles, and they clawed at us as we ran. Fists slammed into my gut, and fingernails scratched across my face. Warm blood sprang from a wound on my cheek, and it trickled down my skin. I didn't care about myself, but I'd be damned if I let my friends get hurt.

"We have to turn back!" I protested.

Ava continued dragging me along. "We— ow— can't!"

"There's no end in sight!" Kallie cried.

Something smashed to the ground, and glass cracked. It sounded like Marcus' headlamp.

"Ava—!" I started, but my shoe caught on something solid, and I went tumbling forward. Ava and I crashed to the cave floor, and I fell on top of her.

Blow after blow landed on me as the ghosts beat us up. I tried to spring to my feet quickly, because I knew from all the fights I'd been in that you *never* stayed down. But there were just so many ghostly hands colliding with me that I couldn't move. I curled on top of Ava, doing my best to protect her from the blows. Nearby, Rishi shrieked, and Oberi howled. I heard a *thud*, then Kallie gasped, as if she'd just been shoved hard against the wall of the cave.

"Charlie, we have to keep moving!" Ava demanded.

I couldn't. If I moved, she'd be hurt. Pain radiated across my back as bruise after bruise took shape, and the ghosts continued pounding down on my raw skin. Fingers sank into my hair and tugged hard on the strands. I reached up to yank them off of me, but as soon as I tried to touch them, they vanished. A second later, they were back. There was no fighting against the ghosts.

"Marcus, how do we vanquish them?!" Ava screamed from beneath me.

"Sage, salt, and— augh— cedar oil!" he cried.

"Tell me you have some!" Kallie shrieked.

"I— fuck!" Marcus cut off. He must've conjured various items out of his stash, because several things clanked to the cave floor all at once. "Hell, that hurt!"

A sharp pain rippled through my back. "Do the spell!"

Marcus scrambled to pick up the items he'd dropped. He swore, and it sounded like he'd landed hard on his knees. He grunted several times. The ghosts were taking a real beating to him. Hell, I wished I could beat up these motherfuckers and save him, but I couldn't move.

"Sage... salt... I've got it all!" Marcus announced in a pained voice. I heard the sounds of salt crystals pouring into a bowl, then smelled the cedar oil. Something clicked, but Marcus gasped a second later. Whatever it was fell to the ground yards away. "My lighter!"

"I've got Fire!" Ava offered, but when she tried to extend her hand, one of the ghosts kicked it. Her hand flew into my face, smacking against my nose.

"I've— ow!— got it!" Marcus strained. The lighter clicked again, and the scent of burning sage filled the tunnel. He began chanting. "*I am love... I am light. You cannot hurt me! I am love... I am light. You cannot hurt me!*"

I heard the bowl scrape off the ground as Marcus, I assumed, took it into his grasp. After he repeated this several more times, he stopped wincing to catch his breath. It must've been working.

"Guys, come on!" Marcus demanded. "I can't keep shoving this bowl into their faces without help!"

Kallie started chanting along first, then Ava and I joined in. "*I am love. I am light. You cannot hurt me!*"

Marcus' voice grew, until it echoed off the walls of the tunnel. His boots squeaked as he stood. "*I am love. I am light.* YOU CANNOT HURT ME!"

The ghostly hands on me drew back, though the pain continued to ebb and flow throughout my body. The ghosts gave a deafening, hallowed cry, and Marcus took off running down the tunnel.

"I AM LOVE. I AM LIGHT. YOU CANNOT HURT ME!" His voice faded as he chased the ghosts away. Rishi screeched and tore off after him. The tunnel fell silent, apart from Marcus' echoing voice.

I groaned as I rolled off Ava. She panted, as did Kallie. Oberi rushed between Ava and me, pressing his nose to either of us in turn. I lay on the cave floor, enjoying the cold pressure on my sore back.

"Holy fuck," Kallie gasped. "That was intense."

"But we made it," Ava said. "That's one trap down. Only a few more to go."

Hell, what if we couldn't make it out of those ones?

But I told Ava I'd help, and I didn't think I'd find my way back on my own, so I had to keep going.

Time passed. I worried Marcus had been taken by the ghosts, until I heard the sound of footsteps. Marcus and Rishi returned, panting over us. "They're... gone."

I pushed myself to my feet. I was sore everywhere, but I'd gotten used to it with all the fighting I'd been doing this semester. It was the others I was worried about. "Thanks, bro."

"Yeah," Kallie added. "That was very... brave."

Was that admiration I detected in Kallie's tone?

"Is everyone all right?" I asked.

Ava sighed from beside me. "Sore, but I'll live."

"Sore?" Marcus squeaked. "Ava, you have blood running down your face."

My stomach hollowed, and I reached out for her cheek. Blood coated my fingers, and she yanked away.

"I said I'll live," she snapped.

"We should get that patched up," I insisted.

"It's fine," she countered.

"I stole a first-aid kit from the infirmary earlier this semester," Marcus said. "Hang on."

He conjured and distributed gauze pads and disinfectant wipes. We cleaned up the blood— it seemed everyone had at least a few scratches that were oozing— and continued down the tunnel.

The walk was quiet. The only sound came from our boots on the cave floor, and the rustle of our mining uniforms. I half expected the ghosts to return, but they didn't.

After several long minutes, Kallie asked, "How much farther do you think—?"

Click.

My friends all shrieked at once, and Oberi stilled from beside me. My heart gave a start.

"What?" I demanded.

"Our lights went out!" Kallie cried. She smacked her helmet, as if that would get the light to turn back on.

I stilled. "I don't have a good feeling about this."

"Relax," Ava said. "I've got Fire to light the way."

A few beats passed. I heard Ava snap her fingers several times before she cried, "What the fuck? It's not working!"

"My illusion magic isn't, either!" Kallie's voice wavered. She smacked her hands together, but apparently, nothing happened.

Marcus gasped. "I can't create light orbs! Our magic is useless."

Kallie groaned. "The Elves must've put a ward on this place, in order to take away all magic. It's part of the task. Whatever booby trap we were coming up on, we've landed in it. Our powers are going to be useless against whatever lies ahead."

"What was the next clue, pidge?" I asked quickly. "What are we up against?"

"It's the... the *riddle in the dark*!" She fumbled the words, like she'd forgotten for a moment. "None of us can see!"

I felt her panic through our bond at the loss of her sight— like the feeling of being drowned. I was sure Marcus and Kallie felt the same way. Marcus whimpered, and Kallie panted beside him. Their eyes wouldn't help them onward. Each of them were helpless in the pitch blackness of the cave.

But I wasn't. This was everyday life for me, being unable to see where I was going. I had this part handled.

"Then it's easy," I assured Ava. "It's no different for me. I'll lead you guys through it."

"You're... you're right." Ava took my hand and took in a deep breath. "We've got this."

Rishi meowed beside me— as a cat, he wasn't worried. There were a couple of large rocks in our way, and I rolled them aside with my Earth magic.

"Hey, why is your magic working, and ours isn't?" Kallie complained.

"Maybe that's part of the puzzle— *a riddle in the dark*," I theorized. "Perhaps you have to surrender to the dark to break the enchantment blocking your magic. And since the darkness doesn't matter to me, I can access it when you can't. I'm just gonna roll with it."

We started forward, but as soon as we did, the sound of rock sliding over rock met our ears.

Kallie drew a sharp breath. "What's that?"

"It sounds like..." I reached out toward the cave wall, and my stomach instantly dropped as I felt resistance from the stone wall. I tried to push back against it, but instead of the rock remaining still, I realized it was *moving*. "Shit. The walls are closing in on us!"

Ava's tone wavered. "Use your magic to stop it."

I tried. I pushed my Earth magic against the walls, but it didn't help. It must've been some sort of enchantment my magic couldn't override. "Everyone grab hands. We have to move!"

I dragged Ava forward, and the rest followed close behind. I could sense with my Earth magic that the tunnel was beginning to narrow. It was slow enough that it'd take several minutes to crush us, but fast enough that I questioned whether we'd get out in time. The cave walls began to wind and twist, leading us in all different directions.

My heart hammered as the sound of our footsteps echoed off a wall in front of us. There wasn't a lot of Air down here in the caves to navigate by, but I could sense the cave walls with my Earth magic. There were two openings ahead, like the end of our tunnel branched off in various directions.

"Hold on." I came to a stop at the openings of the new tunnels.

Ava ran into me, and Kallie and Marcus stumbled into her. Oberi barked, as if to say we had to get a move-on.

"We have to keep going, or we'll be crushed!" Ava insisted.

"The tunnel branches. I need a second to figure out which way to go." I tried to concentrate, and I reached out with my Earth magic to get a sense of the tunnel layout. It was still working somehow, though it couldn't stop the walls from crushing us. Down the left tunnel, my magic slammed into something solid, but it kept going down the right one.

"This way!" I dragged my friends down the right tunnel, nearly breaking out into a run.

"It's a labyrinth!" Ava cried, sounding horrified.

My heart twisted as I realized she was right. This place was a maze, purposefully set up to trap and crush whoever got stuck down here.

I couldn't respond to Ava's cries, because I was so focused on mapping out the tunnels up ahead. One wrong turn could cost us precious time, and if we took the wrong route, we would get squashed down here.

A few yards ahead, the cave split off into three directions, but two of the lanes connected in a loop. I led my friends down the left tunnel, which continued on. Every tunnel was smaller than the last, inching smaller and smaller by the second. We turned several more times before a noise caught my attention.

It was quiet at first— so subtle I wasn't sure my friends had heard it. *Click, click, click.* Though the tunnel had narrowed to mere feet across, I slowed my step. My friends stilled beside me, and Oberi growled lowly.

"What is it?" Ava leaned into me anxiously.

I tilted my head to listen closer. "There's something ahead."

"I... I think I see a light..." Ava said slowly.

The clicking sound sent a chill down my spine. I couldn't describe it, other than to say it sounded like bone sliding against bone. Something slithered across the cave floor, and a hiss came.

"Everyone get back!" I cried as I threw my arms out in front of my friends. "It's an animal."

"We'll fight it," Ava said bravely. She stepped forward, but I stopped her.

"Your magic isn't working. Let me." I lifted my hands. My magic didn't work on the enchantment of the labyrinth, but it still worked on the loose rocks scattering the cave floor. I used my magic to lift them into the air, then shot them at the creature.

The rocks should've squashed the creature, but instead, they connected with a *thud*, and the animal responded with a spiteful hiss.

Oh, shit. This creature was *way* bigger than I'd anticipated. It slithered forward at a quick pace, and I was finally able to assess it with my Air magic.

It was a serpent— and the fucker must've been at least fifty feet long!

"Run!" I screamed.

There was no other way but backward. We ran, our screams echoing off the cave walls. Several crashes sounded as headlamps tumbled off my friends' heads. We didn't have time to go back for them. I tossed rocks back at the snake with my magic, but his scales must've been as thick as armor, because he did nothing but shake it off and advance on us.

"Help me out, guys!" I cried.

"Nothing's working!" Ava screamed. "My magic's still out."

"Same!" Kallie panted.

"I can't do a fucking thing!" Marcus screamed.

"Oberi?!" I demanded.

He barked, and panic came through the bond. His magic wasn't working, either, which meant shifting into a Fire unicorn and frying the serpent's ass was out of the question.

I gritted my teeth. *Fuck!* We were either going to be crushed by this cave or eaten by this monster. I did the only thing I could think to do.

I skidded to a halt and whirled around. The serpent was right on my ass, but I moved so fast it didn't have time to respond. I did something *really* fucking stupid, and jumped onto its head.

If I thought my weight would keep it down, I was sorely mistaken. The best it did was slow the creature, to give my friends a chance to flee.

But that didn't matter, because there was no running from these shrinking tunnels.

The serpent's head must've been the size of a horse, because it felt as big as Oberi when she was in unicorn form. I straddled the creature, but I couldn't get my arms all the way around its neck. It shook its head from side to side, slamming me from one wall of the cave into the other. I held on tight and ran one hand over the serpent, searching for a weak spot. My hands moved over smooth, cold scales, then to exposed bones that protruded from its spine. Horns grew from the top of its head. It continued to slither down the cave with me on its back. Ava cried out in horror from up ahead, like she couldn't believe I'd jumped onto the snake.

"Charlie!" she screamed.

"I've got it handled!" I cried, though that wasn't totally truthful.

I shoved my hand toward the serpent's eyes. Something hot seared my palm, and I jerked back. Its eyes burned— as if they were on fire. That must've been what Ava had seen in the tunnel!

When my hands touched its eyes, the serpent freaked. Its head snapped from one direction to the other, then drove upward, slamming my back into the ceiling. The wind was knocked out of me, and I couldn't hold on any longer. My hands slipped from the snake's horns, and I tumbled over its head. I slammed to the ground and rolled, until I came to a stop at Ava's feet. The serpent snapped its jaws toward me. It came so close I felt its fangs skate across my skin, and its cool breath chilled me.

But it missed me, and went for someone else.

Ava's cry filled the tunnel, and my stomach lurched as I felt her pain ricochet across our bond. She crumbled to the ground beside me, nearly landing on top of me.

"No!" I screamed as I caught her.

She continued to shriek. "I got bit!" she cried.

"Oh, gods!" Kallie freaked over Oberi's loud barks.

A fiery anger surged inside of me, and heat flared in my gut. *Ava's Fire*, I realized. I could access it through the bond.

I didn't think. I just acted.

The serpent snapped its jaws again, but I was faster. I lifted my hands and yanked at Ava's magic. Fire blasted out of my fingers. The heat warmed my skin, so much that it was nearly unbearable.

The smell of burning flesh filled my nose, and a hellish shriek echoed down the tunnel. I didn't know that serpents could scream, but this was no ordinary snake. Fire crackled over its skin, and it thrashed on the cave floor, its tail slapping into one side of the cave, then the other. The snake hissed one last time as it let out a breath and died, the smell of its burning flesh infecting the tunnels.

Ava whimpered beside me. "Charlie," she said weakly. "The… venom."

I turned to a statue. All hope had drained out of me. We were stuck in this shrinking tunnel— with no option to turn back, or we'd be crushed. In moments, the tunnel would be only inches wider than my body. We would die.

"We have to do something!" Kallie demanded. Though her voice came from beside me, it sounded distant as the floor rumbled beneath us.

"What do we do?" Marcus asked in that same distant tone.

It didn't seem to matter now. Ava had been poisoned. Even if we escaped, the venom would work its way through her system in minutes. She'd be lost to me.

What the hell had I agreed to by coming down here?

Oberi grabbed my shirt in his teeth and yanked. I barely felt him. He placed his paws on my shoulder and shoved me.

"Charlie! Charlie!" Marcus tried to get my attention, but my head spun. I noticed the sides of the tunnel touch both of my shoulders, but it didn't seem to matter.

My momentary lapse must've frustrated Oberi, because he growled, then bit my ear so hard it drew blood.

"Ow!" I cried, finally snapping out of it.

Listen to me, Charlie! a voice demanded firmly. I had no idea who said it, because it didn't sound like Marcus or Kallie. I couldn't even place it as male or female.

But the voice was firm and familiar. I'd only heard it once before, but that wasn't what made me recognize it. It was the feeling behind it— like that voice had been speaking to me every day for months, and I'd never realized.

It was *Oberi!*

You need to snap out of it! he insisted. *Ava's in danger. We all are. Only you can get us out of here, and it's not going to happen with you sitting on your pretty little ass like this is a fucking picnic.*

Hell, he was right. If we had any chance, I had to get moving— and fast. Oberi nudged his nose into my chest, and I sprang to attention. My Earth magic surged, and I felt an opening in the tunnel up ahead, through a couple twisting hallways.

"We're close to the exit!" I gasped.

I jumped to my feet. Ava tried to stand beside me, but she collapsed. I yanked her body to mine, and she wrapped her limp arms around me as I boosted up her legs.

"Let's go." I rushed forward as fast as I could. The Fire continued to scorch the serpent's body. I used Ava's Fire magic to calm the flames, and we sprinted over charred flesh. The snake's bones crunched beneath my feet.

"Fuck, fuck," Kallie breathed. "The tunnel's going to crush us! We won't make it!"

"We have to hurry up," I growled. "The exit's just ahead! I can *feel* it!"

I kept on running, and Oberi barked to beacon everyone forward. The tunnel shrank so small that the fabric of my mining uniform ripped as I tried to barrel my way down the tunnel. I turned to the side, shuffling my feet as quickly as I could. It was a good thing Ava was so tiny, or I wouldn't have been able to carry her down the narrow passage.

I held my breath. Up ahead, I felt the tunnel widen. But it seemed that the tunnel shrank another inch with every step I took. Debris from the ceiling peppered my face, and the floor shook even more violently beneath me. I wasn't sure if we were going to make it.

Rishi grew frightened and began meowing loudly. "Ow!" Marcus cried. "He's scratching me! I can barely hang on to him."

"Just... a little... farther..." I broke out into the wide cave, but I was moving so fast that I tripped over my own feet. Ava and I tumbled to the ground.

Oberi yipped as he sprinted out behind me. Marcus' breath strained as the tunnel began to squash him, but Kallie must've given him a push, because she groaned, and the two of them tumbled into a heap on top of us, along with Rishi.

The walls of the labyrinth we'd escaped slammed shut with a *boom*. I drew heavy breaths. Shit. That had been a close one. We'd nearly been squished.

"My magic works again!" Marcus exclaimed, and I heard a *flick* as he cast a ball of light.

I didn't care about our magic right now. I only cared about Ava. She lay on the ground, sucking pained breaths between her teeth.

"Where'd he bite you?" I demanded. I began running my hands over her, until I felt the tear in her pants and the wet blood soaking the fabric. The snake had gotten her right in the calf.

"Charlie, stop!" she cried, but I didn't listen.

I yanked on the fabric, and it tore. I ducked my head to begin sucking out the venom. She tried to shove me off, but I didn't stop. Blood filled my mouth, along with searing heat from the venom. I drew back and spit the blood onto the cave floor.

"Charlie, it's no use!" Ava protested, shoving me again. This time, she shoved so hard that she actually got me off of her.

"I'm trying to help," I insisted. "We can suck the venom out."

"It's too late," she said. "I grew up in a city filled with magical creatures. I know enough about them to know the only way to heal this is through magical means. If you keep trying to suck it out, you'll poison yourself!"

"Like I give a damn," I fumed.

"Oh, yeah, because dragging your heavy-ass dead body back through these caves isn't going to slow us up," she snapped, though her voice wavered.

"Better me than—"

"Guys, this isn't the time to fight right now," Kallie said, cutting us off. She sounded worried.

I whirled toward Marcus. "What do you have? Anything we can brew a potion with?"

"Just the first-aid kit," he said in a rush.

He fumbled with a few items, and Kallie quickly stepped in. "We've got nothing for the venom, but this should help with the blood," she said.

Ava sucked a breath as Kallie wrapped gauze around the wound. I ran my fingers over it to see how much it helped, but the blood was already starting to ooze through.

"This is it?" I demanded.

"That's all I could get my hands on." Marcus sounded bothered.

"We have to do something *more*!" I raged.

"There's only one thing we can do," Ava said in a wobbly tone, and I heard her push to her feet. "We have to keep going."

TWENTY-TWO

Charlie immediately bristled. "Are you crazy? We can't go on if you're hurt."

"Fuck yeah, I'm crazy," I snapped. "I know we're close to another key. I can feel it."

"I can feel you *dying* through the bond!" Charlie cried. "That venom is working through your system quicker than you want to admit!"

"Stop being dramatic," I said, but my head spun. The bite marks on my calf were several inches deep, and nearly an inch across. Blood oozed down my leg through the bandage. The snake had gotten me good.

The cave was illuminated by the light of the magic orb Marcus had cast. We'd all lost our headlamps while running through the tunnels. I tried to cast a fireball, but it flickered out uselessly. The venom was already sucking away all my energy. Hives crept across my skin, and my breathing became labored as my throat swelled. My chest was tight. I felt like I wanted to throw up. Curling up on the cave floor and taking a nap seemed like a great idea right now. I was so sleepy, I could barely keep my eyes open.

Worst of all was the tingling feeling in my leg, and the pang each time my heart took a beat. My very veins were filled with fire, inching up my body and coursing around my form. My muscles were tight and strained, and my thoughts were foggy. I knew this wasn't good.

"We need to turn back," Charlie said. "You need medical attention straight away."

"How do you want to go back? The tunnels behind us are sealed shut," I said. "There's nowhere to go but forward."

Charlie remained silent, and Marcus added quietly, "She does have a point."

"Then we need to find a different way back, and that's going to take time," Charlie said firmly. "We don't know how much time you have left."

I took a short breath, and it nearly caused me to topple over. "Look, that snake was a *serpens spelunca*. It's a rare breed of cave snake. I know about them, because I've studied a few when my parents took us on trips to *Hok'evale*. They live in the cave systems there, though the one that attacked us is a different kind. An Elven mutation, perhaps?"

"What's *Hok'evale?*" Marcus asked.

"It's an Anichi village fifty miles from Kinpago," I explained. "Most cave snakes don't have deadly venom. They just use their venom to slow down their opponent, so they can hunt them easier. The symptoms will probably go away within thirty minutes after my blood metabolizes the venom."

"What if it's not what you assume it is?" Charlie demanded.

I frowned. "Then I'm dead within the hour, and it doesn't matter anyway."

"And if you die, what if Oberi and I die, too?" Charlie asked. "You want to condemn us along with you?"

"We don't know if our bond works like that. You could go on if Oberi survives. Stop trying to be manipulative to save me." I put a hand on the cave wall, to keep myself upright. I was *really* freaking tired.

"Do you guys want to take that chance?" Marcus worried.

Charlie's stone-hard expression was clear. He had it in mind to drag me back to the Institute, no matter what I wanted.

But I wasn't willing to give in. We wouldn't get another chance like this. This was our only shot at getting the next key, which I was *sure* was down here.

"You're being selfish," Charlie spat. "You're putting the three of us at risk for a dumb key."

"Selfish? I'm trying to save the world, here!" I snapped.

Charlie gave a harsh laugh with no humor in it. "Hell, pidge, I'm so sick of you being stubborn. You just won't give in."

"I never will," I growled, but it came out more like a gasp, because the wound in my leg throbbed. Charlie noticed, and his expression tightened at my pain.

"Let's make a compromise," Kallie broke in. "We keep going, just another mile. If we don't get the key by then, we'll turn around and get Ava help. Maybe Charlie can dig us out."

"Done," I said, before Charlie could argue further. "Let's go."

Oberi changed into a Fire unicorn, and I forced my aching arms to work as I hauled myself onto her back. The tunnels were wide and tall here, and therefore, there was room for me to ride. Marcus' orb of light hovered in front of us, leading the way. Rishi jumped up and tried to bat at it like a cat toy, until Marcus told him to stop.

We walked in silence for a time. Kallie and Marcus wandered ahead of us, speaking in hushed tones.

Charlie didn't say anything for a bit, until he suddenly scowled and snapped, "That doesn't help, Oberi."

"What?" I floundered forward, falling against Oberi's neck. "What did you just say?"

"Oberi can talk to me now," Charlie said. "She broke through the bond."

Shock rippled like water over my skin. "I didn't hear her."

"You didn't?" Charlie stiffened in surprise. "I thought you did. She was talking to me after you got bit."

"No. Have her say something again."

There was a beat of quiet, and Charlie asked, "Hear that?"

Hurt grew in my abdomen, and it wasn't from the venom. "I didn't hear a thing." Why wasn't it working?

Charlie took a hasty breath, then crossed his arms. Oberi bobbed her head in front of me and stomped a hoof.

"What did she say?" I asked.

Charlie let out a huff. "She told me to put my big boy panties on and stop whining. The little shit. I don't know why she's taking *your* side. Your bullheadedness is gonna kill us all."

What Oberi had said was funny, but I couldn't crack a smile. I stroked her neck. "Why can't you talk to me, girl?"

Oberi nickered, like she wanted to— but was saying I wasn't ready yet.

Oh, but *Charlie* was ready. That was nice. I felt offended— as if Oberi had chosen Charlie over me.

I pushed the resentment down. We shared Oberi. I shouldn't be feeling this way. I should be happy for Charlie, that he and Oberi had such a big moment.

I didn't. I just felt jealous, because now I didn't feel good enough.

We continued down the tunnel, and the Elven runes on the walls increased in number, until they were scrawled to the ground and over the ceiling. This was getting eerie.

Marcus shivered. "Don't you think we should've come across another trap by now—?"

He stopped so abruptly that Kallie almost ran into him. She went to bite an insult, but her words fell flat as she realized there was someone standing in the tunnel ahead of us.

"There's someone else down here," Kallie said curiously. "Hello! Do you need help?"

The figure stepped into the light, and Marcus went completely pale. It was a girl, a couple of years younger than us. She had thick brown hair, and a petite frame. She quirked a smile and said, "Hey, Marcus. It's been a while."

Marcus made a few choking sounds before he blurted out, "Erica?"

I realized the girl looked so similar to Marcus. This had to be his younger sister. But what was she doing down here?

She couldn't be here. There was just no way. She wasn't real. She was an illusion.

"This is another trap," I said. "The *temptation by illusion*. The spell must work so that you're tempted to take whatever it is you want most."

"She looks so real." Marcus reached out to touch her, but Kallie grabbed his hand.

"Don't," Kallie said. "I've seen magic like this before. You touch the illusion, it means you're accepting it as your own. Then we're all dead."

Marcus blinked. He went to go around the illusion, but she blocked his path.

"Erica, I know it's not really you. Just get out of the way," Marcus said. His shoulders slumped.

"I just came to tell you that everyone wants you back," Erica insisted. "You should return to Octavia Falls."

"I can't go back. I'm a convicted mass-murderer," Marcus said tightly.

Ancestors, that was a harsh thing to say out loud. I always forgot that even though Marcus was the meekest among us, he'd committed the worst crime.

"Mom got your sentence erased. You're free to go," Erica said. "Don't you *miss* all of us? All your friends are waiting for you. We've been so sad ever since you went away."

"You're lying. People have forgotten all about me," Marcus said, though his voice was strained. He was starting to crack. Rishi stood beside him and yanked at his pant leg with his teeth, but Marcus didn't even notice.

"Of course they haven't," Erica said, and she took a step closer. "You have the power of all five Casts. People think you're a hero. They won't even notice me anymore, once you come back."

Marcus gave a harsh laugh. "Yeah, okay. You're perfect. I looked like such a fuck-up, standing next to you."

"Of course you didn't," Erica soothed. "The townspeople want to accept you, I promise. Don't you want to make things right with Anya's family? Her brother *needs* you. Kellen won't survive if you aren't there to help him."

At the mention of his mentee, Marcus began to shake. Kallie put a hand on his arm.

"Marcus, don't listen," Kallie warned. "She'll say anything to try and trick you."

"You know I'm just looking out for my big brother," Erica responded. "You can't survive in prison. Just take my hand, and I'll take you home."

The burning look on Marcus' face told me he really wanted to. Kallie's hand on his arm was the only thing holding him back.

When Marcus didn't move further, Erica added, "Everyone has forgiven you for what you did. I promise."

As she said that, something in Marcus broke, and his expression shattered. He turned his back on the illusion. "I don't need to earn everyone else's forgiveness. I need to forgive myself first. And I'm just not ready to do that yet."

The fake Erica frowned. I expected the illusion to fall away, but instead, Erica moved to the side, allowing us to pass by. As we continued down the hallway, the fake Erica floated behind us— like a mesmerized ghost.

"Why didn't the illusion vanish?" I whispered to Kallie.

"I don't know," Kallie replied. Her eyebrows furrowed.

Marcus refused to look at the impersonation of his sister floating behind him. I tilted on Oberi's back. I nearly fell off, until Charlie grabbed me before I did.

"Pidge, stay awake," he said gruffly.

He jostled me, and I gagged. A bit of bile rose past my lips, and I spat it on the floor. Kallie gave me a worried glance.

Charlie bit his lip. "We need to go back."

"We keep forging on." I gripped Oberi's fiery mane and held tighter. We weren't quitting. Not yet.

Another figure emerged from the darkness ahead. I squinted to see who it could be, until my heart dropped into my stomach as the illusion stepped into Marcus' witchlight.

It was *me*. A complete clone of me, identical in every way. The fake version of me batted her brown eyes and flipped her dark hair, pursing her lips as she came forward.

Charlie had noticed our stunned silence. "Ancestors, what *now*?"

"Charlie," Fake Me called in a sultry voice. "Charlie, it's me. Your pidge."

Charlie went completely white. He put a hand on Oberi's side to steady himself as the illusion said, "Charlie, come home. Dinner's ready. I made your favorite."

"That bitch is *not* me!" I cried. "It's an illusion!"

The Fake Ava didn't hear my words, and continued onward, taking a step closer. "I got a nice fire going. It's really cozy. I know you like it when the house is warm."

A twinge of irritation crossed over my forehead, and I said, "This ho doesn't know what she's talking about. Charlie, don't listen."

I reached for him, but I was too weak to lift my arm from Oberi's mane. The venom had me spent. Charlie didn't take my hand, which gutted me.

"I don't have a home," Charlie responded hollowly. "I don't belong anywhere."

"Don't be silly. You have a home. You belong with me," Fake Ass, Bitch Ass Me purred. "You're so tired, aren't you? Let's take a nap. I fixed the hole in your favorite quilt— you know, the one I made you? Everything's nice and dry."

Charlie's fingers twitched, like he wanted so badly to reach out and touch *her*. It was so crazy that Charlie was falling so easily under the illusion's spell when the real me was right beside him.

"Charlie," I whimpered. I was starting to get dizzy— worse than before. The whole cave was spinning by this point.

Charlie noticed, and put a hand on my back before he said to the Fake Ava, "I can't go home with you. It's not who you are."

Fake Me scowled— damn, I had the bitchiest face when I was pissed — and moved aside. She fell in line beside the false Erica as we continued down the tunnel, hovering behind.

Charlie's hand on my back grounded me, and the dizziness slowly began to fade— though some of it stuck with me as I raised my head off Oberi's neck. "Good job, fighting off that illusion," I told him.

"I know when things are too good to be true," Charlie said quietly. "You can always tell."

My heart cracked a little. "What do you mean?"

"You're not the type to settle down, pidge. It was all too easy to convince myself it wasn't real." The color began to return to Charlie's face. Inwardly, I felt guilty.

I'd never be homemaker of the year, that was for certain. I was adventurous, and liked exploring, and wanted the world at my feet. Once I got out of the Institute, I had a mind never to stay in one place too long. My biggest desire was to travel. I wasn't the type to be waiting at home with supper ready when Charlie came back from his day job, that was for sure.

But Charlie had been tossed around from place to place all his life. It seemed wrong to ask him to keep doing that, for me. He wanted something *secure*, and in my life, all I desired was something fluid. My lip wobbled, and I turned my head away from Charlie.

This isn't going to last, Ava.

This relationship is doomed to fail.

He wants to feel safe, and you're dangerous.

Oh, great. If possible, the venom made the voices in my head even louder. Just great. I wondered if I'd start hallucinating next, because that's just what we needed.

"Who's that?" Kallie asked. She didn't recognize the next illusion ahead, which meant that whoever the spell was impersonating was probably for me. I didn't feel like talking to whoever it was, and let my eyes drift closed, giving a light snore on Oberi's back.

"Don't let her fall asleep. We might not be able to wake her back up," Kallie said.

Charlie jostled me roughly, and I batted him away. "Go away," I moaned. "Wake me when we get there."

"Ava, you need to make this illusion leave," Charlie said firmly. He shook me again, which didn't do much of anything to rouse me.

I didn't care if the Great Spirit himself was blocking the way. I wasn't moving for anyone. The venom was running thick in my head, making my thoughts incoherent.

An impish giggle rang across the tunnel, along with a teasing voice. "You always had a thing for broke-ass bums. He's cute, though. Definitely your type."

That voice was like a slap to the face. I jolted upward on Oberi's back. A wicked chill permeated my bones as I took in the figure's mass of dark curls, green eyes and mess of freckles. On her wrist she wore a red and green band— just like mine.

"Fuck no," I breathed. "I'm not doing this."

I yanked on Oberi's mane, to get her to turn around. Forget the key— it could stay down here, for all I cared.

But Oberi didn't move. She stomped her hoof, as if telling me to stay put, and I was too exhausted to get off her back and run. Marcus looked completely lost, although Kallie's eyes flickered from me to the illusion, working out the details. Charlie rubbed the small of my back in tiny circles, like he'd guessed exactly what I was facing and was trying to comfort me.

"Leave me alone!" I shouted at the illusion. It remained where it was, the figure just as solid as the day I'd lost her.

Monica spread her arms wide, in a dramatic pose. "Surprise, bitch! You didn't think I was *really* dead, did you? I was playing a prank. I can't believe you fell for it."

My eyebrow twitched. I barely held in a sob as I cried out, "Yeah, some prank, wasn't it, dying in my arms. *So* fucking funny."

"Oh, don't be that way. It *was* funny." Monica waved a hand, in that careless way of hers. "Aren't you just glad to see that I'm alive?"

I couldn't help the way my lip wobbled. "I'm *so* pissed at you."

Monica gave a quirky smile. It was then I let out a laugh. "Good one. I should've known you'd pull something like this."

"Ava," Charlie warned, but his voice was like a wisp on the wind. The illusion was *good*— very good. I believed in that moment, with all my heart, that Monica was really here with me and everything that had happened had been a bad dream.

I was floating. I was no longer with my friends, in this dark cave. I was back in my bedroom at home with Monica, and she was standing across from me like she'd never been gone. Colors changed and morphed until I could see the scene around me clear as day.

Monica smiled. "Don't you see I never left? I could never leave you."

"You wouldn't," I whispered.

I fell off of Oberi. Charlie let out a gasp behind me, but he was far away, basically on another planet. My legs wouldn't support me as I began crawling toward Monica, reaching out a hand. I wanted to touch her *so badly*.

"Ava—" Kallie said. She grabbed my shoulder, but screeched as my skin burned her hand.

My Koigni magic was protecting me. I wouldn't let anyone drag me away from Monica ever again.

Monica nearly sang as she spoke her next words. "Come on, Ava.

We need to get our nails done. They need to look perfect for our next video. Your album is almost complete. I know everyone's going to love it. Just take my hand, and we can wrap up the last song."

Our last song. I'd never finished it. It'd been too painful to finish my album without her. After all these years, it remained half-done, abandoned on my computer at home.

But maybe all those years had just been a fantasy, and nothing bad had happened at all. The Institute, the Darke Games... it'd all been a bad dream.

Monica bent over and extended her long fingers to me. Our grasps were within inches of connecting. She gave a mischievous grin as she said, "Let's go back to Kinpago. We can hunt John down and wrap him in a tarp. I've got a baseball bat with his name on it. He'd look good floating at the bottom of the ocean. I'm gonna *kill* him for hurting my best friend."

I immediately drew back my hand, flinching with Monica's words. I had to admit in my heart then that this was an illusion, and that Monica wasn't here. All of that had happened after she died. She hadn't been around to witness it.

I slid away from Monica, recoiling from the illusion's stare. "I know this isn't real. You aren't here, Monica. And I can't love you enough to bring you back. If love was enough to save you, you never would've died."

Monica's face shimmered, like she was wounded by my admission. Tears sparkled in her gaze as she retreated away from me, and it devastated me. I wished I was as blind as Charlie, so I didn't have to see her face.

Charlie scrambled forward. My skin was still warm, but not hot enough to hurt anyone anymore. "Pidge." He lifted me to my feet, but I was still too weak to stand. He placed me on Oberi's back. I barely held in a sob.

Marcus appeared miserable. "I'm sorry," he told me. He touched my knee lightly, and I wiped my face on the back of my sleeve.

I felt stupid. At least Marcus had conjured up an image of someone who was still alive. He wasn't so silly to keep holding on to the past. It wasn't like he'd imagined Anya. Charlie hadn't brought back Marty, either. I was so embarrassed.

"Kallie, are you okay? I didn't want to burn you," I told her.

"I'm fine," Kallie said as she cradled her hurt hand. "I know you didn't mean it."

Monica floated behind us, with Erica and Fake Me in tow. The false Ava and Monica held hands as they hovered. It was bizarre and heartbreaking. I kept my gaze locked forward as the specters continued floating behind us.

"We have to keep moving," Charlie said. "Ava's running out of time."

Hardly cared if I did, at this point. I felt worthless.

But Kallie's illusion, whatever it was, was still ahead, and I wanted to be there to support her through it. We continued through the tunnel, until we came to the last figure hiding in the darkness.

Oh, great, another clone. Except this time, it was of Kallie herself.

And damn, she'd sure dressed herself up. She had a glittering gold medal around her neck and a crown on her head. Her blonde hair fell in massive curls, and her makeup was done to perfection. She wore a big purple gown, and a bright smile on her face that was too white and clean. Her boobs were bigger, her middle was thinner, and there wasn't a blemish or spot out of place.

She looked so *fake*. It was gross. Marcus appeared disgusted at the sight of the perfect Kallie, taking a step back and recoiling away.

Kallie's eyes narrowed when she faced herself. "*You*," she sneered.

The illusion flipped her hair and gave a girlish laugh, which I hated — it was far too feminine for Kallie. "Here I am."

"Move out of the way," Kallie said. "I killed you."

"You didn't kill me. I've been with you all along," Perfect Kallie said. "Everyone knows *I'm* the version that you should've been."

"I lost my chance," Kallie replied. "It's over now."

Perfect Kallie raised a sculpted eyebrow. "I don't give up. That's why there's a crown on my head, and not yours."

"I don't even know if I *wanted* the crown! I just did what was expected of me!" Kallie shouted.

"You wanted a chance to show your *flawless* brother up!" Perfect Kallie spat. "I'm giving you another one. You can't just throw it away! Aren't you tired of living in his shadow? Because I am, and I made sure he knew it."

Kallie's nose wrinkled. "I'm nothing like you."

"You can be!" Perfect Kallie straightened her shoulders. "I'm better-looking, I'm nicer, I'm thinner and everyone likes *me*. You could be me, too, if you just tried hard enough."

Kallie's face twisted. "No, I can't. I can't keep pretending to be someone else. It got me landed in the Institute. I won't go there again."

Perfect Kallie scoffed and rolled her eyes. "Well, at least my parents love me. They despise you."

Kallie flinched. She bounced on her feet, clearly indecisive about what she should do.

Marcus broke in. "I don't *like* that version of you," he said, gesturing to Perfect Kallie. "That's not who you are."

"But she's what I've always wanted to be," Kallie insisted as she spun toward Marcus. "Maybe she's right. Maybe I could be different if I just worked harder."

"She's not real. Why do you want to turn yourself into someone you're not?" Marcus asked.

Kallie didn't answer, and the illusion took it as an opportunity.

"Take my hand," Perfect Kallie said gently. "Then you'll become everything you were always meant to be, and get rid of all the parts that you hate. I promise I'll make all the bad parts of you disappear. Then your family will love you again."

Kallie's hand quivered. I thought she was going to use her magic to break the illusion, but then—

"*Kallie!*" Marcus screamed as she reached out and grabbed the illusion's hand. Once she did that, the cavern exploded into chaos.

The figures floating behind us morphed. They changed, bodies twisting and skin mutating until the figures appeared to be hovering corpses, flesh hanging off bone and insects festering out of holes in purplish, blue skin. Their eyes were gaunt and horrifying as the figures charged at us, arms outreached to wrap us within their decomposing forms.

Ugh, ancestors, decaying flesh was *not* a good look on me.

Kallie's illusion changed, too. Perfect Kallie melted into a corpse with a torn dress as she launched herself at her clone. Our Kallie changed into a shifter and yelped, spinning away from the floating corpse with a wolfish whine. Marcus screamed as he ran in circles, trying to get his decaying sister to leave him alone. Rishi launched himself upward and clawed at Erica's soggy face, but she smacked him off. Marcus gave a cry as Rishi hit the floor of the cave.

"Goddammit, Kallie!" Charlie roared. He was trying to pry Fake Demon Me off of him, who had wrapped her hands around his neck and was squeezing tight. Not that far off from what I wanted to do in real life, to be honest.

My worst nightmare stalked in front of me as Corpse Monica staggered my way. Spiders furled out of her eye holes and nose, and skin dripped off her form. The sight made me want to cry. Monica's body had been burned, her ashes scattered under the burial mounds in Kinpago, but many times I'd woken up screaming, imagining her remains slowly wasting away in a coffin underground.

I tossed fireballs at her, warning the corpse to get back, while Oberi waved her horn. The corpse remained at a distance, although I couldn't get rid of the terror welling in my chest as I observed the haunting figure.

Kallie was on her back, whimpering as the image of her own corpse held her down.

"You can't let me go! You *need* me!" Perfect Kallie screamed. Dark blood dripped from her teeth, spilling onto the wolf's silver coat.

Kallie closed her eyes. She changed back into her human form, and let out a wicked scream. A burst of purple magic erupted from her hand and rippled through the cavern in a shockwave.

Once the violent spell hit the corpses, they immediately turned to dust. Charlie dusted ash off the front of his clothes, while Marcus crawled to Rishi, who meowed to let him know he was okay.

I let out a breath of relief. Kallie had broken the illusion. Her magic was strong enough to overpower it, though she'd sure taken her sweet time breaking it out.

Even so, Kallie was spent. She lay flat against the ground, and didn't get up. Marcus stumbled forward and helped her to her feet. She leaned against him, like she could hardly fit to stand right now.

I leaned forward and cried into Oberi's neck, remembering the depiction of Monica's rotting body. That had been *horrible*. It'd be something that would stay with me forever.

Charlie ran a hand through my hair. "It's okay to cry, pidge. I know that was rough."

I sniffed and wiped my nose. This damn prophecy was going to kill me.

"How'd you beat it?" Marcus asked. He jostled Kallie, who looked as tired as I felt.

"I needed to save my friends more than get what I wanted," Kallie said. "The illusion wouldn't break until I decided that. I tried, and it didn't work until then."

"Well, if it counts, you've always been perfect to me," Marcus mumbled.

Kallie gave a thin, wavering smile. I took it as a hint not to give up on them quite yet.

"I hope you guys have got the next trap handled," Kallie moaned. "I couldn't conjure a cup of tea, at the moment."

"There can't be much more ahead," I insisted. My tongue was growing so swollen in my mouth it was hard to talk. It was clear by now that the venom I'd been injected with wasn't the paralyzing kind— more like the deadly kind. I was fading away by the second.

Charlie noticed how thick my voice sounded. "Ava, we're going back, *now*," Charlie said roughly. "I'm not giving you a choice."

I couldn't protest. The last trap had really wounded me, and not in a physical way. It had been ten times worse than getting bit by the snake. I was ready to go back to the prison. Even the Institute looked welcoming, compared to these dark caves full of memories I didn't want to go back to.

Yet before I could agree, my magic tingled at the edges of my skin, and I felt the sensation of moving liquid less than a hundred feet from the way we'd come.

The others noticed it, too, hearing the sounds of rushing water. Panic coursed over their expressions as they listened to the sound of crashing waves.

A trapdoor must've opened in the caves. And currently, it was flooding in hundreds of gallons of water.

"Run!" I cried, but it was too late. I lifted a hand to try and stop the water from coming into our tunnel, but the venom in my veins had overpowered my magic, and I wasn't strong enough to redirect the water in another direction.

Our tunnel immediately filled up with water, and the undertow was so strong that all of us were swept off our feet. Marcus' witchlight went out as the water crashed over it, and we were immediately washed away, pitched into darkness.

Screams could be heard, until they were drowned out as my friends' heads went underwater. I reached out for Charlie, who didn't have a clue which way was up. He tumbled over and over in the rushing water as we were carried down the tunnel's length at a frightening speed. The water had yanked him away from me, to a place I couldn't reach. Oberi's hooves pounded against the spray as she struggled to keep her head above water. Somewhere ahead, Rishi gave a yowl.

Then the bottom of the tunnel dropped out, and we began falling. Kallie and Marcus screamed all the way down as we dropped twenty, thirty feet.

I thought for sure there'd be hard rock at the bottom, and that all of us would smash upon the stone. But my feet hit water, and our bodies were plunged into the depths. I swam upward, taking deep breaths as my head breached the surface. I heard Kallie and Marcus floundering not too far away, as well as Rishi. Marcus cast another witchlight, and it hovered above us, casting illumination around the area. We'd fallen into some sort of underwater cavern— except that it wasn't that big, and water was still pouring in, raising the water level by the second.

I didn't hear anything from Charlie. I was terrified he was dead. I reached out through our bond. I felt his life stubbornly clinging on to mine, about ten feet below me. I took a deep breath and swam downward, until I saw him. He spun in circles, unsure of which direction to swim.

I indicated I was coming through our bond, and he paused briefly to wait for me, so he wouldn't kick me in the face by accident. I knew the movement took all of his trust as he waited for me to rescue him, slowly losing air. I wrapped my hand around his wrist. I swam us both upward, until Charlie's head burst through the water and he began taking deep breaths.

Now that I knew Charlie was near, I looked around frantically. Despair welled in my chest as I realized my Familiar was missing.

"*Where's Oberi?*" I screamed. Charlie flailed, turning this way and that as if he couldn't sense where she had gone.

I didn't know where my Familiar was, and Charlie didn't either. Both of us were lost without her. Where had she gone? Was she struggling to breathe beneath the surface, and I just didn't know?

"I can't swim!" Marcus screamed. He flapped in the water helplessly as Kallie's head bobbed against his chest. She was on the verge of passing out.

Marcus couldn't cast any more magic while trying to keep himself and Kallie afloat. Rishi sat on his head, mewing frantically due to the rising water. Marcus gasped as water streamed past his mouth, and Kallie's head dipped under.

I lifted my gaze and watched the waterfall streaming into the cavern. At this rate, the cavern would be filled within minutes, and we couldn't swim forever. We'd all drown if I didn't get us out of here.

There had to be a way. My scrambling eyes caught a ledge. It led to a stone doorway, which had to go beyond, into another tunnel.

But it was fifty feet away. We wouldn't be able to swim that far before the cavern filled up completely.

The venom was weaning away at my strength, but I had just enough magic left in me to make miracles happen.

"Ava, take Kallie and Marcus and get out of here!" Charlie cried. His head went under, and he choked on water.

Determined resolution set in me. I only had enough time, enough energy, to save three people.

Didn't mean I had to save myself.

I was dead because of the venom, anyway. At least I could rescue my friends. I pushed my powers outward, containing Kallie, Marcus, and Rishi within a jet of my magic.

"Pidge, what are you doing?" Charlie said in a panicked voice as he felt my Water magic wrap around him.

"Go," I said weakly, and I pushed my powers outward in a burst of energy. My Water magic carried my friends away in seconds, blasting them from our location to the ledge on the other side of the cavern. I heard Charlie scream my name as I sent him away, and my head went under.

I didn't have the strength to keep myself above the surface. I was a great swimmer, but I couldn't even paddle at this point. The venom pulsed through my veins, stealing my life moment by moment. Marcus's witchlight flickered above me, on the verge of going out.

My eyelids drooped. I was content to drift downward, and let the rushing water carry me away.

A form began taking shape ahead, and something swam toward me. A fish, maybe? It was so dark and murky underneath the depths, I couldn't be too sure.

Then the creature became illuminated by the light. It was a *narwhal.* The whale's skin was dark blue, with flecks of white on its sides and belly. The narwhal was thirteen feet long, and had a horn emerging from her head between her black eyes. The creature was so beautiful and majestic that I wanted to cry just looking at her.

The narwhal let out a musical croon, and bobbed her ivory tusk in the water in a way that I knew. The narwhal's black eyes glimmered, and she did a twisting circle before me as she swam to my side.

Oberi. I knew it was my Familiar the moment we locked eyes. I put my arms weakly around the narwhal's form, and she wiggled her tail, giving a powerful burst of energy as we swam toward the ledge. With Oberi's powerful tail, we crossed the fifty-foot gap in less than twenty seconds. She launched herself out of the water, and we landed on the ledge beside the others.

I slid against Charlie's knees and began coughing up water. I curled onto my side as I heaved for air.

Charlie grasped my shoulders and stuttered above me, "Damn you, pidge. I thought I'd lost *both* of you."

I had nothing to say about that. The thought of leaving Charlie alone in the world was too unfathomable to bear.

"Oberi's Water form," I gasped. "We found it. She's a narwhal. She saved me."

Charlie froze. He reached out to touch Oberi, to see if she was truly real. Charlie's hand caressed Oberi's smooth, slick skin, which became fur as she changed back into a husky. Oberi licked Charlie's hand and let out a happy bark.

Oberi was a *mutabeecha*, a shifting Familiar with multiple forms. She could have a form for each of the five elemental Houses— and with her Air and Spirit forms still left to find, what else could she possibly surprise us with?

A pounding sound came from behind us, and Rishi whined.

"This cavern is still filling up!" Marcus cried. He pushed at the door on the stone ledge, struggling to get it to move.

Kallie groaned. She was on her hands and knees, and she shook her head. With a whimper of pain, she changed into a wolf and charged at the door. Her shifter strength broke it open, and Charlie was able to drag me through. The others followed. Kallie slammed the door shut behind us with her paws just as water started to seep over the stone ledge, though she slunk to the ground with a shake as she changed back.

I was still on the ground, and now, my body was starting to convulse. I rolled over. Black bile streamed out of my mouth. I coughed a few times before I flipped onto my back. Oberi whined, and Charlie scrambled to pull me into his arms.

"We gotta get out of here," he insisted. I was hardly coherent as I felt Charlie stand. "Ava needs help."

"There might be a way out ahead," Marcus suggested, though he sounded hopeless. He helped Kallie shuffle along. The world began fading in and out as we moved forward.

Charlie jostled me. "Stay with me, pidge." His voice was strained and desperate. He really thought I was going to die.

Maybe I was. Maybe I'd pushed too far one too many times, and I was finally meeting my fate.

We abruptly stopped. My head lolled against Charlie's chest, and I heard Kallie say, "What the hell is this?"

My eyes creaked open. I noticed before us was a massive wooden door, very similar to the stone gate we'd encountered a few weeks ago. The carvings and symbols in the door were the same, except this door didn't have any keyholes, only ornate handles that were shaped like the cave snake we'd encountered earlier. The door took up the entirety of the cave— you couldn't go forward without opening it.

The key *had* to be behind this door. But it was locked. Marcus yanked on the handles, but they refused to open.

Kallie panted, leaning against the wall as she observed the massive door. "We can't go back. If we don't want to starve to death, we need to open it."

"How?" Marcus was starting to lose his temper— which was weird to see, because usually, he never got angry. He paced back and forth in front of the door before giving a growl of frustration. "We can't have come this far only to be blocked by a fucking door!"

Marcus kicked at it, clearly at his limit. Rishi gave a cry.

Charlie put me down against the floor. "Stay here, pidge."

Like I was going anywhere. Charlie put his hand on the door, to study it. Kallie sat on the ground to take a break, while Marcus fumed. Oberi lay next to me, placing his head on my lap.

"This was part of the clues we found, wasn't it, Ava?" Kallie asked. "*And a door that will only open with the blood of one that is mine?*"

"Yes," I breathed. It took all my effort to force out the word.

"How does that help us?" Marcus spat. "We don't know how to get past this—"

"Marcus," Kallie sighed.

"*Fucking door* in the first place!"

As Marcus continued to rant about *the fucking door*, Charlie appeared puzzled. He put a hand to his chin, thinking. I wondered what was on his mind.

Kallie dragged herself to the door. She put her hand upon it, which was bleeding from the fall we'd taken into the lake. As she smeared her blood against the door, we all waited for something to happen, but nothing did.

"This doesn't make sense," Kallie gasped. "Doesn't the door want demigod blood? That's what it's asking for."

"These tasks were set up for demigods, weren't they?" Charlie asked. "That's what we figured out before we came down here. We're demigods, so we should be able to get through."

Something in my head clicked as I recalled my grandfather's words. "Maybe the traps weren't set up for demigods," I gasped. "Maybe..."

I grimaced, and put a hand to my chest. My lungs felt so constricted now. I forced out, "Maybe they were only trials that *Elves* could pass. That's why we had such a hard time getting through them. So that means the door can only be opened by someone who has Elf blood."

"And how does that help us?" Marcus raged. "We don't *have* a fucking Elf with us, all we have is you, me, Kallie, and Char—"

Marcus stopped speaking. Kallie lifted her gaze.

Charlie said nothing, and I struggled to say, "My grandpa told me that there's always a way out of traps, but we've overlooked something. Traps allow people to pass through that are *meant* to go onward. These traps were set up for Elves, by Elves. We should've died trying to get through them, but we didn't. What if we had an Elf with us all along?"

"What are you saying?" Kallie blinked. Charlie was so still.

"Charlie was the only one who still was able to use magic when we crossed the ward into the maze," I pointed out. "None of *us* could. You'd have to have Elven blood to override an enchantment set by them. That has to mean—"

Charlie mused, opening and closing his hand. "Do you think it's possible?"

I swallowed— my throat was closing up, making it hard to breathe. "You've always been remarkable. Why not?"

Charlie nodded. As he moved forward, he kicked a sharp stone with his shoe. He reached down and grabbed the stone off the floor, then cut into his palm. I winced as I felt the sting through our bond. He placed his hand on the door and smeared blood across its surface.

The door began to rumble. Kallie and Marcus' mouths fell as the stone door began to open. Charlie staggered backward, while Oberi jumped up and began barking uncontrollably.

I smiled. "That's my Charlie," I whispered.

Except there were people waiting for us on the other side of the door. My stomach dropped as I saw a dozen people march into the tunnel, surrounding us. They were both male and female, with long, silver hair and elegant faces. They were beautiful to look at— all different shades of skin tone, with upturned noses and pale eyes, forms tall and lithe. They moved with a gracefulness that was eerie to observe. I'd never seen such gorgeous people.

And their ears— they were sharp and pointed, silver circlets with gemstones perched on their flawless heads. They wore silver armor, with swords at their sides. Each carried large square shields that had the design of a golden tree in the middle, its branches wrapped protectively around seven keys.

The tallest of them stepped to the center and threw back his head. His eyes locked on Charlie. "You're coming with us," he said, leaving no room to argue.

I didn't know what happened after that, because my body couldn't take any more. My heart tightened painfully in my chest, and I passed out. I heard Charlie call for me as I slumped to the ground, and Oberi's whine pitched high in my ears.

My time had run out. The venom had finally taken its hold. There was no saving me now.

charlie

TWENTY-THREE

"Pidge!" I screamed as Ava fell.

I felt her slip into unconsciousness through the bond, and my blood turned to ice. I rushed toward her, but one of the newcomers held me back. I struggled, but the stranger was strong. I'd spent so much energy getting through the traps that I couldn't fight them off.

"Let me go!" I cried.

"The antidote!" a man yelled to another. "She needs it now— before it's too late."

"Antidote?" I demanded. It could be another trap.

"You're not giving her anything!" Kallie snapped.

"Leave her alone!" Marcus added. The two of them must've been held back, too, because their feet scuffed against the cave floor, like they were struggling.

"Calm down," the man holding me insisted. "We're only trying to help. You must give her some space."

"Like hell," I growled. I didn't know who these people were, and I certainly didn't trust them.

I yanked my elbow free and threw it backward, into the guy's face. He dropped my other arm, and I rushed to Ava's side.

But someone was already there. Ava gurgled as liquid slid down her throat.

"What did you *do*?!" I burst. The ground beneath us began to shake beneath my rage. If this was another test, I wasn't sure I could handle it.

A woman with a smooth voice answered. "It's like General Ibrahim said— an antidote."

I yanked Ava's limp body into my arms, cradling her head to my chest. Ava was completely still, but my whole body shook. Everyone had gone quiet, except for a small whine that came from Oberi. His paws padded across the cave floor as he came up to me. He laid his head on my shoulder, as if offering me comfort.

"Ava, please!" I begged, shaking her a bit.

I held my breath, but the following moments stretched into eternity. I could feel her slipping, the venom eating away at our bond. This had to be another illusion. I couldn't lose her.

Sobs racked my chest, and I stroked her soft hair, but her skin had gone cold— as if all the Fire within her had died.

"Don't leave me, pidge," I whispered.

The tiniest cough bubbled out of her throat, and I started. My spine straightened, and I ran a thumb over her lips, as if to see if she'd actually made that sound, or if I'd just imagined it.

Her lips parted as she rasped, "Never."

Relief surged through me, and I squeezed her tightly, burying my face into her hair. "Ancestors, you're safe!"

"You weren't lying," Kallie said, sounding shocked. "You really did give her an antidote."

"Of course," a man said— General Ibrahim, I presumed, by the authoritative tone he used. "We would never seek to harm you."

Marcus scoffed. "I would beg to differ, based on the traps we went through to get here."

I drew a breath of relief and lifted my head. "Who are you? You're not from the Institute, clearly. How did you find us down here?"

"They're.... Elves," Ava whispered breathlessly.

"You're—" I couldn't get the words out.

"It's true," the woman across from me said.

She reached out, and a cool hand touched mine. I jerked away, but

Oberi nudged me with his nose, as if to say that it was safe to grab her hand. I let her take it, and she guided my fingers to her ears. I gasped when I felt that they were pointed.

"I am Colonel Amilda," she introduced. "We are members of the Emperor's Guard."

I shook my head. This couldn't be. "But the Elves went extinct a hundred years ago, during the Great Supernatural War."

"Most of us, yes," General Ibrahim stated. "The few who survived were forced into hiding. Please, let us help you, Charlie."

I hesitated. "How do you know my name?"

General Ibrahim spoke so calmly that it was hard to feel anything but safe in his presence. "We've been waiting for you."

I realized they must've been watching us navigate the tasks. We'd passed— which meant they must be here to lead us to the key. Though I had major trust issues, I felt that I should follow them. They had, after all, just saved Ava's life.

I stood, then helped Ava to her feet. Though the antidote had helped with the venom, it hadn't cured her blood loss. I could tell by the way she swayed on her feet that she was ill. Beside me, Oberi shifted into a Fire unicorn, and I hoisted Ava onto her back.

"We'll follow you," I stated. "It's just... where exactly are we going?"

General Ibrahim gave a friendly laugh. "Where else, Charlie? To Forevermore."

My heart stalled in my chest. It took me a second to process what he'd said. By the time my heart started beating again, the Emperor's Guard was already heading down the tunnel. Oberi's hooves clicked on the ground as she started forward.

"Hang on," Ava said. "You mean you're taking us to a *key* to Forevermore?"

I rushed behind Oberi. The Elves were quite tall and walked briskly. Marcus huffed as he tried to keep up.

"A key?" General Ibrahim sounded confused. "No, not at all. Welcome, my friends, to Forevermore."

The second he said it, I felt the air shift. We stepped out of the tunnel and into a huge cavern. My Air magic reached high to the ceiling — at least a hundred yards up. The cavern was so wide that I couldn't reach across the great expanse with my magic. By my estimates, this cavern certainly was large enough to house an entire city. My friends gasped in unison.

"By the gods," Kallie muttered under her breath.

"Holy shit," Marcus said at the same time.

Ava grabbed my sleeve so quickly, she nearly toppled off Oberi. "We found it! We found Forevermore!"

All this time, we thought we were searching for a *key* to Forevermore. I never expected to find the whole damn city here in the caves.

Something was very strange about Forevermore. My magic told me we hadn't left the caves, but I felt the warmth of the sun on my skin. The sounds of the city echoed off the walls of the cavern. There had to be thousands of people down here. Friendly chatter came from nearby, and the sound of flutes and stringed instruments surrounded us. The scent of freshly baked bread filled my nose. The whole place felt comforting... as if I'd stepped through the doors to a home I'd never had.

"How have you hidden yourselves this long?" Ava gasped. "Ancestors, did we step through a portal?"

"There wasn't a portal," Kallie said. "I would've felt it. This is more like..."

"An illusion," I finished for her. "We're still in the caves. I can feel it."

But I felt other sensations, too. A gentle breeze passed by, and birds chirped from a nearby tree branch. I inhaled the scent of blooming cherry trees. It was like we were underground *and* outside, all at the same time.

General Ibrahim was already farther ahead. He hadn't heard us. "This way," he said kindly.

I kept my hand on Oberi's side, and she guided me forward. I heard the trickling of water and laughter up ahead. We slowed near the water, and a child laughed gleefully from below me. A splash sounded, and warm water splashed onto my face. I felt water wash over my shoes as we stood next to a pool. All I wanted to do was sink into the warm, welcoming water.

The child snickered. "Their ears look funny."

"Simon, please," General Ibrahim reprimanded gently. "These are our guests."

The children splashed a few more times, then jumped out of the pool and began chasing each other around. Their laughter faded down the street.

"This is the Golden Pool of the Goddess," General Ibrahim explained. "Our Goddesses themselves, Idril and Caralyn, have bathed in these waters. These pools are blessed with healing energy. A few minutes in the pool, and you should all be good as new."

"Are you serious?" Kallie squealed. "This pool is *epic!*"

"The bathhouse has changing rooms and robes," General Ibrahim continued. "You may change there. Edwyrd will be by soon to escort you to the Emperor's Palace."

"We're meeting the Elven *emperor?*" Ava gasped, like it was a great honor. I was still so starstruck by the illusion that I hadn't found my mouth to speak.

"Yes, of course," General Ibrahim replied. "He'll be delighted to finally meet you. Enjoy the pool."

The Emperor's Guard left then. The four of us, along with Oberi and Rishi, stood there for a moment. I didn't think any of us could quite wrap our heads around this place.

Ava was the first to speak. "I can't believe this is *Forevermore.*"

"I can't believe I'm an Elf!" I cried. I had to be, because it was the only way I could've opened that door. It was a lot to take in. I'd only learned I was an Elementai a few months ago. Now I discovered I was part of a *second* supernatural race. It was both exciting and terrifying. I didn't know what to make of it.

"I have no words," Ava admitted. Then she gasped. "*Charlie!* We should've guessed you had Elf blood all along. The Elves are masters of energy manipulation. They can take magic from other races. You must've taken that shifter's magic during your fight with him at the club! *That's* why it was a fair fight, and you were just as strong as he was!"

I was in awe as the realization hit me. "I think I took some of Deuce's powers too, when I fought him," I added. "I just didn't siphon enough to win the fight at the time."

"And I bet you being able to take my Fire and Water magic had nothing to do with our bond," she added. "Since you've got Elf blood, you were able to use my powers with ease. I can't believe we didn't notice. Even your ears are a little pointed. I thought it was just a cute little feature."

Ava giggled as she caressed my ears, and I said, "I mean, it's not like we knew the Elves were still alive. It would've been ridiculous for us to assume I was one at the time, though I gotta say, this is all really badass."

"It's freaking amazing," Kallie said. "Come on. Let's go get those robes! This pool looks divine."

Oberi started forward, and I tilted my head toward Ava. "Is it really golden?"

"Oh, Charlie, it's *beautiful*," Ava raved. "The whole city is built out of gold and diamonds. Each building has jewels built into the sides. The fountain has crystal-clear waters, with a golden statue of the Elven Goddesses built in the center. There are waterfalls everywhere, and intricate archways are built straight into the cave walls. It's incredible."

"I can tell," I said. Though I couldn't see everything she could, I could sense the beauty of Forevermore through my other senses. There was so much laughter and music that I couldn't help but smile.

Ava must've been feeling a lot better after she received the antidote to the venom, because she slid off Oberi's back and led me into the bath-house. It smelled divine inside, like roses and honey.

"Wow, these changing rooms are incredible," Kallie raved. "I love the rose-gold taps."

"I've never felt anything so soft!" Marcus cried.

"What is it?" I asked.

"You'll love it." Marcus guided me to a plush sofa, and I sank into the fluffy cushions. I couldn't stop running my fingers over the velvety fabric, because it was just so amazing to touch.

Something clinked as Kallie picked it up from a counter. "Check out these perfumes. Lilac. Honeysuckle." She sniffed something. "I don't even know what this is, but it smells amazing."

"Wow, these robes are super soft," Ava said. "The sign says to take one if you need it. It's not a perfect translation, but close enough." She handed me a pair of swim trunks, a towel, and a robe.

"If the Elves still write in their native tongue, how come they speak English?" Marcus asked.

"They haven't been gone *that* long," Kallie reminded him. "Think of how many hundreds of years they spent trading with other races. Even the fae in Malovia learn English, because it's easier to communicate with other races."

Marcus blew a breath at the insult. "Hey, witches aren't the only race who chose English as their first language."

"Hey, kids," Ava jabbed playfully. "Now's not the time for arguments. We're in the most beautiful city ever built. Let's enjoy it."

We went off into separate changing rooms, then returned to the golden fountain. When I stepped into the water, it was like sinking into a warm bed at the end of the day. The water was pleasant in every way— thick, like salt water would be, and soothing against the skin. The pool bubbled, like a hot tub would. Ava guided me over to a ledge, and we sat on it. The ledge was deep enough that the water came to my chest. I sank into the water, until everything but my head was submerged. My muscles relaxed, and the tender bruises all over my back began to heal.

Oberi barked from the edge of the fountain, then spoke in my mind. *See you in the deep end, sucker.*

He took off running. I heard a big splash as he shifted into a narwhal and canon-balled into the deep water on the other end of the fountain. The shift was easy to notice now, as I felt the energy change between our bond. Oberi's splash had been so big that waves swayed against us all the way on this end of the pool. Ava giggled.

"What is it?" I asked.

"Oberi looks like she's having a ton of fun," Ava snickered. "Rishi's batting at her horn from the edge of the fountain— ancestors, Rishi almost fell in!"

We all laughed. I could only imagine what Rishi would do if he fell in the water. Marcus couldn't swim to begin with. I bet his cat wasn't any better.

"The Elven kids are loving Oberi," Ava said. "They're all swimming over to feel her horn."

"It's actually a tooth," Marcus piped up. "Did you know that? Narwhal horns are tusks that grow from their canine tooth. It has all these nerve endings in it that helps them navigate their environment. Most female narwhals don't have tusks, but Oberi must be special."

"Okay, nerd," Kallie laughed.

"I saw it on TV," Marcus grumbled.

"I didn't say being a nerd was a *bad* thing," Kallie added.

Ava laid her head on my shoulder. She breathed a blissful sigh.

"How do you feel, pidge?" I asked.

"Much better. Feel this." Ava took my hand and guided it over her leg, where the serpent had bitten her. The skin was smooth— as if the snake bite had never happened at all.

"That's incredible," I said breathlessly.

"The pool really does have amazing healing powers," she said. "It must be true that the Elven goddesses bathed here."

Kallie hummed, like she was completely in her element. "This whole *place* is incredible."

"How much of the city do you think is real, and how much is an illusion?" Marcus wondered aloud.

"Most of it's real," Kallie stated with certainty. "I can feel it with my own illusion magic. The buildings, the people... all that is real. The sun and sky are obviously illusions, along with some of the plants."

"Not *all* the plants?" Marcus asked.

"I can feel some of them with my Earth magic," I said. "I bet they're able to grow them under artificial lighting."

"Right," Kallie said. "But the biggest trees could never grow underground like this. Those, I'm guessing, are for aesthetic purposes."

"They're very good illusions," I stated. "I can smell the cherry blossoms."

"Eh," Kallie said, like fancy illusions were no big deal. Forget her. This place was breathtaking.

Footsteps approached, and someone stopped next to the pool. Ava and I turned toward the newcomer, and he cleared his throat.

"Charlie," he greeted brightly. "It's great to see you again."

I furrowed my brow. "Forgive me. I'm not great with voices."

"Yes, of course. My apologies. I am Edwyrd of Forevermore, guard to the Emperor's legacy," he introduced. "You may call me Eddie."

I gaped. It was the guy who'd found me after the cave-in earlier this semester— the one who'd helped me navigate my way out and get back to the prison bus. *That's* why he was down in the caves to begin with— because he lived here. He was an Elf all along!

It took me a few moments to find my voice. "Eddie? How the hell are you, man?"

I hoisted myself out of the pool and held out my hand to shake his. His grip was firm, and he shook my hand fast, like he was excited.

"I'm great, now that you're in Forevermore!" he said.

I tilted my head. "What do you mean by that?"

Eddie laughed lightly. "There is much to tell you. If you are done here, we can discuss things while we walk."

My friends and I didn't want to leave the Golden Fountain of the Goddesses, because really, it was freaking cool. But we also wanted to hear more and explore the city, and getting some answers was more important than having fun.

Everyone climbed out of the pool, and Ava used her Water powers to dry us off. We wrapped the silky robes we'd found in the bathhouse around ourselves. The fabric was smooth against my skin, and felt fit for royalty. Oberi changed into unicorn form, and Eddie began leading us through the streets of Forevermore.

"That fountain was amazing," Ava remarked. "I didn't know the Elves had healing powers."

"Oh, it's quite rare," Eddie explained. "The waters themselves are blessed. For an Elf themselves to have healing powers, they must drink from the waters. But not everyone who drinks from the blessed pool will develop healing abilities. It is reserved for the most gifted of our kind."

There was so much to experience in Forevermore that it was clear the magical fountain barely scratched the surface. We passed by vendors selling freshly baked cookies, and the scent of coffee drifted out of a cafe. My mouth watered, and Marcus' stomach growled.

"Forgive me," Eddie said quickly. "You must be very hungry."

He stopped at a vendor's station. "Hello, Elvira," he greeted.

"Edwyrd!" a woman replied brightly. "How are you this fine evening?"

"Never better," Eddie said. "My emperor has returned from the surface."

Elvira gasped. "By the Goddesses, he *has*? That is grand news!"

"Yes, isn't it? An Elvish Delight for each of my friends, please," Eddie requested.

"I'm sorry, but we don't have money," Ava told him quickly.

Innately, my guts twisted. I'd lived my whole life passing by street vendors because I couldn't afford the food. The last thing I wanted was to miss out in Forevermore.

"That's not an issue here," Eddie told her. "Our ancestors spent centuries amassing their wealth. There is plenty to go around. Here, we exchange pleasantries for goods."

My heart swelled with hope. What a marvelous thing it would be, to live without the need for money.

"Please, enjoy an Elvish Delight," Eddie offered.

Elvish Delight, Oberi snickered in my mind. *Sounds dirty.*

I scowled at her. *Try not to ruin this for me, would ya?*

Eddie placed something in my palm that was as big as my hand, but weighed almost nothing. Beside me, Marcus moaned in pleasure as he took a bite. Kallie followed, moaning so loudly it almost sounded like she was having an orgasm. I deemed the food safe and brought it to my lips.

My tongue rolled over something light and sweet. It felt like a cloud in my mouth, but the burst of flavors was unlike anything I'd ever tasted before. I bit into the heavenly dough, and a sweet, fruity jelly oozed out of the center. Powdered sugar coated my lips, and I licked it up. By the ancestors, I'd never had a pastry that tasted so good. Ava sighed beside me, like she couldn't find the words to describe the taste. We were all quiet for a while as we finished our pastries. Even Oberi had snagged one, though she'd swallowed it in seconds and was nudging me for a piece of mine.

Elvira laughed. "She's such a beautiful creature. Here, sweetheart. Have another."

Oberi tossed her fiery mane backward, shaking it so hard the wisps of Fire touched my arm. She happily scarfed up another pastry.

The pitter-patter of children's footsteps approached, and a young child cried, "A *unicorn*!"

Ava bent to their level and spoke kindly. "Have you ever seen a unicorn before?"

"Never," one of the kids answered, sounding so excited she couldn't contain herself.

"Well, today's your lucky day," Ava said. "Would you like to pet her?"

Oberi's excitement surged through the bond. She was obviously enjoying the attention.

Ava stood back and watched as the kids played with Oberi. She chuckled lightly. "They're trying to put flowers in her mane, but they're burning out."

"This one is for *you*!" a child said chipperly as they approached me.

"For me?" I asked. I reached out my hand, and the child placed a flower in my palm. I pressed it into my nose. It was unlike any flower I'd smelled before. It had to be some sort of Elvish plant, because it smelled like raspberries, which reminded me of Ava. "Thank you."

Eddie laughed under his breath. "Come. We don't want to keep the Emperor waiting."

"You said he just returned from the surface," I said as we followed Eddie. "How long has he been gone?"

Eddie laughed again, though I didn't know what he was so funny— something I couldn't see, I figured. "A very long time."

There was so much to take in as we continued down the street. People nearby conversed in both English and Elvish. The Elvish language was beautiful, with smooth vowels and a soothing accent. I felt like I could meditate at the sound of the voices alone, even though I didn't know what they were saying.

"Kallie, look at the flags!" Ava cried in wonder. She squeezed my hand and described them in detail. "They're like prayer flags, hanging in rows from one of the golden towers. They're all different colors, with beautiful Elvish runes on them. I can't translate them all, but that one for sure is *love*, and that one is *peace*."

Eddie said he worked for the Emperor, but it seemed that he was royalty himself around here. People paraded through the streets, singing and dancing around us. Cheers echoed through the cavern, growing in intensity as we neared the palace.

Someone grabbed my hand and twirled me around. Ava began singing along to a nearby flute, improvising the melody. Something rained down on me from above, and I thought it was flower petals, until I caught a piece and realized it was confetti, mixed with flower petals.

By the ancestors, this place was so full of *life*. It was everything the Institute wasn't. Ava was having so much fun that she took my hand and skipped alongside me.

"Oh, wow," Ava gasped. She dropped my hand and came to a halt. "What is that?"

"Oh, that?" Eddie said, like he passed by it every day. "It's the Mirror of Ingress."

"It's *huge!*" Ava said breathlessly. "I wish you could see this, Charlie. The mirror spans all the way to the sky, and disappears into the illusion. It's so long, I can't even see the end of it, and is wider than a skyscraper."

"It contributes to the illusion," Eddie explained. "It helps make the city seem bigger, and provides us passage in and out of Forevermore."

"It's a *portal!*" Kallie squeaked.

Ava gasped. She took my hand and guided my fingers to the mirror. It felt like warm, thick water, and was smoother than the robe I wore. Ava ran her fingers across the mirror, and I felt the ripples from her touch.

Eddie laughed, like our amazement amused him. "It's like you've never seen a portal before."

"It's not exactly common at the Institute," Marcus deadpanned.

Ava turned to Eddie. "You guys actually come to the surface?"

"Sometimes," he admitted. "Though it's very rare."

"How come no one has ever noticed you before?" she questioned. "Everyone thinks the Elves are extinct."

"We only leave when we have to," he said. "We're able to cast illusions to disguise ourselves, but it's a complicated spell, and one that doesn't hold very long. With so few of us, we can't risk getting caught, so we typically only leave through the mirror to bring resources back to Forevermore."

"So, I could've met an Elf before and never known it," Ava mused.

"It's possible, but very unlikely," Eddie said. "Let's keep going. We're almost to the palace."

The stone street beneath us sloped upward, and I heard the trickle of a stream beneath us as we passed over a bridge. A beautiful bird song drifted through the wind.

"Your illusions are impressive," Ava complimented Eddie. Ava had thrown herself into so much Elven research this semester that I could tell the city fascinated her. "What other magic do the Elves possess? There's so very little written about your people."

"Our magic is very versatile," Eddie explained. "Like the Fae, we come from Edinmyre, so our magic is similar."

"Your illusions don't hold, though," Kallie observed. "They don't become solid. I can feel it."

"Yes," Eddie confirmed. "Our illusion magic works well on the senses, but we cannot bring those illusions into reality like the fae can. Our greatest attribute is the ability to block or transfer someone else's magic. That's why noxite is so effective at blocking magical powers."

"What do you mean?" Ava asked. "What does noxite have to do with the Elves?"

"Oh, you don't know?" Eddie replied, like it was common knowledge around here. "Darke Island was the site of the Elven genocide. During the Great Supernatural War, we fled to the Island for refuge. We were hunted down and slaughtered. As the blood of the slaughtered Elves leaked into the soil, it transformed the minerals on the island and infused them with our magic. Noxite is only found on Darke Island because it's the only place that has seen so much Elven blood. Luckily, noxite doesn't work on us, because it *comes* from us."

Wow. That was a lot to take in.

"Other powers... let's see..." Eddie mused. "We can adopt powers that aren't our own."

"Adopt them how?" Kallie asked curiously.

"If we have magic to draw from, we can make it our own," Eddie said. "Take a dragon shifter, for example. If one happened to be nearby, I could take his magic and become a dragon myself— but only for the period in which I am siphoning his magic."

"That sounds dangerous, and actually quite terrifying," Marcus remarked.

Eddie chuckled. "Why do you think the fae tried so hard to kill us during the Great Supernatural War? We are somewhat of a magical conduit, and that's why they were afraid of us. They didn't like that we had the power to end bonds, either, because they feared we might sever bonds to their mates. But that power is so rare, you'd have to practically be a demigod to perform it. Even most Grand Masters can't do it."

"Grand Masters?" I asked.

"Another thing you should know about Elves is that some of us are gifted with a unique power, something that's different from all other Elves," Eddie explained. "Our Grand Masters are those who possess these special gifts— such as mind reading."

"You don't have a special gift?" I asked.

"Not that I've learned of," Eddie replied. "Though I wouldn't expect to become a Grand Master. Not inside my role."

I frowned. "Just because you're a guard doesn't mean you can't develop special talents."

"You misunderstand," Eddie said. "It's not about my training. It's what I was born into— as all Elves are born into a specific calling. It's why we're able to operate so efficiently without money. Everyone has their calling, which they would lay their life down for. Take Elvira, for instance. It would be an insult to suggest she do anything but bake pastries, because she loves to cook and wouldn't have it any other way. I was born to serve the Emperor and act as his bodyguard."

"Is that what you truly want, though?" Ava asked curiously.

"Yes," Eddie said, like he couldn't imagine anything else. "I would die for my master."

Cheers became louder as we approached the palace, and the sound of trumpets came from above. The air shifted as we entered a large foyer.

Beside me, Ava slowed. "That chandelier is incredible. I've never seen so many rare gems."

"It is quite nice, isn't it?" Eddie mentioned.

We continued on through the halls of the palace, and Ava narrated the decor for me. "It's even more grand than the Orenda Academy castle. Everything is plated in gold, and the archways are carved so intricately. I can only imagine how long it took them to build."

We slowed, and Eddie exchanged a few words with someone. I heard a pair of doors open, and Eddie led us into a large hall. At the head of the throne room, someone drew a sharp breath.

"Your highness," Eddie addressed the man. "May I present to you Charles Wahkin, son of Cameron Wahkin... and legacy to the throne."

I froze. *What the hell* did he just say?

Eddie grabbed my arm and nudged me forward. "Charlie, say something."

"I... what?" I scrambled for the words, but I *couldn't* have heard him right.

Ava's breath wavered. "Did you just call Charlie...?"

"The prince, essentially," Eddie said proudly.

The man at the front of the room stood from his throne and approached me. "Charlie, it's so nice to finally meet you. I am Emperor Cassiel— your grandfather."

My mouth gaped open, but I choked on my words. This wasn't possible. All my life, I thought my whole birth family had died. To find that they hadn't... it just about shattered my world. It didn't quite feel real.

"No way. Charlie can't be—" Kallie's words halted in her tracks, as if something just clicked.

"But Charlie..." Marcus trailed off. We were all so shocked, none of us could find the words.

My head spun, and I placed my palm to my forehead. "This can't be."

"It is true," Eddie said. "The Elven prophecy has finally been fulfilled."

My blood ran cold at the mention of yet *another* prophecy. I could hardly speak. "The... prophecy?"

"Long ago, at the end of the Great Supernatural War, a prophecy was given," Emperor Cassiel explained. *"The emperor's legacy will return, and bring light to a new dawn.* It is you— my grandson— who will save the Elves."

"B-but I'm not an Elf. I'm an Elementai," I stammered. I was in denial, because I already knew I had to have Elf blood to get through the doorway to Forevermore. But... the emperor's *grandson?* He had to be lying, or at the very least, mistaken. How could he be my grandfather?

"You are both," Emperor Cassiel said.

I didn't believe it. But at the same time, it made so much sense.

Eddie had said Elves could siphon powers from other magical races—like how I could siphon Ava's powers and use them. We'd already discussed that this went beyond our bond. I knew I'd won so many of my fights because of my Elven powers. I'd been siphoning strength from my opponents without realizing it.

And then there was the fact that noxite didn't affect me as much as it did everyone else. I knew it had something to do with being a demigod, but I could break through it easier than any of my demigod friends. It was because of my Elf blood. I *knew* I was an Elf since the moment I opened that door.

But... the prince? That just took things a step too far. It was easier to deny it all than accept pieces of it as the truth.

You cannot deny this, Oberi said, for only me to hear.

But I can't be a prince, I argued. *This is all happening too fast.*

Destinies have a way of unfolding very quickly, Oberi said slyly.

This can't be my destiny, I told her.

It is, and you must believe it, Charlie. I will support you every step of the way, but you cannot run from this.

I knew what she said was true. But still... I wouldn't accept it.

"Don't you understand?" Eddie asked brightly. "Why do you think everyone was cheering in the streets?"

I gaped. "I-I thought they were cheering for *you.*"

Eddie chuckled. "No, silly. They were cheering for *your* return."

Ava took my hand in hers and squeezed it. "Charlie, this is great news! You have a *family.*"

I knew she was trying to be supportive, but all I could do was shake my head. "I don't understand any of this."

"Allow me to explain," Emperor Cassiel offered kindly. "I was a young Elf when I fought during the Great Supernatural War."

"That must make you over a hundred years old," Marcus remarked.

Emperor Cassiel sounded amused. "Yes. I'm a hundred and twenty, which is still quite young for an Elf. We are immortal, meaning we do not age once we reach adulthood. At the time of the Great Supernatural War, Darke Island was a place for refugees. The Elves weren't the only ones to make Darke Island our home. Witches, Elementai, and others sought refuge here as well. But we were found, and most were killed during the genocide. A few of us escaped into the caves, and we've been here ever since."

My guts twisted at the story. I couldn't imagine.

"Your grandmother was one of the Elementai who escaped with her parents during the Great Supernatural War," Emperor Cassiel continued. "She was only a baby then. Many years later, when your grandmother was grown, she saved me from a *serpens spelunca* attack. I was in the caves when the serpent bit me. Your grandmother was Yapluma, and trained as an alchemist here in Forevermore. She developed an antidote to the venom, and saved my life. We were married soon after, and we had your father several years later."

"I thought my father was from Kinpago," I said, trying to make sense of it all.

"Your father rebelled, as most young men do," Emperor Cassiel explained. "He left Forevermore and went to Kinpago, where he could learn his Elementai magic and bond with his Familiar. It was there that he met your mother, Kelly Catori. As you very well know, your mother was Nivita, and at that time, the Elementai did not allow members of separate Houses to marry. Your mother was put to death, and your father was sentenced to life in prison. You were sent away, and we had no way of finding you. That is... until you showed up in our caves."

"Is that why you went to the surface?" I asked. "To find me?"

"The surface?" Emperor Cassiel sounded confused.

"Eddie said you'd just returned from the surface," I explained. "He said you'd been gone a long time."

Eddie chuckled. "I wasn't talking about Emperor Cassiel. I said *my emperor*. I meant *you*. As I told you, I was born to serve the Emperor's legacy— that's you, Charlie."

My eyebrows shot up. I thought when he'd mentioned it before, he'd meant he was born to serve the emperor himself— not the *prince*.

"Did you know who I was when you found me in the caves?" I asked. "Why did you let me go back to the Institute?"

"I did not know at the time," Eddie admitted. "With Elves, what we are born into becomes a sacred, magical contract. But I'd never experienced the magic before, so I didn't understand it. I went out in the caves that day because I... I just *had* to. I couldn't explain it. Now I know that my magic was pulling me toward you, calling me to serve you in your time of need. You're my alpha— my master."

"Alpha?" I repeated. "Like a wolf pack?"

"In a sense, yes," Eddie confirmed. "I said we were very similar to the fae. They themselves shift into wolves and have their pack hierarchy. We too have a hierarchy. I was born to serve you. I did not know who you were or what the magic meant that day I found you wandering the caves— not until I returned to Forevermore and researched your history. But by the time we figured out who you were, we weren't sure how to get you out of the Institute. We were planning to help you escape through the mines, but hadn't figured out all the details. Now you're here."

"Wow," I breathed. "It's a lot to wrap my head around. Being your alpha makes it sound like we're bonded or something."

"In a way," Eddie said.

I took a step back. This was a little weird. "How can that be? I'm bonded with Ava. It's not like a... romantic bond, is it? I'm not gay."

Eddie burst into laughter. "No, Charlie. *I'm* gay, but it's not that kind of bond between us. It's more that I am bound to the magic and obligated to obey and protect you. I cannot disobey you, even if I want to. I was born to serve you."

"I don't want anyone to be obligated to protect me," I protested.

"Sorry, but you don't have a choice," Eddie replied. "It is a great honor to be your guard."

There was no arguing with Eddie on this one. Magic or not, he believed me to be his greatest purpose. It was strange, considering no one ever gave a damn about me before. Now this random Elf from a mythical city wanted to follow my every order? I must've gone insane.

If you were insane, would I be standing here talking to you right now? Oberi huffed, like she was offended by my thoughts of insanity. As crazy as this all was, I knew Oberi was real, and I could feel the strength of our bond. It confirmed for me I wasn't imagining any of this.

Stuff like this doesn't happen where I come from, I told her.

Where you came from is not where you are going, Oberi said. *You must accept the truth.*

"So, I'm part Elf..." I mused. "It makes a lot of sense, actually. Like how we got through your traps, and how I can resist noxite so much more than everyone else."

"Unfortunately, noxite will affect you, as it did your father, due to your Elementai side," Emperor Cassiel remarked. "But my guards overheard your conversation in the caves. You are a demigod?"

"That's what I'm told," I admitted. There was no point in lying if they already knew.

"Then you shall learn to overcome the effects of noxite," he said. "It will simply take practice."

"Emperor," Ava addressed him softly. "There's something I'm very curious about."

"You may ask anything you'd like," he offered.

"Well, we thought we were coming into the caves to find a *key* to Forevermore," she told him. "You see, we found a stone gate in the forest near the Institute. There were seven key holes on it, and based on what we've been able to gather from various Elven runes on the island, we thought Forevermore was beyond the gate. Is this the *true* Forevermore?"

"Forevermore is not simply a place," he stated. "It is a *feeling*, one that resides both here and beyond the doorway. This city *is* Forevermore, which is another word for *sanctuary*, or *safe haven* in our native tongue. Forevermore is anywhere we are, as long as we feel safe. We are aware of the gate you speak of, though we have not been able to pass through it ourselves."

"What exactly would you hope to find on the other side?" Kallie asked curiously.

"The afterlife, of course," Emperor Cassiel replied, as if it was the most common thing in the world.

My jaw dropped. No wonder the gate was designed for demigods.

"The gate was created by the gods hundreds of years ago," Emperor Cassiel explained. "Before the Miriamic Coven was even formed, the keys belonged to the entirety of the supernatural community. Seven keys were made, to ensure we would share the power of the gateway. Up until this point, we as a supernatural community were united. The door was meant to bridge the gap between us and the gods, so that everyone may connect with them. But the power was far too strong, and we discovered that only gods and demigods could use the door. It caused division and anger among the supernaturals. The keys only drove us further apart when they were stolen by the Unseelie fae. After that happened, the keys, unfortunately, were lost to time."

He drew a deep breath, before adding, "The Elves sought refuge on Darke Island a hundred years ago in hopes that perhaps we would find the keys, commune with the gods, and stop the Great Supernatural War. But we never found them."

"But *we* could!" Ava cried out hopefully. "We could still do it— find the keys, talk with the gods, and bring peace! The Elves could come out of hiding. These wars between the supernatural races would end. We could prevent the prophecy all together!"

"Pidge," I started to say, but she cut me off.

"Charlie, the prophecy says another war is coming," she reminded me, though she sounded excited. "If we find all the keys, we can open the door and use the gods to unite everyone *before* another war breaks out."

"I... that actually might work." I thought about it for a moment. If the door was as powerful as my grandfather said, then perhaps there was hope. Maybe my piece of the prophecy never had to come true.

"This is precisely why Charlie's arrival is so important," Emperor Cassiel said. "The full wording of the prophecy states, '*The emperor's legacy will return, and bring light to a new dawn. A second war will break Forevermore, but it shall be restored by the power of the demigods. It is his choice to damn the realm, or save us all.*'"

My mouth went dry. *Bring light to a new dawn... a second war... damn the realm, or save us all.* It was Ava's prophecy all over again, just reworded in a different way.

Eddie noticed my stunned silence. "Don't you see, Charlie? The prophecy has always been interpreted as the emperor's kin, who is also a demigod. You're both, *and* the first demigod since the last war. It's talking about you."

Ava sounded excited to have more information about the prophecy. "How is Charlie supposed to restore Forevermore?"

"Recall that Forevermore is a place of sanctuary," Emperor Cassiel explained. "We have always believed that our city will eventually fall, but that we will find our sanctuary beyond the doorway, in the Blessed Haven."

"The Blessed Haven?" I repeated, trying to wrap my head around all this information.

"The Blessed Haven is a realm that encompasses *all* afterlives," Emperor Cassiel said. "The Elven gate leads to this heavenly city, which in itself contains all of our afterlives, including the Great Hunting Grounds from Arcanean culture, the Ancestral Lands of the Elementai, and Alora from Miriamic lore. Anyone may enter The Blessed Haven, just as anyone can enter The Eternal Torment— also known as Hell, the Underworld, or the Abyss. We have always believed this city we're standing in to be a temporary home. Our true home— our *true* Forevermore— lies on the other side of the gateway, in the Blessed Haven. There is no other home for us. The fae took over our first home, Edinmyre, and the people of Earth do not want us here. We have been waiting a long time for a demigod to lead us to our eternal Forevermore."

Pride surged through me. I'd never felt so important before. *I* could be the ones to save the Elves— the prince that could lead my people to heaven. My birth family needed me, and I could finally do some damn good.

But my pride quickly twisted to resentment. There was more to the prophecy than anyone knew— the piece that Maddie had given me.

A choice will be made by the twin of her soul
To save her and damn the realm
Or curse her, and save us all
A fate worse than death
Is the chosen one's destiny.

They didn't know it, but the emperor was asking me to choose between the Elves... and Ava.

"So, we just need to find the rest of the keys, and the Elves will be saved!" Ava cried, sounding thrilled.

"Yes," Emperor Cassiel said. "But finding the keys to the doorway has proven to be an impossible endeavor."

"We already have three," Ava blurted.

"Three?" he breathed, like he couldn't believe it.

It was then a male voice cut in from the other side of the throne room. "He's here?"

Heavy footsteps rushed into the room. "Forgive me. I've only just heard."

"Ah, yes," Emperor Cassiel said calmly. "So nice of you to join us."

The man approached me and took my face in his shaking hands. The movement made me go still. I didn't know what was happening, until he spoke in a broken voice. "Charlie," he breathed.

"Cameron, give the boy some space to breathe," Emperor Cassiel pressed.

"No," Cameron protested. "I've waited too long to see him again. I want to hold my son."

My mind went completely blank. I couldn't believe it— this was just too much to bear. "Dad?"

<h1 style="text-align:center">ava-marie</h1>

TWENTY-FOUR

Finding Forevermore was nothing compared to the bombshell that had just been dropped.

It was unfathomable. After twenty years, Charlie's dad was still alive.

Cameron and Charlie shared some features, but his skin was lighter, and his hair was brown instead of black. But at the same time... the way he moved was *so much* like Charlie.

Cameron's lip wobbled as he observed Charlie's features. "By the Goddesses, you look just like your mother."

Cameron went to take Charlie into an embrace, but that didn't work, because Charlie reacted. His body stiffened, and immediately, I knew this wasn't going to be good.

"Get the hell away from me!" Charlie pushed him away. Cameron staggered backward, his expression wounded, as if he'd expected this situation to go much differently.

Charlie took a few steps backward, breathing raggedly. Oberi stepped in front of Charlie, lowering her horn as if telling Cameron not to take a step closer.

Marcus and Kallie looked between them, not sure of what to do. They glanced at me, obviously expecting me to do something. I stepped beside Oberi.

"You're not going to touch him," I said harshly.

A golden alicorn entered the room. I figured he must've been Cameron's Familiar, because the stallion stood across from Oberi and bobbed his horned head. The alicorn and unicorn faced off, stomping their hooves and letting out snorts that were far from friendly.

Cameron looked on the verge of tears, so Emperor Cassiel spoke for him. "As I said before, Cameron ran away from Forevermore nearly twenty-five years ago, to Kinpago. He rebelled, and found Charlie's mother while living amongst the Elementai."

"I didn't *rebel*. I had no interest in being Emperor," Cameron said spitefully.

That's the same fucking thing, I thought with irritation.

Cameron took a breath. "But that's all in the past now. Let me explain it to him, Father."

Emperor Cassiel fell silent, and Cameron went on, speaking directly to Charlie. "I was half-Hawkei, so I believed that Kinpago could be my home. I didn't intend to find a wife when I arrived. Kelly was... a brilliant Nivita. I was enchanted by her. We fell in love, and she knew of my past, but I wanted no part of my legacy to take the Elven throne. I thought that we could live a life of secrecy amongst the Elementai, and avoid my father. I knew if he found us, I would be forced to return to Forevermore. So Kelly and I married in secret, and tried to live a quiet life amongst the tribe. No one knew I had Elven blood. Then Kelly had you, Charlie, and we knew we had to be even more careful— interhouse children were seen as an abomination among the Hawkei. Your mother loved you so much, the thought of losing you gutted her."

Charlie said nothing, and Cameron gave a heavy sigh. "I knew my father was searching for me, but the Hawkei Elders found us first. Interhouse relationships were illegal at that point in time, and since I was Yapluma, and your mother was Nivita, we were guilty as charged. At the time, Air and Earth were not allowed to be together. I'm sorry to say that your existence proved our guilt, Charlie. The trial they put us through was a farce. You were taken away from us, and we didn't know where they sent you. Your mother was put to death, the penalty for bearing an interhouse child, and I was made to watch."

Cameron's voice cracked, and I put a hand on Charlie's arm. He felt so stiff and cold. I couldn't imagine what Cameron had been forced to endure, but it seemed like what Charlie had gone through was even worse. He'd been so still since the mention of his mother, as if her name wasn't something he could bear to confront.

Charlie's father came closer, and I got ready to protect Charlie if need be. But he didn't move to grab Charlie again. He just kept talking. "After the execution, I was dragged off to a Hawkei prison within the tribal grounds, given a life sentence for being in an interhouse relationship. But my father had finally located me by this point, and sent the Emperor's Guard to free me. Once they broke me out, I was forced to come back here, instead of being allowed to search for you. When I returned, a prophecy was given, stating my son would one day come to Forevermore."

Cameron frowned. "It wasn't enough. I attempted to find you, but your adoption record was sealed, and you were moved so many times from foster home to foster home that by the time I located you, you were already gone. Once you left the system at eighteen, it became impossible to find you. It was like you vanished."

"I moved across the country, to get the hell away from California," Charlie said. "I wanted nothing to do with that place."

"I can understand, but it made it harder to find you." Cameron appeared wary. "After all my efforts, I still could not locate you. So I left it up to fate. And I've been here ever since, waiting for the day my son would return."

The silence was so thick in the throne room that it was nearly suffocating. Charlie didn't say anything, and Cameron tried again. "I'm sorry that I left you alone all these years—"

"*Sorry?*" Charlie sneered. "Sorry isn't good enough. Why didn't you come back for me?"

"I wasn't allowed to leave," Cameron said. "Due to my previous bout in Kinpago, I was guarded night and day. The security of Forevermore is imperative, and my foolish actions had nearly exposed the Elves. I was not allowed to cross through the Mirror of Ingress to get to the surface world. I am not only a prince, but I am also a refugee, and therefore wasn't permitted to leave Forevermore. I attempted to escape several times to look for you, but I was always stopped."

"He speaks the truth, Charlie," Emperor Cassiel said sadly. "We wanted you here with us, but by the time the Hawkei tribe had given you up to the foster care system, we could not find you, and continuing to search for you would put our entire city in danger of being exposed to the supernatural world."

"That's a bullshit excuse," Charlie snarled. "If my son was out there, I'd do *anything* to get him back. I would've torn down this whole city to find him, crown or no crown."

Then, Charlie took a sharp breath. "I can somewhat understand your reasoning, Grandfather. You are an emperor, and have a whole city to protect."

Charlie's voice was raging as he directed his anger at Cameron. "But *you*. There's nothing that can excuse what you did to me. You could've snuck out, found a way, but it wasn't important to you. You had twenty years to do so, and you never even tried *once*. You sure didn't have any hesitations about leaving Forevermore when it was to suit your own self-ishness, but when it came to rescuing me, you sure left me to the wolves."

Cameron's attempt to soothe Charlie was worthless. "I wanted to find you—"

"I was *starving*!" Charlie cried. If the whole kingdom hadn't heard him shouting before, they did now. His voice echoed through the throne room, shaking the walls. "Nobody gave a fuck about me! I had nowhere to go, no one who loved me! Hell, I had to prostitute myself just to get a warm place to sleep most nights!"

Kallie's and Marcus' mouths dropped open. He'd never told them that. My heart twisted and fell into my gut as he brought up that painful memory. I could feel his rampant emotions smashing through our bond. He was angrier than I'd ever known him to be. I just wanted it all to stop, so I could take his pain away. I'd take the pain *for him*, suffer every day, just so he wouldn't feel like this. Enduring a broken heart was nothing compared to watching Charlie be in agony, but this was beyond my power to fix.

Cameron had gone completely pale, appearing horrified. Charlie gave a harsh, cold laugh. "But you wouldn't know that, huh? You weren't around. You didn't care."

"I *did* care," Cameron insisted. "I did the best I could to find you!"

"Yeah, right. You're a coward. You ran away from your duty, and you ran away from me."

The floor beneath us began to shake, and cracks rippled through the gold walls.

Charlie's Earth magic was going to crumble this castle to the ground. Oberi gave a nervous nicker, and I rubbed Charlie's arm. I had to calm him down, if I didn't want us to be crushed beneath the rubble.

"Charlie, it's over now," I reminded him softly.

He flinched at my words, but at least the ground stopped shaking, and the palace remained standing. Charlie was breathing so hard I thought his throat might rip in half. Cameron, bastard he was, decided to keep talking.

"I can't make up for the mistakes I've made," Cameron said heavily. "I can only try to fix what we might have now. Charlie, please, look at me."

"I *can't* look at you," Charlie spat. "I've been blind for twenty years."

Cameron reeled back, and Emperor Cassiel's eyes widened. I was confused for a moment, before I remembered that Charlie hadn't gone blind until after they'd taken him away from his parents. They'd had no idea. I glanced at Eddie, wondering why he hadn't spoken up.

"I didn't tell them," Eddie confessed. "I didn't want to betray Charlie in any way by revealing information he might not be ready to say."

"I didn't know," Cameron said thickly. "You hide it so well."

Charlie scoffed. "Yeah, well. Another trick I learned on the streets. You can't let people know you're vulnerable, or they'll take advantage."

"I understand," Cameron said, though it didn't sound like he did. "What... what happened?"

"I don't know," Charlie replied sullenly. "It was shortly after they threw me in foster care. I woke up on Christmas morning and couldn't see anymore. I don't remember it."

Cameron had been rendered speechless, thank the ancestors. Every word out of his mouth just made everything worse, and no matter his reasons, I couldn't forgive him. He'd abandoned Charlie. In my opinion, that made him my worst enemy.

Emperor Cassiel bobbed his head. "I see. But this changes nothing. You still have an obligation, Charlie."

"An obligation to what?" Charlie said snidely. Eddie bounced anxiously, like he was ready for a fight to go down.

"Elves are immortal, as in we don't age, but we can still be killed," Emperor Cassiel said. "One day, the time of my reign will come to an end, and your father will ascend to the throne, making you the Crown Prince. Due to his Hawkei blood, your father won't live forever. When he dies, it is *you* who will take the throne, and rule Forevermore, until your heir rises after you."

The blood drained from Charlie's face. He appeared stunned. His hands started to shake. I feared he was on the brink of another meltdown.

Kallie spoke up for the first time. "That seems like a long time to rule," she said. "Malovia isn't run like that."

"The Elven monarchy doesn't work the same way the fae monarchy does. Instead of replacing a king every twenty years, an Emperor stays on the throne until he dies. In many years past, Elven emperors and empresses would rule for centuries before passing the crown on to their child, usually after dying in battle, or on missions," Emperor Cassiel explained.

"Missions?" Marcus questioned.

"As I'm sure you're all aware, the Elven Union was the biggest crime family in the supernatural world," Emperor Cassiel explained. "Our wealth, our gold buildings, the gems you see, all of it was amassed through heists and robberies throughout the centuries. It was dangerous work. Many emperors and empresses were killed during the heist of a famous painting, or the theft of a collection of jewels. It is the way many of our rulers perish."

"So you're basically a glorified mob boss?" Marcus asked cluelessly.

Emperor Cassiel frowned, and ancestors, I wanted to hit Marcus. Kallie did it for me— she slapped his shoulder, and Marcus balked, as if he realized his mistake.

Shit, this was the *emperor* here. You didn't come in and insult him in his own palace.

Marcus stared at the floor, and Emperor Cassiel gave a gruff noise.

"Be that as it may, we Elves have not had the opportunity to go on missions again since the genocide. We have more than enough here in Forevermore after our previous heists, but remaining concealed is currently more important."

"I'm studying criminal justice. I want to be a supernatural bounty hunter, not a prince for a group of thugs I don't even know," Charlie seethed.

"If you wish, you may pursue any passions you have, *after* you've fulfilled your prophecy," Emperor Cassiel said. "But before that happens, you will lead us to the Blessed Haven, as was promised."

"Like hell! I have my own dreams I want to follow!" Charlie shouted.

"I know this is all a great shock to you, but you have a responsibility to deliver us to the afterlife," Cameron said. "The Elven people have been expecting you for a long time, and that takes precedence over anything personal."

Charlie's jaw tightened. "I don't have to hear this. Eddie, get me the hell away from him."

"Right away, sir. I'll escort you to your private quarters. They've already been prepared." Eddie took Charlie's arm and led him away. Oberi trotted after them.

I was torn between following Charlie and giving him space. I didn't know what to do. Cameron went to go after them, but I put a hand on his chest and shoved him back.

"If you don't want a fireball to the face, you'd better stay away from Charlie," I warned. I ignited a blue fireball in my hand, and prepared to launch it at Cameron.

A female Elf stepped forward. She had to be Cameron's personal Emperor's Guard, but I didn't give a damn. I'd fry her, too.

"There's no need for violence here," Emperor Cassiel said calmly. "We'll give Charlie some time to process the situation. In the meantime, I think it's best if we show you to your rooms."

"Rooms?" Marcus yelped.

"Of course. You didn't think we'd allow you to come to Forevermore without making sure you had a place to stay," Emperor Cassiel replied.

He nodded to a servant at his side, who bustled forward and bowed to us.

"You mean... we're not going back to the Institute?" I asked.

"It wasn't in my knowledge that you *wanted* to go back," Emperor Cassiel replied. "It is a prison school, after all. And due to the security of the city, I'm afraid we can't allow you to leave. You must stay here, for your own safety as much as ours."

That was worrisome to me, but not to Kallie. She brightened immediately at the mention of staying in a palace once again, whereas I shared a wary glance with Marcus. As pretty as this place was, we were prisoners here as we were at the Institute. They weren't going to let us go.

"I'll have food sent to your rooms," Emperor Cassiel said. "You've all had a very long journey, and need time to rest."

"Follow me this way, please," the servant said. Marcus, Kallie and I drifted after the servant. My fingers twitched as I noticed Cameron watching us lonesomely, as if he wanted to follow.

Tough. I wasn't accommodating at all to the absent father bullshit, and Cameron had seriously pissed me off by hurting Charlie. He could go suck a dick.

As we passed all the elaborate paintings and sculptures in the hallway, Marcus was absolutely gushing.

"This is an authentic Van Gogh!" he cried, pointing to a painting of poppies on the wall.

He hurried across the hallway and pointed to another group of paintings. "*And* a missing Rembrandt, *and* a lost Picasso! Some of these paintings have been lost for decades!"

"Yes, the Elves are great appreciators of all forms of art," the servant replied. "We have a college here that is devoted to studying the masters. Our theater program was the best in the world, before we had to go into hiding."

Marcus squealed. Looks like he'd changed his mind in staying in Forevermore in two point five seconds.

"Mother Miriam's bosom, is that a portrait by *Raphael?*" he all but screamed. Rishi meowed as Marcus squeezed him, like it was a dream come true.

I rolled my eyes. Marcus was totally getting a hard-on for all this art.

I bet all the rare missing paintings in the world were in Forevermore. The Elves really had a talent for getting away with crimes.

"Your rooms are connected to the quarters of Prince Charles. He has his own section of the palace, built for his friends and his bride," the servant explained.

Bride? I opened my mouth to ask something else, but my words died in my throat as I saw Eddie come running up the hallway.

"Ah, Miss Ava. There you are," Eddie breathed. "I left Charlie in his room with your Familiar. He needed some... time alone."

My stomach plummeted.

Eddie gave a nervous smile. "Anyway, I thought that in the meantime, I should take you to the Empress Suite."

"Empress Suite?" I blinked. Kallie and Marcus gaped.

"Oh, yes, you don't know." Eddie blushed, and his eyes shifted toward my friends. "May I have a moment with you, miss? A private word?"

I was about to say no, but Kallie waved her hand at me, as if to say it was fine. Kallie sure was making herself comfortable around here. She didn't seem to think there was any danger. I followed her lead, and said, "Okay. I'm listening."

The other servant led Kallie and Marcus away, while I followed Eddie. He took me around a pillar, before he faced me sheepishly and wrung his hands.

"Pardon me, miss, but as I am an Elf, I can see bonds, even if I'm not strong enough to break them," Eddie said. "You share a soul with my master. And I couldn't help but notice how close the two of you are. He loves you, and you love him."

"What's your point?" I jutted out a hip, preparing to receive yet another surprise.

"There's one thing we didn't *quite* talk about in the throne room," Eddie said. His voice got quieter with every word. "You see, the people weren't just welcoming Charlie. They were welcoming you, too."

"Me? Why?" I was certain they didn't even know who I was.

Eddie nibbled his bottom lip. "Um, well, we haven't had an Empress in the city in some years. Emperor Cassiel's wife died some many years ago, and Kelly Catori was never brought to Forevermore. We haven't had an Empress in the city in such a long time, and the position is very dear to Forevermore. We worship Elven *goddesses*, so the Empress is considered to be the spiritual leader for the people, the mother of our race. In some ways, the Empress is more important to the Elves than even the Emperor himself."

I could see where this was going. "People want it to be me, don't they?"

"It's not supposed to be creepy, or anything," Eddie said, and he put his hands out. "Your arrival gave the people hope that there could be an Empress in Forevermore again. A new heir, perhaps."

A coldness crept over my body. Eddie studied me carefully, and I sighed. "This is really a conversation that I should be having with Charlie."

"Yes, of course." Eddie bobbed his head. "Anyway, I think I should show you the suite—"

"No, you know what? Take me to him," I said. "I need to talk to Charlie."

Eddie frowned. "I'm sorry, miss. His instructions were to not let anyone see him, and I cannot disobey an order from my master."

I tapped my chin. "Okay... then... direct me to his quarters. And then just... leave me alone."

Eddie smiled. "I'm certain I can do that, miss. This way."

Eddie took me down a complicated set of twisting hallways and spiraling staircases that went upward, all the way to the top of the palace. When we got there, Eddie threw open a set of golden double doors. I gasped as I walked into the elaborate space, which was decorated with ornate rugs, beautifully crafted furniture, and a floor-to-ceiling window that overlooked the entirety of the city. It had to be as big as my parents' mansion back home.

At this time of day, twilight was beginning to cast darkness over the city, the horizon spanning in hues of orange, purple, and yellow. I knew it was just an illusion, but it was pretty all the same.

Charlie's quarters were more like an actual house than a set of connected rooms. He had this tower all for himself and his court. I could hear Marcus and Kallie chatting in the parlor room next to the living area.

Eddie told me the Empress Suite was in the room beside Charlie's, but I didn't care to look. Once he was gone, I tried opening the biggest door in the place, which I was sure had to be Charlie's room. The door was locked, but I knew he needed me right now. My magic warmed the lock, and it melted away as I pushed open the door and stepped into the room.

Charlie's bedroom was just as grand as the rest of his quarters. It had an ornate four-poster bed, and a balcony that looked down upon the palace courtyard below. The windows were open, letting in a warm breeze.

My heart was cut to ribbons as I saw Charlie sitting on the edge of the bed, hunched over and quivering. He was *crying*. Sobs broke out of his chest as his shoulders shook. I'd never seen him like this. Charlie was so tough and so strong. He never let his emotions show. To see him so raw and vulnerable broke something in me I hadn't been aware of. It made me tremble to witness.

Oberi was in husky form, and he lay on the bed with his head on Charlie's lap. Charlie stroked his head as he cried, like he needed the comfort. Oberi's eyes were so big and black, and it stung my soul.

Charlie jerked up at the sound of the door closing as I shut it behind me. He stopped weeping almost immediately, as if he was worried someone would see.

"It's Ava," I told him quietly. His shoulders slackened, but only a little. "I'm here for you."

Charlie sniffed. "Eddie's a shit guard if he can't do the one thing I asked him to."

"I'm different." I sat beside him. "It's okay to cry."

"I'm not crying." He tried to turn away from me.

"Yes, you are." I lifted his chin and wiped his face. "You can't hide it from me."

Charlie's voice broke. "I killed my mom."

I felt both sides of our bond twist in pain. "No, Charlie, you didn't."

"Yes I did! Because she had me, she was killed. I thought both of my parents had died because they were in an interhouse relationship— figured my dad had died in prison— but that wasn't true. They let my dad live, and murdered my mom, because she gave birth to me."

"Your mom *chose* you," I insisted, and I continued to wipe the tears away. "She knew the risks of having an interhouse child, but she gave birth to you anyway, because she loved you. My mom chose me, too. I'm an interhouse child, just like you. Both of our mothers would've died to save us. It was only a cruel twist of fate that your mother did, and mine survived."

"My dad should've done more," he cried. "He should've protected her."

"He probably did the best he could," I told him. "But you can't blame yourself for your mother's death. She *wanted* you, Charlie. What she sacrificed proves she did."

"My dad sure as hell didn't want me," Charlie said, and Oberi gave a whine. "He left me to rot."

"I'm not saying you can't blame him. But being angry with him is only hurting yourself," I insisted.

"He could've prevented everything that happened to me, and he did *nothing*," Charlie said. "I could never leave my son to fend for himself, especially as a child. I would've done whatever it took to make sure he was in a place that was safe."

"But your dad isn't you." I took Charlie's head and laid it on my chest. I wrapped my arms around him, and held him tight as my fingers danced through his hair. "Sometimes the people in our life make shitty choices, and we have to pay for them."

"How would you know?" Charlie asked. "You always had parents who loved you. How could you know how I feel?"

His accusations didn't bother me. I knew he wasn't in control of his feelings right now.

"Because I'm the shitty family member," I admitted quietly. "I'm the one who makes bad choices."

"No, you're not," Charlie objected. "You care about everyone."

"You can love someone and still do terrible things to them," I reminded Charlie. "My parents were good, but I was bad. They loved me and did everything they could to support me, and I turned my back on them more times than I can count. Sometimes, I didn't even mean to. I just did. And it was never to hurt anyone. I didn't want to cause my parents pain. I just... couldn't stop the darkness inside of me."

"You were a child. My dad's an adult," Charlie said fiercely. "He could've chosen better."

"Maybe he wasn't capable of it." I wiped away more tears with the sleeve of my robe, which was starting to become soaked.

"He could've tried for me."

"He tried the only way he knew how."

I felt like this was my fault, and I was the one causing Charlie so much pain. If we hadn't been looking for the keys, we never would've found this city, or his dad. I hated myself for putting him through this.

"I know what you're thinking. You can't blame yourself," Charlie said with a shudder. "I would've met my dad eventually. Maybe it's better this way, that I met him now instead of later."

I felt wrecked on the inside. "My prophecy led to all this."

"Your prophecy is tied to me, too," Charlie choked out. "Don't you realize how closely the Elven prophecy and yours are worded? *The emperor's legacy will return, and bring light to a new dawn.* Yours literally says, *The balance between the light and the dark will be brought together by the light of the new dawn.* It's talking about you and me Ava, together. Everything we do is intertwined, whether we want it to be or not. It's like we can't avoid it, and it's too much to handle."

My heart hollowed out. I didn't want Charlie to feel like this— that our fate was too overwhelming. It was breaking him right now. It seemed like it was going to crush me, too.

"Whatever destiny decides, it's led us here," I insisted. "And finding Forevermore isn't a bad thing. Even though it seems like it right now. We thought the Elves were wiped out, but they're still alive. That gives the supernatural world hope that things aren't as bad as they seem."

"I'm not even a real Elf. I'm more Elementai than anything," he mumbled.

"You *are* an Elf, Charlie. As difficult as it is to face, you've got so much Elven blood in you," I began. "You're gifted at singing and music. You're intelligent, and cunning, and let's be honest, you're a damn good criminal. Those are all Elven traits. You had your people living in you all along, and you didn't even know it. You were never truly alone."

"I spent my entire life living as a street rat, and now I'm the heir to a royal throne," Charlie said bitterly. "How can I be an emperor? It's not me."

"Maybe that's a good thing," I said gently. "You understand suffering. You didn't lead the pampered life of a prince, so you know how it feels to struggle. You can help your people so much easier, because you've been there, and you understand how they feel. If anything, that makes you a better candidate for the job, not a worse one."

Charlie took a moment to ponder this. His tears dried. He sat up before he said, "But I don't want any of this. I'm tired of being the criminal. I want to *hunt* bad guys now, not be one of them. And now my grandpa wants me to be the boss of the biggest crime family in the supernatural world."

"The Elves don't really do that anymore. They can't. They're in hiding," I pointed out. "You could just... rule the city and keep everything quiet, like it has been for a hundred years, then lead them on to heaven like you're supposed to. No crime involved."

"What about you?" Charlie asked. "What do you think of all of this?"

I put my hands on his shoulders and squeezed. "I could be a mob boss's wife."

Charlie's lips twitched. "You said *wife*."

"Why not? I think the title of Empress suits me perfectly." I could waltz around the palace with a crown and a big pink dress. It'd be brilliant.

"You know that's not all of what the job entails."

"So? I can do it." My heart pounded wildly. I couldn't believe I was considering having Charlie's heir, and furthering the royal Elven line. I wasn't even sure if I *wanted* kids, before this moment, but it was like my mind had been made up for me. It was so much to consider so fast, but I was a ride-or-die kind of chick. Whatever Charlie needed me for, I was here.

His lips tilted downward. "What about your duty to the Water tribe as chieftess? You're a firstborn. You're obligated to lead the Toaqua tribe after your father steps down."

My heart fell. I was torn between the two options— I couldn't have, or do, both. I'd be forced to choose— my own people, or Charlie's.

Which meant I could be pressured someday to become chieftess, or give Charlie up. He needed an Empress by his side... and it couldn't be me if I had other duties.

The thought made me sick to ponder, so I pushed it away.

"It's not something we need to consider right now," I said softly. "You wouldn't become an emperor for a really long time, anyway. Who knows? Your grandpa is a full-blooded Elf. He's immortal. Maybe he never dies, and you cork off before he does. Then you'll never have to take the throne."

Charlie smirked. "Wouldn't that be great."

"In the meantime..." I held a breath. "Maybe you should try mending things with your dad."

Charlie gave a skeptical sound. "I don't want anything to do with him."

"That's fine, too." Personally, I couldn't give a flying fuck if we never saw Cameron again. "We should probably just relax for the rest of the night, and put all this heavy stuff aside. I bet you'll feel better in the morning."

Charlie crossed his arms around his middle. "Yeah. Probably."

Oberi jumped off the bed. He put his nose to the ground and sniffed around the room, observing his surroundings. When Charlie stood up, Oberi walked beside him, to escort him to the bathroom.

"I'm gonna wash my face real fast," Charlie said. "Can you give me a second?"

I felt a pit of loneliness form within me as I realized he was trying to pull away. "Sure. I'll be waiting."

I heard the faucet turn on as I wandered out of the elaborate bedroom. I found Kallie and Marcus in the main room, sitting on the chaise lounges and having a feast. The servants had dropped by several carts that were loaded with food. There was salmon, prime rib, and an abundance of vegetables that the Elves grew underground. It smelled delicious. I popped a steamed asparagus into my mouth, and nearly died with how good it tasted. The Elves' cooking was a hell of a lot better than the stuff they served at the Institute, that was for sure.

"Is he okay?" Marcus asked as I stood over a cart, trying to decide what I wanted. He'd poured himself and Kallie a few glasses of wine. He tried to hand one to me, but I waved it off.

"No," I answered honestly. "He's taking it really hard."

"A crown's a lot to handle, even if you always knew you had one," Kallie said as she relaxed in the warmth of the fireplace, which the servants must've gotten going. "I feel for him."

"You're certainly right at home," I told her sourly.

"I've spent the last year of my life trying to get back into a palace," she shot at me. "Now that I'm in one, I'm milking it for all it's worth."

"And what about you?" Marcus asked me as he fed Rishi bits of salmon. "How do you feel about the whole situation?"

I shrugged. "I'm ready to bear the fruit of his loins."

Marcus sputtered, while Kallie smirked. "You sure went from *I'm too cool for dating* to *I want his Elf babies* really fast," she teased.

"I don't make any decisions unless they're spontaneous." I shrugged and ate a piece of chocolate as I splayed out on the lounge like the future queen I was. If I was preparing to be an Empress, I'd better start practicing.

"You aren't exactly the mothering type," Kallie quipped.

"*So?!* I can push a baby out my hoo-ha, just you wait and see!" I shouted obnoxiously.

Marcus spat out his wine, and it dribbled down his chin and onto the couch. Kallie cackled.

The door opened. We all got really quiet as Oberi led Charlie into the room. Charlie sat down on an armchair. I began making a plate for him. I set it on the coffee table beside him, and he started eating. I physically felt his mood lighten through our bond as he consumed dinner, which made me a little more at ease. Oberi seized a steak off one of the carts and began devouring it all by himself, chomping the meat into bits so he could savor every delicious bite.

"It's *not* cooked too well. You're being picky," Charlie shot at Oberi. Oberi snuffled and choked up a bite of prime rib, which Rishi scampered over and swallowed. I wrinkled my nose.

"Aren't we going to decide when we're leaving this place? We can't stay here forever," Marcus said.

"Uh, there's no decision to make," Kallie said. "Emperor Cassiel said we *can't* leave, so I guess we just have to listen."

She didn't have me fooled. She'd leave if she wanted to, but clearly, that wasn't an option to her, seeing as how she was back to being treated like a princess again.

"Our families are going to worry about us. We can't just up and vanish," Marcus argued.

"Why not?" Kallie asked. "I'm sure we can get a message to our parents somehow, telling them we're safe. It'll be fine."

I thought Marcus had a point. "We have people back at the Institute," I objected. "What about my brother, and Opal, and Chancey and Ivy?"

"We'll figure out a way to get them here," Kallie said. "It's just going to take time to break them out."

"But no one has ever broken out of the Institute," Marcus said nervously.

"Hello! *We* escaped the Institute!" Kallie all but cheered. "We did it! We won— we fucking beat the Warden! We never have to go back to that dump, ever!"

Elation ricocheted through my stomach as I realized Kallie was right. We *had* escaped the Institute. The Warden had no idea where we were, and because he didn't know where Forevermore was, he'd never find out. We didn't have to go on the run to escape our sentences. We could literally stay here for the rest of our lives, enjoying Forevermore and avoiding the rest of the world. Screw the prophecy.

Though I don't think this suited Charlie. He sat back in his seat, like the idea of remaining here longer than a few days bothered him.

Kallie and Marcus got drunk off the rest of the wine, and fell asleep on the lounge chairs. Servants came and took our plates away. They asked if we wanted anything else, but Charlie told them that he was tired, and they left us alone. Oberi slept on his back on one of the giant pillows by the fire. Rishi curled up on Oberi's stomach, nose touching tail. Both creatures were completely out of it.

I led Charlie back to his bedroom. It was dark inside, lit only by the light of the false moon coming through the balcony.

Charlie let his robe fall to the floor and slipped underneath the covers. I hung my robe up on one of the hooks lining the wall, and slid into the bed beside Charlie fully nude.

Ancestors, this was the most comfortable bed I'd ever laid in. The pillows felt like clouds, and the silk sheets caressed my bare skin. I curled up in a ball on my side, enjoying the floating feeling the bed gave.

"The bed's really soft. I know you like that," I offered. "And the food's good, too. You have a home now. It's everything you wanted."

"I wanted us to earn that for *ourselves*," Charlie said. "Not have it be handed to us."

I didn't think it mattered how we got what we wanted, so long as we had it, but it apparently mattered to Charlie. I dared to snuggle closer to him, though I didn't touch him.

I thought we'd go right to sleep, but a half an hour passed, and neither one of us seemed to get any rest. Forevermore was so quiet at night. It was different from the noise of the prison. There were always guards banging on doors and inmates shouting at each other through the walls, even at night. Without the background noise, I couldn't drift off.

"I can't sleep," Charlie announced, giving a defeated sigh.

"I can't either," I confessed. "Today was a lot to take in."

Charlie made a sound of agreement. His fingers reached out, to tickle my stomach. "It doesn't help that your beautiful, naked ass is right next to me."

"You're naked, too." I snickered.

"What a coincidence." Charlie reached out and brought me close to him.

Our bare bodies pressed together under the sheets, skin rubbing against skin, and it was the most heavenly thing in the world. I felt Charlie's dick harden, and the area between my thighs began to ache. *This is the moment!* I knew it was.

"You're already wet," Charlie whispered as he reached down and felt between my legs.

He slipped a finger inside, and butterflies fluttered inside my head. I gave soft moans as Charlie massaged me, moving his fingers in and out. Tingling sensations ran from my apex all the way down my legs. Without thinking about it, I reached down and began rubbing Charlie's dick. I took it in my hand, and he began gasping with me as we pleasured each other's bodies.

So this is what we'd been missing, forced to live apart at the Institute. How wonderful it was to share a bed, and finally get some private time to be just *us,* instead of being forced to steal away hasty moments whenever we could.

My back arched off the bed as Charlie sank his fingers in deeper, but it wasn't enough. I took my hand off his dick and placed it on his chest. "Charlie?"

"What is it, pidge?" he murmured. He was busy kissing my hair, which he loved to do, and I loved it when he did so.

"I want to go all the way."

Charlie froze. He pulled his fingers out of me and paused, his face a complex riddle. "Are you sure you're ready for that?"

"Yes! I want it." I pulled him close. "Don't you want it, too?"

The puzzle still bore true on his expression. "Yeah. But we need to be careful. Are you taking any medication?"

"I... can't take birth control," I confessed. "It messes up my hormones and makes my bipolar worse."

Charlie rolled over and opened a drawer that was attached to the side table beside the bed. "I guess that means we can't do anything. We don't even have— fuck all, I don't believe this."

Charlie pulled a condom out of the drawer. I giggled. "Looks like the servants wanted to make sure we were well-stocked."

He got really quiet. "Ava, are you *sure?*"

"Yeah," I said nervously. "I'm certain this is the right moment."

"Well... okay." Charlie put the condom on.

My mouth went dry, and my body felt paralyzed as I watched him do it. He boosted himself over me, and I squeezed my eyes shut. I tried to take deep breaths as I felt Charlie's weight press down on me from overhead. I ran my hands over his back and tried to remind myself over and over that this was *Charlie,* and not *him,* but it was hard to do. I could still remember what that bastard had left inside of me, and the memory of it was enough to make me sick.

Nothing had happened yet, but this already felt like too much. Charlie came to a pause. "Ava, you're tense. I can sense you're scared."

"I'm fine," I insisted. Ancestors, I fucking wanted this! He just needed to get it over with.

"You're not ready, and I'm not ready, either. I'm not comfortable pushing you that far."

Charlie pulled away. My body relaxed and wept with lust at the same damn time.

Disappointment seeped into every inch of me, pinning me to the bed. "I feel like a failure."

"You're not. We'll do something else." I heard a snapping sound as Charlie took off the condom and threw it across the room.

He certainly didn't seem bothered, but I was. Charlie began kissing my breasts, but I couldn't concentrate. After I failed to respond, he set his chin on my chest and said, "You're scowling, pidge."

"How can you tell? You can't see me!"

"Because I *know* you." Charlie propped himself up on a pillow. "What's this really about?"

"I can't have heirs if you can't put your dick in me," I grumbled. I was already feeling the pressure, and Eddie had just told me about all this shit a few hours ago.

"Are you serious?" Charlie's mouth dropped open. "I'm not even sure if I *want* kids."

"It doesn't matter. You're expected to have a child, to carry on the Elven monarchy," I said.

"I don't have to *do* anything," Charlie said. "As far as I'm concerned, they lost any right to an heir once they left me to fend for myself. If this is the life I choose, so be it, but I'm not convinced this is the right choice for me yet. And it's definitely too soon to know if this is the right path for you."

"If this is our life, I want to start living it," I said. "I don't want to wait."

"Why do you always have to be so impatient?" Charlie began to rub my thigh. "There's no rush."

"I don't see any point in procrastinating the inevitable."

"I do," Charlie said. "I want to enjoy every moment with you that I can get. I don't want our relationship to be riddled with responsibility."

"But it already is," I insisted. "The prophecy—"

Charlie shushed me, and I fell quiet. "None of that matters," he said. "All that matters is us."

My lip wobbled. "What if we never...?"

"It'll be okay. One day we'll get that far," he said. His gentle fingers roamed my skin. The movements were soft, like he was playing the piano he loved.

Charlie slowly moved down my body. I savored the feelings as his lips caressed my center and immediately made me boneless. He kissed and tasted me until I was calling out his name, my hands fisted in his black locks to drive him onward. In a mad craze, I grabbed him and threw him on his back, splaying a hand on his chest as I went down on him. I took his length down in one motion, and he hissed with delight. The noises he made drove me crazy as I lathered pleasure on all the right places.

Sucking his dick was one of the great pleasures of my life. I had to admit it— I loved giving him oral. I don't know what was so thrilling about it, except that I knew it gave him ecstasy unlike any drug on this planet, and that turned me on. I didn't lift my mouth from his cock when he came, preferring to take it all down like his come was the elixir of my existence. I felt his orgasm explode through our bond, and it was so powerful, it nearly made me dizzy.

I wanted to make him feel like this every day for the rest of his life. I wasn't sure if I was trying to make up for what he'd never had, or just promising him he'd have a better future, but regardless, I just wanted to promise him as much love as possible. I needed to give him so much love that he thought he'd might drown in it, and even then, I don't think it would be enough to express the complex feelings I had that were radiating in my heart. I could cut myself open and spill it all out for him, but it wouldn't be enough to explain it, because I couldn't make sense of it myself. Charlie just *was*, and his existence was enough to make me want to live for him.

Choosing death was easy. Dying for him wouldn't be so hard, but living for him— I'd never wanted to live for anyone, no matter how much I cared about them. I adored people, but I wanted to live for myself, do my own thing, be in control of my freedom.

He was different. For the first time, I was considering someone else's future rather than my own. It made me want to make him endless promises that I knew I couldn't keep.

Charlie fell asleep in my arms not long after, but sleep still eluded me. I waited until he'd been out of it for a few hours to slip out of bed. I grabbed a knitted blanket that was lying on an armchair and wrapped it over my shoulders and around my naked form, proceeding to the balcony.

I looked down upon Forevermore. Even in the darkness, it shimmered. There seemed to be no flaws to it. In the distance, the massive Mirror of Ingress shone against the rock. The golden floral frame that outlined the mirror beckoned to a new beginning.

Maybe we really could stay in this perfect place for the rest of our lives. It wouldn't be so bad. It'd be bliss, even.

Yeah, right. You can't be held in a cage, even a pretty one.

You'll do something to ruin it, Ava.

It'll drive you out of your mind to remain in a paradise.

I scoffed and leaned on the bannister. The voices could be right. It was just too heavenly. The straight and narrow had never suited me well. I'd get bored. I needed to have that rebellious feeling. Maybe if the Elves were still out there committing crimes, living a fast and loose life, I could get along here, because I would go with them.

But that was all behind them now. After the genocide, the Elves had committed themselves to a quiet life, not one of sin.

You'd be wasted talent.

I sighed. Whatever the case, it was too much to decide tonight. I knew I wasn't getting any sleep, so my mischievous nature kicked in. I wondered how many guards were stationed around the area, and how vast this palace was. There had to be *so* many places to explore.

I was shaken out of my reverie by the sound of an explosion. The stone balcony shook beneath me, and I had to grip on to the sides of the railing to avoid tipping over. My head jerked up. I realized with horror that smoke was beginning to filter through the sky, filling the cave and blocking out the light of the false moon. I looked closer. My heart contracted in my chest when I realized that the gate to the city we'd come through earlier had been blown open. Figures began marching through the open space.

Even from this distance, I recognized the uniforms of the guards that so often patrolled the Institute. There were hundreds of them, marching through the streets of Forevermore, raiding shops and yanking people out of their homes.

I knew exactly what they were after. In one singular line, the guards began to rush through the city in the direction of the palace.

I recognized someone amongst them. Though he was far away, I would know that imposing stature anywhere.

Fuck! Fuck, fuck, *fuck*!

I ran back into the room, the blanket falling off my shoulders. I shook Charlie awake. "Charlie! Charlie, get up!"

Charlie stirred, rubbing at his face. "Pidge, what's going on?"

"The Warden is here!" I yanked open the wardrobe, looking for clothes to wear. I found the servants had stocked the drawers. I yanked out clothes for Charlie before hastily dressing myself in jeans and a long-sleeve shirt, already preparing for a fight.

"What?" Charlie balked. I tossed him a pair of jeans with some boxers, socks, and a t-shirt. He yanked them on before I found shoes at the bottom of the Wardrobe. We shoved them onto our feet before I grabbed his hand and pulled him into the living area.

Marcus and Kallie were cuddling on the couch, still fast asleep. Somehow, they'd ended up entwined in each other's arms, completely out of it. I think they'd been too drunk to notice what they were doing.

Great. They decided to look cute the moment our lives were in danger. Typical of them.

"Get up!" I screamed, and I tossed a pillow at them. "The city is under attack!"

The pillow smacked both of them in the face. Marcus pulled his head off Kallie's cheek— he'd drooled on it. Kallie stirred in a daze. Both of them shot upward when they heard the sound of screams resonating outside. More explosions echoed through the city. I could hear the sounds of the Elves fighting back, swords clashing together as guns were fired in the city streets.

Kallie was not bothered by the Marcus-slobber in the slightest. She wiped it off her cheek and said, "Dammit! Forevermore hasn't been attacked in over a hundred years, and the night *we* show up is when shit goes down!"

"We're bad luck, just face it," I told her. Charlie had gone pale, losing color with every dying scream that resonated through Forevermore.

Oberi and Rishi were both awake. Oberi had started barking like crazy, while Rishi ran in circles. It was at that moment Eddie flung open the door.

"Charlie, we need to get you out of here," Eddie began. "The city isn't safe anymore."

"But what about the Elves?" Charlie asked. "We can't leave them to fend for themselves."

"The city is evacuating." Emperor Cassiel entered the room, looking grim. He was flanked by Cameron. He, Eddie, and Charlie's dad were all dressed in Elven armor, swords at their sides. "We have contingency plans for things like this. We need to get as many people as we can to the Mirror of Ingress. Getting them through the portal is the only chance we've got."

"We can't abandon Forevermore!" Charlie shouted. "This is the only safe place the Elves have!"

"We always knew this day would come," Emperor Cassiel said sadly.

Fuck, it was too soon! The Elven prophecy spoke of a second war breaking Forevermore, but I assumed we had more time— like, a *lot* more time.

"The city isn't safe anymore," Emperor Cassiel said. "And you, Charlie, are our top priority."

"Why me?" Charlie asked harshly.

"We can't let anyone know that you are the heir to the Elven throne," Emperor Cassiel said firmly. "If the *world* knows who you really are, they'll kill you. And everything we've worked for will be lost."

"So we just give up the city?" Charlie asked in despair.

"It is as the prophecy foretold. Forevermore has been exposed. We are going to have to move our people somewhere they won't be discovered, until the prophecy can be fulfilled and we are safe once again," Emperor Cassiel said. "Everyone already knows what to do. We can only pray that the people of Forevermore follow the plan we've had in place for over a hundred years, and that nothing else goes wrong."

Charlie appeared heartbroken, and I felt my heart break *for* him. He had just found Forevermore, found a home, and it was already getting taken away from him in less than a day. Cameron shifted uncomfortably, but didn't move to say anything.

"Let's go. We don't have much time." Emperor Cassiel led the way out of the room. Once in the hallway, we were immediately swarmed by dozens of guards. I assumed that this was the Emperor's personal security. They didn't mess around, either. The guards hustled us along through the gold hallways and out the great gates of the palace, into the city streets toward the Mirror of Ingress.

"Do you think we'll get there in time?" I asked.

So many people were panicking. Elves were packing everything they had into bags, rushing through the streets toward the Mirror as if it was their only hope for salvation. I took Charlie's hand, leading him beside me so he wouldn't run into anything or get lost.

"We have a chance, that's what matters," Emperor Cassiel told me, although his tone sounded hopeless. My spirits dampened. The Elves had been prepared for such a moment, but unfortunately, they had hoped this day would never come. As a result, the escape was poorly executed.

"Where are you taking us—?" Charlie asked, but his words were abruptly cut off when a stream of guards stormed in front of us.

I knew them. I recognize so many faces from the men that patrolled the halls of the Institute. There was blood on their uniforms. They hadn't come here to overtake the city. They'd come here to kill.

Professor Hemlock was right when she said that finding Forevermore would be a grave mistake. I wished I had listened to her.

"Defend the Emperor!" a guard yelled.

Immediately, the area turned into a bloodbath. Elven battle magic whizzed by us, fired by the Emperor's Guard, but it was chaotic and didn't hit its target. The Institute guards fired their guns into the crowd, and this time, it didn't look like they were shooting noxite, but actual bullets.

So many Elves went down. The spray of blood and the stench of innards began to rise around the street as one by one, bodies collapsed onto the stone.

It made me sick to watch, to smell. I suppressed a fit of nausea and summoned a fireball. I began tossing my blue Fire at the guards. Once it hit their uniforms, they immediately ignited, becoming torches of screaming flame against the darkness of the cavern.

Marcus began firing offensive spells, and Charlie's Air magic beat back the guards, blowing them out of our way as we ran. Once the guards were behind us, Charlie used his Earth magic to create concaves in the earth, pits that sucked the guards down and prevented them from following us.

A couple of guards saw what Charlie was doing and went to stop him, but Eddie immediately placed himself between the guards and his prince, unleashing his sword with a wild yell. Eddie cut down anyone who got close to Charlie, breathing raggedly as if daring anyone to try and hurt his prince. Eddie had seemed so gentle, but it was clear that once Charlie was in danger, the Elf could turn deadly in a second. If it meant protecting Charlie, Eddie was out for blood.

Kallie used her illusion magic to summon a sword. She charged ahead of the group with a wild yell, and killed any guards that got in our way. She was a ruthless force, a faerie gone mad with the heat of battle. She swung her sword with one hand and used her other to cast harsh spells at the same time, making a small pathway that we could escape through.

The Elves weren't completely defenseless. They cast spells and used defensive magic of their own, trying to push the guards back. But so many of them had never been in a fight, and most were just trying to stay alive as the Institute's guards continued to press in from every corner.

Forevermore had been peaceful for over a century. Now that it was under attack, most of the citizens didn't know what to do. I had to duck as several Elvish spells shot over my head, shattering windows and blowing off doors as we charged through the raid. Kallie and the Emperor's Guard made a way for us to get through, but with each step, that way became smaller and smaller.

The closer we got to the Mirror of Ingress, the worse things got. There were thousands of Elves crowded around the portal, each of them attempting to slip through to get away from the guards. It was complete pandemonium. There was so much blood on the streets that it ran freely like a river over the cobblestone, staining the beautiful streets. The guards had run out of bullets by this time, and had abandoned using their guns, resorting to magic instead.

A couple of the Elves were using their powers to take magic away from the guards. They absorbed shifter super strength, vampire speed and angel light magic, rendering their enemies powerless and using it for their own. But not all the Elves knew, or remembered, how to use their magic, or could steal the magic of others. They'd just been in hiding for too long.

My stomach churned as I witnessed a vampire guard jump onto a female Elf. He began sucking her dry. I rushed to help her, a fireball in hand, but by the time I had flung it at the vampire guard, she was already dead.

The vampire guard turned toward me, blood streaming down his face. When he saw that I was ready to fight, he didn't challenge me, but simply went in a new direction to find his next victim. With superspeed on his side, he vanished into the crowd instantly. I lost him, unable to stop the vampire from hunting the rest of the innocent people in this city.

Marcus was doing his best to disarm as many guards as possible. He held a battle orb in each hand, and ricocheted them through the square like he was juggling, knocking guards out the minute his orb connected with their heads. Rishi clawed at the eyes of guards, and Oberi changed into a unicorn, lowering her horn and shooting off fireballs as quickly as she could cast them. Her Fire smashed into nearby buildings and ignited them, lighting the city on fire in what seemed seconds.

Shifter guards that could transform into creatures like dragons and griffins were ripping the Elves apart. Rage flashed upon Charlie's face. He lifted his hand, and with a wild yell cast a spinning whirlwind at a whole battalion of guards. It lifted them up, tossing them over the length of the city and sending them to ancestors-only knew where. I summoned water from a nearby fountain and splashed it upon the feet of nearby guards, freezing them in place so they couldn't move. The guards wrenched at my ice, but my magic held them.

Then the night illusion over the cave broke, and the false moon went out, leaving the cave completely dark. Elves cried out in terror. The only light in the caves that remained was the fire that had overtaken the buildings. Fear overtook me. With the fires eating up all the oxygen in the cave, we'd soon cease to breathe. But neither could we put them out, because if we did, that would leave us all in total darkness. I lifted a fireball over my head, to light my path as I continued onward.

Charlie was stubborn, continuing to fight even when it was clear that all was lost. He cast Air funnels in any direction that he heard a guard, although I was sorry to say that some of those tunnels ended up hitting Elves instead of enemies. Charlie had no idea where he was casting. He was shooting off spells in every direction. He was so frantic to save Forevermore, he was hurting more Elves than he was helping.

"Charlie!" Cameron screamed. "We have to leave them!"

"We can't abandon everyone!" Charlie replied. He seemed at the edge of madness, a delirium in his eyes that told me he would die here if it meant preserving the lives of people that he now felt responsible for.

"You are the heir to the throne and the prophesied one!" Cameron cried. "The survival of the Elves depends on you staying alive!"

Cameron didn't wait for Charlie to protest. He grabbed Charlie by the arm and hauled him away, toward the Mirror of Ingress. Since Charlie was blind, he didn't know where his father was taking him. I felt rage at Cameron for forcing Charlie to follow his orders, but I knew if we stayed here, all of us would be dead.

Institute guards swarmed into the cave, and they were beginning to outnumber the citizens of Forevermore. I wasn't sure how many people the Warden had hired to come down here, or what he had promised them, but I knew if the Elves had any hope of survival, it wasn't beneath Darke Island.

As we got closer to the Mirror of Ingress, space became nonexistent. Bodies were packed so tightly together that I couldn't move. I felt squished between the frantic Elves who were trying to escape through the portal. Air left my lungs as I was slowly suffocated within the crowd. Kallie, Marcus, and Charlie were already far ahead of me. Somehow, I had gotten left behind.

"Ava!" Charlie screamed, desperately fighting against his father to get to me. He didn't know where I was, but he knew through our bond that I was in deep trouble, and that I wasn't beside him.

I had so little breath from being crushed within the crowd that I couldn't call out to him. Someone shoved into my back, and I fell over. I screamed aloud as I felt people stepping on me from above, mashing my lungs and delivering bruises to my bones. I was going to be trampled by the panicking crowd.

My eyes rolled in the back of my head, and everything went dark as I passed out.

I was startled awake by the sound of the earth breaking beside me. The ground shook with a powerful quake, and everyone in my immediate proximity fell over. I heard Oberi's strong whinny as she came rushing to me, and suddenly, Charlie was there. He lifted me up into his arms and cradled me against him, brushing back my hair. "Pidge, are you all right?"

"I'll make it," I breathed. It felt like I had bruised lungs. I put a hand to my pained side as I said, "The Mirror, Charlie. We're nearly there."

He gasped, and tried to heft me up beside him so I could show him the way. Except there was a problem. I was so beaten, I could barely walk. I still needed time to recover from being trampled, but there was no time. The Mirror was only a few yards away, but it still looked so far.

I wasn't sure how long I'd been unconscious, but it must've been a few minutes, at least. By this time, the city had started to empty. I watched as Elves stepped through the portal, disappearing to somewhere else— we hadn't been told where.

By now the guards were blocking the way, forming a line to prevent any more Elves from getting through the Mirror of Ingress. It appeared most of the citizens had gotten out, but the Elves who hadn't escaped or been killed were being arrested, put into handcuffs by guards. Noxite didn't work on Elves, but handcuffs were still handcuffs, and they were strong, fortified with strong metal to hold supernaturals. It terrified me that I didn't know what the Warden wanted to do with them, or why he wanted to take them prisoner.

Emperor Cassiel and Cameron both waited by the Mirror of Ingress, petrified as they observed the distance from them to Charlie. Cameron cradled his arm, like it was broken. Charlie must've hurt his dad to get to *me.* Kallie and Marcus stood beside them, unsure of what to do or how to break the line of guards blocking our way.

I knew we could make it. We just had to—

"I believe the time for your rebellion has come to an end," a hated, condescending voice cooed behind me.

Charlie turned us both, and I came face-to-face with the man I despised most in the world— the Warden. He wore no blood or dirt from battle, as if he preferred to let others do his dirty work for him. He wasn't even wearing defensive armor. He had on a clean suit, his hair combed back as if this was a business meeting and not a raid. His cruel face was cast in firelight as he approached, like some demonic being from hell itself.

I managed to find the strength to stand as I turned toward the Warden, summoning a fireball in one hand and a water ball in the other. "You'll never take me alive," I threatened, fully intent to shove both down the Warden's throat.

"You touch me, this is all over," the Warden replied coolly. "You are outnumbered, Miss Mitoh. I advise you to put your magic down. If you come quietly, this will go smoothly."

"Come quietly? I'd rather die," I growled. The Warden had destroyed Forevermore. I wasn't getting out of this cave without destroying *him.*

"I don't think that's wise," the Warden said. "I thank the four of you for setting off all the traps and showing me the way to the city. I have failed to find Forevermore for years, but you guided the way. Well done."

The Warden gave a dark laugh. "You should be a little more careful during your phone conversations, Miss Mitoh," the Warden said coyly. "You never know who might be listening in, though I never expected you might be a *chosen one.* How gifted you are. You are more special than I ever imagined you to be."

Marcus was right. They *had* been tapping the phones. The Warden *knew* about my prophecy. Some way or another, he'd found out— probably by eavesdropping on my conversations with my parents— and he'd been watching me. He'd been hoping I'd lead him to Forevermore all along.

I gritted my teeth, and the Warden rambled on. "Did you *assume* we didn't look to see where the noxite cuffs tracked you during your little exploration on the field trip?" the Warden asked. "I knew you and your companions went to the Elven gate in search of Forevermore, and that you'd want to start poking around the island to look for it. After that, it was all too easy to stage the ruse that we needed more volunteers for the noxite mines. I expected *better* of you, Miss Mitoh. I thought you would foresee the trap I laid, but you wandered right into it."

My heart dropped at his words. We didn't escape the Institute. The Warden had merely allowed us to leave long enough for us to lead him straight to Forevermore.

And we'd given it to him.

I hoped he hadn't figured out me and my friends were demigods yet, or anything about the keys. If he had, we were screwed.

Guards circled around Charlie and me. They pressed in on all sides, preventing means of escape. Oberi huffed and tossed her head. Charlie stiffened next to me, though I wasn't scared. I was ready to light this place up like a stick of dynamite. Forevermore was already ruined. I was determined not to let the Warden get his filthy fingers on it.

"I'm willing to cut you a deal," the Warden said. "Follow us back to the Institute, and we'll return you to the general population of the prison. I'll look the other way at your little escape attempt, as it *did* hand me Forevermore, and we'll forget about all the guards your friends just killed. You can avoid Cellblock 9, and I can take advantage of all the benefits this gorgeous city has to offer."

A bit of hope, then. He wasn't sending us to Cellblock 9, which I'm sure he would do if he knew we were demigods. It was the only thing we still had going for us.

But I had no intention of going back to the Institute. Not now, not ever.

I threw back my head in a delirious laugh. "Do you think *this* is going to stop me?" I challenged, casting my gaze at the guards surrounding us. "I'll burn every motherfucker in this place!"

The fireball in my hand swelled to an enormous size. It became a column of flame that slammed against the ceiling, causing rocks to crumble from above. I forged the water ball in my hand into a blade, and clenched the icy sword tightly in my fingers, determined to drive it into the Warden's heart— once I got done frying him to a crisp.

The Warden raised an eyebrow. "Very well. If you're not going to follow orders, we'll have to do this the hard way."

Charlie gave an abrupt cry, and instantly collapsed. Oberi gave a high-pitched scream as his body hit the stone. I cried out, falling to my knees next to him, and my magic vanished.

Charlie gasped, as if he was struggling against the ocean and trying to breathe. I watched his skin visibly pale, and his body shook with tremors. He elicited soft cries of pain. I placed a hand over my mouth, not sure of what to do. It was like he was *perishing* before my very eyes.

The Warden wasn't moving. He had his hands behind his back, and was standing as rigid as ever. He could've fooled me that he wasn't casting a spell, but I just knew he was the one doing this to Charlie.

It didn't end. Insanity began to tear at the corners of my mind as I felt our bond begin to slip away. Charlie was still there, but he was fading. I felt his life begin to end at the Warden's power. His half of our soul tugged at my own, yanking and ripping as if he was on his way to join our ancestors in the afterlife itself. I watched as the light began to leave his eyes, and completely lost my mind.

"*What are you doing to him?*" I screamed. I looked up, tears streaming down my face as Charlie continued to writhe. Oberi danced and knickered— the flames on her mane had gone down, as if they were being put out and she was losing her Fire.

"Aren't you aware?" the Warden taunted. "Powerful angels have mastery over life-force manipulation, and I am a powerful angel, Miss Mitoh. I am currently siphoning away Mister Wahkin's life force. He is very young, and quite healthy, so it will take some time. But eventually, I will drain what is left of his life with my magic, and he will, as they say, become deceased."

"You monster. Give it back," I demanded, sobbing now.

"I very well *could*, but that would mean you'd have to do what I say," the Warden replied. "And you seemed very adamant a moment ago to put up an unnecessary fight."

"Don't, pidge," Charlie choked out. "Don't go with him."

His voice was raspy and rattled— like he was on the edge of death. It cut me to the core to hear. With each breath, I felt Charlie's tie to me and Oberi grow weaker. He was struggling to breathe. I reached out to hold his hand, and he grasped it, but loosely.

"I know you and your friends are very powerful, but keep in mind that I don't need *all* of you," the Warden said. "You are the one I am most determined to keep in my care, Miss Mitoh, and you have quite a few loved ones for me to work through— your brother comes to mind."

"I hate you," I spat. I wiped Charlie's hair away from his eyes, but wept once I touched his skin. It was ice cold.

"Hate me all you like, but it's not going to change the outcome," the Warden said. "You have five minutes to make up your mind. That should be enough time for me to drain out the rest of Mister Wahkin's life force. What's left of it, anyway."

"Charlie!" I heard Cameron cry. He hurried in our direction, but the Emperor's Guard held him back on the orders of Cassiel. It was obvious the ruler was on the brink of making a tough decision.

"*Go!*" I screamed. "Get out of here!"

Cameron flinched in a moment of indecision, but Emperor Cassiel grabbed his arm. The emperor rushed through the portal, along with Cameron and all the Emperor's Guard. In seconds, they'd passed through the Mirror of Ingress and to another place.

A couple of Institute guards went to follow the Emperor through the mirror. But once the Emperor passed through the portal, the mirror completely shattered. Glass rained down from above, cutting into the uniforms and skin of guards. They screamed, and I felt a small bit of victory at the Emperor's escape. At least the guards wouldn't be able to follow wherever the Elves had gone.

But they were lost to us now. Who knew where they had gone to hide?

I put a hand on Charlie's chest. Horror rushed into my veins as I realized his heartbeat was starting to slow, on the brink of failure. I cast a pleading glance at the Warden.

"Don't hurt him! Punish *me!*" I yelled. "Hurt me!"

"I'm sorry, but you and I both know you have a high tolerance for pain, and if torturing someone else is the only way to get you to listen, then so be it," the Warden hissed. "I told you when you arrived here that I will break you, and make no mistake, *I will break you.*"

Charlie's skin turned from pale to yellow, and I knew the Warden's words were true. He would employ any means necessary if it meant breaking my spirit— even if it meant hurting, or even *killing someone* who was innocent. Someone connected to me, whom I loved.

I heard Eddie scream. He came out of nowhere, rushing forward with his sword aloft, to stab the Warden and protect his prince.

But before he even got close, a couple of guards blocked his way. They yanked Eddie's sword from his hand, and punched him in the gut, making him double over. The guards struck Eddie across the face, and as a punch landed on his cheek, he passed out. Eddie was put in cuffs, dragged away to be held with the rest of the Elven prisoners.

I heard footsteps as Kallie and Marcus hurried to our sides. The guards had let them through and into the circle— but that was our mistake, because now, all of us were trapped.

"Ava, do something," Marcus pleaded. He was on his hands and knees at Charlie's side, completely terrified. Kallie's gaze flashed from me to the guards, as if she wasn't sure if we should fight or give in.

"I love you," Charlie whispered. Tears fell from my eyes onto his face. He wouldn't say that if he didn't think it was time for him to go.

The other half of my soul was so far away now. I could feel Charlie's spirit on the brink, ready to detach from mine and pass into the Ancestral Lands. The movement would rip my soul in half. I was sure I'd die from it.

Oberi's black eyes landed on me, and then I knew. Charlie wouldn't survive this if the Warden didn't stop his assault. He had to lift his magic. Otherwise, Charlie wouldn't make it. He was *dying* before my very eyes, and there was only one thing I could do to make it stop.

The Warden looked down upon me with a cruel gaze. "Are we willing to comply yet, Miss Mitoh?"

I bowed my head. "Yes. Please," I said. "I'll do anything. I give in."

"I'm glad you've come to your senses." The Warden took a step back, and immediately, the spell lifted. Charlie took a deep gasp, as if it were the first breath of life. I wept as I watched the color come back into his face and light ignite in his eyes. His skin became warm again, and as

I laid a hand on his chest, I felt with relief his heart beating wildly against his ribcage.

Charlie slowly sat up, with the help of Kallie and Marcus. His head lolled.

"I feel so sick," Charlie murmured. Nausea crossed through our bond, though it wasn't from me. "I'm too weak to stand."

"Lean on me, man," Marcus said. Both Kallie and Marcus got up, and they hefted Charlie to his feet. He had to lean on both of them in order to stay upright. They managed to get him onto Oberi's back, though he slumped forward immediately. Marcus and I each took a side, to catch him if he fell off. Kallie held Rishi in her arms. The cat's hair stood straight up, like he'd been spooked.

"You're alive." I brushed back Charlie's hair yet again, and tried to see my way through the tears.

"Barely," Charlie breathed, and I kissed his face.

A guard came marching up to the Warden, who'd failed to be affected by the scene. Heartless, emotionless bastard. The guard straightened to attention in front of the Warden.

"Sir, we have forty Elven prisoners, as you requested," the guard said. "What would you like us to do with them?"

"Take those twenty-three and younger to the Institute," the Warden instructed. "All the rest, drag them to the adult penitentiary on the island."

"Yes, sir," the guard said, nodding shortly. He turned back to the group of guards that had contained Eddie. Elven prisoners were taken by force back through the stone gate, handcuffed and completely helpless.

"Sir, do you want us to cuff them?" another guard asked, motioning his head to me and my friends.

"I don't think that will be necessary," the Warden replied. "They've been sufficiently trained."

A burning ember of resentment sparked in me, but it quickly died out when I glanced at Charlie. Twenty guards circled around my friends and me. They marched us through the broken remnants of the city, which was still burning and filling the cave with smoke.

I expected us to go back through the traps again, but once we got out of the stone gate, the guards took us down a different tunnel, one that had been newly dug by a Nivita guard— most likely, that night.

I bet the Warden and a couple of his guards had followed us through the traps. Then, once they'd gotten to the door that led to the city, he went back to the prison and got as many guards as he could, and dug a new tunnel down here to funnel his army into. That's why it took them so long to attack the city after we arrived. We'd been so *stupid*.

The immensity of our mistakes— my mistake, really— warred with me from the inside out. The guards were dragging us back to the Institute, and the Warden was pillaging the city that the Elves had called home for over a hundred years. As we walked, a verse from my prophecy broke into my head.

A discovery of the ancient ones on the island of shadow
Will change the course of our universe

A chill crept over my skin as I realized it had already been done. I had found Forevermore and the Elves beneath Dark Island, and that discovery would change *everything* in the supernatural world. A piece of my prophecy had been fulfilled today.

But not merely my own. Charlie's prophecy, too.

A second war will break Forevermore.

War was beginning. Forevermore had been found, and I knew the Warden wouldn't keep it a secret. He would announce to the world that the Elves were still alive, and I was certain that the discovery of their existence would plummet the supernatural world into calamity once again.

We'd failed. *I'd* failed. And as the Warden claimed his victory, I recalled what he'd done to Charlie... how he'd nearly ended the life of the man I adored, because he was connected to *me*.

I looked at Charlie's broken form, slumped over Oberi, and loved him more than ever. It was then that my thoughts sickened with the worst truth I could ever face.

I couldn't be with Charlie. I couldn't be his Empress, or have his kids. I couldn't even love him like he deserved to be loved.

This prophecy would always get in the way. And now there was more on the line than losing him. His dad was right. If Charlie died, the royal Elven line would die out. The Elves would be without a ruler— and a savior. They'd never reach heaven. It'd be like sentencing their race to death, right after they'd managed to survive their first genocide.

I couldn't do that to an entire supernatural empire. And more importantly, I couldn't do that to Charlie. It was wrong to take his family away from him— the family he'd wanted and craved, hell, the family he had even *cried over* for the past twenty years of his life. Now he had to find that family all over again.

There were thousands of Elves that needed him more than me— people that were now refugees from the Warden's wrath. And he needed them, too.

I'd promised to burn down the world if it meant saving Charlie. But I'd never thought that I'd have to abandon what was between us in order to keep him safe. The world, the prophecy, they weren't the problem.

I was. There'd always be people who would come for me, the Warden or otherwise. I'd pick being with Charlie over rescuing the supernatural world a million times over, but as I saw now, my destiny wasn't going to let me go. One piece of my prophecy had already come true, and there would be more, and more, until we were at the end and all that was standing around me was ashes.

I thought I could abandon my quest in order to preserve what was between Charlie and me, but now I saw that was a futile effort. I was destined to either save this world or destroy it, and at the end of the day, that sacrifice always included Charlie. That wasn't right to put him through. Not after everything he'd endured. He'd suffered enough. I wasn't about to be another catalyst for his agony. I loved him too much to be the source of his pain.

He was fated to be a dark prince. I would *not* be his curse.

My insides twisted, and a feeling like death came over me at the thought of what I *knew* I had to do, but I refused to let myself crumble under the torture. I'd made my decision— though it tore me up to do it.

Yet it didn't agonize me as much as the thought of Charlie dead.

And that's what I clung to. I'd accept it if Charlie was sad, in pain—miserable, even.

But I would not have him gone from this Earth. Broken or not, he'd still be alive.

Whether my heart was still beating at the conclusion of this prophecy remained to be seen. I hardly cared. I knew my fate, and I was doing this *my way*.

If I had no choice but to go through the worst pain of my life, it wouldn't go unjustified. The Warden had lost any chance of forgiveness from me the moment he'd dared to harm my Charlie, and by the ancestors, his actions weren't going to go unpunished. One day, the Warden was going to pay for everything he'd ripped from me.

I'd celebrate when I was laughing over his corpse. The Warden thought he could take away *my* world? Fine.

I'd end his.

TWENTY-FIVE

Having your life force sucked out of you wasn't something I wished upon my worst enemy. My whole life seemed to flash in front of me— every memory, every trauma played out for me to relive. I witnessed everything, starting with the soft feel of the teddy bear I'd been given at my first foster home, the weight of the toy in my arms, and the squish of it as I hugged it close.

The rest of my life seemed to play out in detail. The screams from my foster parents echoed in my ears. The bullying from kids taunted me. The memories of sexual assault as I'd had to sell myself to survive churned my guts.

Then came the memory of Ava. The blazing hatred I once felt for her shook my body, but it quickly shifted into intense passion and desire. The one thing that tore me to bits above all else was the thought of losing her. I was going to die at the hands of the Warden. There was no fighting it.

I should have expected this. I'd lost everything else. Nothing stuck around forever— not even Forevermore. And certainly not Ava. Certainly not this life with her.

I felt as if I'd aged decades in a matter of seconds. When I tried to move, my joints ached and protested. Fatigue washed over me, and my chest hammered like I was having a heart attack. I tried to breathe, but even my Air magic couldn't save me.

In a blink, it was over. For a moment, I thought I had actually died. Then the air returned to my lungs, and I gasped.

I had a vague memory of getting to my feet after the Warden's torture, but it was all so fuzzy. I remembered breaking my father's arm to get to Ava. I hadn't meant to injure him, even though I was hurt he'd never been there for me. A part of me thought I could learn to accept his reasons— even accept *him*— once I had a chance to truly process everything. Though I felt awful about what I'd done, I didn't regret it. I'd said I'd do anything for Ava, and I meant it.

I woke up in the infirmary several days later, though I didn't know where I was, at first. I felt as if I'd been trampled by a stampede of dragons as I pushed myself upright. My fingers trailed over the sheet covering me, and footsteps came from the other end of the large room. I inhaled the scent of disinfectant and realized I was back at the Institute, somewhere in the infirmary.

Beside me, Oberi barked. He jumped onto my bed and licked my hand.

I blew a sigh of relief. "We made it out of Forevermore."

Where did you think you'd gone? Oberi asked sarcastically.

"I'm not sure," I admitted. I hadn't really had any concept of time. "Is Ava okay?"

I reached out through the bond for her and felt her close by. Excitement twinged through the bond, like she was happy I was finally awake... but she shut it down a moment later. I tried to reach for her again, but she'd thrown up a brick wall between us.

My guts sank at the rejection. I had no idea why she felt the need to shut me out. After everything we'd been through recently, I needed her right now.

If she isn't okay, I'm not sure who's been bringing you those flowers, Oberi said dryly.

I reached to the table beside my bed to see what he was talking about. My fingers touched soft petals. It was the end of the semester, and springtime now. Ava must've picked them out of the prison yard and brought them here. Some of the flowers were wilted, indicating how long

I'd been here. I took one of them in my fingers and tugged on my magic, to test how badly the Warden had truly hurt me.

The flower stem curled in my fingers, and petals rained down onto the bed. The flower died, though my body surged with powerful magic.

I was just too sad to bring it back to life.

Ava had shut me out. My father and grandfather were gone, and I'd only just found them. As scared as I'd been about learning the truth of my heritage, I'd thought I could make Forevermore my home. The city had been a wonder beyond my wildest dreams. I'd never slept in a bed so comfortable or tasted food so sweet.

But it was too good to be true, and I'd lost it— like I always did.

"Lie back down," a nurse said as she came to my bedside. "You aren't well."

No shit, lady, Oberi huffed in my mind. *You gonna stand there and state the obvious all day?* He was clearly perturbed.

"It's fine," I said, more to Oberi than the nurse. "I'm fine."

Except I moved too quickly to lie down, and my head spun. The nurse offered me meds, but I refused. I didn't trust anything the Warden might possibly have prescribed.

The infirmary went quiet, and I had nothing but time to think. It was agonizing. I wished I could just pass out for another week, so I wouldn't have to think about it. I could still hear the screams of Elves as they raced through the city to escape the guards.

I pondered my Elf magic, and how much of it I could truly manipulate. The last thing I wanted was for the Warden to learn I had Elf blood. He'd been experimenting on students to get to Forevermore. I didn't know what he intended to do now that he'd found the city— probably strip it of its gold and riches. But that didn't mean his quest for power was over. If he found out what I was— a demigod and the next in line for the Elven throne— he would use me for sure.

I was released from the infirmary the following day, once I managed to convince the nurses I could stand on my own. Angel magic was *not* something you wanted to fuck with. My whole body ached as I headed toward my cell. I didn't really want to go there, but I didn't know where else *to* go. Ava hadn't reached out to me, and that wall she'd put up held strong. I was too depressed to pay attention to where I was going, so I held on to Oberi as he walked me through the halls.

As I passed by the Villain's Den, loud conversation caught my attention. Something played on the TV, but so many people spoke amongst themselves that I couldn't make it out.

"I bet there are thousands of Elves left," someone said.

I nudged Oberi, and he led me toward the door. I could feel the tension in the room the second I stepped inside. As I listened, I realized the supernatural news channel was playing— a broadcasting station accessed only through private servers.

"*Many are struggling to understand the sudden reappearance of the Elves,*" a newscaster said on TV. "*But the greater question stands: What alliances might form, and what does this mean for the supernatural community? Stay tuned for an expert testimony...*"

I stopped listening when someone called my name. "Charlie! How the hell are you?"

He clapped my shoulder, and I realized it was Chancey.

I shrugged. "Surviving, I guess. What's going on?"

So many conversations were happening at once that I had a hard time picking up on just one. All I could tell was that *everyone* was talking about the Elves.

Chancey took my shoulder and guided me away from the TV. He lowered his voice. "Things have been... strange the last couple of days, ever since you guys got back from Forevermore."

"You know about that?" I gaped.

"Marcus couldn't keep his mouth shut," Chancey said.

I groaned.

"Not like that," he said quickly. "He only told me, Ivy, Opal, and Ez the truth. I guess Kallie and Ava have been avoiding him, and you were in the infirmary. He needed someone to talk to."

"Kallie and Ava are avoiding him?" I asked. "Why?"

"I know how to get my hands on information," Chancey said. "But don't ask me to explain why girls do the stuff they do. I don't know why they're avoiding Marcus. If he has any clue, he left it out of his version of the story."

I think I already knew. Ava was avoiding me, too, and I felt the unease as well. Guilt permeated my bones. I hadn't let myself go there just yet, but it was bubbling to the surface. Sooner or later, I wouldn't be able to push it down.

They were dead. Thousands of Elves had been slaughtered and displaced from their homes, their existence revealed... because of us.

We all had baggage we carried around daily. With this, it just became too much to bear. I wasn't sure any of us had the strength left in us to keep dragging this shit around. The guilt had broken us all.

"How much does everyone know?" I asked.

"They know the four of you broke out," he said. "It was a big deal when you four disappeared after the explosion at the mines. Marcus said Kallie cast an illusion, but you guys weren't back by the time it faded. We all knew something was up. We just didn't know what until you guys returned, and with a bunch of Elves, too. It's... kind of surreal."

"Did they find the rest of the Elves?" I asked, holding my breath. "The ones that escaped?"

"No. Nobody knows what happened to them. Right now, all anyone knows is that the Elves are still out there. We don't know what's going to happen next. Everyone seems to think another war is going to break out."

I stilled. Had we started the war the prophecy spoke of? I'd been trying so long to stop the prophecy and to keep it out of Ava's reach... and it was still coming true. It didn't seem to matter how much I tried to protect her.

There was only one thing left I could think to try.

My stomach dropped out of my abdomen. This would be the hardest thing I'd ever done— worse than the trauma I'd endured as a kid, worse than witnessing the slaughter of the Elves in Forevermore. The Warden could take my life force all over again, and it wouldn't be as bad as what I was about to do.

And yet the decision seemed so easy, because it felt as if the choice had already been made for me.

My throat closed up, but I managed to force out, "Thanks for the info, Chancey. I'll catch up with you later."

I nudged Oberi and spoke to him in my mind, *Take me to Ava.*

Oberi let out a soft whine. *She doesn't want to see you right now.*

I don't care, I replied. *I need to see her.*

Charlie... Oberi used a sharp tone, as if warning me of something. He was taking Ava's side, but I couldn't stand being shut out like this right now.

Fine. I'll find her myself, I huffed at Oberi before storming out of the room. My shoulder slammed into the doorframe, but I yanked the door shut behind me and kept on moving. The door to the Villain's Den was almost always open, but I didn't want Oberi following me.

He barked through the door and screamed in my mind, *Come back here, young man!*

I scoffed. He couldn't tell me what to do.

Navigating the halls of the Institute was difficult without Oberi. I could get to my classes without him, because I knew the landmarks and counted my steps, but when I wandered, I easily got lost. I turned a couple of hallways to lose Oberi, but I didn't really know where I was going.

Pidge, please let me in, I begged in my mind. She couldn't hear me the way Oberi could, but she could feel me reaching out to her.

She shut me down, as if telling me to go away.

Come on, Ava. We need to talk. Where are you?

She shied away from the connection, but a mix of emotions slipped through— sorrow and guilt, combined with a sense of safety.

There was only one place I could think of that would make her feel safe.

I turned around and wandered the halls until I heard voices coming from the cafeteria. Once I knew where I was, it was easier to navigate. I calmed my breath so I could focus on my surroundings. I counted my steps as I wove through the halls. I went up a stairway, until I came to the door that led outside.

I opened the door, and Ava gasped at the sound. My heart surged when I heard her— it felt so freaking good— but it crumbled a moment later. This was *not* a meeting to be happy about.

"Charlie," Ava breathed as I stepped onto the balcony. Chilly air brushed across my arms, and the cloud cover was so thick, I couldn't feel the sunlight. "What are you doing here? I thought I made it pretty clear I wanted to be alone."

"You've had plenty of time to be alone while I was in the infirmary," I reminded her. I wasn't harsh about it, but it came out sounding less than friendly. "We need to talk."

"What I *need* is space," she argued.

I sensed she meant it on a deeper level, and that fucking hurt. I kept my voice steady. "I know you, pidge. You don't need space. You're uncomfortable with the thought of someone caring about you, so you isolate yourself and push me away, because it's easier for you to be alone than fight for me."

Ava went silent. It was obvious my accusation was truer than she cared to admit.

"It's *always* like that with me," I said bitterly. "People don't want me around, just like my dad didn't."

She blew a breath. "That's unfair, Charlie. You know your dad looked for you. And you know I want you. It's just... I'm still trying to process it all."

"Which is *why* we need to talk," I practically begged. I reached out for her, but she yanked away.

"I know," she said in a small voice. "It's just... too hard."

Her words startled me, and my airways began to close. For the briefest of moments, her wall crumbled down, and I knew this wasn't about what we'd been through. She wasn't ready for what was *about* to happen.

Neither was I.

I swallowed down all emotion, because the pain was too much to bear. We had to get this over with, or we'd avoid it forever, which was dangerous for us both.

"Those flowers you gave me weren't a get-well gift, were they?" I realized. "They were goodbye."

I knew they were sad when I touched them, but I didn't quite understand it until now.

She sniffled. "I-I don't know. Please don't make me do this."

Hell, I thought she might tell me I was wrong. I'd *hoped* that this was all in my head, and she could convince me otherwise, but Ava and I had found ourselves at the same place— a place where the pain ran so deep not even our connection, magical or otherwise, could heal it.

"I don't want to make you do anything," I whispered. I couldn't find the breath to speak any louder. "This is my choice."

I knew in that moment that it had to be this way. I wanted to fight for her with every fiber of my being, but I also wanted to protect her— protect us *both*. And to do that, *I* had to be the one to make the decision, because she wasn't strong enough to do it.

"What are you saying?" Ava's voice cracked. She wasn't angry or even surprised. It was like she simply wasn't ready to hear it out loud.

"I'm saying we need to break up." My stomach twisted into knots, and all I wanted to do was break down and cry. I couldn't actually *want* this, could I?

A part of me did, and I had to do it now, or I'd never be able to let her go.

Ava sniffled. "You sure?"

Hell, my heart felt as if it was being ripped out of my chest.

"I think it's what we both want," I said gently. "We both know this isn't going to work."

She hiccupped. "I just... never thought we'd actually go through with it."

"Me, either," I replied solemnly. I pushed down all feelings I could manage, though they forced themselves upward. I thought I might hurl. I felt the need to justify it— more for myself than for Ava, I think.

"It's just... we found Forevermore," I began. "I found my birth family. Forevermore could've been my home, once I got over the shock of it all. But now it's *gone*, like every other home I've ever had. All I've ever wanted was a home and a family, and someone to love. That's why I've been holding so tight to you."

I took a rattling breath. "But you're never going to want to settle down. You love adventure, and I need something permanent and stable, because I never had that as a kid. I need someone who will be by my side forever, someone I *know* will stay, and I don't know if you can offer that. We want different things."

I just kept rambling, like I needed more reasons to convince us both. "Everything I've ever had has been taken away from me... and pidge, I can't stand if you were taken from me, too. If we go into this relationship any deeper, I don't know how either of us will survive it. And I know that if we stay together, the Warden will use us against each other. He already has, and it nearly killed me. The prophecy has already started, and it's going to break us apart one way or another. We've gotten too close. It will be easier for both of us to fulfill our duties if we do this now. I have to make this decision, for both of us."

Her breath wavered, like she knew the truth but it was too difficult to hear. "This prophecy is *so unfair*. I love you, Charlie, but I can't choose between saving you and saving the world. I have an obligation to fulfill this prophecy, but the closer you are to me, the more likely you are to die. And I just don't think I'll be able to fulfill it with you around."

Her words had turned to a whisper, and my stomach twisted. "What do you mean by that?" I asked. I had to know how she truly felt.

A beat passed before she answered. "I don't feel like you support me. Every time I get closer to answers, you seem to have some sort of excuse as to why we can't do it. It's like you've been trying to sabotage me the whole time."

I said nothing, and Ava hitched a breath. "That's because you *have* tried, haven't you?"

I crossed my arms in front of my stomach. I felt so cold. "I took the Elven books from the library, and buried them," I admitted. "I didn't want us getting any closer to the truth."

"You took my key when we were fooling around in the woods, didn't you?" Ava accused. "I didn't lose it. You *stole* it."

My voice had withered away inside my throat. Ava's tone was heart-broken. "I can't... you *know* it's hard for me to be vulnerable in that way. Do you think I can just... take my clothes off and fuck around with anyone without it being *scary*? But I did, because I felt safe, and I thought that was a moment where I could *trust* you. I'm really disap-pointed in you."

I couldn't defend myself. It'd been a shitty thing to do then, and I felt worse about it now.

Ava's voice grew angry. "You're always saying everything is too dangerous, and you're right. It *is* dangerous, but I knew that when I learned about the prophecy. I'm willing to face the danger, but I get that you're not. Even if you don't want to fulfill *your* prophecy, I have to fulfill mine. I don't want to force you to follow me when it could get you killed."

I gaped. How did I even begin to explain this? "Pidge, you think I said all that stuff because *I* was scared for myself? Hell, no! I was scared for *you!*"

"I know it's dangerous—"

"No, you don't know," I choked. "You have *no* idea how dangerous this truly is."

"I'm not—" she cut off when she realized something. "Wait… do you know something about the prophecy that I don't?"

I pressed my lips together and didn't speak.

"Charlie, you have to tell me," she demanded.

"I'm not supposed to," I said. "It could hurt you even more. Your aunt said it would compromise the outcome of the prophecy."

"How can I do my job as the chosen one without knowing *everything* about the prophecy?" Ava demanded. She sounded agonized that her aunt had hidden this from her.

"Because if you knew what the rest of it said, you wouldn't keep pursuing it."

"Then you'll have your wish," she stated. "You don't want me doing this anyway."

My heart gave a jolt. I'd been so scared of telling her the truth, thinking that doing so would doom her, but maybe she was right. Maybe *this* was the choice my prophecy piece spoke of. *A choice will be made by the twin of her soul… It is his choice to damn the realm, or save us all.*

Perhaps *this* was how I fulfilled my piece. Breaking up sure as hell felt like a fate worse than death. Damn it all, I knew I'd do anything to save Ava, even if it meant letting her go.

"*A choice will be made by the twin of her soul,*" I began. I'd memorized the words months ago, but they still tore me apart to hear aloud. "*To save her and damn the realm, or curse her, and save us all. A fate worse than death is the chosen one's destiny.*"

I gave a heavy sigh. "The prophecy says that I'm going to hurt you in order to save the world— deliver you a fate worse than death. Your aunt foresaw it."

A sob broke from my chest, but that was all I allowed. I shoved the rest downward, because I couldn't handle anything more. "Pidge," I rasped. "I can't keep doing this. If this is what saves you—"

"It's not me I'm worried about," she cut in. "If it comes down to saving the world and saving you— which it will— I'm going to choose *you*. The only way the supernaturals can survive is if you're not around me, so you don't end up dead. I'd damn the whole world to hell if it meant choosing you."

"I hate that it's hurting you to choose between me and your destiny," I admitted.

Ava swallowed audibly. "I'm sorry, Charlie. But when I was forced to choose to save you from death instead of stopping the Warden to save the Elves, I just realized I can't do both. We damned a whole magical society because we love each other, and it can't happen again."

I dropped my head. "I feel awful. It's our fault the Elves were exposed."

It felt so strange to agree with her. I knew I should be fighting for her, because I loved her so damn much, but we couldn't fight for each other when it meant damning everyone else. We blamed ourselves— we blamed *each other*— for what happened to the Elves. And the last thing either of us wanted was for our relationship to end the world. Because we were villains, and we knew it would.

And so, we had to end it first.

Ava hiccupped. "I'm *so* sorry, Charlie."

Fuck, she was crying. Instinctually, I reached out and pulled her into a hug. Instead of drawing away, Ava laid her head on my chest. Her tears stained my shirt, but I just held on tight to her. I wanted this moment to last forever— no matter how much it hurt— because I knew this was the last time I was ever going to hold her.

"Wh-what are we going to do about Oberi?" Ava asked in a wavering tone.

It was obvious what she meant, though neither of us said it. We were connected through a soul bond, and Oberi would always be that bridge for us. But as for the rest of it... it was just too painful. Ava and I could no longer be friends. Hell, I didn't know if *any* of us would be friends anymore. Not after what we endured in Forevermore. I wasn't just losing Ava. I was losing Kallie and Marcus, too.

"We'll share custody." I forced a chuckle, but my lame attempt at lightening the mood fell flat.

"That's probably best," she agreed. "I guess this is goodbye."

Her words forged a chasm between us, and I physically felt the hole that formed in our bond. The two halves of our souls split, as if they couldn't bear to be together anymore. It was so strange— like the time before I'd met Ava. I hadn't realized such a big part of me was missing, but now that we were no longer one, it was as if my identity had been ripped in half, and she took most of me with her.

My legs went weak at the thought of losing her affection. It drove me halfway to hell just thinking about her being with someone else, imagining some other man pressed up against her skin and making her feel the way that only I could. We'd shared everything with each other, and it didn't seem to matter.

Don't go. I wanted to beg her not to leave me. I wanted to tell her I was sorry, and ask her to stay with me. I wished to be reminded of what it felt like to experience her love. The thought of being alone in the world once again, without a family or even someone to care for, made me want to throw up. I couldn't stand being alone anymore. I wanted... her.

But I wanted to hurt less. And I knew the longer we drug this out, the more we fought, the more we tried to stay together, the worse it would be. Two people could be in love but bad for each other, and that's what Ava and I were. I had to protect myself from getting hurt worse than I already was. To avoid being destroyed completely, I had to push her away. It tore me up how she was choosing to leave me, just like I'd decided to leave her. That we agreed this wasn't going anywhere was almost worse than being dumped.

I always knew I was going to lose her, anyway. Might as well just let her go now.

My stomach hollowed, and my voice sounded empty. "Yeah. I guess it is."

Ava shook in my arms as she drew away. "Goodbye, Charlie," she said, before turning away and leaving me standing there. Her footsteps left holes in my heart as she abandoned the balcony and ran away.

Something broke inside of me, but I couldn't stand to feel it. I didn't want to cry anymore, or suffer anymore loss.

So instead, I just... went numb. I felt the air around me and heard the door close behind Ava, but inside, I didn't allow myself to *feel* anything. It scared me, but not as much as the ungodly pain of letting her go did.

What have you done? Oberi roared in my mind. He was on the verge of complete panic.

I was too broken to respond.

Stay where you're at, he demanded. *I'm coming to find you.*

I threw up a wall between us, because I couldn't bear to hear him tell me what a huge mistake I'd just made— and I knew in my heart he would.

I forgot how I got back inside the building and down to the main level. I must've been wandering around for over an hour, though I had no sense of time and no sense of direction. I couldn't even sense Oberi through the bond, though he had to be looking for me. I didn't know what to do, or where to go.

It terrified me.

"Charlie," a voice called down the hall. I didn't recognize the voice at first— didn't even recognize my own name.

"Charlie," the voice repeated. Footsteps approached, and I finally came to attention.

"Who's there?" My voice didn't seem like my own.

"It's Eddie," the Elf announced. He'd been among the prisoners the Warden had brought back to the Institute. "What are you doing wandering around? I heard you'd been released from the infirmary. I've been looking for you for hours."

I tried to force myself to breathe, but I'd gone so numb even that didn't seem possible. "I got lost," I said flatly, though it held more meaning than I intended. "Where are we?"

"A deserted hall at the back of the Institute," Eddie said. "Are you okay?"

I shook my head but answered, "I'll be fine. Why were you looking for me?"

"I'm your guard, remember?" Eddie sounded really worried.

"Yes, of course," I said. "But you're not my servant. You don't have to follow me around."

"The Institute is a dangerous place," Eddie pointed out. "I won't let you get hurt."

I already have, I wanted to say, but I didn't. Instead, I changed the topic. I had to think about something— *anything*— but Ava. "Any news on the Elves?"

"I have no means of contacting anyone," he admitted. "But I'll tell you what I *do* know."

I leaned in closer, because I was curious. Eddie took my shoulder and guided me into an alcove. Though I didn't hear anyone else in the hall, it was obvious he wanted to claim every bit of privacy we could, in case someone overheard.

He spoke in a quiet whisper. "Your grandfather always knew the day would come when Forevermore was found. The Mirror of Ingress was *always* meant to be our one-way ticket out of the city should that day come. We were taught at a young age if that happened, we should scatter the globe and take refuge in other supernatural communities. We learned about them all— fae, witches, vampires— and studied their locations, so that we could find them and blend in if we needed to. But the Elves know they can't hide forever."

"So what are they going to do?" I asked.

"The Elves need someone to fight for them," Eddie said. "Right now, they're waiting."

I tilted my head. "Waiting for what?"

"For *you*."

I gaped. "For me? What the hell?"

"Charlie, the Elves need a prince to lead them into battle," Eddie hushed. "There's going to be another Great Supernatural War. The magical races are already preparing to fight one another all over again. It's all over the news. It's only a matter of time before chaos erupts."

"And what do you want me to do about it?" I took a step back, as if I could physically retreat from my fate.

"You need to gather the Elves that are scattered around the globe, and prepare them to fight back against our enemies. Your grandfather knows you aren't ready for this," Eddie said. "But when you are, our people will look to you to lead them. The Elves can't survive another genocide, Charlie. They won't make it. The only way to survive is to fight, until you can lead us to the Blessed Haven."

"Why can't my dad do it? Or my grandpa, or—"

"They aren't a demigod. You're the future," Eddie insisted. "Our people saw you fight when the Warden found us. The prophecy announced your arrival. They know you have great power— more power than your father, or even Emperor Cassiel. If you abandon them, they'll consider our race a lost cause. They'll give up. Can you really do that to an entire empire?"

I got really quiet. I'd already failed the Elves when my friends and I had exposed them to the world. I didn't think I could fail them twice.

"You're my master, so I'll follow you whatever you decide," Eddie said. "But consider that if you turn your back on the Elves, they'll have no one to defend them from this war that's coming. They'll have no one to lead them to their eternal Forevermore, to our heaven and our destiny. So what are you going to do, Charlie? Are you going to save them... or are you going to walk away?"

END OF BOOK TWO

Continue on to read a special excerpt from Book Three: *The Infernal Underground*.

HIDDEN LEGENDS

Read more from the Hidden Legends universe! Each Hidden Legends series takes place within the same world, but in separate and unique societies. Every series stands on its own, and they can be read in any order.

ELEMENTALS, DRAGONS, & MORE

Academy of Magical Creatures by Megan Linski & Alicia Rades

SHIFTERS, FAE, & SORCERESSES

University of Sorcery by Megan Linski

WITCHES, DEMONS, & REAPERS

College of Witchcraft by Alicia Rades

Never miss a new release! Join our newsletter at
hiddenlegendsbooks.com/fanclub/

THE INFERNAL UNDERGROUND
CHAPTER ONE

Charlie

A year ago, I had hope of getting out of this prison alive.

Now, I had nothing. No hope. No fear. Nothing. I had too much time to think these days, so I just... didn't. I shut down.

It was all too easy to go into autopilot while labeling boxes during my Work-Study hours. The Warden obviously didn't want me working in the mines anymore-- not after the stunt the Villain's Club pulled last semester, when my friends and I had exposed Forevermore. I'd been reassigned to a packaging facility located in the prison wing furthest from the classrooms. The guards had shoved a label gun in my hand and had me labeling boxes eight hours a day, every day.

Box. Label. Box. Label. Box. Label.

That's all I let go through my head. It was easier to focus on the process than ponder any real problems-- like how to save the Elves, or how to get over... *her.*

Tonight, though, my thoughts raced. I tried to shut them down, but they wouldn't go away.

The sound of machinery whirred around me, and the heavy scent of metal filled my nose. A box moved down the conveyor belt to my station.

I felt for the corner, then pressed the label on with the gun. I could feel the noxite inside the box draining my energy. I didn't know what was actually *in* the boxes. It could be raw noxite, cuffs, darts, really anything. The guards never said, and we weren't supposed to ask.

No one spoke here in the facility, though I could hear other students shuffling around the large room, working their factory jobs. It was a dull job, but better than the mines, at least.

I hadn't been to the mines since I'd found Forevermore with Ava-Marie.

Hell, Ava.

I hadn't run into her since we'd broken up. The mere memory of her fingers gliding over my skin caused my entire form to go ridgid, and my guts to twist. No magical torture could be so intense as the recollection of my hands running through her long hair. The thought of her beautiful voice, which I'd missed so much, almost dropped me to my knees. It had been months, but instead of getting better, the agony of losing her had only gotten worse. It was like my soul was being torn to shreds, hacked bit by bit by pieces of glass that were too fragmented for me to pull out, and I bled every time I tried.

Don't think about her.

Iron bars came down as I shut the ever-encompassing thought of *her* out of my mind. I wouldn't allow myself to go down that pit to hell. No thanks.

I had no classes over the summer, just my Work-Study credit I earned from labeling these stupid boxes. During the summer semester at the Institute, classes were suspended and inmates were expected to work forty-hours a week-- or more-- on our Work-Study courses.

I was supposed to keep attending counseling sessions, but no one had seen Professor Takahashi since the Elves had fled Forevermore. I didn't know why he'd left, but I was sure it was for a good reason. Whatever it was, it was certainly more important than counseling a couple of college-aged criminals.

I took it as a blessing. The Institute hadn't found anyone to replace Takahashi, so I hadn't been forced to go to counseling and talk to *her* all summer. I'd been avoiding her as much as possible, for reasons too painful to consider.

When I wasn't labeling boxes, I was training for the fight club. I didn't really want to do it anymore. What was the point? I'd only been doing it to save money to provide for my girl when we got out of this hell hole, and she was gone now.

Although fight club certainly paid better than my garbage Work-Study job-- if you could call it a *job*. I was pretty sure I made less than ten cents an hour, though no one had ever given me an official number. Prisoner wages were shit.

But I didn't need the money anymore, not now that she and I had split. Money just didn't matter. I'd lived without it before. I could do it again.

But I couldn't get out of fight club, even if I wanted to. When I'd *hinted* I wanted to quit, Captain had yanked a punching bag off its chains and threw it at me. He wasn't the kind of vampire you wanted to mess with. It was easier to fight my peers than it was to fight him. So I just took the beatings, because at least I felt *something* when I was being pummeled by a dragon shifter.

The rest of the time, I was just... numb.

Don't think. Don't feel. Just breathe.

Every breath I took felt suffocating.

My bonded partner wasn't the only person I was avoiding. I avoided the guys at fight club as much as I could, too. I put in my training hours at night, when most students were in bed. The guards left my door unlocked so I could sneak down to the training center after my late Work-Study shift. I'd train all night, then sneak back into my room before *her* cell unlocked from beside mine. I'd sleep most of the day, until my Work-Study shift started at two o'clock.

And I repeated that over and over. Like I said, it'd become too easy to fall into an autopilot routine. Any spare moment I had, I spent with Eddie searching for information about the keys to open the Elven gate on Darke Island, but we hadn't found anything.

I was prophesied to bring the Elves into paradise, by opening that Elven gate using seven keys, one from every supernatural race, and leading them on into heaven.

Though at this point, it felt more like I was leading them into hell.

I'd basically given up. What was the point, anyhow? The Warden had won.

Box. Label. Box. Label.

A buzzer went off overhead, and I breathed a sigh of relief. That was the cue for the end of my shift. I shoved the label gun back in its holder at my station, then got the hell out of there, because I didn't want to stay a second longer than I had to. It was gross how the Institute used us for cheap labor, under the guise of *rehabilitating* us.

Rehabilitation, my ass. If anything, I'd gotten *worse* since I'd shown up here. I'd joined a freaking fight club, for the ancestors' sake!

She'd been right, and I should've never joined. They were using me.

But there was no going back now. I was in this until I graduated or until I fucking died here.

Right now, dying felt like the better option.

The good thing about fight club-- besides the guards looking the other way when I did shit that should've earned me an infraction-- was free reign to punch something whenever I wanted. After my Work-Study shift, I always needed a good punching bag to beat the shit out of. I swear, it was the only thing that kept me sane in this place.

The quickest way to get to the secret training room from the packaging facility was to cut through the prison yard, near the siren lake, rather than weave through the maze of hallways. I could always navigate the outdoors better anyway, because of my magic.

Better than that-- she was hardly ever outside, and it helped me to avoid her.

I could tell it was late when I left the building, because the air was cool, and the bugs that only came out at night sang their mating calls loudly. I counted my steps as I left the building, and paid attention to landmarks throughout the prison yard, listening for the sound of my footsteps echoing off the obstacles around me. It's how I navigated the Institute as a blind guy when my Familiar, Oberi, wasn't here to guide me.

Not far from me, I could hear the waves of the lake lapping against the shore. I reached out with my magic to sense a large tree up ahead. As I approached it, I grazed my fingers against the rough bark, which was a habit now. I liked to touch my landmarks to confirm I was headed in the right direction.

Screech!

My heart lurched as a high-pitched alarm filled the prison yard. Voices began shouting, and the wind whipped around me. It wasn't my magic; it was someone else's. Instinctually, I ducked behind the tree to conceal myself from whatever the hell was going on.

"Get him!" someone shouted. The voice was rough, and belonged to a guard for sure. They were coming straight toward me. For a second, I thought they were talking about me, but curfew wasn't for another few minutes. I'd done nothing wrong.

"Get back here!" another guard shouted.

"Don't let him get away!" someone screamed.

Hell, I realized. Someone was making a break for it.

Good for them, I thought. They were braver than I. No one got out of the Institute, and if you tried, you were sent to Cellblock 9. Marcus and Kallie had tried to escape once, but they'd gotten lucky. Professor Warbright had talked down the guards for them. I wouldn't want to risk it-- not after what we'd discovered about the Warden last semester.

We'd discovered that he'd been running experiments on students, trying to find a demigod for some nefarious purpose. We hadn't gotten any evidence, but I knew it was true. Any sorry sucker who got dragged off to Cellblock 9 was a victim of those experiments. I was sure of it.

There were so many voices footsteps racing across the prison yard that I couldn't make out how many guards were in pursuit. They were closing in fast, coming closer and closer to my hiding spot.

"Take him down by any means necessary!" one guard screamed to the others.

"My magic's gone!" another yelled back.

"Then shoot him!"

"He's an *Elf!*" the guard spat back.

I held my breath. One of the Elves was trying to escape, and if he'd managed to take a guards' magic, he was going to make it. I hoped he did. It was the first time in forever I felt *any* kind of hope.

Elves were immune to noxite. The darts wouldn't slow him down.

But the fence around the property did. It was the only thing keeping the Elves prisoner. I'd asked Eddie about it once-- why he and his friends couldn't just steal the guards' magic and get the hell out of here. Hell, he could break us all out if he wanted.

But Eddie had assured me that stealing someone else's magic was difficult, something none of the Elves at the Institute had mastered yet. At least, not until tonight. As Eddie had put it, *"We may be immune to noxite, but there's still barbed wire keeping us from jumping that fence."*

There was hope. If an Elf had figured out how to overpower the guards, they could steal someone else's magic and fly out, or break straight through the gates with vampire strength.

Hell, I hoped it was Eddie, but I knew he wouldn't attempt to leave without me. He was born to protect me... psh... the *Elf prince.*

Yeah, I was the grandson of the Emperor. Still hadn't quite wrapped my head around it myself. And to be honest, I was still feeling a little bitter about the whole thing. I'd found my family, but then I'd lost them again.

Even worse, finding my heritage had cost me the love of my life. Nothing good ever happened to me, and if it did, it always came with a cost too high to bear.

My heart hammered as I listened closely. It felt good to *feel* something. The wind picked up around me, whipping my long hair around my face. I could hardly hear the conversation between the guards anymore. I tried to calm the wind with my elemental magic, so I could figure out what the hell was going on, but it barely died down. That meant whoever was whipping up the wind storm was nearly as strong as I was.

It was the Elf. I just knew it. He'd taken one of the Yapluma guards' Air magic and was using it to keep them away, so he could make his escape.

"I got him!" a guard shouted.

The Air around me swirled chaotically. It was as if two Elementai were warring against one another-- a guard against the Elf, I was sure.

"You're not going anywhere," a guard growled across the prison yard.

The Elf laughed manically. "You want to bet?"

He must've given up on the Air magic, because the wind died down. The next thing I knew, a deafening screech filled the yard. I threw my hands over my ears and curled against the tree I hid behind. It was louder than the alarm blaring overhead and made it feel as if my brain was rattling around in my skull.

When I thought it was over, I dropped my hands from my ears. All throughout the prison yard, guards groaned in agony. The Elf had stolen a siren guard's cry.

The sound of wings unfurling met my ears, and they began to flap. I could tell by the sound that they were huge and feathery, like angel wings. Most angels could only fly around the center of the prison yard. Once they got close to the noxite gates, their wings gave out.

But this guy was no angel.

"What the hell!?" a guard yelled. "He's stolen my wings!"

I smirked. Good for him!

"So long, suckers!" the Elf laughed. He flapped his newfound wings and flew directly over me. My jaw hung slack as I listened to him fly away, far above the barbed wire fence, and into the forest beyond.

Holy ancestors. He'd done it. He'd *escaped the Institute.*

I beamed. If this Elf could escape, then it meant others could as well. *I* could get out of here!

I pressed my back to the tree, where the guards couldn't see me. I was still trying to catch my breath, because I was so shocked by it all. I couldn't believe someone had gotten away. This was a big fucking deal.

"You bastard!" a guard screamed.

"*You're* the one who let him steal your wings. If you were stronger, he wouldn't have escaped."

"This is *your* fault!" another accused.

"Oh, yeah? You wanna fight about it? I'll give you a fight--" The guard must've shifted mid-sentence, because the next thing I knew, a dragon's roar filled the prison yard.

One of the guards laughed. "What do you think you're gonna do with those dull dragon claws? Half of us are vampires. I'd rip your head off and suck you dry. I don't care how filthy your blood tastes."

Hell, the guards could be worse than the inmates sometimes.

"Stop screwing around and go after him," another guard growled. "He's on an island for God's sake. He can't go far!"

The guards were *pissed*! They hurried off in pursuit of the Elf, but they had to go out the gate, because even the guards couldn't get past the noxite fence. The Elf had a major head start, though. I didn't think the guards would find him, even on Darke Island. If the Elf got past the ward surrounding the island somehow, he'd be home free.

I sat behind my tree a while longer, listening to the fading sounds of the guards' footsteps. When I was confident they were gone, I rushed out from behind my hiding spot and hurried into the building.

I was still reeling over what I'd just witnessed that I wasn't quite paying attention to where I was going. I quickly got lost in the maze of hallways.

Hell, where was I? I stopped to take in my surroundings. It had to be minutes from curfew by now. The halls were dead silent.

Then I heard the sound of paws padding down the hallway. My heart surged when I felt Oberi's presence through our bond.

"Hey, boy," I greeted. I knelt down and scratched him behind the ears.

I frowned when I noticed his fur was matted and felt a bit rough. It seemed Oberi hadn't been brushed all summer, which made me sad... because it meant *she* was sad. Oberi didn't ask to be groomed when my other half was feeling down.

Oberi barked and panted happily. Usually, he didn't visit me until after I got back from training. It was unusual for him to find me this late at night, since he usually spent the night with her. He must've noticed something felt off.

"It's okay, boy," I told him. "I'm safe."

I noticed your lost ass needed saving, Oberi cracked.

I frowned. He could get sassy when he wanted to. "I need to find Eddie. Can you lead me to him?"

Oberi barked. I placed my hand on his back, and he started guiding me through the halls. I heard voices ahead, and I figured we'd entered one of the cellblocks. Oberi slowed and guided me into what I figured had to be one of the cells.

"Charlie?" Eddie asked, sounding surprised. I wasn't so good with voices, but Eddie and I had spent a lot of time together over the summer. I'd learned to recognize his voice easily. "What are you doing in my dorm? Curfew's in two minutes."

"Something's happened," I said breathlessly.

Eddie's bed springs squeaked as he jumped up from his bed and shut the door. He spoke in a hushed tone. "What is it? Have you found something on the keys?"

I scoffed. At this point, I wasn't sure we'd *ever* find anything. "It's not that. You heard the alarm?"

The fabric of Eddie's uniform rustled as he crossed his arms. "Only the whole prison heard it. Wait... you weren't involved in that, were you?"

"No, but I heard what happened. One of your buddies escaped."

"Fuck," Eddie growled under his breath. He sounded exasperated as he sat back down on his bed. "It was Gavyn, wasn't it?"

"No idea," I said. "All I know is that it was an Elf. He overpowered the guards and stole some of their powers. I thought you said none of the Elves at the Institute were strong enough for that."

"We weren't," Eddie admitted. "But Gavyn's been training with his magic all summer, in secret."

The lock on Eddie's door clicked, and I knew there was no leaving now. I was stuck in here with him all night. Not a big deal, since the guards never checked my bed anyway. I figured I might as well get comfortable. Oberi guided me to the chair beside Eddie's desk, and I sat.

"You sound upset," I remarked. "I thought you'd be happy for him. You're always talking like you want to get out of here."

"Of course I do, but not like this." Eddie sighed. "After the Elves were captured in Forevermore, we got together and talked about our options. Gavyn *always* wanted to get out. He talked about it constantly. But none of our magic was strong enough, and we knew we wouldn't *get* strong enough to get everyone out at once. We needed to practice first. We agreed to stick together, seeing as we don't know where to find the rest of the Elves. The deal was either we all go, or no one goes. Gavyn apparently did not listen."

"But if one Elf gets out, so can the rest of you," I remarked. So could *I*, since I was part Elf. For once, I actually had a spark of hope.

Unlike me, Eddie was realistic and logical. "We're still pretty young Elves, and while we can do *some* magical manipulation, it's not enough to get all of us out. That's why we agreed to stick together. Even our illusion magic is shit. Gavyn has betrayed us. Even if we did get out of the gates, we'd have to be strong enough to get off Darke Island. There's a ward around the whole island, you know."

Hell, he was right. Even though I hoped Gavyn was strong enough to overpower that somehow, too.

"One Elf escapes, and the Warden is going to come down on the rest of us," Eddie pointed out. "You just watch."

I didn't want to believe that Eddie was right. I wanted to believe we had a chance at getting the hell away from here, where the Warden couldn't run his experiments on us, and where he'd never figure out what I was— an Elf prince, and a demigod.

But it didn't take long before Eddie suspicions were confirmed. The next morning, a letter slid under Eddie's dorm.

"*All students are required to attend an assembly in the Room of Mirrors at eight a.m. sharp,*" Eddie read aloud to me. "*Anyone not in attendance will be charged an infraction and a six-hundred dollar fine charged to their account.*"

Hell, a fine that huge would put most students' accounts in the negative. Most of us made less than ten dollars a month, working the shitty Work-Study jobs they forced us into.

"Can the Warden do that?" I questioned. "Charge a fine?"

"I don't want to find out," Eddie remarked.

I didn't want to attract the Warden's attention. Once Eddie's door unlocked, we went to the cafeteria to get some food, then headed to the Room of Mirrors. It was the same room where the Warden had hosted his welcome speech my first day here, and where the Villain's Ball was held after the Darke Games every year. The vast room was used for various school functions, but it got quite crowded when the whole student body was packed in here.

Bodies pressed in on me from all angles. Oberi stayed close to my side in his husky form. He seemed calm and relaxed, which worried me, because he hadn't been this way since before she and I had broken up.

I realized it probably meant *she* was nearby, and he was happy we were finally in the same room together again. I listened closely to the voices around me, but I couldn't pick her out of the crowd. I hoped she was across the room and couldn't see me. I wouldn't be able to know she was approaching until she was right on top of me, as our bond had weakened considerably since we'd been apart. The magic between us was almost... gone.

Ava's three rows up, Oberi mentioned. *You should go talk to her.*

I scowled. *How many times are we going to have this conversation?*

As many as it takes.

I huffed. Oberi had been trying to talk me into getting back together with Ava all summer. Every fucking day of the week, actually.

It was never going to happen. We were bad for each other. We had made the right decision.

Or so I told myself.

"Are you okay?" Eddie leaned over and asked me.

"Yeah. I just have to deal with *his* sassy ass all day." I poked Oberi.

Better to be a sassy ass than a grumpy ass, he shot back.

I was sure that was Ava's half of our soul talking. Oberi didn't really think before he spoke.

"Welcome, students." The Warden's cool voice boomed over the room, and the student body began to quiet. A few people still made noise, because most students here had a problem with authority. On the other hand, the majority of us were scared shitless of the Warden, so it didn't take long before the room fell silent.

My guts twisted at the sound of his voice. The Warden had tortured me last semester and nearly killed me. I despised the man.

"I have called this assembly today to share news of an incident that transpired last night," the Warden said. His voice came from high up on the balcony. He made it sound like he was trying to sympathize with the students, but his attempt came across stale. He was shit at pretending like he cared about any one of us. We were just numbers to him.

"Last night, a student by the name of Gavyn Woodward attempted to escape the Darke Institute," the Warden announced.

Gasps traveled around the room. I furrowed my brow, because I hadn't expected the Warden to tell the truth. The Institute was supposedly impossible to escape. I would've expected him to maintain that illusion.

"Settle down," the Warden said in a threatening tone. The whispers filling the room settled, though they didn't completely die down. "It's important that you realize this student was no ordinary supernatural. He was an *Elf*."

He spoke the word *Elf* like it was some sort of curse. It was obvious he despised us.

"I tell you this to keep you safe," the Warden said-- like he gave two shits. "What Gavyn Woodward did last night in his attempt to escape was deplorable. He created a wind storm, stole a siren's scream, and slaughtered six guards using an angel's life-force power."

People gasped again, and the whispers grew.

My eyebrows furrowed. That had never happened. Gavyn had stolen an angel's powers, but only their wings, not their life-force abilities. The only way that was true was if the guards had found Gavyn on Darke Island after he'd escaped, but I didn't know how they could've caught up with him. The Warden was twisting the truth to suit his message. It made me sick.

"Unfortunately, drastic measures had to be taken to protect everyone here at the Institute," he said. The Warden was trying to make himself seem like the *good* guy. I wasn't buying it. His voice turned sad, but I could hear how fake it was. "I am devastated to announce that Gavyn Woodward died last night in his attempt to escape."

The whispers around the room grew louder. My lips tightened at the Warden's lies. I wanted to tell everyone he was *wrong*, that Gavyn had actually escaped without killing anyone, but that was a good way to piss off the Warden.

"The safety of our students and staff is of the utmost importance," the Warden continued. "I do not take kindly to *any* threats within the Institute. Rest assured that anyone who threatens the safety of the students or guards *will* be dealt with by any means necessary."

Students murmured around me, but they seemed to *agree* with the Warden. They thought he was protecting them.

But I knew better. This speech was a threat to the Elves. To *me.*

"Know that you are safe here," the Warden said, like we were supposed to be *grateful.* "Anyone who is deemed a threat will be *punished.*"

He said it with such finality that there was no denying what he meant. Anyone who stepped out of line, or who showed too much power here at the prison, would be killed. The Warden could do anything he wanted to us, all in the name of keeping us *safe.*

And people fucking bought it. I could hear them whispering around me.

Gavyn got what he deserved.

The Warden is doing his best.

Some kids can't be saved.

My nostrils flared, and I just wanted to scream.

Stay calm. You can't tell anyone what you know, Oberi insisted.

My hands curled into fists at my sides. Oberi was right. It wasn't like exposing the Warden for his lies would change anything. He'd twist some story to make me out as a *threat* so he could run his sick experiments on me. And if he found out I was a demigod, we were all doomed.

The Warden could keep his lies.

This time.

With the Warden's threat hanging in the air, he excused us. Students filed out of the room and headed in different directions. The conversations around me were deafening.

We didn't make it far before Eddie pulled me aside, and we ducked into an empty classroom. The door shut behind us, and I felt like I could finally think in the silence. Oberi nudged against me, like he was trying to comfort me, but I was fuming.

"The Warden is lying," Eddie raged.

"I know," I agreed. "Gavyn didn't kill anyone when he escaped. I'd have heard *something.*"

"Of course he didn't," Eddie insisted. "Gavyn wanted out, but he was no murderer. I know him. We grew up together. He wouldn't do what they said he did."

I gritted my teeth. "The Warden is trying to scare us."

"The Elves aren't bad people," Eddie practically pleaded. "We just want peace."

"I know that. But it's not me you have to convince."

Eddie began pacing. "The Warden started a war when he raided Forevermore. He's using Gavyn's escape to perpetuate that war. It won't stop unless we do something."

I raked my fingers through my hair. "I want to. I just don't know what we can do. I'm not totally immune to noxite like Gavyn is. I can't go up against the Warden on my own and get everyone out, even with what I am."

I made sure never to say what I was aloud-- a demigod *or* the Elven prince-- in case someone overheard.

Eddie stopped pacing. "You're assuming you have to do this on your own."

I huffed, then lowered my voice to a whisper. "Well, don't I? My prophecy says so."

Eddie had practically drilled the prophecy into my head.

The emperor's legacy will return, and bring light to a new dawn. A second war will break Forevermore, but it shall be restored by the power of the demigods. It is his choice to damn the realm, or save us all.

"No," Eddie clarified. "You will lead us, but nowhere does the prophecy state that you must do it on your own."

I was so frustrated, I could break something. I held myself back. "Who's going to help?" I demanded. "We have no allies here."

Eddie spoke softly. "You have Ava."

When he said her name, my heart stopped. I didn't talk about Ava, not even to Oberi. I'd barely heard her name in months. It was too much to hear. I could feel my chest ripping apart, as if a wolven shifter was digging inside of it to devour my heart. I'd rather feel nothing at all.

"I don't have Ava," I spat. "We broke up. Remember?"

"That doesn't mean you can't be allies," Eddie insisted. "Your destinies are entwined, and you know it. It's time you two stopped acting like you can do this on your own. If you can't face each other, everyone will perish."

Eddie was always kind to me, but he sure had a way of making me feel guilty.

"I didn't ask for this!" I growled.

"Nobody asked for this," Eddie said calmly. "Please stop acting like you have to go at this alone."

"I'm not alone," I argued. "I have you."

"And others! The Elves are here to help you. If we just had a little instruction, then maybe our powers would grow strong enough to save everyone. Someone like you, Charlie."

I paused for a moment to digest his suggestion. "You want me to teach the Elves how to use their powers?"

"Yes," Eddie said. "You're more powerful than any of us. This war was always going to lead to a revolution, and we need you and your friends to lead it."

I knew what he meant without him saying it. We needed *demigods*. It was part of the prophecy.

Hell, I hadn't spoken to Kallie or Marcus since we left Forevermore, either. We weren't friends anymore-- none of us were. I didn't know if they'd help Eddie and me save the Elves.

Ancestors, I'd been *so lonely* since the summer had begun. I hadn't said a word to any of my old friends-- not Ez, Opal, Ivy, any of them. I didn't even talk to Chancey, and he was in fight club with me, for ancestors' sake. The thought of speaking to any of them again was soul-crushing. I just wanted to be left alone, to deal with this hurt.

But Eddie was right. We hadn't gotten anywhere on our own, and if we didn't do something soon, the Elves would die, and the rest of us wouldn't be far behind. My ex-friends were the only ones who would help us.

I couldn't open the Elven gate on the island without them, anyway. Ava, Kallie, and Marcus all had a key-- the Elementai, fae, and witch keys that would help open up the portal to heaven. Though who knew if they'd actually *want* to give them to me, after the destruction we'd caused last semester?

It didn't matter. If I wanted to save the Elves, I had to get the Villain's Club back together-- no matter how much it hurt.

Even worse... I'd have to face Ava again.

I'd spent an entire summer feeling nothing, but once I faced Ava, I was certain every emotion I'd ever had about her would come rushing back, and I'd be helpless to stop it.

Forget the Warden. I was sure that she alone was going to be the end of me.

Continue The Infernal Underground to reunite the Villain's Club and stop the Warden!

BONUS OFFERS

Find coloring pages, games, quizzes, and bonus content at
hiddenlegendsbooks.com

Join *Orenda Academy of Magical Creatures* on Facebook for all things
Hidden Legends!

Check out the *Prison for Supernatural Offenders Official Playlist* on
Spotify!

Never miss a new release! Join our newsletter at
hiddenlegendsbooks.com/fanclub/

ABOUT THE AUTHORS

Megan Linski (left) and Alicia Rades (right) are best friends and the authors of the Hidden Legends universe. Both are USA Today bestselling authors of young adult and new adult fiction. Megan Linski is a coffee connoisseur who enjoys ice skating, horseback riding, and shopping. Her stories feature themes of community and friendship while advocating for the rights of the disabled. Alicia Rades is a mother who loves baking cookies, reading tarot, and binge-watching Netflix. She has a passion for personal development and strives to incorporate emotional-empowerment themes into her books. Both girls love nature, animals, sexy romances, and eating cheese.

9 781948 704878